Secret North

G.J. Walker-Smith

Secret North

Print Edition

© 2014 G.J. Walker-Smith

Cover by Scarlett Rugers, http://www.scarlettrugers.com
Formatting by Polgarus Studio, http://www.polgarusstudio.com

Other Books by G.J Walker-Smith
Saving Wishes (Book One, The Wishes Series)
Second Hearts (Book Two, The Wishes Series)
Sand Jewels (Book 2.5, The Wishes Series)
Storm Shells (Book Three, The Wishes Series)
Silver Dawn (Book 4.5, The Wishes Series)
Star Promise (Book five, The Wishes Series)

Contact the author:
https://www.facebook.com/gjwalkersmith
gjwalkersmith@gmail.com
gjwalkersmith.com

For Paul, my Boy Wonder.

CONTENTS

1. STORY OF THE DAY

Ryan

There was nothing appealing about turning thirty. Putting the brakes on and staying twenty-nine obviously wasn't an option. I woke up that morning to the horrible realisation that I was now Ryan Décarie, aged thirty.

I was more than content to let the day slip by without mention, but my family had other ideas. I had voicemails waiting from all of them, even Grandma Nellie. I sat at the counter in the kitchen with the phone on speaker, half-eating breakfast while I played them back.

"I bought you a gift but I can't remember where I put it," Nellie warbled. "I got you socks. Everyone needs good socks. And gin. Everyone needs good gin."

I set it down on the counter to listen to my mother's message. "Happy birthday, my son!" Even from a distance, she was loud. "Don't forget about dinner tonight, and don't bring any wretched girls. I'd like it to be a pleasant evening."

I reached across and tapped the screen, skipping to the next message before she added any more stipulations.

My father's message was generic and short, but at least he'd called me. Adam's message was short too, but only because Charli snatched the phone from him mid-sentence. The fairy-themed ramble I was expecting from her didn't happen. "Happy birthday, Ryan," she crowed. Bridget commandeered the phone then, and the morning brightened in an instant.

I carried my bowl to the sink, listening to my funny little niece's birthday message. "Happy, happy day, Ry!" she shouted. "In all the fairest land with the king's horses." She was losing me fast, but I was laughing. "Wishes in the pockets for you on Tuesdays with the little trees."

I rinsed my bowl, picked up the phone and walked to the bathroom to brush my teeth. Bridget's message was showing no sign of ending. I listened to another minute of her mashing together every nursery rhyme she'd ever been told with the odd 'happy, happy day' thrown in.

Eventually Adam called time. "He'll be late for work, baby," I heard him say. "Say goodbye."

"Bye, Ry," chimed my favourite voice in the whole world. "Happy, happy day!"

Bridget Décarie was a four-year-old package of awesome. She seemed to have adjusted to life in the big city better than her parents, even her father who'd spent most of his life here. I put it down to the fact that the kid's heritage was more complicated than a city roadmap. Bridget had no choice but to be adaptable. She was part French, part American, part Australian, part English and part fairy. Adam had brought his little family back to New York eight months earlier. I wasn't entirely convinced that they belonged here, but I liked having them around – especially Bridget.

Retaining the title of favourite uncle wasn't really a coup considering her other uncle was just a few weeks old, but I always gave her my best anyway. In return, I was exposed to a whole new world. Hanging out usually involved afternoons at the park, something I'd never done pre-niece.

Life at Bridget's tempo was slow and easy, and I enjoyed the change in pace. The blondes I usually hung out with were fast and a different kind of easy. She was also ten times smarter than any of the girls I knew. If not for her, I would never have known that seahorses are the slowest moving fish. I liked to think the education was mutual. I was the one who broke it to her that seahorses don't eat hay.

Another thing Bridget taught me was to always look up at the sky when you first step outside. Her reason made so much sense that it scared me: "You can see the story of the day," she explained.

As soon as I stepped out of my building that morning, I looked to the sky.

The story was bleak. It was warm and uncomfortably humid, and I could hear faint rolls of thunder over the busy traffic. It was terrible birthday weather, even for someone as unenthusiastic as me.

The story of the day got better when the entertainment kicked in.

I was still standing on the stoop when a cab violently screeched to a halt outside my building. The back door flew open and a ramped-up brunette tumbled out, loudly demanding that the driver unload her luggage.

I don't pretend to know a lot about women's fashion, but a tight black skirt and four inch heels didn't seem sensible for someone gearing up for a fistfight. And that was exactly what I was expecting to see when the driver got out of the cab and fronted up to her on the sidewalk. It was a brave move on his part, considering he was a foot shorter than her.

"Pay your fare!" he yelled, wagging his finger.

"I lost my wallet!" she spat. "That's why you're kicking me out!"

The driver marched to the back of his car, muttering in a language I couldn't make out.

I understood the rowdy brunette perfectly, and every one of the crude insults she hurled at him. He obviously understood too. He took a cardboard box out of the trunk and dumped it at her feet, sending the contents spilling across the pavement.

Not one person stopped. They just stepped to the side to avoid the carnage and kept walking. I couldn't have moved if I'd wanted to. I'd seen street performances before, but nothing like this, and certainly not right outside my building.

"You pay!" he demanded.

She threw her arms out wide. "No money, stupid!"

Fearing that she was about to do him some real damage, I grabbed a twenty-dollar bill out of my wallet, stepped into the line of fire and thrust it at the driver. Without saying a word, he snatched it and jumped back into his cab.

A quick getaway in Midtown Manhattan was never going to happen. It took a full minute for him to break into the passing traffic and pull away. Angry Girl stood on the sidewalk, hurling insults at him the whole time. Her vocabulary was outstanding. She didn't repeat herself once.

Once he was gone, she started gathering her belongings off the ground. She didn't acknowledge me or the fact that I'd just settled her fare. "You owe me twenty bucks," I told her.

Maintaining her crouched position on the pavement, she looked up at me.

"I didn't ask you to pay him," she said, composing herself enough to speak. "I would've gladly beaten the crap out of him."

I crouched beside her, picked up the last of her bits and pieces and dumped them in the box she was gripping.

"Thank you."

"You're welcome." I stood up, extended my hand and helped her to her feet. Unsure of whether I should pick it up or not, I stared at the box on the ground. I knew exactly what I was looking at. If someone had tipped the contents of the top drawer of my desk into a box, it would've looked exactly the same – minus the Garfield pencil case. It was a last-day-on-the-job box, which had undoubtedly added to the day from hell she was having.

"So, what's your plan from here?" I asked.

"I'm not sure, but it's a solo plan," she replied, crouching to pick up her box. "Your work here is done."

She was such a cranky bitch – and I'd missed her more than I'd realised.

"You haven't changed one bit, Bente Denison. You're still mean."

"I doubt you have either," she replied, balancing the box on her hip. "I'll bet you're still a pretty boy man-whore."

I grinned. "At least you think I'm still pretty."

She smiled at me for the first time in five years, and it was still spectacular. "To be honest Ryan, that's all you've ever had going for you."

"Where are you headed?" I asked, taking no offense.

"Nowhere," she said glumly. "I'm heading nowhere."

I wasn't quite sure how to console her. Bente had psychotic tendencies. One wrong word and she'd probably deck me – though she'd look good doing it. When she was smiling and happy, she was a very pretty girl. When she was angry and threatening bodily harm, she was freaking gorgeous.

"Why don't you come back to my apartment? I'll call you a driver."

Bente squinted at me, weighing up my offer. "Where's your apartment?" I pointed at the building behind her. "You live here?" she asked, turning to look. "In a city of eight million people, I get thrown out of a cab outside your door?"

"What can I say? It must be your lucky day."

She laughed, and for a brief second the drama disappeared. "You're still an egotistical jerk."

Calling her bluff, I took a backward step toward the door. "Just trying to be nice. Good seeing you, Bente."

I was almost at the steps when she called out to me. "Ryan, wait."

I killed my triumphant smile before turning back to face her.

She dropped her head and cleared her throat. Being humble had never been easy for her. "I would appreciate your help."

I stepped back to her and took the box from her grip.

"Thank you," she said quietly.

"My pleasure." And it was.

2. SERIAL KILLER

Bente

It was five years since I'd last seen Ryan Décarie, and running into him now felt like a punishment. There was only so much a girl could endure. I'd been fired, lost my wallet, and somehow stumbled across the man who to this day I considered to be my biggest mistake. To top it all off, I looked like crap. I stared into his bathroom mirror, trying to work out how to pull myself together.

Washing my face was a good start. I thought I'd done a decent job until I patted my face with one of the stark white towels hanging on the rail. I hung it back up, folding it over to hide the black streaks I'd left on it. I now owed him cab fare and dry-cleaning. Glancing around the bathroom gave me a quick reality check. It rivalled any swish hotel I'd ever seen: marble counter top, chrome fixtures and the biggest shower I'd ever seen. Confident that he could cover his own dry-cleaning expenses, I messed the towel up again and headed to the living room.

Ryan was in the kitchen. "Feeling better?" he asked.

"Much, thank you."

"I called for a car," he told me. "It should be here within the hour."

"Awesome. Thanks."

We stood on opposite sides of the counter, separated by a large chunk of black granite and an awkward silence. There shouldn't have been any silence. We hadn't seen each other in years. We could've spent hours catching up, but neither of us said anything. I kept quiet because I was stubborn. I could only guess what his reasons were.

Unable to look at him any longer, I wandered to the centre of the room, making no secret of the fact that I was checking it out.

I'd never been to Ryan's place before. I'd slept with the man twice, but had never scored an invitation to his home. I wasn't sure if that made me a bigger whore than him, so I didn't mention it.

"Nice place." I glanced back at him.

He flashed me a crooked grin but didn't reply.

I wasn't just being polite. His apartment was gorgeous. Rough exposed red brick walls were softened by honey coloured floorboards. Black leather couches dominated the centre of the room, matching the huge TV screen mounted on the wall. Big canvas prints strategically displayed on the other walls added colour. It was boyish, chic and untouchable, much like the owner, who was busying himself by making coffee.

I continued sticky-beaking, and it wasn't long before something caught my eye. The wooden toybox in the corner of the room looked so out of place that I couldn't help checking it out. It was filled to the brim with dolls and almost all of them were broken. I picked up a particularly tortured-looking redhead. "Your doll collection has seen better days, Ryan."

"Technically they're not mine," he replied, grinning wryly. "I share them with my niece."

I levered myself onto a stool at the counter. "Is your niece a potential serial killer?" It wasn't such an odd question considering the state of the doll I'd just laid on the counter. It was missing both arms and legs.

"Bridget has trouble dressing them," he explained. "She wrenches their limbs off to get their clothes on. Sometimes they lose their heads too."

"So you're the repair guy?"

He put his hand to his heart. "Second only to her dad," he said proudly. "I love hanging out with her."

I looked down to hide my confusion. I'd known Ryan a long time. He was selfish and self-serving. I'd never seen a hint of the type of man who'd find joy spending time with a four-year-old.

"Have you met her?" he asked.

"Of course." I picked up the doll and began fussing with its scrappy hair. "She's a cutie."

Ryan was right to be smitten. The little girl was as mad as a hatter, just like her mother, but somehow grounded like Adam, without the serious douchey parts.

"Charli knows you're back?"

I nodded. "We're friends. We talk all the time."

"She never told me you were back."

"Why would she tell you?"

Ryan suddenly looked a little wounded. "I would've called if I'd known," he said. "We were friends too."

"I used to work for you," I clarified. "Sometimes I used to like you. The problem was, sometimes you used to like screwing me over."

I didn't like where the conversation was headed. Ryan had treated me horribly in the past. I'd learned from it and moved on. Dredging it up again made absolutely no sense.

"Is it too late to say sorry?" he asked.

I wasn't prepared for the question, so answering took time. My thoughtful stare seemed to unsettle him. He shifted from one foot to the other.

"It's never too late to apologise," I said finally. "As long as you mean it."

"I do mean it," he assured me.

I wasn't sure if I cared either way, despite the flutter that rippled through my chest as he spoke. "Apology accepted, then."

Ryan turned to finish the forgotten cups of coffee. "So are you planning to stay in New York for a while?" he asked over the hum of the coffee machine.

"As long as I can find work again," I replied. "I've only been back in town two weeks."

He set two mugs down on the counter. "You got fired after two weeks?"

I glowered. I hadn't mentioned anything about being fired. It annoyed me that he'd jumped to that conclusion, even if it was right.

"What makes you think I got fired?" I asked defensively.

He just pointed at the box near the front door.

"My boss was a creep," I explained.

That was an understatement. My boss was a freaking nightmare. I'd put up with his wandering hands and creepy grab-ass attempts for days longer than I should have because I'd desperately needed the job.

"So *you* got fired because *he* was a creep?"

I grinned wryly. "No, I got fired because I wasn't very acquiescent. He hit on me once too often."

"So you hit on him?"

"With my knee."

He winced. "Ouch, Bente."

I brought my mug to my mouth to mask my smile. "That's what he said."

He didn't have a chance to offer up a smartass reply. The intercom buzzed, halting the conversation.

"Your ride is here," announced Ryan, walking toward the panel near the front door. He pressed a button and told the driver I'd be down shortly.

I took a long sip of my coffee, grabbed my bag and followed him to the door. He handed me my box.

"Thanks for today," I said. "You saved it from completely going to hell."

He held the door open for me. "Keep in touch, okay?"

I smiled. "Not a chance."

He smiled back. "You just got through telling me that I saved your life. Does that mean nothing to you?"

"I never said any such thing, Ryan," I scoffed. "You must be getting hard of hearing."

"It's possible," he conceded, shrugging. "I turned thirty today."

I took a step back. "It's your birthday?"

His smile grew broader. "All day, apparently."

"Well, happy birthday." I shifted the box to my other hip. "I hope you're doing something nice to celebrate."

"I am, actually. I'm having dinner with a sweet little blonde I'm rather fond of."

"Great." There wasn't an ounce of sincerity in my tone. "I'm happy for you."

I brushed past him, escaping his space by getting into the foyer. The big jerk had the gall to call me back, and like an even bigger jerk, I turned around.

"If you're free tomorrow, perhaps you and I could have dinner," he suggested. "You can choose the –"

"You haven't changed at all, Ryan," I interrupted. "You screwed me over once before, but at least you were sly about it. If you think for one second –"

He cut me off with a rushed explanation. "My date tonight is with Bridget. We're having a family dinner at my parents' house."

I suddenly felt two inches tall, and far too embarrassed to look at him as I mumbled my weak apology.

"I was teasing," he said gently.

My eyes drifted up, locking his. "I don't like being teased – not by you."

Ryan's mouth formed a line. I knew he'd read between the lines perfectly. He pulled out his wallet and handed me a business card. "Please think about dinner," he urged. "I won't call you. No pressure."

The slow approach was very unlike the Ryan I used to know. He was notoriously gung-ho about everything, especially when he wanted something. I had no idea what to make of it.

I took the card from him. "I'll think about it."

He broke a sexy crooked smile – the very same one that had gotten me into trouble too many times before. "That's all I ask."

3. EVICTION

Ryan

I wasn't expecting any more visitors that morning, and judging by the shocked look on their faces, Bridget and Charli weren't expecting me to answer the door either. Charli stood with her key in hand, ready to let herself in. Bridget lurched forward and hugged my leg. "Happy, happy day!" she announced.

I opened the door wider, picked Bridget up and flipped her upside down. "Thank you," I replied, carrying her through to the kitchen.

Charli dumped a bag of groceries on the counter. "We didn't think you'd be home. We came to make you a cake."

"And to happy day you some more," added Bridget.

I righted her, lowered her to her feet and kissed the top of her head. "Thank you," I repeated. "There's no one else I'd rather be happy day-ed by than you."

Bridget took off running, making a beeline for her toybox.

I turned my attention to Charli. "What's wrong with your kitchen?"

"There's no room to cook in it."

It was a perfectly acceptable response. There was no room to live in the cave they called home. Moving back into Gabrielle's apartment was supposed to be temporary, but eight months later they were still there. Househunting had been put on the back-burner in favour of hectic jobs and hanging out with their girl.

"You need to find a bigger house, Charli."

"Adam's too busy and I wouldn't know where to start."

I smirked at her. "Maybe he could ask his boss for some time off."

She set the box of cake mix down with an unnecessary thud. "He's lucky if he gets a lunch break most days."

Against his better judgement, Adam had accepted a job at our father's firm. The hours were long and from the little he'd told me, the job sucked. Dad's expectations were high and Adam's heart wasn't in it. It made for a bad combination.

Charli took the tyranny personally. "He's punishing him, you know."

"For what?"

"For leaving in the first place," she said irately.

"Adam is a grown man, Charli," I pointed out. "If he's not happy there, he'll leave."

Bridget reappeared, forcing a change in conversation. She climbed onto the stool beside me and picked up the doll that Bente had left on the counter. "You've been playing with my girl?"

"No, I had a friend over this morning," I explained. "She liked her a lot."

The little girl studied the doll closely. "She took her arms off."

"Bridget Décarie, *you* took her arms off," I retorted. "Her legs too."

She scrambled off the stool. "Don't let your friends play with my girls any more, okay?"

"Yes ma'am."

I doubt she saw my salute; she'd already hightailed it back to the toybox.

"What friend?" asked Charli.

"Why do you care?"

"Well, I need to know whether the doll needs disinfecting."

"It's my birthday, Charlotte. Be nice."

She pulled a face and began searching through the cupboards. "So who was she?"

"Bente."

She spun back to face me. "Bente Denison?"

"How many Bentes do you know?" I muttered. "Why didn't you tell me she was back in town?"

"I didn't think you'd be that interested," she replied guiltily.

I stared her down. "Liar."

Charli opened a drawer and grabbed a wooden spoon. "I know you have a soft spot for Bente," she conceded, aiming the spoon at me, "but the soft spot you have for screwing around always wins out. I wasn't going to pave the way for you to rip her heart out again."

I walked into the kitchen and found her a bowl. "I like her," I declared. "I've always liked Bente."

"Are you going to see her again?"

"I hope so."

"Be kind to her, Ryan," she warned. "She doesn't deserve any more grief from you."

***

Charli's only input in the cake making was cracking two eggs into the bowl. She retreated to the living room and left Bridget and I to it after that. I didn't care. She's a hopeless cook.

Operation birthday cake was a battle of wills. I gave Bridget instructions, and she ignored them. "You're cooking it wrong," she insisted.

"Be quiet and stir."

Despite the drama, the cake tin was finally loaded into the oven and clean-up began. Bridget lost interest at that point and went back to her box of severed doll parts. Charli remained sprawled on the couch as if she owned the joint, and the ensuing conversation led me to think she sometimes wished she did.

"Ryan, I think you and I should make a deal," she suggested, staring at the high ceiling.

"What kind of deal?"

"A business deal."

She might not have seen me roll my eyes, but I was sure she heard me laugh. "I've made enough business deals with you to last me a lifetime."

Ignoring me, she continued her pitch. "I think you should move into our apartment so we can move in here."

"I'm sure you do," I replied, still chuckling. "Find your own house."

"Adam owns half this place, right?"

"Technically."

"Then technically I own half too. I'm evicting you."

"Yeah. Good luck with that, Tinker Bell."

She sat upright, trying her best to appear serious. "You're becoming very unreasonable in your old age."

Bridget chimed in from across the room. "Are you old now, Ry?"

No one on earth got away with shortening my name – except her. She wasn't going to get away with calling me old, though. "No, Bridget. I am not."

Charli giggled. "Did you know that my dad was only eleven when you were born?"

"Charli, Alex wasn't much older than that when *you* were born."

She had no smart comeback. I wasn't lying.

***

My clean-up efforts were in vain. Once the cake was cooked and cooled, Bridget went to town decorating it. There was more frosting on the counter than the cake, but she was thrilled with the result, which made it easy to overlook the mess she'd made.

"Great job, little one," I praised.

"We can eat it now?" she asked hopefully.

I looked to Charli for an answer.

"No," she told her. "We're taking it to Mamie's tonight."

My mother had been planning my birthday dinner for days. Supplying dessert was tactical. It meant we didn't have to fear the marzipan topped pound cake she usually subjected us to. For some reason, she considered it to be one of her signature dishes, and to this day, not one of us had had the heart to tell her how truly revolting it was.

4. THE WASP'S NEST

Bente

No one thought my sister could top the ridiculous name she'd cursed her eldest daughter, Fabergé, with, but four years later she outdid herself by naming her second daughter Malibu.

Malibu Vienna Denison to be precise. With a name like that, she was bound to have attitude. Malibu was a growly, bad-tempered bundle of terror, but in the eyes of her mother she could do no wrong. In fairness, turning a blind eye is probably necessary when it comes to raising two precocious girls by yourself.

No one really knew how Ivy ended up a solo parent. Both girls seemed to be immaculate conceptions. One minute my sister was single. The next she was pregnant and single.

I'd never asked about their fathers. I didn't even know for sure that there were two daddies; it was just an educated guess based on the fact that Malibu and Fabergé looked nothing alike. Fabergé was olive skinned with dark hair like her mother. Malibu had red curly hair and very pale skin.

"It's the Irish in her," declared Ivy.

I offered no input. I had no idea what the little girl had in her.

***

Living with Ivy and her girls was akin to serving out a prison sentence, and now that I was unemployed my plan of moving into my own place was nothing more than a pipe dream.

I was doing my time in Fabergé's room while she bunked with Malibu. Neither girl was happy with the arrangement. When Fabergé started moving her things across the hall, World War Three broke out. It started out with pinching and slapping and ended in tears on both fronts. Witnessing it made me glad that I had no children. It also made me want to step out into the hall and deliver a few slaps of my own. I only held off because the rent was cheap and I needed a roof over my head.

★★

As soon as I arrived home, I headed to my room. I dumped my box of office supplies at the foot of the bed, crumpled in a heap and dissolved into tears.

Ivy knocked on the door a short while later. "Everything okay?"

"Fine," I called, trying to sound composed. "I'll be out soon."

That might've been a lie. I was going to need days to recover from the morning I'd had.

My mind wasn't even on the horror of losing my job. I'd hated it from day one. I was a journalist not a receptionist, but beggars can't be choosers. I accepted the first job I was offered to get me back to New York.

But in truth I'd barely given McGivern Realty another thought since I'd walked out the door. My mind was on a previous employer. Dealing with Ryan Décarie is like being stung by a wasp: it hurts like a bitch but you learn a lesson and vow never to go near the wasp nest again.

Today the wasp came to me, and instead of running in the opposite direction, I gave the nest a big ol' kick.

I sat up and grabbed my box, searching through it for the business card he'd given me. It was a pointless exercise. His number hadn't changed, and even though I hadn't called it in years I still knew it by heart.

That made tearing the card up a pointless exercise too, but it still felt good doing it.

5. CHOCOLATE CAKE GIRL

Ryan

Considering the effort Mom had gone to, arriving on time was the least I could do. Charli and Bridget showed up late, and much to Charli's annoyance Adam didn't show at all.

"You must understand, Charli," said my father in a gentle but condescending tone. "Work comes first. It's the way of the world."

"Not our world," she replied strongly.

The king didn't intimidate Charli in the slightest, no matter how hard he tried. It impressed me. Adam and I had dealt with him our whole lives and were nowhere near as good at shutting him down as she was.

"Your world must be a wondrous place," he replied dryly.

Jean-Luc's battle was no longer with Adam. He had him right where he wanted him. When Adam agreed to take a job at Décarie, Fontaine and Associates, our father considered it a victory. The prodigal son was returning home to make good. The fact that they'd only come back because of Charli's position at the Merriman Gallery never rated a mention. Jean-Luc once told her that she was fortunate to have found a project to keep her occupied.

He still maintained that he was fond of his feisty daughter-in-law, and I believed him. She just frustrated the hell out of him, which was perfectly understandable. She frustrated the hell out of most people.

Charli made a lame excuse to leave the room, perhaps to stop herself speaking again. Dad turned his attention to Bridget who was sprawled under the coffee table, playing with her toys.

"*Bridget, viens voir Papy*," he beckoned.

"I'm working under here, Papy," she replied, making me smile.

"I have something for you," he coaxed.

Predictably, the little girl scrambled out from under the table to find out what it was. I groaned aloud as he reached into his wallet and presented her with a fifty-dollar bill.

Her little eyes lit up and she thanked him.

It was a stupid, pointless gesture and I proved it in an instant. "What have you got there, Bridge?"

She climbed on to the couch beside Dad, waving the bill at me. "Paper money," she replied.

I smiled roguishly at my father. "Awesome."

He frowned and I knew I'd made my point. He'd have gotten the same reaction by giving her a dollar bill.

My mother appeared a few seconds later with more spoils for Adam's little princess. "Come, Bridget," she instructed, holding out her hand. "Mamie has something for you upstairs." It really wasn't any wonder that Charli avoided letting Bridget hang out with my parents for any length of time. The level of excess they showered on the kid grated on me, and I wasn't the one trying to raise her.

Bridget and Mom disappeared and Charli returned. My father wasted no time in trying to put her in her place. "I don't enjoy tension, Charli. I hope you've calmed down."

She sat beside me, giving her the best vantage point to glare at him from. She didn't say a word, which was far more powerful than any reply she could've given. We endured an awkward few minutes of silence before Bridget and Mom returned. Mom held her hand and paraded her around, showing off the new coat she'd dressed her in.

"*Magnifique!*" praised my father.

"Doesn't she look lovely?" crowed my mother, speaking mainly to Charli. "I saw it this afternoon and couldn't resist. It's a fraction too big –" she tugged at the cuff of Bridget's sleeve, "– but it should fit her by winter."

Charli was so rigid that her voice sounded strange as she thanked her. Bridget didn't seem to be faring much better. She escaped her grandmother's grasp and piled onto her mother's lap. If I'd been any further away, I wouldn't have heard Bridget's whisper. "I don't like it, Mummy."

"Shush," replied Charli, equally as quietly.

***

Dinner was done with fairly quickly. Mom served her stock standard stodgy roast beef and finished up with the cake Bridget had made. It was lopsided, overloaded with sprinkles and little fingermarks, and still more appealing than any dessert my mother could've cooked. It wasn't an unbearable evening, but I was glad when it ended. I decided to make the most of the clear, warm night and walk home.

I would've walked the girls home too but Charli had other plans. She ordered Bridget to stay put, stepped off the sidewalk and hailed a cab with the expertise of a true New Yorker.

"You're getting a cab?" I asked incredulously. "I'll walk you home."

"We're not going home," she replied, hoisting a slab of cake at me. "We're going to surprise Adam at work."

"My daddy likes cake," added Bridget.

I didn't feel the need to warn her that the building would be locked. If anyone could talk their way past security, it was those two. I opened the back door of the cab for them. "Have a nice night, ladies."

Bridget clambered in and Charli handed her the plate of cake before turning back to me. "Happy birthday, Ryan," she said, kissing my cheek. "Spend your wish wisely. Buy only what you need."

I should've bowed out of the nonsense and walked away, but I couldn't help asking my next question. "What do you think I need?"

She flashed a smile. "Someone to bring you chocolate cake when you work late."

"Yeah, right." I dropped my line of sight to the pavement.

"It's true, Ryan. You're ready for her." She dipped her head, chasing my eyes. "Find her. Go forth and find chocolate cake girl."

I couldn't help laughing. "I'll work on it."

"You should," she replied, suddenly serious. "I wish that for you."

"Me too, Ry," called a little voice from the back seat of the cab.

"Get out of here," I teased, opening the door wider. "The meter's running."

6. CHAPERONES

Bente

Nothing could be more pathetic than an unemployed twenty-six-year-old woman hiding out in her niece's Hello Kitty-themed bedroom. Especially when said woman was sitting on the floor, debating whether or not to call the only man who'd ever broken her heart.

And yet here I was. And that's where I'd been for the last two hours. The whole situation was pathetic. Calling Ryan was a dumb idea, but I found myself doing it anyway.

"Here goes everything," I muttered out loud.

I'd barely got the words out when he answered. "Bente. Hi."

"How did you know it was me?"

"Lucky guess." I could hear the smile in his voice, and instantly relaxed because of it.

"I'm just wondering if your offer of dinner still stands."

"Yes, of course." He punched out the words. "Tomorrow?"

Pretending to check my schedule was pointless. After the events of that morning, he knew better than anyone that I didn't have one. "Yes, something casual and low key, okay?"

"You don't want to be seen with me, Miss Denison?" His dark tone and cheeky words were reminiscent of the Ryan I used to know, the same Ryan who has a knack for turning my insides to mush.

"Not in public."

"Okay, fine. How about we make it really low key and take chaperones? I'll bring my little niece and you can bring yours."

Eight-year-old Fabergé wouldn't even entertain the idea. My thoughts turned to dreadful Malibu. "Sure," I replied, struggling to sound pleasant. "That sounds great."

Ryan told me to pick the time and place. "Just make an early reservation. Bridget has a curfew."

His serious tone made me smile. "Do you take Bridget out often, Ryan?"

"No, she usually takes me out," he joked.

"I'll call you tomorrow with the details, okay?"

"I look forward to it," he said. "Talk to you tomorrow."

Clearly he was gearing up to end the call, but I wasn't quite done with him. "Ryan?"

"Yeah?"

"Happy birthday," I whispered.

I didn't breathe again until he spoke, which seemed to take an eternity. "It is now."

"Goodnight Ryan."

"Bente?"

"Yeah?"

"Do you like chocolate cake?"

I had no idea how to answer him so I went with the truth. "Actually, I'm more of a pecan pie kind of girl."

"Good to know," he replied. "Goodnight Bente. Sleep well."

That was impossible. I'd just arranged a dinner date with a mean, selfish monster – and Ryan.

7. ANIMAL

Ryan

Something about Bente Denison had always fascinated me. She was nothing like the women I usually spent time with. She was a fiery, opinionated brunette. I usually favoured spending time with compliant blondes whose affections could be bought with expensive gifts and talking dirty.

I'd been out of the game for a while. I can't really explain why. Somewhere along the line, casual meaningless affairs had become boring. Bente was the first woman to catch my eye in weeks, and game playing was the furthest thing from my mind. I used to enjoy the fact that she had a low tolerance for me. Now just thinking about it made me break into a cold sweat.

If Bente was having second thoughts about our dinner date, she didn't let on. She texted me early the next morning to let me know the details of the kiddie friendly restaurant she'd booked. Everything was organised. All I had to do was ask permission to borrow my niece. I decided to do it face-to-face and corner Charli at work.

She wasn't surprised to see me. I'd bought a few pieces from the Merriman gallery since she'd been working there, and had my eye on at least ten more. That's the problem with good art – the more you see, the more you want. I'd run out of walls to hang anything else so I was reduced to window-shopping, which I did quite often.

The Merriman gallery was one of my favourites. It was sparsely stocked, very upmarket; and best of all, everything on display was for sale.

"Good morning Fairy Pants," I crooned as she walked toward me. "You look very grown up in your big girl clothes."

She pulled a face. She also tugged at the hem of her blouse so I knew I'd gotten to her. "Do you want something or are you just being painful?"

"I'm here because I want something – namely your daughter."

She didn't seem alarmed in the slightest. "So you're really going through with this?"

"With what?"

She flapped her hand at me. "This little play date thing you've organised with Bente."

I didn't bother questioning how she knew about it. Bente and Charli were friends. They'd probably chosen the time and place together.

"You're the one who told me to find chocolate cake girl."

"Yes, I did," she agreed. "I just don't like the interview process. Bente is my friend, Ryan. I don't want to see her get hurt again."

"I like her, Charli," I insisted. "What's wrong with reconnecting?"

She tilted her head. "Nothing, if it's genuine."

I held up three fingers. "Scout's honour."

She still didn't look convinced. "Just play nice, okay? And keep an eye on Bridget. She doesn't get along very well with Malibu."

"What the heck is a Malibu?"

"Bente's little niece," she explained, screwing up her face. "She's awful."

I'd been preparing to deal with Fabergé. I had no idea there was a Mark II.

"How awful?" I asked.

Charli didn't answer. She walked away, leaving me no choice but to follow her to her desk at the rear of the gallery.

"Tell me," I demanded.

She sat and momentarily leaned forward. "You'll see," she said ominously; then she leaned back and abandoned the creepy frown. "Bring my kid back in one piece or you're in big trouble."

It may have been the first time she'd ever actually scared me, and it took effort not to let it show. "Thank you, Charlotte," I said, edging away. "I'll pick her up at six."

***

Bridget didn't seem to share my excitement when it came to our dinner plans. She was, however, excited by the boots she was wearing.

"See the sparkles?" she asked, pointing at her feet.

Her penchant for wearing galoshes – even in the middle of summer – hadn't wavered since she'd first learned to walk. Her parents didn't discourage her, despite my mother's warning that her feet would spread to fit the boots.

"She'll begin to waddle like a duck," she moaned.

"But she'll be a cute little duck," defended Adam.

The blue sparkly boots didn't bother me. It was her slow walk that drove me crazy, but Bridget's pace was still quicker than trying to get through peak hour traffic, so we got out of the cab a few blocks early.

"Why do I have to come?" she whined.

I'd asked myself the same question more than once in the last half hour. I couldn't really complain considering it had been my suggestion in the first place.

"You're my wing girl, Bridge," I explained. "It's your job to make sure I don't say anything dumb."

Her walk slowed to a virtual crawl as she thought things through. "Like whales?" she asked. She put her hands to her mouth and wiggled her fingers. "They go 'squeep, squeep, squeep'."

I couldn't help laughing. "I don't know what kind of whales you have in Australia, sweetheart, but that's not like any whale I've ever heard."

***

Bente had chosen a restaurant called Ginger's. It wasn't really my type of place. It was loud, bright and packed with small children and tourists – a

25

bit like Times Square as a whole, which is why I usually avoided going there. Even Bridget seemed a little scared, especially when a person wearing a padded cow suit greeted us at the door.

"Ginger, I presume?" I asked dryly.

"Very funny, guy." The gruff reply from inside the suit terrified Bridget even more. She clung to my leg and refused to take the colouring sheet he tried handing her. I took it instead and told him we had a reservation for six-thirty.

"Sit anywhere you like," said the cow.

I'd already decided that if Bente wasn't there, we were leaving. When I scanned the crowded room, I almost wished she wouldn't show. Unruly kids were bouncing around, and there was a long queue at the self-serve soda machine and an even longer line to the bathrooms. Finally I spotted her at a table in the corner. With a firm hand on Bridget's shoulder, we wove a path through the tables.

"Hi." She greeted me with a sheepish grin. Hopefully that meant she realised how ghastly her choice of venue was.

"Hello," I replied. "I'm sorry we're a little late."

"It's no bother." She turned her attention to the little girl who was gripping my hand like grim death. "How are you, Bridget?" Getting no reply, Bente moved on. "Ryan, this is my niece, Malibu."

The little girl sat next to her aunt, paying us no attention as she fiercely scribbled on her colouring sheet. I was struck by how different she looked from Fabergé. Her snowy white skin and curly red hair reminded me of orphan Annie.

I tried to speak but she beat me to it. In a barely comprehensible growl she demanded something to eat, and followed it up with a hardcore scream. This was no orphan Annie. She was more like Animal from the Muppets.

"In a minute," chided Bente. "Mind your manners."

"I want to go home," whimpered Bridget in a tiny voice.

Me too, I silently replied.

I lifted her up and sat her between Bente and I. The further I kept her away from Animal, the better. If Bente noticed my strategy she didn't let on. "I haven't been here before," she said, almost apologetically. "Ivy said it was a good place to bring the kids."

Her kid, maybe. I happened to like mine.

"It's fine." I glanced around the room. "I've already come up with a counteroffensive, depending on how agreeable you are."

She looked around. "I'm prepared to hear you out."

I doubted her amenability had anything to do with my charm. She was probably just as desperate to get the hell out of there as I was.

"Well, while the children are eating, I'm going to call for two cars," I began. "In one hour, you're going to deliver you kid back to her mother and I'm going to do the same with mine."

"I don't want to go home!" growled Malibu.

"I do," whimpered Bridget, clinging to my shirt.

Bente stared at me. "That's some plan, Ryan."

I straightened up. "It's an awesome plan."

"What happens after that?"

"Well, that's where things will take a turn for the better," I explained. "The driver will then drop you off at a restaurant of my choosing, and we'll start this date over."

She picked up a paper menu and pretended to read. "I never said this was a date."

I grinned. "We both know it's a date, Bente."

She smiled at the menu she was holding. "We'd best order the girls some food then," she suggested.

8. BABY SHOES

Bente

My stomach was in knots, but it had little to do with the unappetising food that had just been served to the girls. Malibu pulled her burger apart, spreading her dinner so far across the table that her fries were mixed with her coloured pencils. But at least she ate. Bridget barely touched anything.

"Please eat something," pleaded Ryan, sliding her plate closer.

"I don't like it," she replied in a tiny voice.

"Do you want to take it home?" he asked.

She nodded. Ryan called a server over and asked him to box up the left-over food.

"This too, please," I said, pointing at Malibu's dinner.

"I'm eating it!" she yelled, making me wince. I didn't care. I was more than ready to shut the meal down and get out of there.

"We can wait for her to finish," offered Ryan.

"Or we could get out of here and start enjoying the evening."

"I'm enjoying!" screeched Malibu.

I cocked one eyebrow at Ryan. "Ready?"

"Born ready." He stood, picked Bridget up and grabbed her box of food.

My escape was a little more complicated. First I had to wrestle Malibu's box of food from her, then suffer the indignity of watching her roll around on the dirty floor while her epic tantrum played out. All eyes were on her, which was the exact reaction she was aiming for. The pink sundress she was wearing was now filthy, stained by the mucky floor she was writhing on. I stood, dumbfounded and unsure of my next move.

Ryan hitched Bridget higher on his hip, handed her the box of leftovers and grabbed my hand. "Let's go."

"I can't just leave her here," I replied, appalled.

"Trust me," he murmured. "She'll follow."

We'd almost made it to the door when Malibu crashed full force into me, throwing her arms around my legs.

I'd heard her before I felt her. "Don't leave me!"

"Keep walking then," ordered Ryan without looking at her. Unbelievably, Malibu released her grip and trailed us out the door, but victory was fleeting. Once we were outside, she took her shameful display up a notch by setting her sights on Bridget.

"I hate your dumb baby shoes."

Bridget didn't reply but her little knuckles whitened as she tightened her grip on Ryan's shirt.

"Baby shoes," repeated Malibu, throwing in a poke of her tongue for good measure.

Ryan had had enough. He lowered Bridget to her feet and took a step forward, towering over the little horror. "You listen to me," he demanded in a low tone. "Do you like your aunt?"

"Yes," spat Malibu, unperturbed.

"I like her too," he replied. "Do you like me?"

"No!"

"Well here's your problem," he explained. "If you don't start behaving yourself, I'm going to marry your aunt. You know what that will mean for you?"

Malibu shook her head.

Ryan leaned down closer to her. "It means I'll be your uncle," he menaced. "I'll move into your house and you'll have to see me every day."

"No!" She finally sounded appropriately terrified. "Don't do it!"

Ryan glanced at me and winked. I managed a small smile. "Behave yourself then," he ordered.

Malibu nodded madly but said nothing. It was Bridget who found her voice. She tugged on Ryan's sleeve, making sure she had his full attention. "*Non, tu ne peux pas la marier, Ry.*"

Ryan smiled down at her. "*Dans ce cas, d'accord, Bridget. Je ne la marierai pas ce soir.*"

He pronounced her name differently when speaking French. Unlike me, she wasn't enamoured by his gorgeous tone. Her worried frown remained.

We loaded our respective children into the waiting cars. I glanced around, convinced that people were staring. Patrons at Ginger's generally don't depart in chauffeured town cars. The Décaries didn't seem to share my embarrassment; obviously it was nothing out of the ordinary for them. I'm sure dining at Ginger's was, though.

"So I'll meet you in an hour?" asked Ryan.

"Yes, where?"

"Your driver has the details."

I tilted my head and sighed. "I don't know about this, Ryan. You're so secretive. Secretive destinations, secretive conversations …"

He put his hand to his heart. "I am completely transparent."

"Yeah? What did Bridget say?"

He looked back at his car, making sure his niece was in it and out of earshot. "She asked me not to marry you. I don't think she's keen on having Malibu in the family." The corner of his mouth lifted. "I told her I wouldn't marry you tonight. That's the best I could do."

I nodded, slightly dumbstruck. "I'll see you soon," I stammered.

He held a finger up. "One hour."

9. CONQUER AND KEEP

Ryan

I don't know what possessed me to call Bridget's parents and let them know that she was on her way home – but I was glad I did. We'd obviously interrupted something very non-PG. The first thing I noticed when Adam answered the door was his inside-out T-shirt.

Bridget wrapped herself around him like a vine. "I'm back again!"

"Yes you are," he beamed insincerely, putting his hand on her head. "It's as if you only just left."

Bridget abandoned her grip on her dad and took off into the apartment. I was afraid to venture further than the doorway. "Thanks for the nice time, Bridge," I called. "I'll see you later."

"Okay," came a distant reply.

"This is her leftover food." I thrust the box at Adam, giving him no choice but to take it. "My advice would be to ditch it. It didn't look good to begin with."

"Right."

The longer I stood there, the harder it was to keep a straight face.

"One word, Ryan," he warned. "Say one word and –"

I held both hands up. "I'm not saying a thing … except that you really need to work on your time management skills."

The door closed in my face and I chuckled my way back to the elevator.

***

I'd arranged for the driver to take Bente to Nellie's. The look on her face as she walked in led me to think she was disappointed by my choice of venue. Her outfit screamed disappointment too. She'd changed out of her jeans and was now wearing a silky red dress that perfectly matched the colour of her lips.

My heart sank a little. She'd reiterated her need to keep things casual at least ten times. Maybe I got it wrong.

I met her at the door. "Everything okay?" I asked.

She forced a smile. "Fine."

I knew enough about women to know that fine didn't mean fine. I also knew that calling her out on it wasn't smart, so I said nothing. I took her hand instead and led her to a small table near the kitchen door. It wasn't an ideal spot. In fact, it was probably the worst table in the whole place, but the others were occupied and I wasn't a big enough jerk to move anyone.

I pulled out her chair and Bente sat down, scanning the room with her eyes. "Business is obviously booming," she noted. "It's a full house tonight."

The kitchen doors crashed open, making us jump. A server rushed past, carrying four plates.

"Business is good," I awkwardly confirmed.

"This wasn't quite what I was expecting when you suggested a change in venue, Ryan."

"No?"

She shook her head and almost smiled.

I leaned back and busied my hands by fussing with the edge of the tablecloth. I'm not a fidgety person but I was having trouble looking her in the eye. Bente is easily irritated. I usually loved that about her, but in this instance it worried me. She was probably fighting the urge to slap me.

"You were the one who insisted on keeping it casual. Nellie's is low key."

"Ginger's was low key too," she retorted.

The kitchen doors crashed open again, but neither of us reacted.

"You're sending mixed signals, Bente." I frowned at the tablecloth. "I thought you'd be happier here. We don't serve salmonella and the floor is clean. So if you're unhappy enough to take a leaf out of Animal's book and hurl yourself on the floor, your pretty dress will stay clean."

Her glare gave way to a look of disbelief. "You call my niece Animal?"

My insults were usually intentional but not this one. "I said that out loud?"

She huffed out a sharp laugh. "Totally out loud."

"I don't mean it in a bad way," I lied. "She reminds me of Animal, the Muppet." Even I knew the hole was getting deeper. "The drummer Muppet. He's quite talented."

"Just stop talking, Ryan."

I nodded, and dropped my head to hide my smile. When I glanced up for a second, I saw she was doing the same thing.

Neither of us spoke for a long time. The silence was excruciating but Bente finally put me out of my misery. "She is a bit like Animal," she conceded, rolling the stem of her glass between her fingers.

I didn't agree, because I'm not a total idiot. I changed the subject instead. "We can go to Billet-doux if you want," I offered. "Or somewhere completely different. Your call."

"I'm not sure what I want," she mumbled. "I have no clue what I'm doing."

At least I wasn't the only one out of my depth. I'd never put so much effort into trying to win over a date in my life.

I'd dated a lot of women – too many to admit to a number. The way I operated hadn't changed since my teens. I chase, I conquer and I release, usually the next morning. When it came to conquering and keeping, I was clueless. And I'd known from the first minute I'd laid eyes on Bente that she was a keeper. I just hadn't been ready for her before.

I thought quickly, trying to come up with some semblance of a plan to stop the evening completely unravelling. "Look," I began, "the way I see it, we have two options here. We can keep it casual if you want to. We'll order the special and spend the night discussing politics and the weather."

She scrunched up her pretty face, clearly unenthused. "What's the second option?"

My heart began thudding, willing my brain to come up with option two. "I will make this the most romantic, memorable evening you've ever had," I declared.

"Wow." She smiled at the cutlery she was pretending to straighten. "That's sounds like an offer almost too good to refuse."

"Two minutes," I blurted. "All I need to make it happen is two minutes. Just say the word."

She lifted her head and glanced around. Not only were all the tables full, a queue was forming at the door, which was great for business but not so great for romance. It made my offer sound like a complete crock, but I was still hopeful of pulling it off.

"I'll take option two, please." Her words came out sounding like she was daring me to do something wicked, which was very fitting. The only plan I'd come up with was about as wicked as they come.

"Excellent choice, Miss Denison," I told her, trying to sound confident. "Are you ready?"

"Born ready."

With a nod, I stood and walked the short distance to the fuse box hidden behind a pot plant. I opened the door, took a long moment to study the interior, and turned back to face her. "Option two, right?"

She wasn't looking smug any more, but I took the stiff nod she gave me as a yes, reached inside and pulled the fire alarm.

A thrumming bell rang out. It was much louder than I expected it to be, but not loud enough to drown out the bedlam in the room. Confusion among the patrons quickly set in. Some panicked, abandoned their meals and rushed out the door; but some stayed put. I was surprised: the food was good, but not that good.

Thankfully, my staff were a little more on the ball. The kitchen doors crashed open over and over as they rushed in and out searching for the fire.

Bente stared at me in wide-eyed disbelief. "What the hell did you just do?"

I took her face in my hands and crushed my lips against hers. "You look so beautiful tonight. You should know that."

It probably wasn't the most appropriate time to be making such a declaration. We were in the midst of chaos.

"Thank you," she choked. "I'll remember those as your parting words. You're going to jail, Ryan."

"No one's going to jail." I released my hold and glanced at the mayhem I'd caused. "Okay, maybe I'm going to jail."

"This is your idea of a memorable evening?"

I grinned at her. "Go big or go home, right?"

"You're not going home," she replied, shaking her head. "For years probably."

Someone called my name. I looked up to see the manager waving me over. "Don't go anywhere," I ordered. "If I don't come back, call Adam to bail me out. And when he says no, call Charli."

10. ODD NUMBERS

Bente

When the fire department stormed the restaurant I was still sitting at the table, pondering whether Ryan Décarie was a romantic man or a stupid one. I felt no urge to flee the building. It wasn't as if it was on fire or anything.

"You have to leave, Miss," ordered an approaching fireman. He pulled my chair back and hooked his arm under mine, making sure I stood.

I wandered out, sharing none of the panic of those around me. The flashing lights of the emergency vehicles lit up the night and onlookers crowded both sides of the street, watching the mayhem unfold.

I stood in the crowd for a long time before spotting Ryan further down the street. He was having a conversation with a police officer and two firemen. I didn't approach. I just stood there, studying him.

Ryan has a habit of talking with his hands. The more intense the conversation, the more animated he becomes. He must've been aware of the quirk because both hands were in his pockets, meaning he was in total control of himself and the conversation. I shuddered to think the lies he was spinning to get himself off the hook. They seemed to be buying it, though. There was a lot of nodding going on, and no sign of any handcuffs.

Ryan Décarie could charm the pants off anyone. It was his biggest talent and his biggest downfall. Every woman he'd ever wooed had been attracted by the same thing – bright brown bedroom eyes, sexy crooked smile and a body made for touching. If for some strange reason those attributes failed, he had a fat bank account to sweeten the deal.

The downfall was, no one ever looked past it – or got the chance to. Ryan's relationships were notoriously short lived: one night, two if he thought she was worth the effort.

Claiming to be immune to his charms would've been a lie, but I was older, wiser and far better equipped to deal with him now. Perhaps that's why I'd agreed to give the wasp's nest another kick.

***

Ryan finally spotted me and waved me over. Just as I got to him, another fireman approached and declared the emergency a false alarm. "You might want to get the alarm system checked out," he suggested, lifting the visor on his helmet. "Something's obviously defective."

Just the owner, I answered silently.

"Thank you," replied Ryan. "I'll do that." He curved his arm around my back and pulled me close and that's when I realised his steely criminal resolve was a sham. I could feel his guilty heart pounding.

"You're free to re-open if you want to," said the police officer.

Ryan looked up at the sign above the front doors. "I think we'll just call it a night," he replied, feigning melancholy.

The emergency responders disappeared as quickly as they'd arrived. Once the trucks and flashing lights were gone, the crowd dissipated too. The only people who remained were the shell-shocked staff, waiting for instruction from Ryan.

"Give me a minute?" he asked.

I nodded. Ryan leaned in, lightly kissed my lips and ventured over to address his staff. I used the time alone to pull myself together. No amount of good looks and charm could change the fact that Ryan was trouble. Pulling a fire alarm to clear a restaurant was the perfect example of the kind of behaviour he was capable of.

When he reappeared, I let him know exactly what I thought of his fire alarm stunt. "What if there had been a real fire somewhere? They couldn't have attended because they were busy dealing with your nonsense."

"I'll send the FDNY a sizeable donation tomorrow," he promised.

"And what about your staff?" I demanded. "They rely on the tips they get. They're getting nothing tonight."

His arm swooped around me. I didn't fight his hold, but I wedged my elbow between us to buy the distance required to keep my brain functioning. "I'll take care of them too."

"If you say so," I muttered.

"You worked for me for a long time, Bente," he reminded. "I'm a good boss, am I not?"

"Yes."

It would've been a terrible lie to claim otherwise. Ryan was the fairest of employers, and I had no doubt that he'd make up their lost wages. His current employees obviously thought highly of him too. They were inside clearing the abandoned tables as we spoke.

"You'll make sure they're compensated?"

"Everyone will be made whole," he assured. "And once the tables have been cleared, we'll be free to continue our date. Do you have any other questions, Miss Denison?"

"A few."

"I'm listening."

"Why did you kiss me?"

A frown marred his otherwise perfect face. "I kissed you?"

"Twice."

"You let me kiss you twice?" he asked. "You must be out of your mind."

"I'm beginning to think so." I agreed.

He leaned a tiny bit closer and whispered, "I think we should make it three times. I like odd numbers."

"That may be so but I don't like odd men," I teased, pushing him away.

A woman walked out of Nellie's and headed toward us. She looked nervous, as if she'd pulled the fire alarm herself. Ryan abandoned his shameless flirting and switched to serious restaurateur mode.

"Sorry to interrupt," she said sheepishly. "We're ready to close up."

"I'll take care of it, Michelle," he replied, nodding. "Thank you."

As soon as she was gone, he drew me in close again. "We finally have the place to ourselves," he said in a deliciously low tone. "It took a little longer than the estimated two minutes but I hope you won't hold that against me."

Of all the things I was thinking of holding against him, that wasn't one of them. Thankfully, I thought better of telling him so.

Ryan reached for my hand and led me back inside. It was strangely reminiscent of old times. I'd always loved Nellie's when it was empty. It was kind of creepy and extraordinarily quiet. Setting tables before dinner service used to be my favourite time of day.

We wove through the tables, straight back to the power box on the back wall.

Despite the fact that it made no sense, I spent a terrible moment thinking he was going to pull the alarm again. But of course he didn't. He dimmed the lights instead, casting a golden glow over the entire front of house.

"Privacy and ambience," he proudly announced, throwing his arms wide. "What more do we need?"

"Music," I replied seriously. "There's no ambience without music."

Ryan's face fell. "Ah, I don't think we have any music."

"You have music, Ryan." I walked over to the small alcove under the stairs that led up to the mezzanine level. "You actually have a pretty decent sound system. It just doesn't get used because it's always so loud in here."

I switched it on and a sultry voice filled the room, asking if we'd still love her tomorrow.

"I never knew that was there." He sounded surprised.

"There are probably a lot of things you don't know."

"What's next?"

"You have no ideas?"

His eyes never left mine as I ambled toward him.

"Your co-ordination efforts have been first class so far," he replied. "I'm happy to let you continue."

"Hmm…." I turned my head, pretending to check out the room while I thought. "How about a dance floor?"

"Stay right there," he demanded, pointing at me as he backed away.

He'd ordered me to stay put a few times that night, which spoke volumes. Obviously he knew I should've been running in the opposite direction too.

Ryan quickly made a few modifications to the décor by pushing tables and chairs to the far side of the room. "Better?" he asked, turning full circle in the space he'd cleared.

The romantic part of me thought it was the grandest, sweetest gesture in the world. The more sensible part of me considered the bigger picture.

"Ryan, this night is going to cost you a fortune," I said gravely. "All that lost revenue and –"

"And what?"

I took a long look around the room before replying. "You've trashed the joint."

He stalked toward me. "I'm still ahead."

"So what happens now?"

His whole body pressed up against me, stealing the air in my lungs. "We dance."

11. TRUST

Ryan

Most girls can't dance – they just think they can.

Bente Denison was the exception to the rule. It wasn't the awkward shuffle I was used to. The girl had skill, never missing a step as we danced around the space I'd cleared.

She craned her neck, looking up at me. "Where did you learn to waltz?"

"Private school."

Her eyes narrowed. "I thought you went to an all-boy school."

The mere fact that she remembered such a trivial detail made me smile. "I did." I lifted her hand above her head and slowly twirled her. "Dance classes were quite awkward at times."

She laughed and I drew her back in close. I freaking loved her laugh. Like her voice, it was rich, velvet and sultry. "What about you? Where did your dancing prowess come from?"

"*Dirty Dancing*," she replied, still smiling. "The movie, not the act."

"You learned to dance by watching a movie?"

"No, but that was my inspiration. As soon as I saw it, I made my mom sign me up for dance classes. I think I was about ten."

I tightened my hold, stepped forward and dipped her backwards. "That must've been some movie, Bente."

The low light caught her face, highlighting her gorgeous features perfectly. "You haven't seen it?" I shook my head. "Well that is a tragedy,

Mr Décarie." She stretched out the words in a sexy drawl. If journalism didn't work out for her, she'd make a great phone sex operator. Unlike the Animal slip, I managed to hold off saying this out loud.

"You'll have to show me *Dirty Dancing* some time." I righted her and drew her back in. "The act, not the movie."

Her body melted against mine. Our stance was no longer technically correct for waltzing, but perfect in other ways. Bente moved slowly, running both hands up my upper arms before linking her hands around my neck. "I'm not sure you'd handle it, Ryan."

"Bente, are you flirting with me?" I asked. "Because if you are, we're no longer in the realm of casual dating."

"No, I'm waltzing."

The girl was not waltzing. She was all hips and hooded eyes.

I broke her hold and positioned her in a way I definitely didn't want her. "Partners stand six inches apart. Chin up." I tilted her face. "The connection is through the hands, wrists and fingers, not the hips." I doubted she was buying this. I liked her hips. There was no denying it. "If all-boy schools taught your version of the waltz, there would be mass confusion among the students."

Her head fell back as she laughed and I desperately wanted to kiss her neck. I tensed my arms instead, holding her in the formal position.

"How about the rumba?" she asked. "Do you know how to rumba?"

"No," I murmured. "It's an unpopular style of dance at an all-boy school."

"I can see why. The rumba is a dance of passion," she explained, following my lead as I stepped back and to the side.

We weren't dancing to music any more. I had no idea what was playing in the background. I was too busy following the way her red lips moved as she spoke.

"It's a very slow, serious flirtation between partners on a dance floor," she explained. "Like making love with your clothes on."

"Is that what we're doing?" I whispered.

She grinned, and I was gone. The pose I'd been struggling to keep disappeared as my hands slipped behind her and travelled south.

"The rumba step is compact and smooth," she said, making no attempt to escape my wandering hands. "You need to roll your hips, like this."

"This isn't your first rumba, is it?" I sounded remarkably composed considering she was grinding against me with every sway of her hips.

She looked up. "Is it your first?"

"One of many firsts for me tonight."

She suddenly looked deadly serious, leaving me to wonder what I'd said wrong.

"I wish I could trust you, Ryan," she whispered. "Things would be so different right now."

There weren't enough words to reassure her that I wasn't following my usual catch and conquer program, so I said nothing.

"You've been the perfect gentleman." She patted my chest as if she was praising an obedient dog. "The bad behaviour has come from me."

"Are you testing me, Bente? Seeing how far I'll go before –"

"Not testing you," she interrupted. "Just getting in first. That way I'll have no one to blame but myself when I'm creeping out of your apartment at four in the morning."

I dropped my hold on her and took a step back. I could hear the music in the background perfectly now, and found it irritating. I walked toward the stairs to switch it off, but my mouth got the better of me. I turned back midway. "I know I hurt you. I know it today and I knew it five years ago. But things are different now."

"How?"

"Because I can admit to it." The words came in a rush as I pushed for understanding. "I was glad when you left New York when you did – so freaking relieved you wouldn't believe it."

Her eyes gleamed in the muted light. She muttered some of the obscenities she'd screamed at the cab driver the day before.

"You're not hearing me," I said, throwing my arms wide. "I was glad you were gone because that meant I didn't have to look you in the eye every single day knowing how badly I screwed up. I had no idea how to deal with you."

"And what about now, Ryan?" she asked quietly. "Are you ready to deal with me now?"

"It doesn't scare me any more."

She looked to the ceiling. "What do you want?" She sounded exasperated. "Where do you see this going?"

I made the brave move of approaching her – slowly, in case she decided to throw a chair. "I have no idea; but I don't want you to sneak out at four in the morning," I told her. "I want more than that."

She looked miserable. "You're so smooth," she muttered. "It's like silk in the beginning. It's the ending that's rough."

We stood inches apart, but I held off reaching for her. "It might never end," I suggested. "For all we know, it could be smooth sailing forever."

Finally she smiled – not blindingly – but enough to reassure me that I wasn't in mortal danger. "I just don't tru –"

I cut her off by wrapping my arms around her and pulling her in close. "You don't have to trust me," I said quietly. "You just have to trust yourself. You know things are different. That's why you're here."

I considered kissing her but Bente beat me to it. She stretched up and kissed me instead, really truly kissed me.

"Number three," she whispered, finally breaking free.

12. INVESTIGATIVE JOURNALISM

Bente

I listened to my inner voice and then bravely disobeyed it, prepared to accept whatever heartbreak followed. Ryan Décarie was a guilty pleasure – one that I'd never stopped liking, just stopped indulging in because it wasn't good for me.

I kissed him a few hundred times before we paused for dinner and then a hundred times more when we got back to his apartment.

Being in Ryan's apartment felt nothing like it had the day before. I wasn't interested in checking it out. I was more interested in checking him out.

"Can I get you anything?" he asked, wandering around the kitchen like he'd lost something.

I stood in the centre of the living room, clutching my tiny purse with both hands. "No, thank you."

Ryan stopped the aimless drift and rested both hands on the counter. "I freaking adore that dress," he declared.

I fanned out the bottom of the skirt. "This old thing?" My flippant comment was a sham. His driver had patiently waited outside Ivy's house for half an hour while I'd pieced my outfit together.

"Actually, it's more than the dress," he amended. "I adore you in my apartment, in that dress."

I wasn't sure how I'd ended up here. A casual dinner with our nieces had somehow transitioned to kissing, lewd dancing and the offer of a nightcap at his place. I had to establish a line I wouldn't cross, and I drew it. "I'm not staying."

The corner of his mouth lifted. "I didn't ask you to."

I dropped my head, feeling slightly stupid. "No, you didn't."

"But if you want to," he added, ambling toward me, "I have the perfect place to hang that dress."

His arm slipped around my waist, drawing me close.

"I'm sure you have, but I'm not staying." Even to my ears, it didn't sound believable.

His lips brushed mine, spreading unbearable heat through my body. "I'll call a cab then."

"Yes, please," I whispered.

"My phone's on the counter."

"You should get it then."

"I should," he agreed.

He didn't get it. He got me instead, because my resolve went out the window about three seconds later when he kissed me again. Carefully set lines blurred, my red dress hit the floor, and we were both goners.

***

I'd expected an air of awkwardness the next morning. I'd even prepared for it. Ryan wasn't going to get a chance to politely ask me to leave his bed because I was up before he even stirred. I was getting in first and cutting myself loose. The idea was to play it cool, thank him for the nice time, and lie about getting together again soon.

Once I was dressed, I sneaked into the adjacent bathroom to wash my face and sort out my rat's nest hair. The top drawer of the cabinet didn't make a sound as I slid it open. Finding a hairbrush was my objective, but curiosity side-tracked me.

The drawer was as neat as the rest of the apartment. I picked up a small bottle and studied the label closely. Even then, I was none the wiser as to what shaving oil was – but it sounded sexy as hell.

He had everything from hair products to moisturisers. Perhaps looking drop dead gorgeous took work.

The last thing to catch my eye looked like a big ChapStick. I pulled the lid off, checked it out and concluded that it was still a big ChapStick. "For people with big mouths," I mumbled.

"Not really."

I jumped, dropping it on the floor. The stick rolled across the tiles, coming to a stop at his feet.

Ryan picked it up, showcasing every muscle on his bare back as he stooped. It was an unfair move on his part. Thinking straight was hard enough without that kind of display.

"It's a styptic pencil," he explained, rolling it between his fingers. "It's good for healing shaving nicks." He handed it back to me and I quickly dropped it back in the drawer. "Are you snooping on me, Bente?"

If anything, he seemed amused by the prospect.

"Do you know the definition of investigative journalism, Ryan?"

He folded his arms and leaned against the doorjamb. "I'd like to hear yours."

"It's a form of journalism in which reporters deeply investigate a single topic of interest."

"I'm all for deep investigating, Miss Denison," he murmured in a low tone. "What would you like to know?"

My eyes darted between his eyes and his mouth. "Nothing." I cleared my throat. "I've got you all worked out, pretty boy."

"I've got you all worked out too," he replied, taking a few slow steps closer to me.

"Really?" I asked dryly.

"Yes. You're a shameless stickybeak." The way he hummed the words against the side of my neck made defending myself impossible. "Are you done spying?"

"For now," I mumbled.

"Excellent. We can get back to more important tasks, then." He abandoned the mind-scrambling neck kissing and led me to the kitchen. "Sit," he ordered, pointing at a stool. "Please."

"You're very bossy, Ryan."

I wondered if he realised it. He was forever issuing orders. It should've been a quirk that grated on me, but it didn't.

Ryan disappeared from view while he searched a low cupboard. "I don't mean to be." He popped back up, set a cast iron pan down on the counter and pointed at the stool again.

I gave in and sat down. "What are you doing?"

"You're very inquisitive, Bente," he teased.

"We make quite a pair then, don't we?"

He smiled, and it was magnificent. "*Oui*, sweetheart. We do."

"One night together and you're calling me sweetheart?" I tried sounding appalled, but failed. "That's a bit *Fatal Attraction* isn't it?"

He shrugged. "No more *Fatal Attraction* than you snooping through the drawers in my bathroom."

He had a point, so I changed the subject. "What are you cooking?"

Ryan walked to the fridge and peered inside. He seemed to be having trouble deciding, which was understandable. There was more food in his fridge than in the storeroom of his restaurant.

"How about something fancy?" He glanced at me. "*Oeufs brouillés*?"

"That sounds amazing."

"You're sure?" he asked, sounding worried.

I wasn't sure about anything. I had no idea what it was, but he made it sound heavenly. "If it's out of your league, I'll settle for cereal."

Ryan nudged the fridge door closed with his foot and carried an armload of ingredients to the counter. "Nothing is out of my league when it comes to cooking. I'm a fine chef," he declared, dumping the food down in a heap.

"You like to cook?" The notion surprised me.

"No, I *love* to cook," he corrected. "I'm actually more of a baker. I like to bake. Cakes are my specialty."

I laughed, and then threw my hand over my mouth because it was inappropriate. "I'm sorry," I replied. "It's not funny. It's actually very sweet."

Ryan smiled crookedly. "It's not common knowledge, Bente." He grabbed a whisk from a drawer. "If you tell anyone, I'll deny it."

"Who would I tell?" I grinned. "All you've done is even the score. I told you about my *Dirty Dancing* addiction, remember?"

"I remember."

"So we're even."

"*Au contraire*, sweetheart," he crowed. "I'm still ahead."

***

Oeufs brouillés wasn't anywhere near as impressive as it sounds.

"Scrambled eggs?" I asked, staring at the plate in front of me. "I thought you were going to serve me something fabulous – like a plate of truffles infused with the laughter of a thousand babies."

"That would be amazing," he agreed. "Are you disappointed?"

I turned the plate in a full circle, pretending to study it. "No," I had to admit. "Nothing about the past day has disappointed me."

13. TRAIN WRECK

Ryan

Strange things were happening to me. I had a million things to do that day, and most involved getting Nellie's back in order after my theatrics of the night before. But spending the morning with Bente was much more enjoyable. We sat at the kitchen counter, enjoying breakfast. Conversation flowed, and before I knew it, it was close to midday.

"I should be going," she said, noticing me glance at my watch.

"Why?"

Bente carried the plates to the sink. "Because the day is slipping away. My sister is probably going out of her mind."

Her sister was already out of her mind.

"How long are you planning to stay with Ivy?" I asked curiously.

She leaned against the counter. "It was supposed to be temporary but it looks like I'm in for the long haul now – at least until I can find a new job."

I bit my tongue to stop myself offering her one. It would've been an insult. Bente wasn't a server any more. She'd been a working reporter in Boston for a long time before coming home to New York. "I'm sure something will come up," I said instead.

"Yes, I know it will," she agreed, walking back to me, "but a great new job isn't going to just fall in my lap, which is why I should be spending the day job hunting instead of hanging out with you."

As soon as she was in reach, I swivelled the stool and grabbed her. "I don't think you should leave," I said quietly. "I want you to stay."

She wedged her body between my legs. Her hand moved to the back of my head, raking her nails through my hair. "I have to leave some time, Ryan. There's only so much sex two people can have before they die of exhaustion."

Close enough to kiss her, I brushed my lips against hers. "Are you prepared to investigate that theory? I'd be happy to be your single topic of interest."

Her body instinctively leaned, chasing my mouth. "I'm always up for a challenge, Ryan," she murmured.

***

No one dies from an excess of sex. After two days of intensive research, we proved it. The investigative study might've been ongoing if not for the fact that real life kicked in.

Late on day one, Ivy started blowing up Bente's phone, demanding to know where she was. By day two, her voicemail messages included threats of bodily harm so Bente had no choice but to return her call.

"I'm staying with a friend," she uttered.

Even with a pillow over my head, I heard the reply. "You don't have any friends," Ivy roared. "You need to come home."

I tossed the pillow aside and pulled the phone from Bente's ear. "She's not coming back, Ivy," I said loudly. "Never, ever."

That earned me a sharp elbow to the ribs. It was worth it just to sock it to her nasty sister. "Ryan, shush!" Bente hissed.

"Ryan? Ryan Décarie?" Ivy screamed. "You're hooking up with Ryan Décarie?"

I couldn't help smiling. I hadn't seen the woman in years; obviously I'd made a lasting impression.

Bente sat bolt upright, taking the sheet with her. "I'm not hooking up with anybody. I'll be home this afternoon."

I tried talking her out of it by kissing a line across her back. She wriggled but kept talking. "You need to get a grip, Ivy."

"Ryan Décarie?" her sister spat. "You're the one who needs to get a grip."

Bente barked a few choice words and ended the call. She tossed her phone on the bed and flopped back. I took immediate advantage, kissing a new line along her collarbone. "I don't think she likes me," I noted between kisses.

"Not so much," she agreed. "I wish we could hide out here forever."

"We can," I hummed into the hollow at the base of her neck. "Let's do it."

Her body trembled beneath me as she laughed. That was reason enough to stay in bed forever.

"It's alright for you," she said, giggling. "No one's chasing you."

"You're right. That's actually pretty sad," I lamented. "I could be dead on the floor, and no one cares."

Bente shuffled from beneath me and reached for my phone on the nightstand. "Here." She held it out to me. "Do you need to call a friend?"

I silenced her with a kiss, but I did take the phone. When I turned my head to check the screen for missed calls, she groaned. "I didn't mean now, Ryan."

The screen was one long log of messages. I'd been missing call after call for two days because I'd switched my phone to silent. "This isn't good," I muttered, laying my head back on the pillow.

Bente propped herself up on one elbow. "Something wrong?"

I dropped the phone back on the nightstand. "I have to go into work," I told her. "My restaurants are going to the dogs. If I stay away much longer, someone will add coleslaw to the menu."

She sighed. "So this is how it ends."

I swept her hair off her shoulder. "It's been nice knowing you."

"That's it?" She huffed out a husky laugh. "That's all I get?"

I curved my hand around her waist and rolled her on top of me. "I'll give you much, much more if you stay."

"No, I have to go too."

I put my hand to her cheek and she leaned into my palm. "Pack your stuff and move in here," I blurted. "Or better yet, I'll send someone to do it."

Her flash of surprise matched mine perfectly. It was a ludicrous suggestion. I'd never lived with a girl in my life; except my mother, and I'm pretty sure she didn't count. "Forty-eight hours," she choked. "We've known each other forty-eight hours."

"That's not true. We've known each other seven years. At least think about it," I urged. "It might be amazing."

"It might also be a train wreck."

"Bente, you live with Ivy and the squealers," I pointed out. "The worst train wreck would be an improvement."

She kissed me chastely. "I'll think about it."

***

The only thing worse than leaving Billet-doux unmanaged for two days was having my business partner step in and take charge.

The daytime manager, Noelle, gave me the heads up at the door. "Charli's in your office," she warned, skipping to keep up with me. "I told her that you wouldn't be pleased, but she didn't listen."

"Okay, thanks." Stopping suddenly was a mistake. She nearly ran into me, like an overenthusiastic puppy. "Was there something else, Noelle?"

There was usually plenty where Noelle was concerned. She was very … keen. In the year that she'd worked at Billet-doux, she'd tried a hundred times to catch my eye. I wasn't completely immune to her charms. She was a very pretty blonde with blindingly white teeth, enormous energy and a fondness for the word 'super'. I liked to look at Noelle. I just had no desire to touch her.

"No." She hit me with her stun gun smile. "I'm just super glad you're back. Everyone missed you."

I glanced around the quiet restaurant. Two girls were setting tables and there was a guy polishing glasses behind the bar. None of them looked super excited to see me again.

"Well, I'm back now." I walked away before she could speak again.

Noelle wisely decided against following me. Perhaps she knew what was about to go down. I threw open my office door expecting at least a second or two of expressions of terror, but I got nothing. Charli sat at my desk, staring at my computer as if she had half a clue what she was looking at.

"Get off my chair."

"No. It's my chair too."

"I want a chair," came a little voice out of nowhere.

My eyes scanned the room. "Where is she?"

Bridget's little hand popped up from under the desk. "I'm here."

"Don't you two have anything better to do than hang out in my office?" I grumbled.

Charli didn't pay me so much as a sideward glance. "We're just here to use the printer, then we'll be out of your hair," she declared. "Ours is out of ink."

"My daddy broke it," volunteered Bridget.

I dropped my keys on the desk. "So nothing work related then?"

Charli's giggle sounded positively evil. "Not unless you count princess colouring sheets as work."

Bridget's head popped up. "Did you do the blue one?" she asked. "I love the blue one."

"None of them are blue, Bridge," muttered her mother. "That's the whole point. You've got to colour them in yourself."

"Do you have pencils, Ry?" asked Bridget.

"No." I scooped Bridget off the floor and put her down by the door, hoping her mother would follow. "I'm sure you have plenty of pencils at home."

Charli glanced at me. "Are you trying to get rid of us? Noelle already tried, super hard. She's very territorial, Ryan. It's super scary."

It was impossible not to smile. "It's only scary if she thinks you're a threat."

"Me?" Her eyes never left the computer screen. "Ugh. I'll stick with your younger, hotter brother, thanks all the same."

"You do that, Charli," I agreed. "I really do have work to do."

She let out a sigh, swivelled her chair and grabbed a handful of papers off the printer. "Okay, okay. We're going."

"Thank you."

As soon as she moved I took her place on the chair, fearful that she'd change her mind. Charli slung her bag over her shoulder and grabbed Bridget's hand. "Where have you been, anyway?" she asked. "We haven't seen you in days."

I wiggled my eyebrows. "On a date."

She abandoned her daughter and dumped her bag on my desk again. "With Bente?"

I nodded, sliding her bag toward her suggestively.

"For two days?" she asked.

"She's amazing, Charli."

She narrowed her brown eyes, tilting her head. "How amazing?"

I leaned back in my chair. "On a level of one to chocolate cake?"

"She could be chocolate cake girl?" Her voice rose, making her sound eerily like Bridget.

"I'm looking forward to seeing where it goes," I replied. "That's all I'm telling you."

She put her hand up. "Say no more."

"I appreciate that you're respecting my privacy," I replied formally.

"I'll just call Bente for details." She took Bridget by the hand and slipped out the door, only to poke her head back in a second later to offer up a parting shot. "And you know I don't respect you, Ryan."

14. DUMB PRINCESSES

Bente

I didn't go straight home. Dealing with Ivy could wait. I'd had a blissful two days and wanted to tell someone who'd actually be happy for me, so I walked the short journey to Charli's place.

The only fault with that plan was that she wasn't home. Adam answered the door.

I looked him up and down, quickly concluding that he was on his way to work – or a GQ magazine shoot. He was dressed for either.

Someone should've given Fiona Décarie an award when her boys were born. She'd knocked it out of the ballpark twice when it came to producing gorgeous looking men.

"I can come back," I offered.

"No," he replied, jingling a bunch of keys in his hand. "Stay if you want. The girls should be back any minute. I have to go, though." He checked his watch. "I have a meeting ten minutes ago."

"You're sure?"

"Of course." He glanced back into the apartment. "Just try not to knock the tent over."

I looked past him, spotting a bed sheet canopying the lounge. A row of dolls lined the couch and a kiddie size table and chairs was set up underneath. "Cute campsite."

"It's not a camp," Adam corrected. "It's a school for dumb princesses."

I held both hands up. "I don't even want to know."

He chuckled darkly. "Probably not. I'll see you later, Bente." He made a dash for the elevator. "Have fun in class."

"Wait," I demanded. "Are you calling me a dumb princess?"

He hit the button on the elevator and turned back, grinning. "Not at all. Last I heard she was recruiting teachers."

***

Charli and Bridget arrived home soon after. I was glad to see them. The dumb princesses lining the couch were beginning to creep me out.

"Hey." I jumped to my feet.

"Hi!" beamed Bridget, bolting toward the couch. "See my girls at school?"

"I do see them," I confirmed. "They're all so pretty."

The little girl threw herself over the arm of the couch. "They need work," she said, making me laugh. She ducked under the sheet, freeing me to seek grownup conversation in the kitchen.

"I'm glad you're here," said Charli. "You're just the girl I wanted to talk to." Her tone led me to think she was in possession of more information than she should've been.

"You've spoken to Ryan already?"

She began searching through her bag. "I've just come from Billet-doux. He was almost human. I'm guessing you've got something to do with that."

"It was so good, Charli," I said wistfully.

She stopped rummaging to glare. "Don't give me details!" She looked appalled. "I don't want to know."

"Not that part ... although that was good too."

"Stop right there!"

"Okay, no details," I promised, crossing my heart. That left only one thing to tell her about. "He asked me to move in with him."

Her brown eyes bugged at the news. "Are you kidding me?"

"No. I'm serious."

Charli pulled a pile of papers out of her bag and called Bridget over. "Colour them in, okay?" she instructed. "Don't rip them up, Bridge. I mean it."

Bridget took them. "Small ripping?"

"No ripping," she repeated.

The little girl took off back to her classroom tent.

"She's going to tear them, isn't she?" I asked.

Charli let out a sigh of resignation. "Into a million pieces, probably."

With Bridget occupied, we were free to sit at the table, drink tea and deconstruct Ryan's crazy offer.

"I think it was a spur of the moment suggestion," I told her.

Charli shook her head. "Ryan doesn't make spur of the moment decisions."

"How else would you explain it?"

Her bright eyes bored into me. "He thinks you might be chocolate cake girl."

Coming to Charli for advice probably wasn't wise, mainly because of the language barrier. Fairy-speak confounded me. Normally I'd overlook it and move on, but in this instance I needed to know what she meant. "Charli, just step back onto my planet for a minute and tell me what you mean."

"My daddy likes cake," announced a little voice from the next room.

Charli wiggled her eyebrows. "Ryan does too, apparently."

I leaned back, defeated. "This isn't helping," I complained. "I came here for advice, not a lesson in desserts."

"You're asking me for advice?" she asked incredulously. "Even my kid doesn't come to me for advice – and she's four. Her father's the sensible one. Go to him."

Frustrated, I scrubbed both hands down my face. "Tell me what to do, Charli," I practically pleaded.

She stared at me for a long time, deliberating. "If you already knew the answer, what would it be?"

I shook my head, feeling hopeless. "I don't know."

"It might be the best five minutes of your life, Bente."

Charli's habit of putting a romantic spin on everything wasn't helpful. I didn't want five minutes with Ryan. I'd had five minutes with him before, and then spent the next five years recovering. I wanted something more substantial with no need for recovery time.

"Would you do it?"

"With Ryan?" She screwed up her face. "Hell, no."

"Because he's selfish and fickle and conceited?" My shoulders slumped as I prepared for her answer.

"No." She laughed. "Because he's Ryan."

***

I'd avoided facing Ivy for hours but couldn't put it off any longer. I didn't even make it to the front steps before she ambushed me. Clearly she'd been lying in wait. The hanging plants she was pretending to tend to had been dead for years.

"Ryan Décarie?" she screeched, throwing her watering can over the edge of the porch. "Really?"

I trudged up the steps like a tired old woman. "Yes, really," I muttered.

Ivy beat me to the door, swinging the screen open so hard that it smashed against the house. "He's not welcome in my home." She spoke with absolute contempt. "I have impressionable children in this house."

I almost laughed. If her children were any more corrupt, they'd be in jail. There was nothing Ryan could teach them. I pushed past her. "Fine. I won't bring him here."

My sister had obviously been preparing for a fight. Agreeing with her seemed to mess with her game plan. She'd run out of words. "Fine," she agreed, almost calmly.

"So we're good?" I asked, wondering why she had me bailed up in the hall.

"Why aren't you at work?" she asked, getting a little off track.

"I got fired."

Her eyes widened. I braced myself. "He got you fired?"

I pushed past to the kitchen, uselessly trying to escape. "Ryan had nothing to do with it. How could he get me fired?"

Ivy was hot on my heels. "I wouldn't put anything past him," she snapped. "Have you forgotten what happened last time?"

I would never forget. His past behaviour was still causing damage, not that I'd admit it to Ivy. "People change. It was a long time ago."

I knew Ivy wasn't finished with me but I won a reprieve when my nieces barrelled into the kitchen – well, Fabergé barrelled in. Malibu entered against her will, thanks to the handful of hair her sister had hold of.

"Tell her to stay out of my stuff," demanded Fabergé.

I couldn't quite make out Malibu's reply. It came out in a growly shriek.

I threw both hands up in surrender. I was out of there.

15. THE COUPLE THING

Ryan

As much as it sometimes pained me to admit, my restaurants ran pretty well when I wasn't there. I only spent a short time at Billet-doux before heading over to Nellie's. Paolo greeted me at the podium with a big grin and a thump on the back as if he hadn't seen me in months. I kept waiting for him to broach the subject of the rearranged furniture, but he never mentioned it. I almost wished he had; I might've told him the whole story. Good things were happening and I was feeling an unusual need to share.

"Do I look any different to you, Paolo?" I asked.

The man looked completely trapped, as if there was no correct answer. "New shirt?"

"New beginnings, Paolo."

"Should I alert the media?" The caution in his voice killed the joke he was trying to make.

"No need." I grinned. "She *is* the media."

***

I decided to walk home from Nellie's, which wasn't something I did often. It was a good decision. After a few days of intermittent rain, the humidity had given way to sunshine. The bustling streets of Manhattan are the perfect place to be alone with your thoughts, and I had plenty. Most revolved around the preposterous offer I'd made to Bente of moving in.

Her argument that we'd only known each other a short time was completely valid. Neither of us were renowned for making rash decisions. We were sensible and smart. So why was every fibre of my being hoping she'd take me up on it?

I could think of only one reason. Turning thirty had made me soft.

I was still walking when I received a text from the lady in question.

- Are you busy?

I thought quickly, trying to come up with a witty response.

- No

I failed. Turning thirty had made me *really* soft.

- I think we need to talk

No good could come from a sentence like that. I could almost feel my feet dragging as I slowed to type my reply.

- Dinner? I'll cook for you

I added a smiley face for good measure. I had never texted a smiley face in my life. What the hell was happening to me?

Bente replied with a love heart. Perhaps she was losing it too.

I picked up my pace and rushed the rest of the way. By the time she knocked on my door a few hours later, dinner was prepared.

I put on a confident smile, took a breath and opened the door.

"Hi." Her voice was barely there, and the half-hearted wave she gave me was just plain odd.

"You're greeting me with a wave?" I asked, puzzled. "Do you want me to follow up with a high-five?"

She answered with a quick shake of her head, an even quicker lurch forward and a heart-stopping slow kiss. After spending all afternoon preparing for the worst, it was the most welcome kiss I'd ever received.

Talking wasn't high on my agenda at that point, so it was left to Bente to break the embrace. When she pulled away and walked to the centre of the room, I didn't move.

"I've been putting a lot of thought into your offer and –"

"And what?"

She spun to face me. "Why do you do that?"

"Do what?"

"Cut me off. I was in the middle of explaining and you cut me off. It's annoying."

"I am annoying," I agreed, taking small steps toward her.

Her cross look began to slip. "I am too," she confessed. "I'm also really messy. Shambolic actually. You wouldn't want to live with me."

I dropped my head and smiled at the floor. "Shambolic? That sounds serious," I teased. "I'm sure I'll adapt."

"But you're clearly a neat freak, Ryan." She waved her hands around the room. "You'd have a breakdown in the first week."

"Maybe," I agreed. "But I'm prepared to chance it." I had no idea why.

She shook her head. "It's a really bad idea."

I stared at her, trying to figure out what to say. She was being sensible at a time when I seemed to have lost my mind. I should've been thanking her.

"So you're saying no?"

"I'm not sure," she replied, sounding confused. "Common sense says we should be ending this before it gets out of hand."

"You're breaking up with me?" I couldn't help smiling as I asked the childish question.

"Technically, I think we have to be together before we can break up," she replied, over-thinking things as usual.

"I could do that," I bravely offered.

"Do what?"

"The couple thing," I said awkwardly. "I could do that with you."

The corner of her mouth twitched and I knew she was on to me. "Do you even know what that means, Ryan?"

"No, not really," I admitted, shrugging. "But I'm a fast learner."

"Not that fast."

"Give me a little credit." I sounded far more wounded than I was. Every misgiving she had about me was more than warranted, but it didn't stop me pleading my case. "Just because I've never had a girlfriend before doesn't mean I –"

She cut me off with an angry moan. "You've dated half the women in the free world, Ryan."

"But that's not the same as having a girlfriend, is it?"

Bente's backward steps looked more like a stumble. She fell back onto the couch in a heap. "Oh my God." She buried her face in her hands. "My potential boyfriend is a relationship virgin."

She made it sound terrible. Now I *was* wounded. "I'm not completely clueless," I asserted. "I kind of had a girlfriend once."

She looked at me. "And what happened?"

I tried to keep a straight face. "Her husband found out."

Bente moaned again. "It goes from bad to worse, doesn't it?"

I pulled her to her feet. "I'm kidding, Bente."

"Really?" Her voice was tiny but hopeful.

"Yeah," I assured her. "Her husband never found out."

***

Dinner wasn't exactly a romantic event. It was more like a session in contingency planning. We sat side by side at the kitchen counter, discussing worst-case scenarios.

"If you're not happy, dump me *before* you find someone else," she demanded.

"You'll be the first to know," I assured her. "Should I email or will a text suffice?"

She glanced at me, and perhaps realised I was a little hurt. "I'm sorry, Ryan. I just want you to be sure."

I reached for her hand. "I'm as sure as I can be," I promised. "I just have one question."

She nodded. "Okay."

"Are we going to go all-in and live together or do I have to knock on your crazy sister's door every time I want to see you?"

"Would that be a problem?"

"I don't know," I replied seriously. "Has Ivy got a gun?"

"No, but I think Malibu might."

I couldn't be sure she was joking so I tried harder to talk her round. "Just move in here," I urged. "Take the spare room if you want. I'll visit you there."

Bente took a long sip of wine before replying. "I can't pay rent. I'm unemployed."

I rolled my eyes at her ridiculous excuse. "I'll try my best to cope with the financial burden of having you here."

Her garnet lips didn't smile, but her brown eyes did. "Smartass."

"Just do it, Bente. Don't make me beg."

She looked down at her plate. "Will you cook for me?"

"Every night if you want me to," I pledged. "Will you walk around the house naked?"

Her laugh filtered through my whole body. "Sure. I see no problem with that."

I leaned across and kissed her. "A woman after my own heart."

She bumped me with her shoulder. "I'm going to get your heart, Ryan," she whispered.

"Bring it on, sweetheart. I'm ready for you."

16. SMALL TALK

Bente

It took me two days to come up with a game plan for breaking the news to Ivy. It took me another two to convince Ryan that he should be with me when I did it.

"Can't I tell your parents instead?" he asked. "Surely that would be less traumatic."

"They're on vacation."

My parents had been on permanent vacation for years. Ed and Evie Denison were the king and queen of the cheesy cruise ship scene. My mom spent her days singing karaoke and sunning herself poolside. My dad enjoyed shooting the breeze at all-you-can-eat buffets with other bald old men who shared his fascination for Hawaiian print shirts. They usually make it home for Christmas, spend a few weeks whining about the terrible weather, and then take off again.

Chances are they wouldn't give a damn about my new living arrangements; but Ivy more than made up for their lack of concern. Her heart was in the right place, and I spent most of the drive to Astoria trying to convince Ryan of that.

The second we got out of the cab, every promise I'd made him that things would go smoothly went out the window. I could hear the girls going at it hammer and tongs in the house. Ryan obviously heard it too. "Getting you out of here is practically my civic duty, Bente," he grumbled.

I hooked my arm through his to keep him moving up to the house. "Just play nice." As opposed to my nieces. Through the screen door I could see them strangling each other in the hall.

They separated the second we walked in. Fabergé didn't react to Ryan – unless a blank stare can be considered a reaction – but Malibu unravelled quickly. The colour drained from her already pale little cheeks and she took off up the stairs. "Mama!" she screamed. "She got married with the bad man! Don't let him live here!"

Ryan looked smug, but it didn't last long. Ivy came bounding down the stairs and stopped half-way, giving her the advantage of height and distance. "I told you not to bring him here," she said sourly. "He's already upset Malibu."

Ryan tilted his head to the side and whispered. "Marry me, Bente. I dare you." He must've expected my elbow to his side because he didn't flinch.

"We came to talk to you," I said strongly, "but you're going to have to calm down first."

Ivy clung to the timber balustrade as if she was holding herself back. Her eyes darted between the two of us a hundred times before she finally spoke. "You have two minutes."

"That's generous," mumbled Ryan. Ivy confounded him. He saw her as nothing more than a maniac who hated him for no good reason. I knew differently. My sister had fiercely protected me for as long as I could remember. And if he'd seen the emotional wreck of a woman that she'd had to scrape off the floor after he was done with me the last time, he would've understood.

Despite softening enough to hear me out, Ivy dragged out the drama as long as she could. Ryan and I sat in the small, over-furnished living room while Ivy disappeared to make coffee. Fabergé stood in the doorway, staring Ryan down. Malibu was nowhere to be seen.

"How are you Fabergé?" asked Ryan, making the smallest of small talk. "Long time no see. Do you remember me?"

"No."

"Pity," he replied. "I guess there's no point asking for my phone back then, huh?"

I had no clue what he was talking about, and was fairly sure I didn't want to. I changed the subject. "Ryan is my boyfriend," I explained, sounding incredibly juvenile.

Ryan leaned across and patted my knee. "And Bente is my girlfriend," he added, sounding worse.

Fabergé wasn't impressed. "You guys are lame," she muttered, disappearing from sight.

17. DEATH METAL GIRL

Ryan

We weren't lame. The candy pink velvet wing chairs we were sitting on were lame.

Ivy's living room was a horrendously girly display of pageant trophies, diamante crowns and ribbon sashes. The house looked like a unicorn had thrown up in it.

"Nice chairs, sweetheart." I ran my hands along the velvet arms.

"They're great, aren't they?" My comment backfired the instant I realised she was serious. "They were the only things I shipped back from Boston, besides my dresser."

"These are yours?"

"Yeah," drawled Bente, sounding far too proud.

She wriggled back as if settling in for a nap. The hideous chair swamped her. There was no doubt about it. My very first girlfriend had appalling taste.

"Bente, what kind of music do you listen to?" I asked nervously.

She turned her head. "Why?"

"Just wondering."

She hit me with a smile so gorgeous it almost made up for her lack of taste in home furnishing – until she ruined it by poking her tongue out and following up with the devil horns salute. "Heavy metal mostly.... or really loud death metal when the mood hits." I imagined my downstairs neighbours bashing on my door when her mood hit. "What's the matter?" she asked leaning closer to me.

"Are you lying to me? I'd feel so much better if you were."

Her smile returned in an instant. "If I was lying about one thing, would you rather it be the chairs or the music?"

It was a tough choice. Both were hideous but at least the chairs were quiet. "The music."

"Good news then." She settled back in the chair. "The chairs are mine and I hate death metal."

***

Ivy finally returned, looking no less pissed off than when she'd left. She handed me a mug off coffee, which I would've thanked her for if she'd given me chance. "What's this all about?" she barked.

I nominated myself spokesman and cut to the chase, mainly because Bente was too far away to elbow me. "Your sister is moving in with me."

Ivy cut me her nastiest glare but it had little effect. I took a sip of coffee as if I was leisurely passing time until she spoke. She turned to her sister. "After all he put you through, you're going back for more?"

Her disgusted tone was more painful than any elbow to the ribs. I wanted to defend myself, then realised I couldn't. Her incredulity was warranted. I wasn't owed a second glance, let alone a second chance at a relationship with Bente.

"I know what I'm doing," insisted Bente, sounding completely dishonest. "I want you to be happy for me, Ivy."

"And what about him?" she asked, pointing at me. "What does he want?"

Bente shrugged. "Ask him."

"Well?" she snapped, whipping her head in my direction. "What's in it for you?"

Even my father would've been impressed by her skilful cross-examination. Anything I said was going to come out wrong, so I tried my hand at being honest. "I don't know what I'm going to get out of this. I've never done it before."

"Exactly," scoffed Ivy. "You've no clue what you're doing. You barely know each other."

I set my mug down on the coffee table. "I know a lot about your sister."

"I just heard you ask her about her favourite music," she snapped back. "You know nothing."

I should've known she'd been hanging on every word from the kitchen. Thank God I hadn't used the time to tell Bente what I really thought of her overbearing maniacal sister.

"I know that she got wildly drunk on her twenty-first birthday," I revealed. "That was the night she got the little heart tattooed on her wrist." Ivy straightened up but didn't pass comment. "I know she's allergic to red wine: she comes out in hives. White is okay, though." I glanced at Bente, who acknowledged my wink with a tiny smile. "Shall I continue?"

"No," muttered Ivy.

"Yes," overruled Bente. "Tell me what else you know."

"You're left-handed."

"I am," she confirmed with a chuckle.

It occurred to me that I knew a lot of things about Bente Denison, and they weren't details she'd shared recently. I wish I'd thought to tell her days ago. It might've helped convince her that moving in with me wasn't such a blind leap.

"You like to sing," I added, smiling, "but only when you think no one's listening."

Bente flushed. I reached over and took her hand. "You're not a death metal girl. You're an Etta James girl, right? You used to sing at Nellie's while you set the tables. I used to hear you from Paolo's office."

"I'll bet I know the song," interjected Ivy. "'Anything to say you're mine'."

I smiled at Ivy for the first time ever. "That's the one."

I hadn't known the name at the time, so I Googled the lyrics to find out. I then downloaded it to my phone – but I kept that gem to myself in case it was weird.

"That was her pageant song when she was younger," she revealed. Surprisingly, Ivy's face didn't crack when she smiled. Perhaps she'd done it before.

I turned to Bente. "Pageants? You never told me about the pageants."

Ivy jumped up and moved to the bookshelf. There wasn't a book on it, just a cluttered row of trophies. "These are all Bente's," she said proudly, waving her hand along the shelf. "She dances too."

"Yes she does," I beamed. "Beautifully."

However embarrassing the revelations might've been for Bente, I found it endearing. I'd dated a million women who claimed to be beauty queens, but none of them had ever waltzed like Ginger Rogers or crooned Etta James songs in empty restaurants. Bente was old school charming and classically beautiful – far different from the high-maintenance blondes of my past. No wonder none of them had ever appealed long-term; I'd spent years playing on the wrong field. Brassy, shallow divas weren't my type. Sultry, siren journalists were.

"Can you cook, Ryan?" asked Ivy, snapping me back to the moment.

Bente answered for me. "Yes, he's practically a chef," she shamelessly declared.

"Good." Ivy headed toward the kitchen. "We're barbecuing tonight. You can cook." Coming from Ivy, it was an incredible invitation, even if it was disguised as an obnoxious demand.

As soon as she was gone, Bente piled onto my lap and smothered my face with a barrage of kisses. "Thank you. Thank you. Thank you."

"For what?" I asked, trying to escape the onslaught.

"For winning her over. I knew you would."

I wasn't sure what I'd won where Ivy was concerned. I was just grateful I'd lived through it.

"Bente, I don't know the first thing about barbecuing," I whispered.

"I don't care." She kissed me again. "You know plenty about me."

***

The prospect of barbecuing became a lot more terrifying when I saw what I had to work with. Bente led me outside to a small backyard littered with toys and a broken swing set. Among the junk was a small gas grill propped up on bricks, and it was so raging hot that it glowed.

"When did she light this?" I choked. "Last week?"

"At least you know it works."

The back door swung open and Ivy appeared at the top of the steps. "Don't mix Fabergé's veggie hotdogs up with the rest," she ordered, waving a plate of meat at us. "She'll know if you do."

Bente took the plate. I stayed put until she returned, trying my best not to combust in the meantime. As soon as the door slammed closed, I felt free to speak. "What would an eight-year-old know about vegetarianism?" I asked. "It's stupid."

Bente set the plate on the edge of the grill. The thing was so hot, I swear the cooking process began there and then.

"It's just a fad," she replied, handing me tongs. "All kids go through phases."

"It's weird," I insisted. "Your niece is weird."

"Bridget wears boots every single day," pointed out Bente. "Do you think *your* niece is weird?"

I snapped the tongs at her. "Absolutely out of her little freaking mind."

Paying no special attention to Faberge's veggie hotdogs, Bente dumped the plate of meat onto the grill in a heap.

I knew the thing was unsteady. What I didn't know is that it wasn't level. Before I had a chance to act, a handful of hotdogs rolled onto the ground like they were trying to escape the searing heat. I held the rest in place by pinning them with the tongs. "Now what do we do?"

"Just leave them," she replied, unperturbed. "She won't notice a few missing."

I looked down at the casualties on the ground. "Fabergé might," I said, gravely. "The veggie hotdogs are now *really* veggie."

Bente plucked as much grass off them as she could and threw them back on the grill. "The extra nutrition will do her good."

18. FAIRY CONNECTIONS

Bente

Despite the pandemonium, dinner in Ivy's house is actually pretty structured. We ate at the table every single night. I'm not sure what Ryan was expecting, but a neatly set dining table probably wasn't it.

Although she'd never admit it, my sister was out to impress. The first thing I noticed was that she was using the cutlery usually reserved for special occasions. She'd also laid a tablecloth. Until then I wasn't aware that she had a tablecloth.

Ryan had no way of knowing that she'd gone the extra mile, but he did know when to lay on the charm. "This looks great, Ivy," he praised.

Ignoring the compliment, she pointed to an empty chair. Ryan politely pulled my chair out for me before sitting down. I wasn't sure if she'd positioned him well or not. He was opposite Malibu, who was trying to kill him with a nasty glare. Fabergé was a little more receptive to our dinner guest, but I suspected that would change once she tasted her veggie hotdogs.

Ivy loaded the girl's plates, then took the odd step of doing the same for Ryan. She sat at the head of the table and the weirdest dinner party of my life got under way.

"Do you live in a mansion?" asked Fabergé, out of the blue.

Ryan glanced at me before replying. "No. Why?"

"You have a nice watch," she replied, waving her fork at him. "Did it cost a lot of money?"

Instead of reprimanding her for being rude, Ivy turned to Ryan, seemingly hanging for the answer. I sank down in my seat, mortified.

"It might have," he casually replied. "It was a gift from my parents."

Fabergé shrugged. "I like it."

"I like it first!" growled Malibu, determined to put her two cents in.

Ryan kept his focus on Fabergé. "Well, I like your bracelet. I'll bet that was expensive too. I can tell by the craftsmanship that it's a quality piece."

Fabergé was befuddled. "What's craftsmanship?"

"The way it was made," he explained. "Someone worked very hard to make it so pretty."

Fabergé set her fork down to free up her hand. She twisted the string of plastic beads, proudly showcasing her work. "I made this."

Ryan widened his eyes in mock surprise. "No kidding?"

The little girl's face was laced with pride. "It's true. I put all the beads on the string and this one is a flower button."

Ryan craned across the table to study it. "Oh, so it is. The flower is a nice touch."

"It's a fairy bracelet," explained Fabergé.

"Yes, I know," fibbed Ryan. "I actually know a few fairies. Flowers are important to them. Each flower has its own special meaning."

Fabergé's hazel eyes brightened, probably at the prospect of having Ryan hook her up with a fairy or two.

Malibu was less impressed. "You don't know fairies," she accused.

"Sure I do." He sounded calm but I could tell his gentle tone took effort.

"What do they look like then?"

"Well, the ones I know are blonde. They're very pretty but really crazy. That's why you can't hang out with them for very long. If you do, they start to make you crazy too."

I couldn't be sure if it was the fairy-tale voice or the silly story that made both girls giggle. Either way, it was a good result.

"Can you call them on the phone?" asked Malibu.

"I guess I could, but you wouldn't understand them. They speak in a different language."

"Call them now!" demanded Malibu, abandoning her calm demeanour in a flash.

"Yes, do it!" agreed Fabergé excitedly. "Ask them about this flower." She twisted the flower bead on her bracelet. "They can tell us what it means." The little girl turned to her mother. "What sort of flower is this, Mom?"

"It's a sunflower," replied Ivy.

"Do it!" chanted Malibu, smashing her fork on the table. "Do it! Do it! Do it!"

In a move that surprised me, Ryan rose to the challenge. He took his phone out of his pocket, dialled a number, and set it on the table.

19. CROWD PLEASER

Ryan

I wasn't sure how this was going to play out, but I was determined to convince the precocious little monsters that I had fairy connections.

I spoke as soon as Charli picked up, giving her no chance to blow my charade. "Speak French," I demanded in the language she barely understood. "You're on speaker."

"*D'accord,*" she replied, making me cringe.

Charli's pronunciation was dreadful. She didn't sound French at all. She sounded like an Australian trying to speak French while chewing a wad of gum.

"What do sunflowers mean?"

Despite the fact that I'd spoken slowly and dumbed it down for her, she didn't understand the question.

There was no point persevering with her, so I slowed my speech even further and asked her to put Adam on the phone with one simple word. "*Mari.*"

The little girls leaned over the phone while Charli's rambling, unnecessary reply played out. Both looked awed, but they had no clue what was being said. I wasn't sure I did either. She'd thrown in a few words that were neither French nor English.

Finally Adam took over and I explained the situation as best I could. "I need to know the meaning of sunflowers. Just ask the chief fairy and translate."

"We're in the middle of dinner," he complained.

"So am I – with Bente's nieces." Bente looked across at the mention of her name. "If I can't deliver a fairy story, they're going to attack and eat me. Mom will never forgive you."

"Such a romantic language," breathed Ivy, blissfully unaware that I'd just compared her daughters to wild animals.

"Mom will recover," stated my brother. "I've always been her favourite anyway."

The introduction of Adam's voice seemed to confuse Malibu. "Is he a man fairy?" she asked, speaking straight into the phone.

"No," I replied. "He's an ugly troll. He helps with fairy business, but he's the ugliest and dumbest creature you can imagine. He never even leaves his house because he's so gross."

Everyone at the table cackled. Adam was unamused. The slew of insults he hit me with were unrepeatable in any language.

The background conversation was muffled, presumably because he had the sense to cover the phone while he asked Charli about sunflowers. After what seemed an eternity, he returned.

"It's not a short story," he warned.

"They never are," I replied. "Just tell me."

The story Adam told was epic, but he was relaying it truthfully. There was no way he possessed the talent needed to make it up. I thanked him, asked him to thank Tinker Bell, and ended the call.

"Well?" demanded Fabergé.

I leaned back in my chair. "Sunflowers represent adoration," I announced. Both little girls stared blankly at me and I knew I'd lost them already. "Once upon a time there was a water nymph called Clytie." Neither Charli nor Bridget ever began a story with 'once upon a time'. I felt like a fraud, but battled on. "She was Greek."

Fabergé leaned close to her sister. "That means she was from a land called Greece," she whispered knowingly. Animal nodded as if she was keeping up, but I knew differently.

"She was in love with a man called Helios, but he didn't love her at all," I continued. "He loved someone else."

Fabergé pouted. "Big meanie."

"He was," I agreed. "But Clytie didn't give up. She tried and tried to make him love her."

"Did it work?" asked Ivy, showing the same inexplicable interest that most people did when hearing Charli's La La stories.

"No, he ended up leaving town to get away from her," I told her. "He rode off in his chariot, following the course of the sun."

I'd reached the make or break part of the fable. Most fairy stories involve some level of tragedy. Clytie's was no exception. How the Denisons would cope with that remained to be seen. "She missed him so much that she stripped herself naked and sat on a big rock for nine long days," I said gravely. "She had no food and no water. She stared at the sun the whole time, watching Helios as he travelled through the sky, hoping he'd come back to her." I took it up a notch by adopting a dire expression and a tone to match. "But he never did."

"Did she die?" Fabergé's voice sounded shaky. I hoped she wasn't about to cry and undo all my good work.

"Yeah, did she die?" Nothing about Animal's tone sounded shaky. If anything, she sounded excited by the prospect.

"No. Late on the ninth day, she transformed into a beautiful sunflower. She couldn't speak and she couldn't cry any more, but she could still turn towards the sun," I explained. "So when you see big sunflowers in the garden, you'll notice that they always look at the sun. And now you know why. It's Clytie, watching Helios as he travels through the sky."

There was total silence. The Denison women sat and stared at me. It was Ivy who finally spoke first. "That's the most beautiful story I've ever heard."

Bridget had told me better ones, but I wasn't about to regale them with more and keep the nonsense going.

Fabergé twisted the bracelet on her wrist. "I'm never taking this off," she pledged.

"I want one!" demanded Malibu.

"Shut up," hissed her sister. "I'll make you one if you shut up."

"Both of you shut up," demanded Ivy. "Eat your dinner."

Fabergé dropped her eyes to her plate. "I don't like this hotdog," she complained. "It's got grass in it."

"Well what do you expect?" snapped Ivy. "You chose the vegetarian option."

20. PLAYTHINGS

Bente

At first the plan of moving in together seemed grandiose and crazy. But things somehow worked out. Ryan charmed his way into my family's good graces and a truce was called. Ivy still thought living with him was a stupid idea, but she let me go unchallenged. She'd even helped me pack.

Ryan arranged a courier to collect my stuff and deliver it to his apartment. Colin, the delivery guy, struck me as kind of odd but Charli assured me he'd been moving things for them for years. Despite this, I stopped short of letting him unpack my boxes for me. "Thanks, Colin." I wrenched a small box from his grasp. "I can handle it from here."

He flashed me a smile that matched his creepy face. "No problem, ma'am," he replied. "When you're ready to move it all out again, give me a call."

He made it sound like a given. Clearly this wasn't his first Décarie rodeo.

Once he'd gone, I glanced around the usually pin-neat living room. The only furniture I'd brought were two chairs and a dresser, but the boxes alone would cause Ryan immeasurable pain. Thankfully he wasn't here to see it; he'd already left for work by the time Colin showed up.

By late afternoon I was exhausted. All I wanted was a shower, but I was interrupted by a knock at the door. I scraped my messy hair into an even messier ponytail and answered it.

A trashy but impeccably styled blonde was working her best angle by leaning with one arm raised against the doorjamb. As soon as she realised I wasn't the intended recipient of her pole dancer impersonation, she straightened up.

I had no clue who she was and I wasn't about to ask. Blondie, on the other hand, had a burning question. "Who are you?" She looked me up and down, scowling as if I was something she'd just scraped off the sole of her Manolo Blahnik heels.

"I'm nobody," I said sweetly. "Who are you looking for?"

She craned her neck to look past me. "Ryan. Where is he?"

"He's busy."

She smirked as if she still had the upper hand. "I'll come back later then."

"He'll be busy then too."

I wasn't sure that she was capable of reading between the lines. She didn't strike me as the literary type.

"Are you his girlfriend?" she asked, proving otherwise.

"Yes."

"Ryan doesn't do girlfriends." She spoke as if she truly felt sorry for me.

I felt sorry for me too. Something told me that fending off playthings at the door was an ordeal I'd probably have to endure for a while.

"You've been misinformed. He does do girlfriends, he just doesn't do you," I replied, shutting the door in her face. "Thanks for coming." I raised my voice to compensate for the thick wood between us. "I won't tell him you stopped by." I turned around and leaned against the door as if there was a chance she might bust her way back in. I then took a long moment to think things through.

I wasn't upset with Ryan and I wasn't hurt. We both had a past. The difference was, mine could've been written on a postage stamp and his was an epic twelve-book saga. Dealing with it was going to be a big learning curve. The lesson for that day: never answer the door wearing a coffee-stained T-shirt and sweat pants.

***

When Ryan arrived home I looked much more presentable, which was good because he looked his usual perfect self, despite the fact he was wearing a suit on such a warm day.

"Hey." He quickly kissed me and shrugged off his jacket. "How did the move go?"

"Good, I think."

Ryan walked to the centre of the living room, loosening his tie while he surveyed for damage. I knew the six boxes still on the floor would be traumatic for him. He did well not to mention them, but I explained anyway. "I have a lot of books, Ry. I'm not sure where to put them."

"We'll work it out."

"I can put them in the spare room." He didn't reply. "Or I can send them back to Ivy's."

With a shake of his head, he turned around and pulled me into his arms. "No, don't do that. We'll get some bookshelves or something."

I arched my back to look at him. "Are you okay?"

His hands moved from my hips to my face, holding me in place while he kissed me. "I am so good right now, Bente. You have no idea."

It probably wasn't the best time to mention his visitor from earlier but I found myself doing it anyway. "Are there likely to be more callers like that?"

Ryan completely dropped his hold on me and stepped away. "I'm so sorry. I had no idea she was coming."

"Who was she?"

He chewed his bottom lip. "What did she look like?" he asked finally.

I fell onto the couch in a heap. "You have no idea who she was, do you? There are probably ten possibilities."

"Are you mad?"

I really wasn't, but proving it was going to be next to impossible. Tact went out the window as ire set in. "How did she get upstairs?" I grumbled. "I never buzzed her in."

Ryan stopped chewing his lip and ran his hands through his hair. "She must have the code to the front door."

"Well, does that narrow the field?" I asked hopefully. "If she has the code, you must know who she is, right?"

"A lot of people have it, Bente."

My chest suddenly felt achy and heavy. "I don't have it."

Ryan sat beside me, covering my hands with his as I wrung them on my lap. "I'll give you the code to the front door." He spoke quietly. "I'll give you everything."

I nodded the tiniest bit. Ryan leaned across and pressed his lips to mine, kissing me out of my troubled mood. The instant he touched me, I realised I probably had more of him at that moment than Blondie had ever had.

21. BUYER'S REMORSE

Ryan

A week ago I was single. A few weeks before that, I might've appreciated a woman turning up unannounced. But things had changed and now there was nothing appealing about it. If anything, it was embarrassing. Bente didn't deserve the torment of dealing with it so I made amends by reprogramming the code on the front door. I wasn't sure if it was a move to lock my old life out or to keep my new life in.

The first person to be upset by the change was just three feet tall. I stood in the kitchen listening to the intercom near the door buzz over and over. Bente was on the living room floor, going through boxes. She looked at me with a frown, probably wondering why I wasn't rushing to answer it.

"It's Bridget," I told her.

"How do you know?"

I walked over to the intercom. "Yes?"

"You locked us out, Ry," came the irritated little reply.

I turned to Bente. "Told you."

A few minutes after buzzing her in, Bridget appeared at my door with her dad. After hugging my legs and chastising me again for locking her out, she headed for her toybox.

"Where's your mama?"

Bridget didn't slow her walk. "At the picture shop."

I checked my watch. It was just after four, which made seeing Adam very odd. He never usually escaped his office during daylight hours.

"Day off?" I asked.

"Afternoon off." He made his way into the kitchen. "We had a babysitter malfunction. How are you, Bente?" he asked, noticing her on the floor. "Coping okay?"

She laughed. "Holding my own, thank you."

I silently reprimanded my brother with a harsh scowl, which he ignored. "Buyer's remorse usually take a week or two to kick in," he taunted.

Bridget sat on the floor next to Bente, showing no sign of the shyness that had crippled her at dinner the week before. "You can't play with my girls, okay?" she said, laying down the law.

Bente threw both hands up. "I won't touch them. I swear."

While she was occupied with Bridget, I stole a quick minute with Adam. "I need your help with something," I murmured with a discreet upward nod.

Following my lead, we headed down the hallway to the bedroom.

Adam noticed the dresser as soon as he rounded the doorway. In fairness, the thing was so ugly and out of place he had no choice but to notice it. The clunky wooden piece was covered with a hundred layers of paint, and to its detriment, the most recent layer was teal green.

"Can you do anything with it?" I asked hopefully. If anyone could get it to an acceptable level, it was Adam. No one knew where his talent for carpentry came from. My mother insisted it was her side of the family. My father considered it a useless, pointless hobby and didn't give a damn either way.

Adam pulled open one of the drawers. "It's a really nice piece," he murmured.

"Just tell me you can fix it."

He closed the drawer and pulled open another. "I'll give it a crack."

I frowned at him, rubbing my chin. "How is it that you can speak perfect Australian and yet after all these years, your wife can't grasp basic French?"

The corner of his mouth lifted, forming a sly smile. "My wife grasps French all the time. Just not in public." He turned his attention back the dresser. "When does Bente want this done?" he asked, pushing the drawer shut. "I don't have much time so it might take a while."

"She doesn't know anything about it," I replied. "I'm the one who wants it fixed."

Adam pulled in a long breath but didn't seem to let it go. "She might not think it's broken, Ryan."

I took a look around my bedroom. I'd paid a designer a small fortune to make it look the way it did. I loved the sleek low line black furniture. It was urban and chic and exactly what I wanted. The dresser was like my bed's ugly stepsister. Of course it was broken.

"How could she not?" I pointed at the monstrosity. "Look at it."

"I'm not touching it until she gives the go-ahead." Adam chipped a few flecks of paint off with ease. "You can't make decisions like that on your own, Ryan. Not any more."

"Why not?"

"Because you're not on your own any more, stupid. For some reason, Bente's agreed to take you on permanently. That means you now share a closet and an ugly dresser. Congratulations." He slapped me on the back. "You're a grownup."

***

Apparently Bridget had taken advantage of the minute alone to really lay down the law to Bente. Not only was her box of severed dolls off limits, trips to the park with her uncle were too. I'm glad Bente waited until they left before telling me. I suspected it was something I should've been reprimanding the little princess for, but as usual, I had no idea how. "She also told me that the juice boxes in the fridge are all hers," Bente concluded.

"I never knew she was such a green-eyed little monster." I flopped beside her on the couch. "Why do you have to stay away from the park?"

Bente laid her legs across my lap. "She said I'm too old." She grinned. "I considered snapping all the legs off her dolls as retaliation, but then I remembered she's already done it."

***

My very first girlfriend was not a procrastinator. A week of unemployment was all she could stand, so Bente was heading out to find work.

"I've got a few contacts," she called from the bathroom. "I might be able to call in a favour or two."

"Don't jump at just anything this time," I urged. "You don't need to take the first job that comes up."

The bathroom amplified her raspy R-rated laugh. "Yes, I do." She stalked back into the bedroom half dressed, fresh-faced and beautiful. The second she was close enough; I reached and grabbed her. "I've changed my mind," I said, hauling her across the bed.

"About what?"

"About letting you leave." I rolled, pinning her beneath me. "You're too pretty to leave."

"Let me up, Ry," she replied. "I've got work to find."

I lowered my head, breathing my next words against her cheek. "Say my name again."

"Ryan."

"No, not like that."

She arched her back, pressing herself against me as she obscenely purred my name. "Ooh, Ryan."

"Lovely, but not what I meant," I told her, chuckling. "You shortened my name. I've heard you do it a few times lately. I think I like it."

Her body relaxed beneath me. "Bridget does it all the time."

I kissed her before replying. "Bridget doesn't count."

***

Despite my best efforts at making her stay, Bente left the apartment half an hour later. I had nowhere to be until late afternoon.

I managed to drag myself out of bed to the couch. I sat for a minute, trying to come to grips with the recent changes to the décor. Two pink velvet chairs stood in a corner, breaking every design rule ever written. I almost didn't care how ugly they were because they were Bente's chairs. The part of me that did care was wondering if my brother knew anything about upholstering.

Most of the unpacking had been done, with the exception of a few boxes of books and one box of junk on the coffee table. I fought the urge to sneak a peek for five whole minutes before I actually did it. The most scandalous thing I found was a yoga DVD – until I happened upon Bente's inspiration for learning the hip-grinding rumba.

Her prized copy of *Dirty Dancing*.

My DVD player had barely been used pre-niece. It was now on its last legs thanks to constant re-runs of the mermaid movie she loved. I pulled Bridget's disc out and loaded Bente's, promising myself that this was one film I'd deny ever watching. I'd barely gotten through the opening credits when the front door swung open. That was the first and only hint I got that Adam and Bridget were coming over, which proved that giving them the new code to the door was a mistake. I nearly jumped out of my skin, for no other reason than fear of being caught watching a chick flick. I hid the DVD case under the nearest cushion, pointed the remote at the TV and frantically punched the off button until the screen went black.

"Can't you people knock?" I sounded more panicked than angry.

Of all the mornings to practise her hand-eye coordination skills, Bridget had chosen this one. "I put the key in and turned it." She waved it at me. "It's easy."

Her father wasn't so oblivious. "What did we just walk in on?"

"Nothing."

"You can't stay, Bridge," he told her, staring at me. "I'll make other arrangements."

"No, I want to stay," Bridget insisted. She was already buried headfirst in her toybox.

"You can stay, sweetheart."

"No she can't," protested Adam in a strange muted growl.

"Why not?"

Adam glanced at his daughter before replying. "Because you're a freak."

"Why?"

He picked up a cushion and belted me with it. "What are you watching?"

It dawned on me that he'd jumped to a terrible conclusion.

"Oh my God," I growled, throwing down the remote and jumping to my feet. "You think I'm watching porn?"

"Shush!" he hissed, glancing in Bridget's direction again.

I grabbed the cushion he'd whacked me with and thumped him as hard as I could. "I do not watch porn."

"What's porn?" came a little voice from across the room.

I folded my arms and smirked at my brother. She was his kid. Explaining was up to him.

"Nothing, baby," replied Adam.

"Good parenting, idiot."

"Good uncl-ing, freak."

"Stop fighting," scolded Bridget, only half-paying attention to us. "I'll tell Mamie and you'll be in big trouble."

Determined to win, Adam reached beneath the cushion and grabbed the DVD cover he'd seen me stash there. At that point, I almost wished he had found porn. "You've got to be kidding me."

I snatched it from him. "It's not mine."

"If you say so, princess."

I had no smart comeback. I'd been caught watching *Dirty Dancing*. I deserved to be mocked.

***

The key to hanging out with Bridget is to keep her occupied. Staying busy keeps her out of trouble, which probably explains why we spend so much time at the park.

"I have to shower first," I told her. "Then we'll go."

She followed me to my room, zooming past me at the doorway to take a flying leap onto my bed.

"Please don't bounce on the bed."

"I have to," she replied, mid-air.

I made a grab for her and missed, making her giggle. "Bridget, do you bounce on beds in your house?"

"Course," she answered, as if it was a stupid question.

"When?"

"When no one can see."

Nothing about her reply surprised me. It was probably one of the lesser crimes she got away with. I glanced around the room, trying to work out my next move. Turning my back on her even for a second wasn't an option. I didn't need to occupy her. I needed to contain her.

Bente's ugly dresser suddenly had purpose when I noticed that the low stool was Bridget-height. I set it down a few feet from the bathroom door and patted the cushion.

"Sit here, Bridge."

She stopped jumping, coming to a stop on her butt. "All day?"

"No, just while I grab a shower."

She slid off the bed and took up position on the stool, swinging her legs and looking sweet, small and totally untrustworthy.

"Five minutes, okay?" She nodded. "I'll leave the door open so we can talk."

Despite my misgivings, I stepped into the bathroom and lost sight of her. The silence coming from the bedroom was deafening.

"How are you doing out there, sweetheart?" I called.

"Good."

Even over the sound of the water, I heard my closet door slide open.

"What are you doing?"

"I'm not doing nothing." She even sounded crooked.

"Anything," I corrected. "You're not doing anything."

"That's right," came a distant reply.

The soap barely had a chance to lather. I stepped out of the shower, wrapped a towel around my waist and ventured into the bedroom, still wringing wet.

Bridget was sitting on the stool right where I'd left her, but it wasn't hard to tell she'd been up to no good. The familiar shade of red lipstick she was wearing wasn't confined to her lips. It was spread right across her face.

I held out my hand. "Hand it over." She looked guilty as sin. "Now, Bridget."

"Can I keep this?" The big patterned scarf she waved at me was bigger than she was. "It helps you fly."

She was probably going to need wings when Bente got hold of her.

"Give me the lipstick," I ordered, gesturing with my hand again.

Bridget bunched up the scarf like she was scrunching up a piece of paper. "I can keep this?"

I pulled in a deep breath, trying to work out how to win. I was a lawyer, for crying out loud. Negotiating with a four-year-old should be a piece of cake. "Keep the scarf, give me the lipstick." Bridget produced the tube from the front pocket of her dress. I took it before she changed her mind. "Thank you."

"That's lovely manners, Ry," she praised.

"I'm not happy with you, Bridget," I told her.

"I'm not happy too." Her little face fell but I held my ground and ignored the sad pout.

"That was really naughty."

I wasn't hopeful that she'd be able to wash it off, but I sent her into the bathroom to try. While she was gone I quickly dressed and checked to see if she'd swiped anything else. Finding nothing amiss, I followed her into the bathroom.

Bridget was making a half-hearted attempt to wash her face. "It's stuck on," she said in a quivery little voice.

It was going from bad to worse. Not only did I have to try cleaning her up, tears were coming.

"Show me." I took the washcloth and swiped it across her cheek. "It's not too bad."

That was a lie. Bente's lips were always red for a reason. The stuff was impossible to get off. At an absolute loss, I admitted defeat and called Adam for cleaning instructions. Charli was probably the more knowledgeable option, but much harder to deal with.

"Lipstick?" he asked, amused. "Did she steal it from your purse while you were watching *Dirty Dancing*?"

"She's your kid, Adam. I'm perfectly happy to leave it on her."

"Well, how bad is it?"

I looked down at the girl in question, trying to decide. "You know that movie she likes?"

"*The Little Mermaid?*"

"Yeah." I shifted my phone to my other ear and took another swipe at her face with the washcloth. "Well, she looks like Sebastian… the lobster."

"Crab" Adam corrected. "Sebastian's a crab."

I put my hand under Bridget's chin, tilting her face from side to side while I surveyed the damage. "Either way, she could now get a job as his stunt double."

The picture I'd conjured in his mind was obviously good because he put some effort into remedying the situation, despite the fact he'd left a meeting to take my call. "What goes on must come off, right?" he asked. "Look for anything that says 'remover' or 'antidote' or 'face cleaner'. It'll be there somewhere."

I pulled open the top drawer of the cabinet. Like the rest of my apartment, it had undergone some changes. "There's an abnormal amount of crap in here, Adam," I reported. "Why would she need all this stuff?"

"Don't ask me. Girls like crap."

Girls do like crap. They like ugly furniture, sappy movies and drawers full of cosmetics they don't need. I was so far out of my depth that there was no point pretending otherwise. "Bridge, have a look in here." I pointed at the drawer. "See if you can find something that will get it off."

She reached her little hand into the drawer and pulled out a small pot of something.

"Concealer," I said into the phone. "That means it will conceal it, right?"

"You don't want to conceal it. You want to remove it."

My brother lived with two women, and he was still clueless. That meant there was no hope for me.

Bridget tried again and handed me a bottle of clear liquid. "Eye makeup remover," I read to Adam.

"Good enough."

"Right, I'll give it a shot."

I ended the call and prepared to try my hand at graffiti removal.

After a long few minutes, Bridget finally looked more like herself. A red tinge remained on her face, but I suspect that had more to do with the fact that she'd spent the whole time crying while I cleaned her up.

"Can we go now?" she whimpered hopefully.

I threw the washcloth into the sink. "Yeah. Let's get out of here."

***

The morning took a turn for the better once we got out of the apartment. The story of the day was a good one. It was warm and sunny, and despite the great weather the park wasn't too crowded.

Bridget quickly recovered from lipstick-gate and spent the next half hour running around the playground, trailing her stolen scarf behind her like a cape. I sat on a bench and watched, awed by her energy.

It was the perfect way to kill the morning, and it got even more perfect when I received a text from Bente asking if I wanted to meet up for coffee.

I texted her straight back.

- We're in the park. Come and play

22. DESIGNER WINGS

Bente

I smiled at the text on my phone and kept walking toward the 59th Street entrance of the park. It had been a productive morning. Begging for work isn't something anyone enjoys, but I was confident I'd made progress so it was worth it.

I caught up with Ryan at the playground.

"I didn't know you were babysitting today," I said, leaning to kiss him.

Ryan shuffled across to make room for me. "Nor did I. It was a sneak attack." His inconvenienced tone wasn't the least bit believable. "How did it go?"

"Good," I beamed. "Nothing set in stone but at least I've put the feelers out."

He stretched his legs out and folded his arms. "I'll give you a job."

I would never have asked Ryan to hire me, but was secretly thrilled that he'd offered. "Really?" I asked, cocking my head to one side.

He shrugged as if it was no big deal. "Of course. You're a decent server."

I bumped him with my arm, making him laugh.

"You can start tomorrow," he added. "Don't be late."

"I'll have to make sure my boyfriend doesn't try keeping me holed up in the bedroom then," I said dryly. "He can be very persistent."

Ryan leaned in close. "Sounds like my kind of guy."

His whisper travelled all the way south to my toes. I'd barely recovered when Bridget came running over. The first thing I noticed – besides the pissed-off look on her face – was the scarf trailing behind her.

She was clearly unhappy to see me. Cutting into her time at the park with her uncle was a massive no-no. Using my four hundred dollar Hermès scarf as a cape was a no-no too, but I seemed to be the only one who realised it.

"You gave her my scarf?" I muttered from the corner of my mouth.

"Not really," replied Ryan. "She found it."

Bridget came to a halt in front of us. "Come and play, Ry," she demanded, ignoring me.

"In a minute," he replied. "I'm talking to Bente at the moment."

She grabbed his hand and tried pulling him to his feet. "No, we have to go now. Please, now."

Ryan repositioned his hand so he was now holding hers. "In a minute." He almost sounded cross but Bridget wasn't fazed. She turned her attention to me. "No park for you, Bente." A cutting glare was probably her intention, but she was too cute to pull it off.

I'd been dealing with horrid Malibu since my return from Boston. Bridget had nothing on her, but for some reason, I felt intimidated. Holding my ground wasn't going to be easy, but I had to at least try.

I started by asking for my scarf back. "I know Ryan said you could play with it, but he made a mistake," I explained.

Bridget took a step back. "No. I really love it."

"I love it too," I said. "That's why I saved all my money to buy it."

"I'm sorry, Bente," mumbled Ryan. "I didn't know."

I ignored him, keeping my focus on Bridget, who'd abandoned her frown in favour of a pout. "Please, Bridget. I'd really like it back."

She barely paused to think about it. "No. I don't want to." With that, she took off running toward the playground, my Hermès scarf flapping behind her like a victory flag.

"I can chase after her and take her down if you want," offered Ryan. He was trying to make light of it, but I wasn't finding it funny. Four hundred dollars was chump change to him, Bridget too, but I'd survived on Ramen noodles for months to save for the scarf.

He shifted his hand to the back of my head, tangling his fingers through my hair. "I'll replace it, sweetheart." He spoke casually, as if he'd just fixed everything. "I promise."

"And Bridget gets to keep that one?"

He shrugged but didn't speak, highlighting just how clueless he was.

"That solves nothing."

"I don't know why it's such a big deal. There's no problem," he replied.

He was wrong.

Bridget's little mind had formed the opinion that I was out to steal her favourite uncle. Turning up at the park after she'd warned me not to was interpreted as a hostile move. Asking for my scarf back hadn't gone down well either, but she'd won.

I got the impression that Bridget was victorious most of the time where Ryan was concerned. And that *was* a problem.

***

Taking Ryan up on his offer of going home with them would've been a declaration of war, so I politely made up a lie about having to go to my sister's.

Ivy's house was bedlam, as usual. The girls were fighting upstairs, but at least they stayed there.

"Why aren't the girls in school?" I asked.

"It's the Merry Berry Pageant tomorrow," replied Ivy. "I thought they should take the day off and relax. I want them at their best."

They didn't sound very relaxed, but they were at their best. I heard a loud thud and looked up at the ceiling. "Do you think you should check on them?"

Ivy threw her head back and shrieked, "What's going on up there?"

"Just playing!"

My sister looked at me, completely at ease. "They're fine."

I followed her to the living room, carrying the coffee I'd made. Now that my chairs were gone and her couches had been pushed back into place, the room looked much more presentable – well, as presentable as the pageant palace could be.

Ivy went straight to work. She spread a sparkly dress across her lap and switched on her glue gun.

"Is that for tomorrow?"

"Yeah." She held up a bejewelled orange creation, "Malibu's doing the apricot jelly dance in the talent section."

I nodded. It was the best I could do. I'd grown out of the pageant phase at fourteen. Ivy was still working on it.

"So why are you here?" she asked, brash as ever. "Is he bored already?"

The snide remarks about Ryan were going to be ongoing for a while, but I didn't care. That was Ivy's gentle approach.

"No, he's watching his niece. Three's a crowd."

"What do you mean?"

Confiding in her about my troubles with Bridget was nonsensical. She was hardly in a position to be giving me advice on how to handle her, but I told her the whole story anyway.

Ivy was outraged. "Little minx."

"She's not, really," I defended. "She's usually very sweet."

Ivy put on her glasses and fossicked through a container of plastic gems. "She just needs a good whack," she suggested. "Spare the rod and spoil the child."

I glanced around. "Where's your rod, Ivy?"

She looked at me over the top of her glasses. "My girls are good girls."

That was debatable, but I let it go. "Bridget is too. She's just not used to sharing."

"She's spoiled?"

I hadn't decided yet. Adam's little girl was unimaginably privileged. Being a Décarie meant that she could have whatever her little heart desired. But Charli's little girl lived on another planet, which meant the things her heart desired probably couldn't be bought with money.

"Ryan spoils her." That much I did know. "That's why she's floating around the playground wearing my scarf."

Ivy pointed her glue gun at me. "This is exactly why you're not supposed to move in with a man you barely know. Just a few days in and he's already pandering to other women."

I rolled my eyes at her. "Can we stick to the true version of the story, please?"

"Whatever," she grumbled. "But you need to toughen up. You're the outsider, Bente. You're not like those people." I assume she meant the Décarie family as a whole. "They're going to stick together. That little girl's poor treatment of you is probably just the beginning."

I knew exactly what I was in for. I wasn't the first to suffer through an adjustment period. Charli had had a horrendous time trying to crack the Décarie circle in the beginning; Fiona Décarie did all she could to keep her out. I wondered how Charli would feel knowing that her daughter was now doing the same to me.

"It's going to be fine." I sounded like I was trying to convince myself more than her. "Just you wait and see."

23. MAGIC vs POTENTIAL

Ryan

Allowing Bridget to keep the scarf was a mistake. I'd made a few Bente-related mistakes over the past few days, but to her credit she was hanging in there like a trooper.

As talented as I was at screwing up, I was also pretty deft at making amends. After Adam picked Bridget up, I set about making good – starting with a trip to the Hermès store on Madison.

My rush to get home was for nothing. Bente didn't show up until after seven, by which time I'd all but convinced myself that she wasn't coming back. She wandered into the kitchen and stood beside me at the stove. I put an arm around her and continued stirring.

"Hey. What are you cooking?"

"Hey. It's called Chicken Primavera, but I didn't have any chicken, so it's just Primavera."

Her warm laughter made me relax. Just being with her made me relax. I set the spoon on the counter and hauled her in close.

We stared at each other for a long time. It wasn't uncomfortable. I liked looking at her. I could've kept it up all night, but Bente got bored and came up with something else to do. Her hands moved to my face, holding me in place while she moved in for the kill. Her dark eyes were dangerous but her scarlet lips were deadly.

There was no way a kiss like that was going to end in a glass of wine and Chickenless Primavera. I took a step forward, taking her with me as I fumbled behind her, trying to turn off the stove. Once there was no danger of burning the apartment down, I lifted her off her feet, managing to carry her as far as the couch. Despite my urgency to get her naked I thought I'd managed to lay her gently onto the cushions – until she let out a pained yelp and reached behind her back.

My mind was too scrambled to come up with an acceptable defense for the *Dirty Dancing* DVD in her hand.

"You watched my movie?" she breathed.

I tried to figure out the right answer. Lying won.

"No, of course not."

Bente grabbed a fistful of shirt and pulled me down on top of her. "Pity," she mumbled. "That would've been as sexy as hell."

***

It was after ten when we finally got around to having dinner. I wasn't particularly hungry. My focus was on my dinner companion, who sat beside me at the counter dressed in nothing more than my T-shirt. I held off telling her how lovely she looked. If I'd told Bente she was beautiful every time I wanted to, she'd probably start looking for a motive.

"It's probably a good thing that there's no chicken in this, Ry," she said, pushing the pasta around her plate with the tip of her fork. "It's been sitting on the stove for a while." She had a point. All the good work I'd done to convince her sister that my intentions were good would probably go out the window if I poisoned her. I stood up and grabbed her plate. "Hey," she protested. "I'm eating that."

"No, you're not." I scraped the plates into the trash and loaded them into the dishwasher. "I like you too much to kill you. I'll cook you something else. What would you like?"

"Nothing. I'm good."

"You're sure?"

"I'm perfect, Ryan."

"Yeah," I agreed, sounding scared by the prospect. "You really are."

Her head dropped. "You're just too smooth, Ryan Décarie," she mumbled.

It was hard to tell whether she was kidding or not. I always felt like I was on the back foot where Bente was concerned, constantly disadvantaged due to my past bad behaviour. I wasn't naïve enough to think I could make it all up to her in a week. Acts like giving her prized possessions to my niece meant it would probably take months, but I was determined to keep trying.

It seemed like as good a moment as any to present her with the gift I'd been hiding all afternoon. I opened the pantry, grabbed the small orange box from the top shelf and handed it to her.

Her eyes lit up, making me smile.

"I hope you like it."

Bente pulled the brown ribbon off and lifted the lid. "Oh, Ryan." She picked up the corner of the scarf and fanned it out.

I was still worried. It looked nothing like the one Bridget had commandeered. It wasn't even the same colour. "Is it okay?"

She glimpsed at me only briefly. "It's lovely."

"I want you to know that I'm really sorry," I said, genuinely remorseful. "I shouldn't have let Bridget keep the other one."

Bente stepped off the stool and made her way around to my side of the counter. Both of her arms wrapped tightly around me and she rested her cheek on my back. "Thank you for making it right."

Her hold on me remained as I twisted to face her. "There's more," I said ominously.

"More what?"

"Well, I was pretty sure you'd appreciate the gesture, but I had no clue what sort of scarf you'd like."

Bente dropped her arms to her side, freeing me to move.

I walked back over to the pantry, reached up and grabbed another four orange boxes. I didn't bother handing them to her; I just set them down on the counter.

"This is overkill, Ryan," she choked.

"No, it's hedging my bets," I corrected. "One of those boxes contains your new favourite scarf."

She stripped the ribbon off the first box. "I'll return the others," she offered.

She was taking too long so I unwrapped the next three myself, draping each scarf over her shoulder as I went. "I want you to keep them all," I insisted.

"Do you have any idea how much these cost?"

"Of course I do. I picked each one of them."

Bente looked at the silky mass of couture that I'd draped over her "What will I do with five Hermès scarves?" She bunched them in her hand and waved them at me.

"Do you like them?"

"I love them."

I took her face in my hands. "Then keep them. Wear them all."

"At the same time?" She was probably joking, but I was inspired. I plucked a scarf from her grip, wrapped it around her head and tied a loose knot at her forehead. It was hardly stylish. It looked like I'd just bandaged a head wound. She brushed the fabric aside so she could see. "Nice." She laughed darkly. "That takes care of one. How will I wear the other four?"

I wiggled my eyebrows. "Take off your shirt and I'll show you."

Bente didn't question why. She just grabbed the hem of her shirt and dragged it over her head, somehow managing to do it without displacing her Hermès bandage.

Naked and in my kitchen was a very good look for her. Covering her up was the last thing I wanted to do, but I kept my end of the bargain, grabbed another scarf and wrapped it around her waist, knotting it at her hip.

Modesty took over then and she folded her arms across her chest. "Well?" she asked, taking a downward glance at her new skirt. "What do you think?"

I tried prising her arms apart. "Don't hide from me," I murmured. "I like looking at you."

A pretty blush that I didn't often see burned across her cheeks. "Finish dressing me," she ordered.

"Yes ma'am." I reached for the next scarf, and managed to fashion a top that almost covered her.

"Not bad," she praised. "Not bad at all, but you have two left."

I was done. My mind was already undressing her, so my efforts to utilise the last two scarves were half-assed at best. One minute and two knots later, she was sporting Hermès armbands.

"You should've been a fashion designer, Ryan." She flashed me a killer smile.

"Perhaps," I replied casually. "But my workmanship leaves a lot to be desired." I pulled a corner of her headscarf, undoing the knot. Both of us ignored it as it drifted to the floor.

"Shoddy at best," she agreed.

I grabbed her hips and jerked her forward, pulling her against me. "Perhaps you should hire a professional next time."

"No," she breathed. "I like your style."

***

It was the middle of the night when I woke. I reached across for Bente and grabbed nothing but sheet. The light coming from the hallway was dull. The light illuminating the clock next to the bed was slightly brighter. It was a little after one in the morning.

Bente was sitting at the kitchen counter tapping on her laptop when I walked in. I wrapped my arm around her from behind. "Can't sleep?"

She kissed my forearm, but typed until she'd finished her sentence. "I write a lot at night," she explained. "I have a busy mind. I think it comes from working to deadlines."

I sat down beside her. "Do you like working to a deadline?"

"I do," she replied. "I work pretty well under pressure."

"So what are you writing tonight?"

"Just thoughts and ideas," she said vaguely. "Things to keep me going until a job comes up."

I looked around the living room. "You'd probably work better if you had a space to work in. We'll get you a desk."

"And put it where?" She closed the lid on her laptop. "You've made enough allowances for my stuff already. One more piece might tip you over the edge."

I frowned. "Bente, it's not about making allowances for you. We're supposed to be in this together."

She stepped off the stool and sidled up to me. "We are together."

My hands moved of their own volition, settling on her hips. "I want you to be happy here."

"I am," she insisted, pressing against me. "Me and my ugly dresser are very happy here."

"So you're aware that it's… aesthetically challenged?"

"It's as ugly as sin, Ryan," she replied, chuckling. "I was planning to get it restored but I never got round to it."

I let out a long breath I couldn't remember taking. "My brother convinced me that it had some special meaning and that's why it looked so tragic."

"Like?"

"Like, a dead grandma decorated it, leaving you with the magic memory of teal paint."

"How could she decorate it if she's dead?"

I grinned at her. "I don't pretend to understand magic."

Her head lolled back as she laughed. I usually fought the urge to kiss her when she made that move, but not this time. I pressed my lips to her throat, tasting her warm skin.

She inched my head back. "I'm not Charli," she replied. "It's just an old thrift store dresser with great potential."

"You don't see magic in it?" I asked cautiously.

She smiled blackly. "No."

And therein lies the difference between Bente and Charli. Charli looks for magic. Bente looks for potential.

"Do you think I have potential, Bente?" I have no idea why I asked. Judging by the confusion on her lovely face, she didn't either – but she answered anyway.

"Huge potential." She kissed me. "As soon as I get all the layers scraped off you, you'll be spectacular."

***

Bente wakes early, even when there's no need. I wasn't even convinced it was morning when I awoke to the sound of the shower running. She skipped into the bedroom a few minutes later and climbed on top of me. I brushed her wet hair from my face. "Are you always this hyper in the mornings?" I mumbled.

"No, just this morning." She planted a kiss on my chest. "It's my first day at a new job. I'd like to make a good impression on my boss."

I grabbed the sash on her robe and pulled. "Get back into bed then." I never got tired of her laugh, or the effect it had on me as it travelled through my bones.

"No, get up." She patted my chest. "The day is wasting." She slipped off the bed and headed for the closet. "I'm actually excited about it. I might've missed Nellie's a little bit," she admitted, raking through the clothes. "I even missed Paolo."

It occurred to me that we should've discussed my job offer in greater detail. "Ah, sweetheart, you're not working at Nellie's," I said quietly.

She turned back. "You've changed your mind?"

I propped myself up on one elbow. "Of course not. It's just that I don't have a position for you at Nellie's. The job is at Billet-doux."

"Oh." She took a long moment to think things through. "Okay, then."

"You'll like it there," I assured her. "Probably more than Nellie's." She was much better suited to Billet-doux. The place was almost as sexy as she was.

"It doesn't matter either way, Ryan," she finally replied. "A job is a job."

24. SPECIAL FAVOUR

Bente

Starting a new job is as scary as a first day at school. Ryan wasn't going to be there to hold my hand. He wouldn't have come if I'd begged him to. My first shift was a fairy high tea – the ultimate trial by fire.

A woman named Noelle met me at the door. She was bubbly, blonde and really annoying. I couldn't pinpoint why. Perhaps it was her high-pitched voice. It might also have had something to do with the way her eyes darted around as she spoke.

"I've been waiting for you," she said urgently. I checked the time on my watch to make sure I wasn't late. "It's Ben-ta, right?"

"That's right."

She shamelessly looked me up and down. "I was surprised when Ryan told me he'd hired you. He doesn't usually do the hiring and firing. I can only assume you're a special favour for someone."

"I like to think so," I replied, trying to keep up as she scuttled over to the bar.

Noelle picked a menu off the counter and handed it to me. "It's super important to know the menu back to front," she instructed. "And listen carefully to the orders."

I thumbed through the fancy pages. "No coleslaw?"

I enjoyed my private joke. Noelle did not. She narrowed her eyes. "This is a classy place," she snapped, sounding personally offended.

"I understand."

"Super," she crowed, recovering quickly. "Let's go, Ben-ta. I'll show you around."

***

Fairy high teas are not for the faint of heart. It was like being locked in a room with thirty Malibus and an excess of sugary desserts. I steered clear of the small children, opting to serve their mothers instead.

I was standing at the bar waiting for a round of drinks when Noelle approached. "Nice work, Bente." I could tell she was happy with me because she almost pronounced my name properly. "You're going to fit in really well."

"Thanks."

The bartender loaded my tray with a round of lethal looking mojitos. I'd been introduced to him earlier but couldn't remember his name. In my mind, he was Bar Guy.

"Noelle's seal of approval after just a few hours?" he teased. "Lucky you."

Out of the blue, Noelle let out a squeak, but I didn't think it had anything to do with the bar guy. I followed the direction of her of darting eyes and saw Charli walk through the glass front door.

"What's the matter?" I asked.

"One of the owners just walked in," she replied acidly.

"I'll be on my best behaviour then."

"She won't care either way," she snapped. "Charli doesn't give a damn about this place. I have no idea why she even shows up."

"I like it when she shows up," interjected Bar Guy.

I looked at him. He seemed to be stripping her naked with his eyes as she closed in on us.

"Yes, Charli?" asked Noelle as soon as she was within earshot. "What can I do for you?"

Charli ignored her curt tone. It was too high-pitched to be taken seriously anyway. "Nothing," she replied cheerily, "but thanks for asking."

108

Bar Guy diverted her attention by saying hello.

"How are you, Rob?" she asked, sounding much more like herself.

He swiped a cloth along the length of the glossy wooden bar. "Better for seeing you," he drawled.

I almost felt bad for him. If ever there was a case of unrequited affection, this was it. Charli only had eyes for Adam. She was a one-frog woman, and always had been.

"We're super busy here, Charli," fluttered Noelle.

If that was a hint to leave, Charli missed it. "Can I talk to you for a second, Bente?"

I glanced at Noelle before replying. "Sure." I picked up my tray of drinks. "I'll just offload these first."

Charli was already walking away. "I'll be in my office," she called.

"It's Ryan's office," corrected Noelle, raising her voice to make sure she was heard.

I delivered the drinks to the tipsy fairy mothers and began making my way to the office. Noelle cornered me at the doorway. "Do you know Charli?"

"Yes," I confirmed. "We're friends."

"I see." She cocked her head to the side. "So you're *her* special favour," she accused, relaxing her grip on my arm. "That's why Ryan gave you a job."

I shrugged free of her. "No, no. Ryan's my boyfriend," I corrected. "He gave me a job because I'm *his* special favour."

I didn't wait to see her reaction. I took off down the hall and didn't stop until I reached Ryan's office door.

***

Ryan's office was far less impressive than I expected. The room looked more like a storeroom. There were papers scattered all across his desk and sticky notes stuck to the edge of his computer screen.

"What's wrong?" asked Charli, leaning back in her chair. Perhaps I looked confused.

"Nothing." I closed the door. "I just expected his office to be… tidier."

"I don't think he cares how tidy it is as long as it's functional. He knows exactly where everything is. If I move one thing, he'll know I've been here." She picked up a stack of papers and put them in a drawer. Her errant smile made me laugh.

"No wonder you drive him crazy."

"He told you that?" She actually sounded excited by the idea.

"Once or twice."

She leaned back and drummed her fingers together like an evil professor. "Excellent."

I slumped in the chair opposite her as if I'd been on my feet for hours. "I'd forgotten how hardcore waitressing could be."

"Noelle is hardcore too," she teased. "I'll bet Ryan didn't tell you that, did he?"

"Nope. Never did."

"She has a huge crush on him," she revealed. "She's all sweetness and light when he's around."

"No crush on you, though."

She laughed again, wickedly. "No, she doesn't like me much."

I kicked off my shoes to give my feet a minute of relief. "So did you come down here to rescue me or did you want something?"

I began to fear her answer when her smile morphed into a worried frown. "I heard about what happened yesterday. I feel horrible." She leaned across, reached into her purse and dropped a familiar orange box down on the desk. "Ryan should never have let Bridget take your scarf. I'm really sorry."

I stared at the box. "You bought me a new one?"

"It was the least I could do," she mumbled.

While I appreciated the gesture, I was still annoyed. Bridget was still victoriously sporting a Hermès cape. Charli must've picked up on my ire. "If you'd rather choose your own I'll –"

I sourly cut in. "What does it matter, Charli? Bridget still gets to keep mine."

She was shaking her head before I'd even finished speaking. "No, she doesn't. I took it from her as soon as I found out where it came from."

"So why not just give it back to me?"

"I didn't think you'd want it." Her shoulders drooped. "For some reason, it's covered in red lipstick."

I was so relieved, I felt like crying. I needed Charli as an ally, but until that point I didn't think I had her. "I could kiss you right now," I told her. "I was worried that you wouldn't understand."

"Bente, you know me," she grumbled. "Since when would I think giving Bridget something like that was okay?"

She sounded so irate that I felt the need to defend Ryan. "Ryan wasn't thinking."

"Bridget has superpowers where he's concerned," she explained. "She gets the better of him every time."

I couldn't have worded it better myself, but it didn't make the conversation any less awkward.

Charli slid the box across the desk. "If you don't like it, say the word."

I forced a smile. "I'm sure I'll love it." And if by chance I didn't, I had five others to wear instead. Perhaps that's why I made no attempt to open the box. "I should probably be going," I said, slipping my shoes back on. "Noelle's probably already started docking my pay."

Charli stood too. "I've got to get back as well. I'm on my lunch break."

I didn't think the fast pace of life in New York necessarily agreed with Charli – or Adam for that matter. Both of them always looked a little weary. I called out as she got to the door. "Is everything okay, Charli?"

She turned back. "Yeah, why?"

"Just wondering."

25. ROSE COLOURED GLASSES

Ryan

I'd thrown Bente in at the deep end as far as work goes. Fairy high teas were marathon events, but I was sure she'd handle it. Whether she'd handle Noelle or not remained to be seen.

Confident that she didn't need me there to hold her hand, I stuck to my usual routine and stayed away. I had a different high tea planned, and it would be no less traumatic than the one at Billet-doux. I was planning to tell my parents that I'd stumbled into my first committed relationship.

Past history told me it wasn't going to be an easy conversation, which is why I'd chosen the middle of the day to confess. Dad would be at work so I'd only have Mom to contend with.

I never just dropped in on my parents. I called ahead to let Mom know I was coming, but my casual approach made no difference. My mother knew I had news for her.

"Is everything alright, darling?" she asked, greeting me at the door.

"Yes, of course." I kissed her cheek. "Where's Mrs Brown?"

My mother swatted my shoulder as if brushing off invisible dirt. "She's watching Bridget today."

Mrs Brown had been taking care of Décarie children for years. She was my nanny before Adam was even born, and moved with us from Marseille when we came to New York. Once we were grown, she stayed on with my parents as their housekeeper. Charli and Adam were unwilling to throw their little princess into the big bad world of day-care, so when Mrs Brown offered her services they jumped at the chance.

"I don't like this shirt, Ryan," Mom complained. "It doesn't sit properly."

I grinned at her. "That's because I'm crooked, Ma."

Her demure giggle sounded crooked too. "I've made us some lunch. Come."

Even by Manhattan standards my childhood home was pretentious. I followed her through the lounge and into the dining room. "We're eating in here?" It was ridiculous. The massive mahogany table sat sixteen people. Sitting at it always felt like being in a board meeting, especially when my father took charge.

"Yes, I'd like to," Mom replied. "But if you'd rather eat in the kitchen, we can."

I looked at the setting she'd prepared, and suddenly felt bad. The room was over-the-top and ostentatious, but the way she'd set one corner of the table wasn't. I knew she'd made lunch herself. The unevenly cut plate of sandwiches gave it away.

In some respects, my Mom was just like Charli – making her way through one way of life while trying to keep hold of another. It was a trait that never surfaced until my brother married Tinker Bell. Since then, we saw glimpses of it all the time. Mom never cooked for us as children, but as grown men we were subjected to crooked sandwiches and lopsided cakes on a regular basis.

"No, we can eat in here," I relented, pulling out her chair. "It looks great, Ma."

She sat down and thanked me. "I'm glad you're here, darling. We don't see enough of you."

"I've been busy lately." I sat opposite her. "That's why I'm here. I want to tell you about it." There wasn't any point easing into it. All I could do was put it all out there and wait for the fallout.

Mom slid the plate of sandwiches toward me. "Bridget told me you've met a girl," she revealed.

I stared at her, trying to work out my next move. Bridget's opinion of Bente wasn't exactly favourable. I couldn't imagine she'd said anything nice.

"My niece has a big mouth," I said finally.

Mom took a quarter of a sandwich and reached for a napkin. "She's a constant source of information for me, Ryan," she replied. "If not for her, I'd never know anything."

"I'll tell you everything," I offered, surprising even myself. "No doubt it's a better story than the one you got from Bridget."

Telling her everything didn't take long. Most of the best details weren't suitable for my mother's ears.

"I've always liked Bente," said my mother. "She's a very bright girl."

"She is," I agreed.

"Journalism at NYU, correct?"

I nodded. "She spent the last few years working in Boston. She's only been back in town a few weeks."

"And she moved straight in with you?" Her voice was emotionless, giving me no hint as to how she was taking the news. I didn't trust her calm demeanour one bit. The last girl to steal the affections of one of her sons earned a black eye for her trouble.

"Yes, and it's working out great. I want you to be happy for me."

Mom leaned back. It was a better scowling position for her. "Why would you think I'd be anything but?"

It was hard to take her hurt expression seriously, but I tried. "When Adam brought Charli home –"

"Adam didn't bring Charli home, Ryan," she sourly cut in. "Adam brought his new wife home. How were we supposed to react to the news that our twenty-two year old son had married a girl we didn't even know?"

I was fairly certain that beating her up wasn't an appropriate reaction, but I chose not to share that thought. I went in a different direction instead. "You've already met Bente, and I've no intention of marrying her."

"You're not a clueless child," she replied. "You're a grown man and I want nothing more than for you to find someone special."

I dropped a crust on my plate. "I'm a clueless grown man," I replied pathetically. "I've never done this before."

She smiled for the first time since the conversation began. "You've never found anyone worthy of the effort before." The rose-coloured glasses my mother wore saved her from a lot of pain where I was concerned.

"I've never stuck around long enough to find out," I confessed. "I'm not a good guy, Mom."

She picked up the glass pitcher and poured two glasses of juice. "That doesn't mean you don't deserve something wonderful, Ryan."

"I'll keep that in mind," I muttered.

"Yes, do," she replied simply.

***

I ended up staying longer than I expected, mainly because I wasn't free to leave until the platter of sandwiches had been cleared. It was an impossible task. Mom had made enough to feed a small army. I escaped by agreeing to take some with me. "You can have them for afternoon tea," she suggested, handing them over at the door.

Perhaps she'd forgotten that I was on my way to work – at the restaurant I owned. I thanked her anyway, and made a vague promise of catching up with her again later in the week. It wasn't enough. Intent on pinning me down to a more concrete arrangement, she ordered me to bring Bente to the house for dinner.

"Friday night," she instructed. "I'll invite Adam and the girls too. It will be lovely to have the whole family together."

"Okay," I replied unenthusiastically. "We'll be here."

She started swatting at my shirt again. "And get rid of this shirt, darling. It's truly a terrible cut."

***

Walking into Billet-doux post-fairy high tea is something that's done with trepidation. Some days the restaurant makes it through unscathed. Today wasn't one of them.

Noelle was rushing around, barking squeaky orders at a frazzled-looking waiter trailing behind her.

"That's four so far," she barked in her little Chihuahua voice. "And here's number five." She tapped the back of one of the white dining chairs. The waiter carried it away in the direction of the storeroom. Finally she spotted me at the door. "Oh, Ryan." She breezed toward me. "The dry-cleaning bill will be huge. A few of the chairs have been stained." She grabbed my arm. I wanted to shrug her away, but didn't.

"We have spares," I told her. "Just get the others cleaned."

It wasn't as if it was the first time I'd been left with a cleaning bill after a fairy stampede. It didn't even annoy me any more. The bar sales alone more than made up for it.

Noelle dropped her hold on me. "I'm already on to it," she replied. "You know me, super efficient."

I pretended not to notice the wink that accompanied her comment and moved on to more important things, namely my newest employee who was setting tables at the back of the room. "Will you excuse me, Noelle?" I didn't hang around to hear her reply. I was already making my way toward Bente.

"Miss Denison," I called.

She turned and granted me her trademark red-lipped smile.

"Mr Décarie," she crooned.

In a ploy to stop myself grabbing her and kissing her all over, I folded my arms. "How was your first day?"

She glanced past me, undoubtedly at Noelle. "Interesting."

"Do you think you'll be back tomorrow?"

She dropped a handful of cutlery on the table and took a tiny step toward me. "Unless I get a better offer," she hinted in a whisper.

I dropped my head and chuckled at the floor, acutely aware that Noelle was burning a hole in the back of my head with her eyes. "I have a few things in mind," I murmured.

"I'll bet you do," she replied. "But you'll have to tell me about them later. I'm going home in a minute."

"Pity," I said wistfully. "I was just going to clear the restaurant so you could set the tables in private. I haven't heard you sing in a long while."

Bente picked up the cutlery and continued laying the table. "I'm sure you know where the fire alarm is."

As tempting as her offer was, I behaved like a responsible adult. "I've got work to do."

She turned to me. "Well, that sucks. My working day is done and yours is just starting."

"I'll make sure it's a short day," I promised. "Then we can have a long night."

26. SOCIAL EXPERIMENT

Bente

The first thing I wanted to do when I got home was take a long bath. It had been a long time since I'd spent all day waiting on tables. I'd missed certain parts of it, but not the aching feet.

I started stripping off my clothes as I walked down the hall, stopping dead in my tracks when I reached the doorway to the bedroom.

My dresser was missing. We'd either been burgled by a robber with no sense of style or Ryan had made good on his promise of sending it to Adam for restoration.

There was just no thinking time where he was concerned. Everything had to be done at warp speed. I shook my head at the absurdity and continued to the bathroom.

***

I'm not as good a chef as Ryan, but I tried. Not even I could mess up a basic salad. I was expecting him home at any minute and was looking forward to having him all to myself, so the buzz of the intercom annoyed me.

I pressed the speaker and answered curtly. "Yes?"

"I'm here to see Ryan, please." Of course she was. Who else would she be here to see?

I leaned closer to the speaker than necessary and smashed my finger down on the button. "He's not here, and even if he was, he wouldn't be interested."

There was a long pause. "You're exceptionally rude," she told me. "I think you're rude."

I was rude, perhaps unfairly so, but I wasn't about to apologise. "Look, come back later," I said wearily. "He'll be home in an hour." I couldn't believe I'd made the offer. I was practically inviting trouble.

"I will," she replied. "Thanks."

Intent on torturing myself, I ran to the window to see if I could spot her walking away. The steady flow of pedestrian traffic on the street below made it impossible to pick her out in the crowd. It wouldn't have mattered anyway. No doubt I'd get a perfect view of her when she returned later.

***

I never mentioned Ryan's caller to him when he arrived home, slightly optimistic that she wouldn't come back. We'd almost made it through dinner when my hopes were dashed. Ryan groaned out loud at the sound of the intercom.

"I'll get it."

I wasn't going to argue. There was no way I was going to open the door to whore number two.

"Yes?" he answered.

"Hi, it's me."

Ryan obviously knew who she was. He smiled as he replied. "Hey, come on up."

I set my fork down to stop myself stabbing him with it. That was the only move I made. I sat at the counter, waiting for her to knock.

Ryan rubbed salt into my invisible wounds by greeting her at the door with a big hug. "Where have you been?" he asked. "I've almost missed you."

"I know, I know," she replied, stepping into the room. "I've been so busy lately."

119

"Come," he ordered, steering her forward with a hand on her back. "I want you to meet someone."

I stared the girl down as if she was my worst enemy. There were a few noticeable differences between her and every other woman in his not-so little black book. She was tall with mousy brown hair and thick black-framed glasses. She was pretty, but not the usual type to catch his eye. She was also very forward. She thrust her hand at me before Ryan had a chance to introduce us. "I'm Trieste Kincaid," she announced. "Very pleased to meet you."

I nodded, caught slightly off guard by her friendliness and lack of whore factor. "Bente Denison."

"Bente's my girlfriend," said Ryan, in the same juvenile way he usually announced it.

Trieste's eyes widened. "You have a girlfriend?" she asked. "That's awesome." She turned back and play punched his upper arm. "Good job."

I suddenly felt like a zoo exhibit, or some weird social experiment. "Hello." I waved at both of them. "I'm still in the room."

Trieste snorted as she laughed. It was the strangest sound I'd ever heard. "I'm so happy for both of you," she said, dumping her huge bag on the counter. "You must come to the wedding, Bente."

"She'll be there," replied Ryan, heading for the fridge.

Trieste sat beside me, pushing Ryan's half eaten meal aside, clearly oblivious to the fact that she'd interrupted dinner.

"You're getting married?" I asked.

"Yes, I am." She waggled her left hand at me, showcasing a modest but pretty diamond ring. "William Best is my fiancée," she announced. "I love him to death."

I couldn't help smiling, but kept the reason to myself. Her married name would be Trieste Best.

Trieste struck me as a fairly simple creature, but the girl could talk. In the time it took Ryan to pour her a glass of wine she gave me the rundown on her entire relationship. William was a clerk at a convenience store that Trieste frequented. They'd found love somewhere between the cleaning aisle and fresh produce. "He's the sweetest man I've ever met," she declared, gazing at her engagement ring. "I can't wait to marry him."

It was a cute story, but did nothing to explain her connection to Ryan. "And what do you do, Trieste?"

Ryan jumped in, perhaps saving me from another explanation. "Trieste is an attorney," he explained. "A very clever one."

She rolled her eyes at him, seemingly uncomfortable with the praise. "I'm coming to the end of my clerkship," she said, glancing at me. "I'm hoping they'll keep me on."

"Of course they will," asserted Ryan. "They'd be crazy not to."

It took a long moment to wrap my head around the fact that the scatty girl was an attorney. Once I came to grips with that, I began to wonder what sort of match she'd make for a convenience store clerk.

"For now, I'm just focusing on the wedding," she said, bringing her glass of wine to her nose and sniffing it. "It's taking up every spare minute." She pulled a face and handed the glass back to Ryan. "I really don't like wine. Thanks anyway."

Chuckling blackly, he reached across and poured it down the sink. "Would you like something else? You can have one of Bridget's juice boxes if you want," he offered.

"Yeah, okay. Maybe I'll take one with me too."

Ryan didn't bat an eyelid. Still smiling, he set two juice boxes in front of her. "Anything else?"

"Yes," she answered. "I'd like some money, please." I watched in stunned silence as Ryan fetched his chequebook. Curiosity was killing me, but I waited to see what happened next. "It's a lot of money, Ryan," Trieste said gravely. "Are you sure?"

He dropped the chequebook on the counter. "Do you love it?"

Trieste straightened up and squared her shoulders. "It's exquisite," she gushed. "It's white and glamorous. It's fitted at the waist," she ran her hands down her sides as she explained, "and it's got little –"

"Spare me," he pleaded. "Just tell me how much."

"Five thousand, two hundred and twelve." She cringed as she said it but Ryan began writing the cheque before she'd finished telling him. He tore it off the stub and handed it to her.

"You're sure?" Her voice was barely there. Even in the short time I'd known her, I could tell it wasn't a tone she used often.

"I want you to have the perfect day," Ryan insisted. "Now you'll have the perfect dress too."

If ever there was a moment that I wanted to drop him to the floor and have my way with him, that was it. The hard-shelled, fickle jerk had just made a giddy bride's dream come true by paying for her wedding dress.

She waved the cheque at him. "I won't ever forget this, Ryan," promised Trieste. "You've been so good to me."

His skin flushed pink, all the way down to his neck. The coy smile he flashed me paled in comparison to the one I gave him.

Another layer of his tough exterior had been scraped away, exposing something that reminded me why I'd so eagerly given the wasp's nest another boot.

***

As soon as Trieste left, I pounced, forcing him onto the couch. "I'm so glad you're mine, Ryan," I murmured against his mouth.

"So you'll keep me?"

My hands moved to his shirt, twisting the buttons undone as I spoke. "For a while."

"At least until Friday," he said, dipping his head to kiss me again. "I promised my mom we'd go for dinner. It might be awkward if I show up without you."

I straightened up on his lap. "Dinner with the parents already?"

"Yeah." He reached and tucked my hair behind my ear. "Another first."

I tried to play down the nervousness, silently promising myself that there was nothing to worry about. I pushed his shirt off his shoulders and planted a kiss at the base of his throat. "I look forward to it," I mumbled against his skin. "I've always liked your parents."

"They like you too." He leaned forward, allowing me to slip the sleeves off his arms. "That's half the battle, right?"

"Yeah." I wasn't sure what the other half was, but there was no point asking. It was a situation where being forewarned probably wouldn't mean being forearmed.

I tossed his shirt on the floor and fell back against him, and all thoughts of dinner with his parents disappeared.

27. SECRET NORTH

Ryan

If I live a thousand years, it wouldn't be enough time to figure Charli Décarie out. But I'd worked out a few things. I knew how to flip her switch in two seconds flat, taking her from pleasant to homicidal. Calling her into Billet-doux to sign paperwork first thing in the morning was the ultimate switch flipper.

Paperwork was not Charli's forte. Being a grown up was not Charli's forte either, although today she looked like one. She appeared at the doorway rocking a sleek navy skirt suit and heels high enough to make her adult size.

"You look like you mean business, Charlotte," I greeted.

"Can we do this quickly?" She marched to my desk.

I leaned back in my chair. "Do come in, please."

"You called me, Ryan," she sourly reminded. "I have a meeting with a buyer in half an hour and then I have to rush home so Adam can go to work. Mrs Brown bailed on us again."

Bronson Merriman was a family-friendly employer, so Charli worked pretty cushy hours. My father was not, which explained Adam's horrendous schedule. Every time Mrs Brown bailed they were left in the lurch, and it had been happening frequently. Mrs Brown wasn't a young woman any more; clearly she was struggling.

"She's past it, Charli," I told her. "Mrs Brown can't keep up with Bridget." A Formula One driver couldn't keep up with Bridget.

She nodded dejectedly. "I know. She fell asleep on the couch the other day and Bridget tattooed her with a Sharpie pen."

I laughed, earning myself Tinker Bell's nastiest glare. "Was it in a good place?"

She dropped her head, unsuccessfully trying to hide her smile. "Her arm. She's now sporting Bridget's version of a Celtic band, just like Alex's."

"You can't have your child tattooing the help, Charlotte." I spoke in my primmest English accent. "What will the queen think?"

"The queen was not amused."

It wasn't really funny. If the kid was unsupervised long enough to tattoo someone, she could just as easily have been using the time to jemmy open the window in her bedroom. And she lived on the eighth floor.

"You need to find someone else."

"I know that, Ryan."

"How many days a week do you need a sitter?"

"Monday to Thursday," she replied. "Two to five-thirty."

"What about mornings?"

"I don't start until ten. Mrs Brown can manage for a few hours."

I didn't put a whole lot of thought into the offer that tumbled out of my mouth. "I'll help you out."

Charli staggered backwards. "Seriously?"

"My hours are pretty flexible," I replied. "If I get busy, Bridge can hang out here with me."

"Just until I find someone else, okay?"

"No problem."

She beamed. "You're such a good uncle, Ryan."

"Of course I am." I pushed a stack of papers across the desk. "I've been telling you that for years. Now sign these and get out of my office."

***

My babysitting duties began the next day.

I relieved Mrs Brown at two o'clock as promised, and she'd never looked more pleased to see me. "Good boy," she praised, hugging me at the door.

"Is everything okay?" I asked, looking past her. Bridget was bouncing on the couch, half watching the TV.

Mrs Brown glanced back at her before replying. "It is now." She pinched my cheeks. "Enjoy your afternoon." With that, she was gone. Mrs Brown could move when she wanted to.

I closed the door loudly, hoping to catch the attention of the little girl who'd so far ignored me. When that didn't work, I cleared my throat.

Bridget finally spoke, but didn't slow her bounce or look at me. "Hi, Ry."

"Hi. What are you doing?"

"Jumping."

"Well, can we find something more constructive to do, please?"

She stopped. "I am reductive."

I shook my head. "How about we get out of here? We could go to the park."

She didn't need asking twice. Like Mrs Brown, Bridget could also move quickly when she wanted to.

***

Central Park in summer is glorious – a big flash of green in a city of grey. It slows you down and brightens your mood. It was almost shameful that I only took advantage of it when I was with Bridget.

We wandered in off 59th. I thought Bridget would want to head to the playground but she had other ideas.

"We have to go over there," she said pointing down the tree-lined Mall.

"We're going to the fountain?" I guessed.

She shook her head. "We have to go hunting."

It was a statement that worried me. Her hunting plans could've involved anything from butterflies to other small children. I asked for clarification.

Bridget reached into the pocket of her shorts. "See what I have." I shifted her a few steps to the side so we weren't blocking the path, and waited. Finally, she held out her hand. "Look."

At first glance, I thought the round brass piece in her hand was an old fashioned fob watch that maybe she'd swiped from Mrs Brown. Then Bridget flipped open the lid.

"A compass?" I asked incredulously. "Where did you get that from?"

"My daddy. We went to the army shop."

No matter how many questions I asked, I couldn't get a straight answer from her. Fearing she'd gotten hold of something she shouldn't have, I texted Adam.

-Did you give your daughter a compass?

-Yes.

-Why?

-Because the night vision goggles didn't fit her properly.

I wasn't going to get a straight answer from him either, so I replied with a quick insult and gave up.

-I have no words. You're an idiot

I put my phone away. "Right," I announced, clapping my hands together. "What happens now?"

"We have to go looking," she replied.

I put my hand on her shoulder, steering her forward. "For what, Bridge?"

The explanation wasn't one I was expecting. Her little fingers pointed to the dial. "The numbers tell you where to go."

"The letters." I soon realised there was no point correcting her. Bridget had no idea when it came to orienteering, but in her mind she was an expert. From what I could pull from her rambling, her dad had done his best to explain it to her.

She reminded me of him when she was talking. Like Adam, one word answers were never enough. Even though she had trouble understanding a lot of it, Bridget soaked up information. Then a switch would go off and she'd become a mini Charli, making up details to fit the story in her head.

Bridget's compass had four cardinal directions: east, south, west and a La La suburb called Secret North. Funnily enough, that's where we were headed.

"That way," she instructed, pointing west.

We wandered at Bridget's pace for a long time, but didn't get far. We never ventured off the path either, so I could only assume that Secret North was a fairly broad coordinate.

"How will we know when we get there?"

"Because it will be special."

"Well, what's there?"

"It's lovely." She threw out her arms, almost losing her grip on the compass. "There are flowers on the roof."

"Okay."

"It's your place, Ry," she declared. "I'll find it for you."

I'm not a sappy man but the determination in her little voice hit me hard. I wanted to know more.

"Why is it my place?"

She threw her arms out again. This time, I took the compass from her, fearful she'd drop it. "Because you can see everything from there," she announced.

She'd managed to tell me everything and nothing.

I shook my head, trying to clear my brain of the nonsense.

"Sounds like a nice place, Bridge," I replied, humouring her. "Just let me know when we find it."

"We can hunt all day and all night," she declared.

I glanced at my watch. "I'm just not that diligent, sweetheart. I've got plans."

28. KEYS TO THE CASTLE

Bente

Despite the fact that Ryan assured me it was nothing more than a casual get-together, I spent two days thinking about the upcoming dinner at his parents' house. As a result, I was off my game and earned the wrath of my manager.

"I'm super disappointed in your performance today, Ben-ta," Noelle scolded. "Ryan would be too."

Totally fed up, I took the low road. "Ryan is *never* disappointed with my performance, Noelle." Her whole body tensed and her mouth fell open. I didn't hang around to hear if she was capable of a witty comeback. I walked out the door without looking back.

I didn't feel up to going home. Ryan was watching Bridget for the afternoon and I wasn't up to fending off any more of the miniature blows she liked to dish out. I decided to make an impromptu visit to her mother instead. If anyone knew the dread I was feeling, it was Charli. I'd spent days consoling her after her first few run-ins with the queen so it made total sense to go to her for moral support.

I'd never been to the Merriman gallery before, but the minute I stepped through the door I understood why she loved her job so much. It was calm and quiet and there wasn't a soul around. I would've turned up on a daily basis just for that.

"Wow, Charli," I mused, looking around the vast space. "Can I come back here with my laptop? I could sit here and write all day."

Her heels clicked on the wooden floor as she came toward me. "It's great, huh?"

"Gorgeous."

"Come with me," she ordered, hooking her arm through mine. "I want to show you something."

She led me to the rear of the gallery. The back wall showcased some of the biggest canvas prints I'd ever seen.

"These are huge," I gasped. "Why do they need to be that big?" They seemed awfully ostentatious to me, but in fairness I knew nothing about art.

"They don't need to be, but I'm glad they are," she replied, gazing ahead as if she was caught in a trance. "Tell me what you see."

I felt nervous, probably because I knew I was stuck in some sort of pop quiz. "Is this one of your pictures?"

"I wish," she said wistfully. "Tell me what you see."

I stared at the picture, having no clue what I was supposed to tell her. It was a photo of a coastline. The waves were rough and the beach was deserted. If anything, it looked like a miserable place to be.

"The ocean," I said finally.

"Look at it, Bente," she urged. "Really look at it."

I squinted, wondering if that might make a difference. "It's still the ocean. What do you see?"

She stared ahead, smiling in wonderment. "The ninth wave," she replied. "It's the first time I've seen the ninth wave of a set captured on film."

I wasn't about to ask the significance of the ninth wave. I found her stories confusing at the best of times and I already had enough confusion bouncing around in my head to contend with.

I looked back at the picture, studying it more closely. "There are only four waves, Charli."

She shook her head, pointing at one particular wave. "Yes, but that's the ninth one in the set. I can tell."

"How?"

Her eyes didn't leave the oceanic scene in front of her. "I can see it. And this picture is so beautifully detailed that I can feel it."

Nonsense, I thought.

"And that, my darling, is why you are my number one," interjected a voice from behind.

It wasn't the booming voice that made us jump. It was the clap that he followed up with. We spun around to see a man gliding toward us. He truly was gliding. Perhaps it's an easy manoeuvre in green velour slippers.

As soon as she was within reach, he grabbed Charli's hands and kissed her cheeks. "You like this one, darling?" he asked, waving at the picture we'd been discussing.

"Yes, I love it."

"I knew you would," he sang, dotting the tip of her nose with his index finger as if she was five years old. When he turned to me, I took a step back. "What about you, friend? Do you love it?"

I was too scared to answer in the negative. "It's outstanding," I lied.

He clapped his hands again, making only me jump. Perhaps Charli was used to it.

"It's a veritable steal at seventy-two hundred," he insisted, walking away. "Sell it to her, Charli."

Charli giggled down at the floor. "I'll try my best, Bronson."

I waited until he slipped out of sight before speaking. "Your boss?"

She nodded. "Fabulous, isn't he?"

Fabulous was the only way to describe him. He was short and stout, and had more hair on his face than his head. His tiny round glasses didn't seem to fit, and the oversized white cheesecloth shirt he wore reminded me of a drab housecoat.

"Super fabulous," I replied.

Both of us dissolved into hysterics that showed no sign of ending, even when Bronson reappeared.

"I love happy girls," he told us. "Happy, smiley girls. Why don't you flit away, Charlotte?" he suggested, flapping his hands in the direction of the front door. "Disappear into the sunshine with your lovely friend. Have coffee, share some gossip – or better still have a cocktail or two."

"You're sure?" asked Charli.

"Yes, yes," he replied. "The afternoon is yours. Take it while you're still young and beautiful."

***

I couldn't have planned the afternoon better if I'd tried. Escaping work early meant that Charli could actually partake of some grownup down time.

"Where are we going?" she asked, following me out onto the sidewalk.

"Let's go for a drink," I suggested.

She checked her watch. "I have to pick Bridget up at five-thirty."

I hooked my arm through hers to get her moving. "It's two-thirty," I told her. "I said a drink, not a bender. You'll be back in plenty of time."

"Okay," she relented. "Where?"

"I don't care," I replied, "as long as your family doesn't own it."

***

As far as we knew, the Décarie brothers had no monetary interest in the classy cocktail den we settled on. Considering the early hour, I was surprised by the number of people there. Most of the stools at the bar were occupied, but we landed a fabulous low table and a couple of small couches at the window.

Guilt was written all over Charli's face, so I took it upon myself to order drinks before she changed her mind about being there. The waitress set two strawberry daiquiris on the table. Charli didn't look impressed.

"Daiquiris?" she quizzed, once the waitress was gone.

I picked a piece of mint out of my glass. "I love daiquiris. They're the perfect summer drink."

"It's not a drink, Bente. It's a dessert."

"Good choice then." I raised my glass in a toast. "I like dessert too."

Despite her initial protests, Charli began to relax and enjoy her unexpected lazy afternoon. We were on our second cocktail when the subject of dinner with the Décaries rated a mention.

"This Friday?" she asked.

I set my glass down on the table. "Please don't tell me you have other plans," I begged. "I need you there."

Charli shook her head. "You'll be fine. Fiona is a lot more mellow where Ryan's concerned. She's more than ready to see him settle down."

"Please come," I repeated desperately.

"I have to," she said glumly. "If we're summoned to dinner, we go. That's the rules."

"Whose rules?"

Charli stabbed the ice in her glass with her straw. "I don't even know." She shrugged. "It's just the rules."

She'd worked hard over the years at gaining acceptance *and* standing her ground. Sometimes I wondered which was the bigger victory.

"Do you think Jean-Luc will like me?" I asked in a tiny voice. From the little I knew I had more reason to fear him than the queen.

She smiled, albeit wickedly. "Of course he will. You're well educated and have good future prospects, which is more than he thinks I have."

"Is that why he gives you such a hard time?"

"No," she replied. "I won't submit and behave. And I lead his son astray. That's his problem with me. If you want to fit in Bente, just play by the rules."

"So what are the rules?"

Charli stalled by taking a long sip of her drink. I wanted to rip the glass from her hand. "Well?" I pressed.

"Learn to love the lifestyle as much as you love Ryan," she finally replied. "If you can manage that, you're guaranteed the keys to the castle."

"Do you have the keys to the castle?"

She shook her head. "I don't need them. I use Bridget's keys to gain entry."

The mention of Bridget made me check the time on my phone. Like a couple of gossiping lushes, we'd somehow whittled away three hours.

"It's nearly five-thirty," I told her. "Do you want to go?"

Charli thought for a long moment. "No," she decided. "I'll call Adam. He can pick up Bridge and we can order another round."

She was holding her phone to her ear before I could protest, which was fine by me. I was happy to stay longer. I got the impression that time out wasn't something Charli got often, and judging by the strung-out look on Adam's face most days, he didn't either.

"Hey, it's me," she said quietly. I tried not to listen to the one-sided conversation but it was impossible. "I'll meet you at Ryan's in an hour or two," she told him. "I love you, Adam. So much."

Charli slipped her phone back in her purse. "You're staring like an idiot. What's wrong?"

"How can you be so sure?"

She laughed, perhaps more at my tone than my question. "He's fine. He's leaving the office now and heading over to pick –"

"No," I interrupted. "How can you be so sure that he's the one?"

She'd always known, even before Adam worked it out. I wanted to know how to get to that point. I would've endured the most outlandish fairy story ever told just to know the secret.

"I just know, Bente," she replied, almost smiling. "My life works better when he's in it."

"I want that," I told her. "So badly."

"With Ryan?"

I shrugged, feeling slightly stupid. "I could love Ryan," I admitted. "I just don't know if I'd be loved in return. And if he told me he loved me, I probably wouldn't believe him."

"How long do you think he should be punished?" she asked.

"Excuse me?"

"How long do you think he should have to keep making up for past mistakes? A year? A couple of years?" She paused, but not long enough to let me reply. "That seems like an awful waste of time if you ask me."

I signalled for another drink. "As long as I have to deal with ex-playthings showing up unannounced, my doubts are warranted."

"It happened again?"

Despite the fact that I'd felt the same level of annoyance at her arrival, I couldn't throw Trieste in the same boat as the blonde stripper wannabe.

"No, not really," I admitted. "A girl called Trieste turned up the other night. She's not a plaything."

Charli slumped back and giggled. "No, definitely not," she agreed.

"You know her?"

"Yeah," she replied. "Totally harmless. Ryan and Adam have a soft spot for Trieste. They look after her pretty well."

"Ryan paid for her wedding dress," I revealed.

"Good for him."

"It was a sweet thing to do," I agreed. "And hugely generous. It was a five grand dress."

"It won't break the bank." Her smile slipped. "I don't think we're in any danger of becoming destitute any time soon."

Charli wasn't one for practising what she preaches. She'd never learned to love the lifestyle. Talk of finances seemed to embarrass her.

"The Décaries have a lot of money, don't they?" I spoke quietly as if it was a secret we weren't supposed to discuss.

Charli nodded but her dire expression remained. "It takes some getting used to."

"Ryan bought me five Hermès scarves," I said gravely. "I'm not sure how to deal with that."

"You just do," she brooded. "I like vintage cocktail dresses so Fiona buys them for me. I have more than I'll probably ever wear. No big deal."

"So you just get used to it?"

"You can if you want to," she quietly permitted. "But I'll never get used to it. That's how I know I'm doing okay."

29. KILLJOY

Ryan

If I were a stickler for details, I would've been furious with Charli for breaching our babysitting agreement. Bridget was still with me at six o'clock, thanks to her mother's decision to hit the town with my girlfriend. I wasn't pissed. Bridget's good mood was holding and I was confident of keeping her happy until her father arrived to pick her up.

I rustled her up a quick dinner, but Bridget didn't seem impressed by my efforts. She pulled a face as if I'd set a plate of rat poison in front of her.

"Please try it," I urged.

"I don't like it."

"How do you know? You haven't tried it."

She pushed the plate forward.

"Everybody likes chicken," I insisted, sliding it back in front of her.

"I like chicken nuggets."

"Bridget Décarie, chicken nuggets do not count as food," I told her, aghast. "Do you know what they put in nuggets?"

"Nuggets?" she guessed. I instantly admitted defeat. Entering into a chicken debate with a four-year-old wasn't smart, especially considering the calibre of my opponent.

I managed to strike a deal with her, but at a price. She ate the smallest amount of dinner, and in exchange, I spent the half hour before her father arrived watching *The Little Mermaid* with her.

Adam let himself in.

Bridget clambered over me on to the arm of the couch and launched herself the second she thought he was close enough to catch her. Clearly it was a manoeuvre Adam was familiar with. His arms were outstretched before she made her move. After a quick kiss, he hung her upside down, making her giggle.

"Thanks for watching her."

"Any time," I replied. "She didn't eat much."

"I don't like rabbit," interjected Bridget, still hanging upside down.

Adam righted her and dropped her on the couch. "You fed her rabbit?"

"Yeah." I glanced at the little liar next to me. "Next time I'll take the fur off."

Adam sat down on the last spare space on the couch. "I'm glad I'm not eating here tonight. What are you watching?"

"Ariel," Bridget announced excitedly.

Not much was said over the next few minutes. The mini Tinker Bell sat quietly, as captivated by the redheaded mermaid as the first fifty times she'd watched her. I couldn't explain Adam's reasons for sitting through it – or mine.

Adam spoke first. "Ariel's kinda hot."

"She's whiny," I objected. "Not my type."

"She lives under the water," Bridget explained, shuffling closer to her dad.

"So would your mother, given the chance," I replied.

***

By the time Bente and Charli arrived, Bridget was asleep on the couch, exhausted by the hours we'd spent in Central Park looking for the elusive Secret North. Inexplicably, Adam and I were still watching the mermaid movie. In move strangely reminiscent of the *Dirty Dancing* debacle, we jumped to our feet when the door swung open.

"Hi," beamed Bente, loudly. I shushed her and pointed at the sleeping girl.

"Oh, sorry," she whispered, half leaning into me for an almost-hug.

Adam walked over to Charli, took her in his arms and kissed her as if they were alone in the room. I could've put it down to the hour of Disney inspiration he'd received at the hands of Ariel, but a more honest assessment would be that it was just Charli and Adam being Charli and Adam. "Go home," I ordered. "We don't need to see that."

He loosened his hold on her but didn't let go. Charli twisted in his arms to face me. "Thank you for watching our girl today."

I glanced at Bridget. "She was no trouble. The story of the day was a good one."

"Do you think she'll wake up?" whispered Bente.

The fear in her voice made me smile. "I'll protect you if she does."

"That's not funny, Ryan," chided Charli. "Don't encourage my kid to be a bully."

"What does that mean?" asked Adam, totally clueless.

Charli said nothing, leaving it to me to explain that Bridget's treatment of Bente had been less than welcoming. "She's not very good at sharing."

"See, Charlotte?" he asked quietly. "Only child syndrome."

She glared at me as if I'd just thrown her under a bus.

Tension filled the room in an instant, and I wanted no part of it. Obviously it was a continuation of a conversation that was nothing to do with us. "Right." I stupidly clapped my hands. "Who's up for a drink?" Bridget stirred at the sudden noise but didn't wake. Bente grabbed the throw off the other couch and covered her.

"I am," replied Adam. "I'll get the glasses."

I headed for the fridge and grabbed a bottle of wine. Charli sat at the counter. "So, what did you do today?"

"Just the usual," I replied casually. "Rolled a couple of old ladies in the park for their purses, smoked a few joints near the fountain."

"Uncle of the year, aren't you?"

"Uncle of the freaking millennium, Charlotte," I corrected, making her laugh.

"I have the day off tomorrow," said Bente, taking a seat on the stool next to Charli. "Perhaps I could hang out too, maybe try winning her over."

"You don't need to win her over," said Adam, frowning. "Don't let her give you a hard time."

"It's not a problem," assured Bente. "Malibu and Fabergé put Ryan through worse and he managed to talk them round."

"Yeah," said Charli wryly. "With help from Helios and Clytie."

I slid a glass of wine across to Bente. "I would've won them over without your story, Charlotte," I boasted. "I know a few of my own."

"Of course you do," said Charli.

I held another glass in front of her. "It's true, and because your husband doesn't know the difference between a wine glass and a champagne coupe, I'm all set to tell you one."

"A glass is a glass, Ryan," Adam insisted. "If you were at our house, you'd probably be offered a sippy cup."

I ignored him and began my tale.

"Legend has it that the shape of the champagne coupe was modelled on the left breast of Marie Antoinette," I revealed. "She wanted her court to toast her health by drinking from glasses shaped like her boobs."

My brother picked up one of the shallow round glasses and held it to the light. "Marie had a decent rack," he approved. "But I don't want to know who they modelled the champagne flute on."

Bente laughed. "No, me neither."

Charli straightened on the stool. "I'm very impressed, Ryan."

"Don't be." I poured another glass of wine and handed it to her, preparing to kill my own story with a dose of reality. "It's a crock, just like the stories you tell. Champagne coupes have been around since the seventeenth century, long before Marie Antoinette and her boobs."

"Killjoy," muttered Charli.

"No," I corrected. "Just a realist."

**

I'd learned more about women in the past few weeks than I had in the thirty years before that.

When men make the decision to go to bed, they undress and they go to bed. Women flit between the bathroom and the bedroom fifteen times, open and close the closet a few times – seemingly without purpose – then decide it's a good time to tidy up the bedroom.

They also talk.

"Adam said he's going to need a few weeks to work on the dresser," said Bente, scooping up the shirt I'd just laid over the back of the chair.

"I'm sure we'll cope without it," I mumbled.

"You told him to paint it, right?"

"No, not specifically," I replied. "I just told him to fix it so it matches the rest of the room."

Bente dropped the shirt back on the chair and took a long look around. "He'll paint it black, then," she concluded. "Call him and tell him not to paint it black. That would be horrible."

Hoping she'd take the hint, I reached over and turned off the bedside lamp. Five seconds later the room filled with light again. "Please, Ry," she said sweetly. "I don't want it black."

I grabbed her pillow and threw it over my face. "Fine. No black."

The pillow must've muffled my frustration. She kept talking. "It should be pink – hot pink to match the chairs."

It was going from bad to worse. Not only was she still talking, she was now making ridiculous design decisions.

"Sweetheart, please, can we talk about this tomorrow?"

I felt her climb into bed so I handed her back her pillow. She snuggled into me and for a quick second, I got to enjoy one of the good parts of living with a woman. And then she killed it by speaking again.

"Did you notice anything weird between those two tonight? Charli and Adam, I mean."

I sighed heavily. "Charli and Adam are weird."

Bente lifted her head and rested her chin on my shoulder. "I'm serious, Ryan."

"Why do we have to be serious at midnight?"

"I think he wants another baby."

It was a totally inappropriate conversation for a few reasons. First, it was none of our business. Second, it was far too late to be discussing anything. I tried answering her anyway, in the hope that she'd finally go to sleep.

"I have no idea. Why don't you ask him?"

"Because it's none of my business."

Exactly, I didn't reply.

"Do you want to have a baby, Ryan?" she asked.

My throat seized up at the unexpected question, making a calm reply impossible. "Now?" I choked.

Bente dropped her head, bouncing her warm laugh off my skin. It was so freaking perfect I considered knocking her up there and then.

"Not now, in the future," she clarified. "Do you want children some day?"

It wasn't something I thought about very often, but it was on my list of things to do when I eventually became an adult.

"Yes," I muttered. "I want four sons."

"Four?" she gasped.

"Yeah. And I'm going to call them all Ryan. I'm going to create my own miniature army of Ryans."

Perhaps realising that delirium had set in, she patted my chest. "You might need help with that, soldier."

"You'll help me," I said smugly.

"Not with four," she informed me. "Two, max."

I slid my arm beneath her and cradled her against me. "Are you offering to bear my children, Miss Denison?"

"Maybe."

"Well, I appreciate the offer but I'm just not sure that I'd be content in settling down with my very first girlfriend."

Her whole body moved when she laughed. "You're right, Ryan. I think you should play the field a little first."

30. ENIGMA

Bente

My offer to attempt to win Bridget over was ambitious to say the least, but I was determined to give it my best shot. Ryan spent the morning at Billet-doux, doing whatever it is that Ryan does, and then collected his niece. They hit the park from there and, not surprisingly, I wasn't invited.

I put the time alone to good use, preparing an arsenal of little girl delights. It was a complex operation. My nieces could be easily bought with chocolate and toys but Bridget would not be so easily swayed.

I'd visited Ivy that morning and commandeered a glue gun and a box of sparkles before heading off to buy a Bridget size pair of galoshes. Now I sat on the couch like Suzy-freaking-homemaker diligently attaching sparkles to a pair of boots.

I knew it was going to be a long afternoon, and judging by the look of pure thunder Bridget bestowed on me as she walked through the door, she knew it too. My plan was to ignore her and wait for her to come to me when curiosity got the better of her.

I'd laid out my entire plan to Ryan over breakfast.

"Just ignore me," I instructed. "Pretend not to notice me."

"I'll try," he promised. "But if you get glue anywhere near my couch, you can bet I'm going to notice you."

Despite his anti-crafting stance, he was playing his part to perfection. He said nothing to me when they arrived, which threw Bridget for a loop.

Instead, he sat her at the counter and made her something to eat. While he was staring into the fridge she stole a glance at me, which I pretended not to notice.

Ryan set a juice box and a couple of cookies down in front of her.

"I don't like them," she told him.

"They're the same ones you had yesterday."

"I don't like them any more," she amended.

He walked around the counter, picked her up and lowered her to her feet. That was probably the point that she usually made a run for her girls, but she didn't move.

"What's up Bridge?" asked Ryan, as if he didn't know. He pointed at her toybox. "Go play with your girls."

If she'd walked any slower, she would've been travelling backwards. She wasn't remotely interested in her toys. She was more intent on checking me out. I could feel her behind me, stalking me like a little lion, but I kept gluing like a trooper despite my shaking hands. After twenty minutes I decided that Bridget Décarie was not easily led into temptation. It must've been a trait inherited from her father. Charli would've been dancing around the room in the bedazzled boots before the glue had a chance to set.

Bridget lurked behind the couch. From the corner of my eye I occasionally saw her head bob up, but that was the only move she made. Ryan sat at the counter reading a newspaper. He was hardly struggling with the silence. No doubt he was relishing the peace and quiet.

I set one gemshot boot on the coffee table so she could get a good look at it. The thing was so junked up it practically glowed.

Bridget finally took the bait. She walked around the couch and climbed up beside me. I continued gluing as if she hadn't made a move.

"I love those boots," she said finally.

Ryan swivelled his stool around and grinned at me. I fought hard not to smile back, somehow managing to keep my focus on the project on my lap. "Do you?" I asked simply.

Bridget nodded. "Do you love my boots?"

"Of course," I replied inattentively. "Who wouldn't love zebra print boots? I think they're wonderful."

Her little legs barely reached the edge of the cushion, but she did her best to swing her feet. "Do you love diamonds, Bente?"

"Sure. Do you?"

"I love them on boots."

I had to hand it to her, she was a stellar opponent. Bridget was smartly taking the long way around. If Malibu was in her position, she'd just throw a tantrum and demand that I give them to her.

"I do too," I replied. "That's why I'm making them."

"They might be too small for you," suggested Bridget. "You've got big girl feet."

I looked at my shoes. "Oh, you're right." I spoke dejectedly as if I'd only just realised it. "I don't think they're going to fit me."

Bridget patted my knee. "Never mind," she soothed.

I heard Ryan chuckle and then quickly clear his throat.

"It seems a shame to let them go to waste," I said sadly. "Do you think they'd fit your feet?"

"Yes I do," she declared, already kicking off her boots.

I helped her pull on her new junked-up galoshes and for a very short minute I felt victorious – until she took off running to Ryan.

Then I felt like I'd been scammed by a four-year-old evil genius.

"Look what I have, Ry!" she squealed.

Ryan looked at me, silently pleading for instruction.

I shrugged. It was round two to Bridget.

***

My efforts hadn't been completely in vain. I hadn't bumped Ryan off top spot but at least Bridget was talking to me again. She refrained from biting my head off when I dared to speak to Ryan too, so I accepted it as a good result.

Despite the progress I'd made, I was relieved when her dad finally picked her up. "Ryan, how long are you going to be watching her?" I asked, sinking back into the couch.

He leaned over the back of the couch and kissed my cheek as he passed. "A few weeks, tops." He disappeared down the bedroom but called out a few seconds later. "I think you might want to see this, Bente."

I trudged down the hall slowly, expecting the very worst. For all I knew, I could've been gearing up to view a crime scene. Ryan hadn't ventured any further than the doorway, doing nothing to allay my fears. I poked my head into the room, noticing that a few changes had been made. I'd made the bed that morning, not perfectly, but a damn sight better than it looked now. The covers were rumpled and the pillows were askew.

"If she's taken to messing up our bed Ryan, the gloves are off," I grumbled.

He took me by the hand and led me over to the bed. That's when I noticed the bulge under the blankets. "A horse's head?" he suggested.

I had no clue what to expect when I pulled back the covers, but a pile of broken dolls wasn't it.

"Her girls," I breathed.

"Congratulations," Ryan murmured, kissing the top of my head. "If you're in with the girls, you're as good as part of the family."

"She's not normal, Ryan." My experience with small children wasn't exactly vast, but that much I did know. "She's an enigma. Four-year-olds don't leave you hanging. They don't bide their time, and they don't play their cards close to their chest." Bridget had patience and wisdom far beyond her years.

"You ain't seen nothing yet, sweetheart," he whispered in my ear. "Wait until you meet the four Ryans."

***

Friday night rolled around far too quickly.

I tried to play it cool, but I changed my dress three times in half an hour, finally settling on a simple black Ivy creation. My nerves were getting the better of me, and Ryan noticed.

"You look beautiful," he assured me, "but you're acting like a crazy woman."

"You're a terrible boyfriend," I informed him. "You're supposed to be comforting me in my hour of need."

"Help me out, then," he replied. "I'm new at this."

I set my brush down on the bathroom counter. "Do you think your parents are going to like me?"

Ryan sidled up behind me and wrapped his arms around me. "Look at you." He dropped his head, resting his chin on my shoulder. "How could they not like you?"

It was going to take more than looking good to charm them. I needed to try my hand at being witty and smart, as opposed to being a smartass. Just thinking about it made me feel ill.

"What if I say the wrong thing?"

"It won't matter. Charli says the wrong thing all the time. They're used to it."

It was a pointless comparison. Anything inappropriate that crossed Charli's lips was bound to be intentional.

"I just want things to go smoothly."

He didn't seem to be listening. The thin straps of my dress slipped off my shoulders as he undid the zip at the back.

"What are you doing, Ryan?"

"What does it look like I'm doing?" He swept my hair over my shoulder and pressed his lips to the back of my neck. "I'm comforting you in your hour of need."

I pushed him out of the room, not stopping until he fell back on the bed. Ignoring the damage I was doing to my perfectly pressed dress, I crashed on top of him.

"We have to be there in half an hour," I reminded, muffling the words against his neck.

In a move I didn't see coming, Ryan rolled, stealing the air in my lungs as he landed on top of me. "I only need half an hour."

I was in big trouble. It wasn't the weight of him that made me breathless. It was everything about him. Every promise I'd made to myself about taking things slowly to lessen the pain of the inevitable crash and burn had gone out the window. I was all-in.

***

I had a weird sense of déjà vu when I stepped out of the cab. The Décarie building was a majestic old brownstone that I'd admired a hundred times from the park over the road; its beautiful carved mouldings, wrought iron balconies and huge arched windows always caught my eye. I knew it would be a grand residence – there are no hovels on Fifth Avenue. I just wasn't expecting it to be *this* building.

"You live here?" I asked, making doubly sure.

"No," he clarified. "My mom and dad do."

This inside of the building was just as impressive. I think I stopped breathing once we got in the elevator. It made talking difficult. "Do you think Adam and Charli will show up?"

Ryan shrugged and continued rolling the cuff of his white dress shirt further up his arm. "They should. They were invited."

I thought back to the conversation I'd had with Charli and felt a little better. They *had* to be there. It was the rules. When the front door opened, I felt better still. Charli answered.

Ryan frowned. "You just can't find good help these days."

She tried closing the door in his face but he was too quick and wedged his foot in the way. "Get out of my way, Tink," he commanded. "We've got real company tonight."

"Oh, yes. Fresh blood." She could sound positively evil when she tried. "Welcome." She drew out the word, dipped her head and curtsied.

I suddenly felt terrified. Not even the sight of Bridget bounding into the foyer calmed me. She ran at Ryan, stopping only because he scooped her up. "Hi Ry," she beamed as if she hadn't seen him in weeks.

"Hey, little girl," he replied. "Where's your papa?"

"Talking to Papy," she told him.

I decided to test the Bridget waters and try talking to her. "Hi, Bridget." My cheery tone took some work. "How are you?"

"I have my boots here," she replied, twisting in Ryan's arms to lift her bare foot. "They're over there."

I turned to see the little junked up boots standing near the door. "That's awesome," I replied truthfully.

She agreed. "Very awesome."

It was a pointless conversation that was headed nowhere, but I welcomed anything that saved me from venturing into the next room. Respite was brief. The double glass doors slid back a few seconds later and I stood face to face with Queen Fiona.

She indiscreetly looked me up and down before speaking. "Darlings," she finally crooned, arms outstretched.

Ryan kissed her cheek before lowering Bridget to her feet. I wasn't quite sure of kissing protocol so I waited for Fiona to make the first move. She put both hands on my upper arms and almost connected as she pecked each cheek. "Bente, welcome to our home. You look lovely."

"Thank you," I replied, relieved that I'd passed muster.

"Why don't you go through to the lounge? Ryan will show you around," she suggested. "I must check on dinner."

Ryan waited until she was out of earshot before speaking. "She's cooking?" he asked Charli.

Charli nodded. "Eve-ry-thing."

He turned his attention back to me. "I am so sorry," he said. "I'll make it up to you, but tonight you're going to have to grin and bear it. You're one of us now. Good luck and Godspeed."

Charli laughed. I managed a slight smile.

Ryan didn't give me time to dwell. He took my hand and led me into the lounge.

It took a long moment to take it all in. The room looked nothing like I imagined it would. Ryan's apartment was sleek and modern. His parents' home was the exact opposite, furnished with ornate wooden furniture. Every piece looked antique and heavy, a perfect statement of wealth and grandeur. The only thing out of place was the pair of tiny bare feet sticking out under the coffee table.

Adam walked in, and I was grateful for the friendly face. "Hey, Bente," he said warmly. I added a weird half-wave to my hello. Jean-Luc followed closely behind. He offered me a hand. "Welcome, Bente. It's been a long time."

He remembered me. Hopefully that meant I had a head start when it came to making a good impression.

Jean-Luc invited me to sit. I glanced at Ryan, silently willing him to do the same. He took the hint and sat beside me on the longest leather couch I'd ever seen.

The Décarie men all possessed the same charm and identical killer smiles. They also shared the same knack for putting people at ease with polite conversation. I couldn't be sure if Jean-Luc's interest in me was genuine, but I was glad he was keeping the conversation alive. He asked me about my life in Boston and my new career plans for New York.

"I'm hoping something comes up soon," I told him. "For now I'm waitressing at Billet-doux."

He nodded. "You're a bright girl. I'm sure you'll secure a job worthy of your talents soon – hopefully something more substantial than waitressing."

"There's nothing wrong with waitressing," said Charli, appearing out of nowhere with a tray of canapés in her hand.

"Indeed, Charli," agreed Jean-Luc. "Some people are well suited to service industries. The hue of that silver platter suits you immensely."

Charli held the tray out to him. "You're too kind."

Jean-Luc took a canapé and turned his attention to Bridget, who was still under the table. "*Alors, viens ma petite. Viens manger un morceau.*"

"I'm not hungry, Papy," she replied. "I'm working under here."

Charli set the tray on the coffee table and took up position on the arm of the couch next to Adam. Clearly nervousness wasn't an issue for them. He slipped his arm around her as if they were lounging in their own home.

I took mental notes as I studied Ryan's family. It didn't take long to work out that I'd been worrying unnecessarily. Everyone worked hard to make me feel welcome, and the only insincerity I detected came when everyone praised Fiona's cooking. It had to be a lie. She'd served up the vilest attempt at lasagne I'd ever been subjected to.

The only person on the receiving end of any hostility was Charli, but Jean-Luc's occasional digs didn't seem to faze her. Fiona was quick to defend her and Adam was even faster. I soon worked out that protecting her was unnecessary. Charlotte Décarie was no victim. She gave as good as she got. From what I could tell, she relished winding Jean-Luc up as much as he enjoyed trying to pull her into line.

Unlike Charli, I wasn't interested in making waves. The best road in was the quiet one. Ryan would appreciate the peace, his parents would appreciate the amenability and I'd enjoy the lack of drama.

31. DELIVERY

Ryan

Bente sometimes stayed up late, writing long into the night. Inexplicably, she'd still wake early the next morning, bright eyed and cheery – even on Wednesdays.

Wednesday mornings should've been the bane of her existence. Every week she made an early morning trek to Astoria to have breakfast with Ivy and the girls. Unlike her, I don't cope well with little sleep or breakfast with the squealers so I never went, opting for an extra hour in bed instead.

"It wouldn't kill you to come, Ryan."

"It might," I replied, spreading out over her half of the bed. "Say hi to the squealers for me."

Bente left and I went back to sleep, but the peace was broken when someone started hammering my intercom. I ignored the buzzing for as long as I could before admitting defeat.

My caller was Colin the delivery guy. "I have a chest of drawers to come up," he explained through the speaker.

I wasn't pissed with Colin – I like efficiency – but I had a bone to pick with my brother. Who in their right mind would arrange a furniture delivery at seven in the morning?

Adam would, because he knew it would annoy me.

Colin and his sidekick appeared at the door a few minutes later, struggling to maintain their grip on the dresser. I held the door as they manoeuvred it inside. A small part of me was hoping they'd drop it and do irreparable damage. Another part of me was keen to see what Adam had done with it. As far as I was concerned, it already looked better. A thick layer of protective black foam hid it from view.

"Where do you want it?" asked Colin, breathless.

I walked ahead, leading them down to the bedroom. Once it was in place, Colin's offsider tore off the foam for the big reveal.

"Holy cow," Colin muttered, staring in disbelief.

I couldn't blame him for the reaction. Bente's shabby green dresser had undergone changes since it left my apartment three weeks earlier. The paint was no longer flaky and patchy. It was perfectly smooth and glossy, and the missing knobs had been replaced with girly glass ones.

As expected, Adam's work was faultless. The only thing wrong with it was that it was now the same shade of hot pink as the wing chairs.

"Was it supposed to be that colour?" asked Colin, sounding traumatised.

"Yeah." I folded my arms and took a step back to get a better look at it. "Girls love crap like this."

"I think I'd rather stay single," he muttered.

"Been there, done that," I replied, glancing at him. "I like this better."

32. MYSTERY BLONDE

Bente

Breakfast at Ivy's was an ordeal, mainly because of the bitchy mood she was in.

"Three weeks," she grumbled, waving a spatula at me as she stood at the stove. "You've been living there for three weeks and not once have you invited us over."

I glanced across the table at my nieces, who were engaging in a sword fight with their cutlery. Ryan would never cope with that.

"We've been busy," I said defensively. "Maybe we can tee up dinner or something soon." It wasn't a likely offer, considering we didn't have a dining suite.

"Perfect. Just let me know when."

I shook my head, trying to shift the image of Ivy and the girls sitting in a line at our kitchen counter.

"At his mansion?" asked Faberge, momentarily downing weapons.

I frowned. "We don't live in a mansion. It's just a normal apartment."

Ivy dropped an omelette onto a plate and set it in front of Malibu. "Normal apartments don't exist smack in the middle of Manhattan," she declared.

"Is it shiny?" asked Malibu.

I had no idea how to answer her. Luckily, Ivy jumped in again. "Granite and marble are very shiny," she replied. "And I'll bet there's an excess of both."

My mouth formed a tight line. She wasn't wrong so I said nothing.

"I want to go there!" yelled Malibu, thumping her fork on the table.

"Be quiet and eat," ordered her mother.

***

Ivy kicked me out after breakfast so she could get the girls to school. I pretended to be sad that our morning was cut short, just as I did every week. In reality, I chose to go there mid-week for that very reason. It was the ultimate escape plan.

It was mid morning when I arrived home. I hoped to steal a few hours with Ryan before he left to hang out with Bridget, but as soon as I walked through the door I realised it wasn't likely to happen.

A blonde sat perched at the island counter, decorously sipping a cup of coffee. I could feel my mouth forming a heinous grimace the second I laid eyes on her.

"Hey," said Ryan, walking over to me, arms outstretched. I tilted my head so he only connected with my cheek when he kissed me. If he thought it was awkward, he didn't let on. "I want you to meet someone."

Blondie looked friendly enough, but until I knew exactly who she was pleasantries were impossible.

"Bente Denison, this is Yolanda Montague," he announced.

"Pleased to meet you," I lied.

She cocked her head. "You too, Bente. I've heard a lot about you."

"Really?" I glared at Ryan.

"Yes; you've got him well trained." She smiled. "We've just spent the last hour working in your bedroom."

"Excuse me?" I choked.

She giggled, but Ryan didn't find it funny. Perhaps knowing my acute dislike of flirty blondes, he punched out a quick explanation. "Yolanda is an interior decorator."

Breathing became a little easier.

"Yes," she said, grabbing her purse off the counter. "And I think I've just done a fabulous job on your room." She handed me a business card. "If you can talk him into working a bit of feminine charm on the rest of the apartment, be sure to give me a call."

I looked at the card in my hand. "I will. Thanks."

I wasn't really sure what I was thanking her for, but Ryan must've been excited to show me because he bustled Yolanda out as quickly as he could without appearing rude.

"You. Bedroom. Now," he ordered.

"I love it when you're bossy," I sighed.

I truly did.

Ryan didn't speak. Instead, he scooped me up and carried me down the hall, lowering me when we got to the door. "You're going to love this."

He wasn't being bossy this time. There was a hint of nervousness in his voice that I didn't hear often. It was almost as sexy as his bossy tone.

Ryan swung the door open and waved me in. He didn't move from his spot in the doorway but I paced every inch of the bedroom, trying to notice everything.

The first thing I saw was my dresser, standing against the far wall in hot pink glory.

"Pink?" I gasped, running my hand along the glossy top. "You asked him to paint it pink?"

"What the lady wants, the lady gets," he replied.

I looked at him and grinned, mainly at his sheepish expression. "It's perfect, Ry."

I turned full circle, checking out the rest of the room. In the time I'd been gone, Yolanda had worked some serious design magic to accommodate the revamped dresser. I'd left a stark, boyish room styled in monochromatic black. It was now broken up with gorgeous hot pink, black and white bedding, silver cushions and flowing pink drapes.

I was at a loss for words, and it had little to do with the decorating. "You're sure about this?"

I had to ask. He didn't look very sure. If anything, the infusion of pink seemed to be causing him physical pain. He did his best to hide it by stiffening his pose and folding his arms. "I want you to be happy here," he told me. "This is your home too."

Pure bliss coursed through my veins as the implications of the situation set in. We were a couple – a real couple, capable of commitment and compromise and pink drapes.

Unable to hold myself back, I threw myself at him, planting a hundred kisses on his lips. "I am so happy right now."

He huffed out a laugh. "So you like it?"

"I love it, Ryan," I confirmed. "I love you."

It was three words too many. I felt his body stiffen as if I'd just delivered a kick to the shins. Worse than that, he didn't say anything.

I silently willed him to return the sentiment and save the day, but he stayed silent. A few seconds passed like hours, stripping away all the euphoria until there was only humiliation left.

Ryan dropped his hold on me. "I should probably go," he muttered, fumbling gracelessly with his words. "I've got a bit of work to do at the office before picking Bridget up."

I smoothed down my hair while I battled to find words. "Yeah," I said finally. "Good idea."

Ryan kissed my forehead. It was detached and aloof, and almost as mortifying as his quick exit from the room a few seconds later.

33. PRICKLY BABIES

Ryan

I couldn't believe it. Of all the responses I could've made after being told that I was loved, I chose none of them. What I'd really wanted to do was punch the air and tell her I felt exactly the same way, but like the idiot I was, I'd said nothing.

How was I supposed to get us back on track after that? Disappearing out the door obviously wasn't the solution, but it was the best idea I had at the time.

I spent a few hours holed up in my office at Billet-doux on the pretence of having lots of work to take care of. I ordered Noelle to keep everyone away and killed my open-door policy by slamming it shut.

In truth, I had very little work to do, which seemed like a big dose of karma. It left me plenty of time to dwell on the fact that my very first girlfriend was probably spending the afternoon moving her pink furniture out of our apartment.

My preoccupation continued long after I left the office. It wasn't a good state of mind to be in while babysitting Bridget. She picked up on my mood immediately.

We'd only just entered the park when she questioned me. "Are you sad, Ry?"

She didn't meet my eyes when I looked at her. She was too busy watching where she was walking for a change.

"No," I assured her, "I'm fine."

"Are you sad because I didn't bring my finder today?"

I hadn't given her compass a thought until that minute, which was odd considering she'd been carting it to the park every day for weeks.

"Where is it?"

I was quietly hopeful that she hadn't lost interest. As ridiculous as it was, I wanted her to eventually find Secret North. It was *my* place, after all.

"It wouldn't fit in my pocket today," she explained. "It's too full with something else."

"What do you have instead, Bridge?"

Her slow walk crawled to a stop as she dug into her pocket. The little pink drawstring bag she pulled out wasn't moving, so at least she hadn't trapped any live animals. As interested as I was to know what it was, I held off asking. Bridget's explanations are notoriously long, and get longer when she's pressed. I put my hand on her back to get her moving again and waited for her to speak.

"Sometimes I can't say words," she said waving the bag at me. "I know what they are but I can't say them."

"I know exactly how you feel, Bridge." It was as if the kid had reached into my head, pulled out my anguish and was now playing it back to me. Despite the weirdness, I tried to play it cool. "There are words I can't say too."

She waved the bag again. "I can help you."

"Maybe I can help you too," I suggested. "What words are you having trouble with?"

"Pock-a-picks," she blurted. "I can't say pock-a-picks."

I was stumped. I couldn't even correct her because I had no clue what she meant. "What's a pock-a-pick?"

As soon as she put her little fingers to her mouth, I knew it was an animal – and that there was a *squeep squeep* coming.

"It's a baby with prickles," she explained, wiggling her fingers. "They go *squeep squeep squeep.*"

Bridget is predominantly Australian. Perhaps prickly echidnas *squeep*. "An echidna?" I guessed.

"No, Ry." She shook her head. "That's a puggle."

I felt truly sorry for her. It wasn't Bridget's fault that her mother liked to fill her head with nonsense. Moments like this highlighted exactly how dangerous the wrong information could be. If Charli kept the baloney going, the poor kid was in for a miserable school career.

"Puggle isn't a word, Bridge."

Letting her down gently had no effect. She stomped a boot on the ground, making the contents of the mystery pink bag rattle in her hand. "It is," she insisted. "Ask someone."

I looked from left to right, wondering who she was expecting me to stop. As busy as the park was, I couldn't see a single person who looked knowledgeable in Australian wildlife. "What am I supposed to ask, Bridget?" I asked. "Excuse me ma'am, do you know what a puggle is?"

She raised her free hand, bouncing on the spot. "I know! I know!" she squealed. "It's a baby 'chidna."

I made a mental note to hold off on the sarcasm for a year or two. I decided to dazzle her with science instead. I took my phone from my pocket and Googled it – then had to eat my words because a baby echidna is indeed called a puggle.

"How can you possibly know the things you do?"

She grinned, reminding me too much of her mom. "I'm a smart girl, Ry."

"Too smart, I think."

We continued our slow amble down The Mall, heading nowhere in particular. Bridget didn't speak. I thought we'd left the puggle conversation a hundred yards back, but her mind was still working on it.

"I can say puggle, just not pock-a-pick," she told me.

It was like being stuck in a game of charades. I could think of only one other prickled animal, and prayed for sanity's sake that it was right. "Do you mean porcupine?"

"Yes, a baby one. Can you say it?"

I racked my brain, trying to work out if I'd ever known the name for a baby porcupine. Coming up blank, I admitted defeat and Googled that too. Bridget stopped walking while she waited for my answer.

"Porcupette," I read in utter disbelief. "A baby porcupine is called a porcupette."

"I know." She sounded a little sad. "But I can't say it yet."

Bente was right. Bridget Décarie was an enigma – smarter than her own vocabulary.

I put my hand on her head. "You will, baby," I assured her. "One day you'll be able to say it perfectly."

"What word can't you say?" she asked curiously.

I saw no harm in confiding in her. It wasn't as if I'd confess my stupidity to anyone else. "I'm having trouble telling Bente something really special."

"Like what?"

"Like, I love her."

Bridget giggled. Even she realised how ridiculous it was. "Those are easy words."

"You're not supposed to make fun of me." I sounded far more wounded than I was. "I just told you my deepest darkest secret."

Her sapphire eyes widened as she looked up at me. "Really? A secret."

"A big secret," I confirmed.

She grabbed my hand, pulled me toward a nearby bench and ordered me to sit. "I'll help you," she promised. She remained standing, holding the pink bag out as if she was positioning it for the big reveal. "When I have words I can't say, Mummy puts them in here." I nodded, still unsure of where she was headed. Now that Charli had rated a mention, it was bound to be off the wall and crazy. "If you keep the words close to you, you won't forget them," she explained.

"You have words in that bag?"

Bridget instructed me to hold out my hands, and fumbled to undo the drawstring. I wanted to intervene and do it for her, but held off because I knew she wouldn't welcome the help.

"Ready?" she asked finally.

"Born ready."

The little girl upended the bag into my hands. Ten scrabble letters tumbled out.

One by one, I placed them on the seat beside me, spelling out her word of the day. "Por-cu-pette." I pointed at each letter as I pronounced it.

She slowly repeated it, almost correctly.

"There you go," I praised. "You've got it."

Her face lit up. "I did get it," she said proudly. "Now I can help you."

I looked down at the letters beside me. "These aren't the right letters for my words, Bridge."

"I know where we can get some," she replied, "but it's very dangerous."

If I were smarter, I would've declined the offer and talked her into heading to the playground instead. But curiosity stamped out common sense. "Where?"

"In Papy's room." Her expression was deadly serious. "I've seen them in there."

"His study?"

She nodded.

No wonder she considered it dangerous. My father's home study was off limits to everyone under the age of twenty-one. Adam and I needed a college degree before we were allowed to set foot through the door.

"Have you ever been in there, Bridget?"

"Yes," she confirmed. "Papy doesn't know."

I couldn't help smiling as I imagined her sneaking in. I wondered if she did it for the thrill or if there was a reason for it.

I swept the letters into my hand and she sat down beside me. "What do you do in there?"

"Look for things," she replied. "I have some girls in there too."

Her confession made me laugh. Not only had she infiltrated my father's sacred space, she'd sullied it with broken dolls – and he had no idea.

"Did you hide some words in there too?" I asked, dropping the letters back in her bag.

"No, they were already there. I found them when I was looking. I'll get them for you."

We were quiet for a minute. I wanted to give her some thinking time, in case she had second thoughts and backed out of her break and enter plot. She didn't. Bridget used the time to come up with a game plan.

"You talk to Mamie and I'll sneak and get them."

Despite the fact I was coming dangerously close to aiding and abetting a four-year-old criminal mastermind, I played along. "What if we get caught?"

Bridget stared at me for a long moment while she thought it through. "You run, Ry," she said. "Really fast."

***

We spent the ten-minute walk to my parents' house going over her shady plan. My one and only job was to create a diversion.

"Talk to Mamie for a while," she instructed.

"Okay," I replied. "I've got it."

Mom answered the door, more than a little surprised to see us. "Hello, darlings. What are you doing here?"

I wasn't sure if the absence of Mrs Brown would work in our favour or not. It didn't seem to mess with Bridget's plans. The ease with which she launched into her tale was almost troubling.

"Can we have a juice box please, Mamie?" she asked sweetly. "We've been to the park and it's very hot."

That was a lie: at best the afternoon was mild; but my mother didn't question it. "Oh, sweetheart." She led her inside. "Playing at the park is thirsty work, I'm sure."

I trailed behind them as they headed to the kitchen chatting nonsense. Bridget hung by the kitchen door while Mom grabbed a juice box from the fridge.

"Thank you, Mamie." Her little voice was far too enthusiastic to be believable, but Mom didn't seem to notice she was hamming it up.

"You're welcome, my darling girl," she replied, pinching her cheeks.

162

Bridget glanced at me. I guessed that was my cue.

Distracting my mother wasn't going to be easy. When Adam's little princess was around, everyone else failed to exist in my mother's eyes. As it stood, she hadn't said a word to me since we'd arrived.

I pulled it off by asking her opinion of my shirt.

She brushed my shoulder. "It's fine, Ryan. I like the colour."

Bridget didn't waste a second. Once Mom's back was turned, she expertly slipped out the door. As soon as she was gone, I abandoned the charade and let my mother in on the scheme.

"You cannot condone that sort of behaviour, Ryan." She was aghast. "Your father will be most upset to know she's been in there."

"She's just after some scrabble pieces, Ma," I muttered. "Not the family jewels."

"It's the principle!" she scolded. "You're giving her permission to be sneaky and underhanded. Not even Charli would approve of that."

She was right. Of course she was right. I knew I had to stop Bridget, but it didn't feel good, especially since the whole reason for her *dangerous* mission was to help me out.

At Mom's insistence, I headed upstairs to intervene. The second floor was deathly quiet, which proved that Bridget was practically fearless. A big empty house should have been a scary place for a little kid, but my niece was no ordinary kid. I crept down the hallway, stopping at the doorway of my father's study.

Everything about the room was huge. The carved antique furniture was oversized, the ceiling was high, and the massive bookshelf running the length of the far wall was so tall that a rolling library ladder had been fitted. The only small thing in there was Bridget, who was fossicking in the bottom drawer of a cabinet. I'd all but forgotten the bounty of board games kept in there; they hadn't seen the light of day since we were kids.

I whispered her name, trying to gain her attention without scaring her.

"I'm here," she replied.

"I know. I can see you."

She lifted the lid off the scrabble game, grabbed a handful of pieces and hurriedly loaded them into her bag. "I've got them, Ry," she announced victoriously.

It was probably her good fortune that I was her uncle rather than her father. Adam would've been appropriately appalled by her antics. I, on the other hand, felt a strange sense of pride – especially when she put the game back together and closed the drawer in a bid to clean up her crime scene.

As much as it pained me, I couldn't let her get away with it.

"I can't let you do this, Bridge," I said, stopping her at the doorway.

She waved her bag at me. "I have your words for you."

"I know, sweetheart, but you kind of stole them." My attempt at righting the wrong was half-assed at best. "It's not good to steal."

Her face fell, etched with the pure disappointment of finding out that her hard work had been for nothing. "But I got words for you."

I put my hand under her chin and tilted her head. "Those letters belong to your dad," I explained. "He might be sad if you steal them."

She shook the bag, making the letters inside rattle. "These are Daddy's?"

They sure as hell weren't mine. I'd favoured games that were actually fun, like Battleships or strip poker. Adam was the dork who'd enjoyed scrabble and chess.

"I'll tell you what," I held my phone to her, "you call your dad and ask if you can have them. If he says yes, we're home and hosed." She frowned, and I knew I'd lost her. "It means we're okay to keep them."

"Okay."

I hit Adam's name on the screen and handed over the phone. She paced the hall with the phone to her ear and a hand on her hip as if she was on an important business call.

"It's on speaker," I told her. "You don't need to hold it to your ear."

When Adam answered, she put her finger to her lips and shushed me. "Hi Daddy," she said sweetly. "It's Bridget Décarie."

"Hello, Bridget Décarie." Adam didn't miss a beat. "What can I do for you?"

His daughter's explanation was straight to the point. She'd swiped his scrabble pieces and wanted his permission to keep them.

"They're for my uncle," she explained. "The big one, not the baby one."

Adam's reply got caught in a laugh. "You may have them," he told her, "but don't lose them, okay?"

"I won't," she promised, making me smile by giving me a thumbs-up from the end of the hall.

"I've got to go, Bridge," he replied. "I'm at work. I love you so much."

The call ended and she took off running toward me. I held my hand out and she met it with a slapping high five. "We're home and closed, Ry."

***

The rest of the afternoon passed quickly. We hung out with Mom for a while – long enough for her to attempt to bake cupcakes while we sorted through the scrabble pieces on the coffee table.

"There," I announced, lining up the last of the letters.

Bridget leaned closer. "What does it say?"

I pointed to them as I spoke. "I love you, Bente."

"Ohh," she sang. "She will love you too, for sure."

I wished my life was as simple as the one Bridget lived. For all I knew, I might've exhausted all channels of forgiveness where Bente was concerned. Twenty-six-year-old women were not as easily swayed as their four-year-old counterparts.

***

I delivered my niece home at five-thirty, carrying a bag of new words and a container of burnt cupcakes. I then headed home to learn my fate, killing some time along the way by stopping to buy coffee and a newspaper that I'd already read.

My efforts at stalling were in vain. I still managed to beat Bente home by fifteen minutes, which sucked because it gave me more thinking time.

165

She finally walked through the door looking wrecked – beautiful beyond measure, but wrecked. The awkwardness was made worse by the little wave she gave me as she said hello. I truly hated that gesture. She only seemed to make it when I was in the doghouse.

"How was your afternoon?" I asked.

My generic question was answered with an equally standard shrug, so I tried breaking the ice by approaching her.

"Don't Ryan." She held me at arm's length. "I think we need to talk."

Nothing about her tone sounded encouraging. I contemplated running out the door, but forced myself to take a more adult approach.

"Fine," I replied. "Let's talk."

34. BLACK PLAGUE

Bente

I wasn't angered by his arrogant tone, mainly because I knew it was a crock. Ryan looked terrified. He sat on the couch and I moved to sit beside him, perching forward on the cushion and angling my body so I could look at him.

"I'm sorry about this morning," I said quietly. "I don't know what I was thinking when I said it."

"Are you rescinding your declaration, Bente?"

If the situation hadn't been so serious, I might've laughed at his phrasing. "You're such a lawyer."

"I've been called worse," he replied with a half-smile.

I worked on my next move. He'd hurt me horribly. I should've been willing to accept that the wasp had delivered another sting and walk away, just as I'd done in the past. But I couldn't.

"I do love you," I admitted.

"I'm sorry I freaked out," he replied. "This is so new and –"

I cut him off before he said anything cringe-worthy. "It's not new, Ryan. Not for me." My head fell. "I've always been in love with you."

"You have?" His shaky voice was barely there.

"For years," I confessed. "I just assumed I was allowed to admit to it now. Clearly I jumped the gun."

Ryan shifted, joining me at the edge of the couch. One sudden move from either of us would've sent us toppling to the floor in a heap.

He reached for my hand and held it tightly in his lap. "We've known each other a long time. You're not new to me, Bente. But the way I'm feeling is new. That's what I'm struggling with."

"Do you love me, Ryan?"

I could feel him looking at me but didn't dare lift my head, afraid of what he might say.

"If I say yes, can I keep you forever?"

I smiled, because his dumb question left me no choice. "I only want you to say it if you mean it." I felt like I was backing him into a corner. Ryan Décarie was not renowned for deep and meaningful conversations. Pressuring him to discuss his feelings was adding stress to a structure that had never been up to code in the first place. I let him off the hook. "On second thoughts, don't answer that."

"Why not?"

I lifted my head, immediately noticing the hurt in his eyes. "Because it wouldn't be believable, Ryan."

He shifted my hand from his lap to his chest. "Can you feel my heart?" he asked.

I could, but lied and said no.

"It's hammering," he told me. "It was doing the same thing this morning when you told me you loved me. I was also feeling nauseous and shaky all over. I've never felt that before. What do you suppose that means?"

"You tell me," I whispered.

"Well, I suspect I have the early symptoms of the Black Plague."

The laugh that escaped my lips was quiet and breathy. "I hope not," I replied. "I'm not finished with you yet."

Ryan brought my hand to his mouth and kissed my fingers. "When I tell you I love you, you're going to believe it. I promise you."

***

Everybody has different expectations about how love should play out. Charli and her frog hold hands, count stars and end phone calls by saying "I love you so much." My love life worked a little differently. I'd somehow fallen for a thirty-year-old relationship virgin who couldn't differentiate between falling in love and contracting an obsolete plague.

Moving forward with Ryan required taking baby steps, which is exactly the stride I took as I headed up the hallway to the bedroom after our heart-to-heart on the couch. If I'd known what was waiting for me, I would've run to get there.

On the floor at the foot of the bed was a message spelled out in scrabble letters. At first I thought it was something Bridget had done and forgotten to pick up – until I read it. The girl was smart but not yet literate, so I discounted her as the culprit.

I read the sentence spelled out on the floor:

You are pecan pie girl.

Thanks to Charli, I understood it perfectly. The next sentence was a little harder to decipher so I read it out loud. "I love rou, Bente."

"I ran short of y's."

Jumping at the sound of his voice, I quickly spun around to see Ryan standing in the doorway.

"Is that what happened?"

"Yeah." He smiled, and it was perfect. "I improvised and went with the Scooby-doo angle."

I was overwhelmed and confused. Overwhelmed because it was the sweetest, most romantic gesture in the world. Confused because it had come from Ryan.

"Is it true?" I couldn't believe I'd questioned him. Doubting him was unfair; but Ryan took no offense.

"If you're not convinced, I'll have to work harder," he told me.

"You're sure it's not the plague?" I asked in a small voice.

He shrugged nonchalantly. "If it is, I'll die a happy man."

***

169

Two weeks passed and I was no closer to securing a journalism position, but Billet-doux was working out okay. Noelle drove me nuts, but I took heart in the fact that she seemed to have the same effect on everybody.

Perhaps that's why two servers had called in sick. "It's going to be a busy one," she warned, collaring me at the door. "We're two men down already." She'd made it sound as if they were casualties of war, but I didn't dare laugh at her theatrics.

"I'll do my best to keep up," I assured.

Keeping up was impossible. The place was bedlam that day – two impromptu birthday parties and several business meetings made for a very busy shift. On top of that, Ryan and Charli chose that day of all days to get together over lunch. It wasn't exactly a social gathering. They were business partners. One of them was savvy and business minded. The other liked to take pictures.

I heard Ryan grumble as I passed their table. "I'm legally obligated to keep you in the loop, Charli. At least pretend to be interested." I was moving too quickly to hear her reply, but vowed to keep an eye on them. The last thing I needed was a front-of-house slanging match between owners.

I made my way to a table in the corner. Tables for one were usually easy because they were fast to turn over, but as soon as the guy sitting there looked up at me I knew there would be nothing easy about it.

"Well, well, well," he drawled. "If it isn't Bente Denison."

My skin began to crawl. The last time I'd seen Joel McGivern, he was doubled over in pain thanks to my knee to his groin.

"Joel," I replied curtly. "What can I get for you?"

His smarmy smirk grew broader. "I can think of a few things."

I'd only lasted two weeks as Joel's receptionist. Seeing him again made me wonder how I'd endured it for that long.

Unbelievably, he put his hand on the back of my thigh. I slapped him away and stepped out of reach. "Don't you ever touch me again," I hissed, "or I'll break your hand."

Joel's laugh matched his slimy grin. "Still fiery," he said. "And I still like it."

I turned my head, hoping to catch Ryan's eye. It was hopeless. He was too busy trying to hold Charli's attention. "Order something or get out," I demanded.

Joel continued being a slug. "I've already ordered. You're inefficient as usual. But still, you're probably better suited to bussing tables than being a receptionist."

For some stupid reason, I bit back. "I'm not a receptionist, and I'm not a waitress," I hissed.

He reached for me again. "You're a tease though."

I slapped his hand away, harder this time.

"Tell me something, honey," he purred. "Did you make it home okay on your last day? I imagine you might have had a bit of trouble paying your fare without your wallet."

I burned with pure fury. "You took it," I realised. "What could you possibly have to gain from doing that?"

He tried to whisper his reply but it came out in a gravelly hiss. "You inconvenienced me. I returned the favour. If you want your wallet back, swing by my office any time you like."

There was no way I was going back there. I'd already cancelled my cards, and he could keep the cash. I told him this using every single curse word I could think of, and stormed away before he could respond.

Ryan's office was at the end of a short corridor, well out of the way of front of house. It seemed like a good place to escape to. The tears that hit me as I wove through the tables to get there had nothing to do with sadness or humiliation. I felt nothing other than pure unadulterated hate towards Joel McGivern and his beastly ways. Ryan must've noticed something amiss because he caught up with me before I'd even reached the door.

"Bente," he called, grabbing my elbow. "What's wrong? Why are you crying?"

I felt like a fool explaining it to him, but I tried. "He's the creep I used to work for," I sniffled. "And he's the one who took my wallet."

Ryan brushed my tears away with his thumbs. "Why would he do that?"

"Because he's an ass."

Charli appeared a second later. "Everything okay?" she asked quietly.

"She's fine," Ryan replied, glancing back at her. "Are you up for a little bit of role play, Charlotte?"

Her look of concern quickly slipped in favour of a wicked grin. "Beats going over the monthly accounts."

This was Ryan and Charli at their best. Under normal circumstances, business relations were strained. When they were up to no good, it was the perfect partnership. "Just leave it," I pleaded. "Someone else can serve him. I'll hang back here until he's gone."

Ryan stepped back toward me, took my face in his hands and whispered in my ear. "No one puts baby in the corner." His *Dirty Dancing* reference killed my anger in a flash. I was now fighting the urge to laugh, which was probably his intention.

"I knew you watched it."

He put his fingers to his lips as he backed away. "Shhhh."

Charli followed him to the archway leading to front of house. I couldn't hear the conversation Ryan had with her, but was fairly sure by the way she was nodding that he was giving her instructions. He disappeared a few seconds later and I wasted no time in questioning her.

"He's just going to have a chat with him, Bente," she assured in a creepy slow voice.

"That's it?"

She tore her eyes from Joel's table to glance at me. "And while he's distracted, I'm going to steal his wallet."

"You're what?" My voice sounded strange as I tried to quietly yell the words.

She didn't get a chance to reply. Noelle rounded the corner. "What's going here?" she asked, eyeing us suspiciously.

"Nothing for you to worry about, Noelle," replied Charli.

She wasn't convinced. "We're super busy out there, Bent-ta. You're needed."

"She's okay for a minute," said Charli. "Ryan's taking care of front of house."

Noelle's eyes popped. "What the hell is going on?" she squeaked. "He's not supposed to be serving!" Her adoration of Ryan was positively bizarre. She held him on an invisible pedestal like some kind of restaurant god.

Charli brushed her off. "He's fine, Noelle. Just go back to whatever it is you do."

"Do you even know what it is that I do?"

Charli never took her eyes off Ryan. "Not really."

"Ugh! Why do you even come here?" She used her angry squeak. Things were getting serious. "You're disruptive and annoying."

"I've been told that before," she calmly replied. "But I figure no one's perfect, right?"

Noelle threw out her arms in exasperation. "That's it. I give up."

35. BAIT

Ryan

I couldn't find a single classy feature about the dick sitting at table two. He was in his late thirties, used too much product to slick back his hair and had no aversion to wearing a pink tie. Just for fun, I pretended he was the big shot he considered himself to be, plastered a smile on my face and introduced myself.

"Hello there." I held out my hand. "I'm Ryan Décarie."

"The manager?" he asked, weakly meeting my handshake.

"The proprietor."

A flash of panic crossed his ugly face. I wondered if he thought Bente had sent me over.

"Joel McGivern," he muttered.

I took it upon myself to pull out a chair and join him. I called the closest waitress over. "A bottle of champagne, please. The best."

His panicked look returned and I spoke to reassure him. "You look like you can afford it, am I right, Joel? What line of business are you in?"

"Real estate," he replied.

"Well, clearly it's a profitable venture."

I could see his ego inflating as he straightened his pink tie. "I do alright," he boasted.

Joel McGivern was a tool, but he was actually relatively useful. My brother and I kept a pretty close eye on the real estate market, and were always on the lookout for new projects. The longer I kept Joel talking, the more interested I became. When he mentioned the upcoming sale of a particular Midtown building, he had my total attention. "It's a forced sale," he revealed, smirking. "The old fogey who owns it can't afford to keep it anymore. It'll go for a steal."

I leaned back, mainly to escape the faint whiff of his cheap cologne. "Is that so?"

"Huge building," he continued. "It used to be a club, back in the day."

I had sudden visions of a new restaurant project – one that I didn't have to share with Charli. After stroking his ego with a few more compliments, I coaxed the address out of him. He pulled his wallet out and wrote it on the back of a business card. "If you want to take it any further, you call me," he instructed. "I should be able to secure the listing in a few days – a week, tops."

In a move I couldn't have planned better, he laid his wallet on the table. I busied him again by talking business, paving the way for Charli to make her move.

She swept in quickly, intercepting a notebook and a tray of champagne from a passing waitress. "Good afternoon, gentlemen," she crooned, clumsily setting the tray on the table. I'd forgotten what a useless server she was, but in this instance it didn't matter. Joel didn't notice her lack of skill; he was too busy checking her out.

"Well hello there," he drawled, looking her up and down.

"Like what you see, Joel?" I asked crassly, cutting to the chase. I didn't want to draw out the conversation any longer than necessary in case he moved his wallet.

He stared as if he couldn't quite believe I'd said it. Obviously being a smarmy jerk was supposed to be subtle. "Err, sure," he stammered.

"Yup." I winked at Charli. "She's a looker alright." I felt as slimy as he looked. Using my brother's wife as douche bait was poor form, even for me.

Charli playfully swatted my shoulder, following up with a pout that nearly made me laugh. Joel didn't pick up on our terrible acting, but I wasn't about to question it. As soon as he was distracted by Tinker Bell's flirty giggle, I knocked his wallet to the floor.

Charli made her move less than a minute later. She dropped her notebook and crouched to pick it up. Joel didn't see her tuck the wallet down her shirt, which was surprising since her chest had been the focus of his attention since she approached. After giggling a few more times at his repugnant innuendos, she excused herself and sashayed away.

I was done too. I left him alone to enjoy the meal that he could no longer afford to pay for, and headed back to my office.

36. LOVE NOTES

Bente

When they set their minds to it, Ryan and Charli worked together like a well-oiled machine. The whole operation took less than two minutes. Charli made her way back to me first, waving Joel's wallet that she'd just pulled from her bra. Ryan was only seconds behind. Considering they'd just lifted a man's wallet, they both looked far too pleased with themselves.

"Now what?" I asked.

Ryan spoke first. "Charli will take care it." He made it sound as if they had a body to dispose of. Disturbingly, Charli didn't seem alarmed in the slightest. Ryan kissed my cheek and disappeared back out the front.

Charli grabbed my hand and pulled me into his office. I closed the door and leaned against it as if we really did have a body to get rid of. Charli sat down at the desk and began rifling through the wallet.

"What are you doing?" I hissed, appalled.

"Trying to find an address to mail it to."

I relaxed the tiniest bit. At least she planned to return it. She found his driver's license and copied the address onto an envelope.

"Okay, now seal it up and get rid of it," I demanded.

Her grin was straight out of a horror movie. "I'm not quite done yet."

"Charli, please," I begged, making a grab for the wallet. "This is so wrong."

She yanked it out of reach. "Do you think you're the first girl he's hit on, Bente?"

"No," I conceded. "Probably not."

"And you won't be the last either," she replied. "What if the next victim isn't as good at warding him off?"

I slumped in the chair opposite her. "She'll be in trouble."

"Right," she agreed. "Does he have a wife?"

"Yes, and she's actually quite nice." Mrs McGivern had come into the office a few times while I worked there, always bearing homemade cupcakes or fresh flowers for the reception area. She had no idea what a jerk her husband could be. He acted almost normal when she was around.

The more I thought about it, the more I was content to see Joel get his just deserts. I watched with wary curiosity as Charli found a piece of paper. "How's your handwriting?" she asked.

"Recognisable," I muttered.

"Okay," she picked up a pen, "I'll write it then." Charli narrated as she wrote. "'Darling Joel,'" she began. "'Fingers crossed that the tests come back clear. Mine were okay. Two out of three isn't bad.'"

It was impossible not to be impressed by her wickedness, even if I wasn't prepared to encourage her by admitting it.

"'Lots of love, Roxy'," she signed off.

"Roxy?"

Charli slipped the paper and wallet into the envelope addressed to Mrs McGivern. "Roxy," she purred obscenely. "She's so nasty." She sealed it shut and threw it in her purse just in the nick of time.

Noelle barged in, looking more panicked and skittish than usual. "The man at two can't settle his tab," she snapped. "He says he's lost his wallet."

"So?" asked Charli calmly. "What am I supposed to do about it?"

"You're the boss," she reminded. "Sort it out."

"*Now* you want me to be the boss?" grumbled Charli, rolling her eyes.

Noelle looked in danger of exploding right out of her stilettos. Luckily for her, Ryan swooped in and saved the day. "I've dealt with it," he called from the doorway. "I comped his meal."

"Why?" squeaked Noelle.

Ryan's smirk killed his blasé demeanour. "What can I say? I'm a nice guy."

37. GOOD DEALS

Ryan

Any normal person would've been embarrassed by the situation Joel had found himself in, but clearly Joel wasn't normal. He turned up at Billet-doux a few days later and asked to meet with me. Reluctantly, I instructed Noelle to show him through to my office.

At first I assumed he was there to settle the bill I'd covered for him. But no, he wanted to talk business.

"Did you get a chance to swing by the property I told you about?" There was a desperate tone to his voice. Perhaps he needed the sale now that he was facing the prospect of a costly divorce. "I'll definitely secure the sale if I've already got a buyer lined up."

Joel McGivern was a revolting, unscrupulous man. I shouldn't have been giving him the time of day, but I couldn't deny that I was interested in the property he was trying to push.

"I need to talk to my brother," I told him. "We go fifty-fifty in our real estate projects."

Joel's edginess seemed to intensify. He took his phone out. "Give me his number," he demanded without authority. "I'll call him."

That was never going to happen. I made a vague promise to call Adam myself, thanked Joel for coming and pushed him out the door.

***

Adam's schedule was far busier than mine. Both he and Charli were battling to find more hours in the day, and neither was showing any sign of slowing down.

I'd been babysitting my niece four days a week for the past month. Charli hadn't mentioned finding another sitter, and I doubt she was looking. I didn't care either way. Hanging out with Bridget was good for my soul.

Most afternoons were spent at the park but today we deviated from the program. I took her downtown to visit her dad at work instead. Father–daughter time wasn't my motive. I wanted to talk to him about the deal Joel was pushing.

Bridget and I stealthily slipped past Tennille at the front desk and headed straight for Adam's office. We hadn't called ahead, and if he was annoyed by the interruption he didn't let on. He was on the phone when we arrived. Bridget ran across the room and piled onto his lap. Adam didn't miss a beat, continuing the call as if his daughter wasn't restricting his airway with a chokehold on his neck.

When he put the phone down he turned his attention to Bridget. "What are you doing here?" He tickled her belly, making her giggle like a miniature demon. "It's such a nice surprise."

"It's a good story of the day today," she replied, holding his head in place by pinning his cheeks beneath her hands.

"Indeed," he agreed.

I sat opposite his desk and launched into the real reason for our impromptu visit. "It could be a really good deal," I suggested.

Bridget picked up a pen and Adam moved quickly to find her some paper. "I don't have time to do this, Ryan."

"You don't have to do anything," I assured him. "I just want to know if you want in on it."

Bridget pointed her pen at me. "We want in on it, Ry," she announced. "Just do it."

Adam wasn't as easily swayed as the little wheeler-dealer sitting on his knee, but he agreed to think about it. "Have you mentioned it to Charli?" he asked.

"No, that would involve dealing with your wife," I said, feigning a shudder. "And I make it a habit never to deal with your wife."

"Daddy, can we go to the park?" interjected Bridget.

Adam's eyes drifted to the swathe of papers spanning his desk. "Yes," he replied, surprising me. "Let's get out of here for a while."

***

Battery Park was not one of Bridget's usual haunts. The wind blowing in from the river was cold but it didn't seem to faze her as she hung upside down on the climbing frame like a little monkey.

Adam and I observed from a nearby bench, drinking the coffee we'd bought on the short walk down there. Apart from quick five-minute conversations during Bridget handovers, we hadn't spent much time together lately. My excuse was that I'd been too caught up with the lovely brunette who'd recently moved in with me. Adam's reasons weren't so romantic.

"I don't have much time for anything, Ryan. I feel like a trapped animal," he bleakly confessed. "Every day is the same."

"Are you talking about your job?" I had to ask – his cryptic comment had come out of nowhere.

He took his eyes off Bridget to glance at me. "Yeah, of course."

Getting out of New York for a few years had changed Adam. I doubt he would have ever come back if Charli hadn't been offered a position at the Merriman gallery. In a strange twist of fate, Tinker bell didn't seem to be floundering in New York this time around. She'd found her feet in a job she loved.

"Maybe it's time to find a new job," I suggested.

"I'm thinking about it," he muttered. "I'm just not sure I'm ready to deal with the fallout."

Obviously he was talking about Dad. There was nothing I could say that would be remotely encouraging, so I changed the subject to Bente's dresser revamp. His mood brightened instantly. "She loves it," I told him. "We weren't expecting you to finish it so quickly."

"I worked on it at night. I had to do it fast," he explained. "Charli wanted it out of the living room."

Until then, I hadn't given any consideration to the logistics of the task. Gabi's apartment was tiny, certainly no place for a workshop. It made Adam's gesture even more impressive.

"I really do appreciate it," I told him.

"I'm sure you appreciated the brownie points too."

"I don't need brownie points," I replied chuckling. "I'm doing okay."

"You like Bente, don't you?"

I kept my focus firmly ahead, refusing to look at him. "I think I love her."

"How do you know?"

"Because it feels real," I replied. "When she smiles at me, she means it. I've never had that before."

Adam walked his cup to the trash, chuckling blackly the whole way. "Terrifying, isn't it?"

"A little," I conceded. "I told her I loved her, and now I feel there's no going back."

"You're not locked in for a lifetime, Ryan," he reminded. "It's not like you married her."

"What if I do marry her?" I asked. "How do I know it won't happen again? I might fall in love again one day."

I was new to this love thing. I wanted to know how I could be certain that Bente would be my one and only. If anyone could tell me, it should've been my brother. He'd locked in his happy ending at twenty-two.

"I fall in love ten times a day, Ryan," he informed me. "But it's always with Charlotte."

I believed him. And I envied him. And I wouldn't have admitted it if he'd been holding a gun to my head.

Our impromptu brotherly heart-to-heart came to an abrupt end when Bridget came running over. "We have to go now, Daddy," she demanded urgently.

"Why, baby?" he asked. "What's your rush?"

She crashed onto his lap as if it was the only safe place in the whole world. "The squirrels are trying to eat me."

"I'm sure that's not true," he soothed. "You don't look that tasty."

"Two of them growled at me," she insisted.

"Really?" he asked, gazing in the direction of the playground. "Which ones?"

"The mean ones."

I thumped my fist into my open palm. "Do you want me to go over and have a quiet word with them?" I offered.

"No," she replied in a tiny voice. "Their mum is a mean lady too, Ry. She'll growl and make you cry."

"We should go then," suggested Adam, maintaining his hold on his daughter as he stood. "I don't feel like being growled at today. I get enough of that at work."

38. REJECTION

Bente

No one enjoys being rejected, and it had been happening to me a lot lately. I'd lost count of the number of jobs I'd applied for, but as of that morning, the rejection letters totalled seventeen.

I scrunched up the latest, threw it across the room and fell into a heap on the couch.

Ryan wasn't sharing my dark mood. If anything, he was raring to go. He appeared in front of me, dressed to kill in a grey suit.

"Are you okay?" He bounced a bunch of keys in his hand.

I brought my knees to my chest. "No."

"Another letter?"

"I need a job, Ryan."

He leaned down and kissed my forehead. "You have a job."

Working at Billet-doux was fine. It was the only aspect of my life that was fine. Everything else was spectacular. I just wanted to pull my professional life in line with my personal one.

"Thankfully I have the day off today." I sounded pathetic. "If Noelle calls me in, I'm going to say no."

He glanced at his watch. "Good idea. You can spend the day with me."

"Doing what?"

Of all the things he could've come up with to get me out of my pyjamas, checking out a potential new restaurant site wasn't one of them. "I think I'll pass," I replied wanly.

He kissed me again. "You know something? You're an incredibly beautiful woman, Bente Denison."

"Thank you."

"You're welcome," he replied, heading for the door. "Start attaching photos to your résumé. The job offers will pour in."

"Yeah, from creeps like Joel McGivern."

"Ugh," he groaned, checking his watch again. "Don't remind me."

I twisted to get a better look at him. "What do you mean?"

"I'm meeting him at the property. He's probably handling the sale."

"And you thought I'd want to go?" I asked incredulously. "The man is vile and you're doing business with him?"

He grinned, so brilliantly that I almost forgave him. "Come now, sweetheart," he crowed. "I never said I was going to make it easy for him. I thought you'd enjoy watching him squirm."

The vision of Joel McGivern, squirming or not, would stay in my mind for far too long to make it worth it.

"No, thanks anyway. I'm just going to hang out here and feel sorry for myself."

He made a grab for the door handle before turning back to me. "You're still beautiful, even when you're being melodramatic."

"Thank you. Now get out and leave me be."

39. OLD BROADS

Ryan

The outside of the property on West 52nd looked exactly as I hoped it would, only bigger. It was shabby and run down, exactly the way I like my new ventures to look.

Getting there fifteen minutes before I was due to meet Joel was a smart move. I'd only been loitering outside for a minute when an old man appeared at the top of the steps. "Are you here to view the place?" he asked brusquely.

He wasn't anywhere near as friendly as the loud shirt he was wearing. He looked like he'd just arrived home from one of the cruise ships that Bente's parents frequented.

"Yes." I climbed the concrete steps. "I'm Ryan Décarie."

He moved his fat cigar from his hand to his mouth and shook my hand. "Tiger Malone."

I liked him instantly, despite his gruff demeanour, weird name and bone-crushing handshake. I liked him even more when he offered to show me around before the agent arrived.

He escorted me through a dingy front foyer and into the massive main room located at the back. The inside of the building was a dump, but the potential was huge. I spent a few minutes wandering around, trying to figure out what it would've been like in its prime. The wooden parquetry floor was dull and scuffed and the walls were shabby and peeling, but there were so many endearing features that made me think the place would've been a palace in its day. Most intriguing was the elevated stage at the rear of the room. The heavy red velvet backdrop looked original and the overhead lighting looked to be intact.

"What's behind the stage?" I asked.

Tiger chewed his cigar. "Dressing room area."

"So this place was a theatre?"

A dinner theatre, maybe. There were no rows of fixed seating, but plenty of room for tables and chairs.

Tiger grinned. "It was a bit of everything back in the day."

Tiger Malone was as much a mystery as his building. The ambiguous answer was deliberate. I knew this was a reluctant sale, and I called him on it.

"Not keen on selling, are you, Mr Malone?"

His throaty laugh reverberated throughout the empty space. "The question is whether I'm prepared to sell it to *you*."

I grinned. "I never said I wanted to buy it."

"You want to buy it, kid," he told me. "I can see it in your eyes. You're looking at it with pure desire, like some broad that just turned you down."

We chuckled, but the moment disappeared when Joel McGivern burst through the door.

"You said ten," he said, rushing over to me. "You're early."

"Make haste while the sun shines, Joel," I quipped.

He started rifling through the papers in his girly briefcase. "I've got to get it on the market first," he complained.

"I don't think that's going to happen, McGivern," commented Tiger, blowing a plume of smoke in his direction.

Joel coughed and waved his hand, trying to clear the air. "Do you need more time?"

"No." He puffed for a bit. "I've changed my mind. It's not for sale."

I imagine that the face Joel pulled was very similar to how he would've looked after Bente kneed him in the groin, only more pained.

"I need this sale," he said desperately. "You need it too. You're so far behind on your property taxes that you're going to lose it anyway."

"May be," Tiger agreed, "but it won't happen today."

Joel's face turned a strange shade of purple. I expected him to hit the deck at any second, but he recovered. He wagged his finger at Tiger, warned him he'd come to regret it, and stormed off.

Now that the offer of sale had been withdrawn, I had no reason to stay either. I offered Tiger my hand, which he met with a firm shake. "It was nice meeting you, Mr Malone."

"You too, kid."

I ambled across the huge empty room, taking one last look at the broad who turned me down. Each step I took sent dust particles floating into the air, and the sun bleeding through the high windows made them twinkle like glitter. I wished Bridget was here to see it.

I passed through the foyer and made my way to the door.

Even the front doors were magnificent – solid and intricately carved. Just as I reached for the big brass handle, Tiger called me back. "Do you have a girl at home?" he asked irrelevantly.

I turned back. "Yes, Sir."

"Is she pretty?"

I laughed at his audacious question. "She's gorgeous."

"Can she dance?"

"Like Ginger Rogers," I declared.

"That good, huh?" He tilted his head, puffing more smoke into the air. "I'll tell you what – you bring your girl back here on Saturday night."

"Why?"

"Because I want you to see this place at its best."

I took another look around. Clearly the place hadn't been at its best for at least four decades, but I was intrigued. "We'll be here, Mr Malone."

"You can call me Tiger," he permitted.

"Okay, you can call me Ryan."

"I could," he replied. "But I'm going to call you kid."

40. OUTSIDE THE BOX

Bente

I'd never been very good at self-pity so my plan of wallowing on the couch and being depressed didn't work. As soon as Ryan left, I showered, dressed and abandoned the bad attitude.

Thankfully Noelle didn't call me into work so the morning was mine, and I spent it working on an article that no one would ever read.

Ryan arrived home just after two with a little person in tow.

I knew Bridget was up to something the second I laid eyes on her. She was nowhere near as deft at the poker face as her mother. The sly French commentary between her and her uncle also sold her out. I closed my laptop and set it down on the coffee table. "What are you two up to?"

Bridget answered, but it was no confession. "We're not doing nothing."

"Anything," corrected Ryan.

Bridget took a flying leap over the arm of the couch and thumped down beside me. I didn't dare chastise her for her stuntman move. The mere fact that she wanted to sit beside me was a major win. Ryan looked cagy, and was clearly concealing something behind his back.

"And what do you have?" I asked. I doubt my smile was anywhere near as bright as his.

"A surprise for you," explained Bridget. "You can still be happy-dayed if it's not your birthday."

"Ta daa!" sang Ryan. The big reveal was pecan pie.

"Oh, my favourite! Thank you."

"You might not like it," Bridget warned. "It's got nuts in it."

Ryan set the pie down. "I thought it might cheer you up."

"Thank you," I repeated. "But I'm fine. No point dwelling, right?"

"Absolutely none," he agreed. "And because you recognise that, you get pie."

I didn't really feel as if I'd done anything to earn pie. Lying around the house wasn't really a calorie-worthy activity. "How about we go to the park instead?"

I knew Bridget would jump at the chance – I just wasn't expecting her to be so literal about it. She began bouncing on the couch. "Yes!" she squealed. "We can search."

Ryan wasn't so keen. "Can't we find something else to do, just for a change?" Bridget wasn't taking no for an answer. Perhaps knowing he was in for a long afternoon if he kept her holed up at home, Ryan backed down quickly.

Half an hour later, we were wandering through the entrance of the park. Bridget walked a few feet ahead of us, gripping an old compass as if she truly needed direction.

"Does she know what she's doing?" I whispered.

Ryan gave my hand a squeeze. "Bridget knows exactly what she's doing," he said quietly. "It's the rest of the world that's confused."

"What's she looking for?"

The explanation he gave was vague, but that wasn't his fault. He didn't have much hard information to go on.

She just wasn't normal. To say that Bridget Décarie thought outside the box would be an understatement. The dedication she had when it came to finding her imaginary place was far beyond her years. All kids go through stages, but they're usually short-lived. Fabergé's vegetarian phase lasted three days. Malibu went through a stage of only wearing blue. It lasted an hour and a half.

I shook my head in wonder at the little girl a few feet ahead of us. "How will she know when she finds it?"

"It's supposedly very special," Ryan explained. "There are flowers on the roof, and according to Bridget I'll be able to see everything from there."

The investigative journalist in me kicked in. "If the view is good, it must be somewhere high."

He laughed. "Please don't tell her that," he exclaimed. "We'll go from hanging out in the park to scaling the Empire State Building."

I didn't doubt for a second that he'd take her there if she asked. The relationship between Ryan and Bridget was probably the most honest and pure he'd ever had. I'd long suspected that behind the tough exterior was a softer, sweeter man. I was just beginning to see glimpses of it, but the littlest Décarie only ever saw that side of him.

"Don't you get fed up, Ryan?" I was curious. "Coming to the park every day?"

"No, not really," he replied. "It's good for me."

"It is," I agreed, hooking my arm through his in a bid to get closer to him. "It takes the edge off your douche-like demeanour."

"Wonderful." He punched out a hard laugh. "My very first girlfriend thinks I'm a douche."

"But you're my douche, Ryan."

He kissed my hand. "Yes, I am."

41. ONE HIT WONDERS

Ryan

We walked for quite a while, but as usual didn't cover much ground. The plan was to head back to the playground to kill the last hour before I took Bridget home.

We'd just turned back when a woman walking pushing a stroller stopped us. "Hello Ryan, how are you?"

I repeatedly blinked, trying to put a name to the face. Sneaking a quick look at the toddler sitting in the stroller didn't help. I didn't recognise him either.

"Fine," I replied, "how are you?"

I could tell by the look on her face that she knew I was clueless.

"I'm fine," she replied simply.

I nodded, unsure where to take the conversation next. Thankfully, Bridget provided the perfect distraction by striking up a conversation with her kid. "Hi boy," she said cheerily. "Do you want to see my finder?" Predictably, the little guy made a grab for the compass as soon as she held it out. Even more predictably, Bridget had no intention of letting him anywhere near it. "You can't touch it," she instructed, stepping out of his reach. "Just look nicely at it."

I put my hand on Bridget's shoulder and pulled her back toward me. The smile on mystery lady's face didn't waver but nothing about it seemed genuine. "So, you have a family too?" she asked.

I could see how she'd jumped to the conclusion, but still felt awkward correcting her. "Ah, no. This is my girlfriend Bente and my niece, Bridget."

"Hi lady," Bridget beamed.

I silently begged her to ask the woman her name, but for once Bridget kept quiet. I remained clueless.

"Well," said the mystery woman, giving the stroller a push. "We should let you go."

"It was nice seeing you again," I lied, half waving as she walked away.

"Bye boy," called Bridget.

We'd only walked a few yards further when Bente murmured from the corner of her mouth. "You have no idea who she is, do you?"

I shook my head. "No clue."

"Her name's Vanessa." I stared blankly at her. "She's one of your one hit wonders. You met her at Nellie's one night and took her home."

Despite the terrible tale, Bente didn't seem too disgusted with me, even when I asked her for more details.

"Seriously, Ryan. You don't remember her?"

"No." I was mystified. "I have no idea who she is."

Bente frowned, showing the first hint of annoyance. "You gave her the usual 'I'll call you tomorrow line'."

"So?"

"So, you never called her."

"I never called any of them," I muttered, fighting the urge to cringe.

"Yes, but you picked her up at Nellie's so she knew where you worked," she explained. "She showed up every night for a week looking for you."

"That had to be at least five years ago," I grumbled. "How come you remember her?"

"She was memorable, Ryan – almost stalker material. We used to call her Vanessa the distresser."

I glanced back at the woman pushing the stroller down the Mall, and quickly concluded that I was truly a despicable man.

I called out to Bridget and ordered her not to walk any further ahead before turning my attention to Bente. "Will you wait here a minute?"

She nodded. I lurched forward, kissed her lips and ran to catch up with the stroller.

As soon as she was within earshot, I called out. The look on Vanessa's face as she turned around was one of shock, but she let me catch up.

"Can I have a moment?" I asked.

"What for?"

It nearly killed me, but I forced myself to look her in the eye. "Vanessa, I treated you horribly," I told her. "For what it's worth, I'm sorry. I'm not that guy any more."

After considering my bumbled apology, she finally smiled. It wasn't blinding, but it looked a damned sight more genuine than the one she'd given when she stopped me. "I really appreciate that." She sounded a little melancholy. "No hard feelings."

I nodded, perfectly willing to leave it at that. "Thank you."

"Bye Ryan," she said, already edging away from me. I mumbled a goodbye in return.

I watched Vanessa wheeling her kid down the path for a long time. I wasn't feeling redeemed, but I did feel hopeful. I truly wasn't that guy any more. In time I hoped I'd forget all about him. It was unrealistic to think that every woman I'd scorned would too, but at least I'd managed to make amends with one.

Needing a minute to think, I took my time getting back to the girls. Bridget was clearly tired of waiting. Knowing the leap she was about to take off the park bench probably wasn't going to end well, I grabbed her and hoisted her onto my shoulders. "Get me higher to the sky, Ry," she demanded, with a death grip on my neck. We continued our slow walk. Bente hooked her arm though mine and I held Bridget's feet.

"How did it go?" she asked curiously.

"Okay." I couldn't look at her. "Not my finest hour."

Bente tightened her hold on me. "I think it was."

"I don't know how you put up with me."

"I didn't put up with you back then," she replied. "You were an asshole."

I stopped walking and turned to her. It was a move that made Bridget nervous. She nearly choked me in a bid to hang on tighter. Bente reached up and loosened her grip. "He's got you, Bridge," she assured the child. "And I've got him."

***

Women are dangerous creatures – at least mine was.

The products littering the bathroom counter had the makings of a catastrophic chemical attack. Bente's process of getting ready for a night on the town was complex and unnecessary. She was completely and utterly beautiful. Why she needed to spend an hour trying to improve on that bewildered me.

I stood in the doorway trying to hurry her along. "We're going to be late."

"Where are we going anyway?" she asked, swiping a big brush across her cheek.

"I told you, to a club."

She paused the primping to ponder my explanation. I could almost see her mind ticking over. "A night club?"

I wasn't exactly sure what Tiger Malone's establishment was so I avoided the question and begged her to hurry up.

She finally downed tools and turned to face me. "Okay. I'm done."

For a quick moment, I reconsidered our plans. She was wearing the red dress that she'd worn on our first date. I loved that dress. It did strange things to my thought processes.

"Is something wrong? Do I look alright?" She sounded worried. Perhaps my wide-eyed look of reverence was a strange one.

"You'll do."

Her concerned expression intensified. "I'll change," she said, pushing past me.

I made a grab and pulled her in close. "I'm kidding," I replied. "You're beautiful." I leaned in and kissed her. My effort was good, but nothing compared to hers. The red dress came with its own kissing technique.

"We have to get out of here," I murmured, finally breaking free. "Or I may never let you leave."

***

Our cab driver didn't exactly have to fight for a spot when we pulled up outside the club. The real estate surrounding it was predominantly residential, so traffic was at a minimum.

"Are you sure this is it?" asked Bente, leaning across me to look out the window. Her caution was understandable. The place looked deserted. "It looks rough, Ryan."

I got out and reached for her hand. "It's not rough," I assured her. "Just unpolished."

Bente skipped to keep up as I led her to the steps. "Are you going to buy it?" she asked.

"I don't think it's for sale any more."

She yanked on my hand, pulling me to a stop. "So why are we here, then?"

"Because the cranky old owner invited us here. He wants to meet my gorgeous girl." I leaned in and kissed her ruby lips. "I'm not above showing you off."

I wasn't hopeful of anyone answering if I knocked, so I tried my luck and turned the handle. The old door creaked open. Bente clung to my hand just like Bridget does when she's scared. We took a few measured steps into the deserted foyer as if we'd just entered a haunted house.

Being alone in the room gave me a chance to check it out properly. There really wasn't much to it. A small coat check area to my left, double doors leading into the main room, and a staircase to my right that was roped off with a 'staff only' sign.

"It's lucky we're not wearing coats," commented Bente, running her finger along the dusty counter. "I wouldn't be checking mine."

I spun to face her. "It's great, isn't it?"

She dusted off her hands. "It has a certain something," she conceded.

The whole place screamed intangible charm. Even the old fashioned flowery carpet was endearing, despite the fact it felt sticky beneath my feet.

The more time I spent there, the more I wanted it. It was almost cruel that it was off the market.

My moment of dwelling came to an end when Tiger burst through the double doors. Poor Bente nearly jumped out of her dress, and judging by the look on Tiger's face, he would've appreciated the show.

"Welcome," he announced, gritting his teeth to keep a grip on his cigar.

Bente maintained her hold on my arm and stepped with me as I moved to shake his hand. "Thanks for inviting us," I replied. I still wasn't sure what we were doing there, but got the impression the answers were behind the doors he'd just crashed through. I could hear faint chatter on the other side.

I introduced him to Bente. Tiger Malone was a player. He took the cigar from his mouth and kissed her hand.

"Pretty girl," he gazed into Bente's eyes, "what are you doing with a schmuck like him?"

Bente dropped her head, chuckling down at the floor.

I pretended to be outraged. "You wouldn't be making a move on my girl, would you, Tiger?" It would be a slow move if he was. Tiger Malone couldn't have been a day under eighty. If he were my age, he might've given me a run for my money. He seemed to possess the same *je ne sais quoi* as his building.

Tiger was dressed to the hilt in club owner mode, rocking a black suit that probably had fitted well when he bought it thirty years ago.

"Did you bring your dancing shoes?" he asked, looking at Bente's feet.

She looked at me quizzically. I hadn't mentioned dancing, mainly because I didn't think she'd be doing any. The venue I'd viewed a few days earlier was in no fit state for tripping the light fantastic.

"I'll make do," she replied.

Tiger leaned back on one of the doors, using his weight to push it open. "After you," he announced.

Bente and I had no chance of slipping in unnoticed. We stuck out like sore thumbs, mainly because we were the only ones there with our own teeth. We'd somehow stumbled into a senior citizen's convention.

"You like what I've done with the place?" asked Tiger, slapping me on the back.

I glanced at him only briefly. My focus was on trying to work out what he'd done with the place. The only noticeable change was the addition of some tables and chairs. The floor was still dusty and the paint on the walls was still peeling.

A serious-looking game of poker was being played at one table. Plastic chips were being tossed around and a toxic plume of smoke billowed above. How the old men had lived such long lives with smoking habits like that was beyond me. The other tables were a bit more laid back, but judging by the laughter and constant chatter these people were not typical oldies.

"Is this the music, Malone?" shouted one old man. "Are they the band?"

"Maybe," replied Tiger, throwing his gruff voice across the room. He turned to Bente. "Do you sing, Ginger Rogers?" Bente shook her head but said nothing. It was a first. I'd never seen her at a loss for words before. "They're not the band, Earl," he yelled to his friend. "You're going to have to wait."

"I'm eighty-two," Earl shot back. "How long do you think I have?"

The whole room dissolved into hearty chuckles. I couldn't help smiling, especially when Bente started giggling too.

Tiger checked his watch. "The band was supposed to show at seven," he explained. "I guess you get what you pay for."

"Is this a regular Saturday night for you, Tiger?" I asked.

"Not really," he admitted. "We haven't been open for business in a while."

"Are these people your friends?" asked Bente.

"Some are friends," he replied, looking out at the tables ahead. "And some I wouldn't trust as far as I could throw them." He cupped his hand to his mouth to throw his voice. "I'm talking about you, Grover Irwin."

An old man at the poker table looked up at the sound of his name. From the corner of my eye, I saw Tiger smirk at him. Grover responded in a way I wasn't expecting. He flipped him the bird. Bente turned her head, burying her face in my shoulder to muffle her laugh.

My plan was to make polite excuses, grab my girlfriend and leave. It fell apart quickly when one of the old women waved Bente over to her table. She dropped my hand and wandered over as if she had no choice but to.

"Looks like your lady found some friends." Tiger took a silver cigar cutter out of his pocket and snipped the end off a cigar, which troubled me. I hadn't seen him discard the one he was just smoking. "You might be in for the long haul," he warned. "Women like to talk."

Bente certainly liked to talk. She was already in deep conversation. When she fanned out the bottom of her dress, I realised it was probably fashion-related and boring so I decided to stick with Tiger.

"What's tonight in aid of, Tiger?" I asked. "I don't know why you wanted us here." I'd had no luck in getting any information out of him so far, and that wasn't about to change. The doors swung open. The band had arrived, which pleased the partygoers no end. Even Grover Irwin started clapping and cheering. Old people can really whoop it up when they're excited – but I'd known that for a while. All Grandma Nellie needed to become wild and antisocial was one stiff drink.

"Where do you want us?" asked a guy carrying the biggest upright base I'd ever seen.

"The stage is yours," replied Tiger, pointing at it.

Three more people filed through the door, each carrying instruments, or parts of instruments. It took a couple of trips back and forth before they were set up, and before they started playing there was a bill to settle.

The singer approached Tiger while the sound check was going on. "We can take a cheque or cash," she told him. "Cash is better."

Tiger turned his attention to me. "Are you paying cash or cheque, kid?"

Deep down I wasn't surprised that he'd hit me up for the bill; perhaps that's why I couldn't pretend to be outraged. I asked how much was owed.

"Five hundred and fifty dollars," replied the singer.

I put my wallet back in my pocket. No one carries that kind of cash around, except my father. "It'll be cheque then," I told her. "I'm paying by cheque."

Tiger didn't say a word until the singer was on stage, gleefully waving my cheque at her band mates.

"What do you think?" he asked.

"I think you're a shrewd old bastard," I told him.

He chomped his cigar, teeth gleaming. "It'll be worth it," he said. "Wait till you see this place come alive."

42. HISTORY

Bente

This would have to go down in history as one of the strangest evenings I'd ever had. Clearly Ryan had no idea what we were in for when he accepted Tiger's invitation, and I was glad. I don't think we would've gone if he had. The band was wonderful, and they couldn't have asked for a better audience. Despite their advanced age, every person in the room could dance. *Really* dance.

Ryan pretended to be upset when I dragged him away from Tiger and out onto the dance floor. "It's not even a dance floor, Bente," he grumbled.

I pressed myself against him and linked my arms around his neck. "It is tonight," I replied, raising a smile.

"Did you know that the last time a band played on that stage was in 1982?" he asked.

"No." I smiled. "How would I know that?"

"You wouldn't." He shook his head the tiniest bit. "Tiger just told me."

Ryan stepped to the side, positioning me to glance across at Tiger. He was sitting at the poker table with cards in one hand, a cigar in the other, and a glass of whiskey in front of him.

"He's owned this place since the late fifties," Ryan continued. "Apparently it used to be the place to be back then."

"So what happened?"

"I get the impression he's a bit of a wheeler and dealer." His low murmur tickled my ear. "And the dice haven't rolled his way for a while."

Probably since 1982.

I dropped my hold on his neck and put my hand on his shoulder. Ryan pulled us into a more traditional dance pose by taking my hand.

"But he won't sell? Why?"

"Look around, sweetheart," he urged. "This is his baby. It's probably all he has left in the world."

I took my time and glanced in every direction as Ryan danced us around the huge floor. "So who are all these people?"

"According to Tiger, they all used to frequent this club back in the day. See the lady in the purple dress?" He twirled me around so I'd get a better look. "Her name is Connie. She was the coat check girl in the sixties. The old broad next to her is Marta. She was a cocktail waitress."

I could believe it. Marta was the lady who'd called me over. We'd had a long conversation about my dress. "Don't be afraid to hitch up that skirt, princess," she told me. "That boy looks like he could handle it."

The run-down old club had a history older than Ryan and I put together. I felt strangely humble being there, and I wasn't the only one who'd fallen under its spell. "I want to buy it so bad." Ryan breathed the words into my hair.

"What would you do with it?"

He twirled me as he mulled over my question. "Bring her back from the dead," he finally replied. I wondered how, but held off asking. Ryan didn't look like he needed the torture. It was probably one of the first times he'd ever stumbled across something he couldn't have.

I didn't get a chance to console him. Marta spotted us looking at her, wandered over to us and cut in. "May I?" I think she was asking me, but it was hard to tell. She only had eyes for Ryan.

If Ryan was unhappy, he didn't let on. He was at his best when charming, and Marta wasn't hard to woo. Dancing was a sexy skill, and thanks to his private school education, Ryan could dance. The fact that he was gorgeous and debonair didn't hurt either.

I wasn't up to finding myself another dance partner. I avoided making eye contact with the old men checking me out from the sidelines and made my way to the stage instead. When the band wrapped up their version of "Tears On My Pillow" I asked the lead vocalist if they took requests. "Maybe a bit of Etta James?"

"You want to hear 'At Last'? We get that a lot."

I shook my head. "No, 'Anything To Say You're Mine'. Do you know it?"

On cue, the band started playing the song that had been mine for as long as I could remember. I was so excited to hear it that the next words tumbled out of my mouth in a rush. "I want to sing it."

The lead singer didn't seem too put out by my demand. She motioned to the microphone and stepped aside.

43. LITTLE RED FIRECRACKER

Ryan

Some things are just wrong – like Bridget's penchant for chicken nuggets and Tiger Malone's disgusting cigar habit. But some things are *really* wrong, like the injustice of finally witnessing a live singing performance by my sexy-as-hell girlfriend while I was trapped in the arms of Marta the ancient cocktail waitress.

I wrestled free and bowed out.

"You watch your little red firecracker," permitted Marta, patting my chest. "You know where I'll be when you're ready."

I wasn't likely to ever be ready for Marta, but I nodded and thanked her. I would've helped her to a seat if I'd had the will to move but I couldn't tear my eyes from the stage.

Bente's raspy voice was liquid gold. The way she leaned into the microphone and absently gestured was gorgeous too. I wasn't the only one who thought so. By the time she was midway through her song, all eyes were on her. Even the poker players took a break to watch.

There wasn't a hint of nervousness about her, which proved her mind was elsewhere and she was unaware of the attention she was receiving. The rare lack of inhibition made for the sexiest display I'd ever seen. The desire to get her home and naked was strong, but not the prime emotion. I felt proud, lucky – and completely and utterly in love.

Marta was right. At that moment she was a little red firecracker, but I enjoyed the other side of Bente more – the soft, bright, forgiving woman who chose to overlook my terrible past indiscretions in favour of loving me.

I didn't notice Tiger beside me until he spoke. "Did you know she could sing like that?"

I glanced at him and smiled. "Yeah. She doesn't do it often, though."

"You should encourage her more," he urged, staring at the stage. "The bright lights suit her. Nothing grows in the shade."

***

The second the song ended, I took Bente in my arms and lifted her off the stage. She seemed embarrassed by her audience's chants for an encore, and my weird caveman response was to save her.

"Are you going to carry me out of here, Ryan?" she asked.

"I might." I lowered her to her feet.

Bente turned back to the band and thanked them, and I leaned across to speak to the singer. "What time are you finishing?"

"You paid us until midnight."

It was just after ten. I grabbed all the money I had in my wallet. "Play until two," I told her.

She looked at the handful of elderly rockers, still dancing although the music had ended. "Do you think they'll last that long?" she teased.

I grinned up at her. "I think they'll out-dance your singing."

The girl straightened, smiling. "Challenge accepted."

I practically dragged Bente toward the door. The music started again and I was hopeful the distraction would make for a clean getaway.

"Where's the fire?" Bente joked, nearly running to keep up.

"In places you can't even imagine, sweetheart."

Her x-rated laugh did little to help the situation but having Tiger stop us at the door quickly put the fire out. "I want you to come back on Monday," he instructed.

"I can't, Tiger. I have restaurants to run."

"You'll be here," he said knowingly. "At three. Not a minute later."

I didn't stop to argue. All my focus was on getting my little red firecracker home.

***

I had nothing to gain by going back to the club. I would've been well within my rights to ignore Tiger's demand; the only reason I went was to show it to Bridget. If anyone would get a kick out of the glittery dust and flowery carpet, it was her.

"Then can we go to the park?" she asked.

I trailed behind as she climbed the steps. It took forever to reach the door but I didn't complain. I was getting used to spending the hours between two and five moving at Bridget speed. "If we've got time," I promised

"I have my finder in my boot today." She held the iron balustrade and wiggled her foot at me. "I don't have any pockets."

"What else do you keep in those boots, Bridge?"

She looked down. "Just toes and feet."

My ensuing laugh was cut short when the front door swung open. Bridget got such a fright that she stumbled backward off the top step. I scooped her up in the nick of time.

I couldn't blame her for being frightened. Tiger Malone cut a menacing form, standing in the doorway puffing smoke like an old dragon.

"Does Ginger know you're seeing other broads?" he asked, grinning at Bridget. Bridget buried her head in the crook of my neck.

"How are you, Tiger?" I asked, intentionally ignoring his question.

Bridget lifted her head to whisper in my ear, "Is he really a tiger?"

Mr Malone might have been old, but there was nothing wrong with his hearing. "I'm not really a tiger." His low tone was probably designed to calm her. In truth, it sounded more menacing than his normal voice – but it paled in comparison to the horror of his next move. He whipped out his teeth and waved them at Bridget. "Do these look like the teeth of a tiger?" he garbled.

A normal child would've screamed in horror. Malibu Denison scared Bridget, but a toothless old man did not. She giggled – softly at first – but when Tiger started guffawing she lost the plot completely, cackling as hard as I'd ever heard her.

"What's your name?" he asked, pulling himself together and putting his teeth back in.

"Bridget Décarie."

"Bridget, huh? Are you French?"

The attempt at being funny was wasted on her. She answered honestly. "Sometimes."

"Well, I'll be damned." He laughed again. "A baby Bardot."

They were fast friends after that. Tiger even gave her a special backstage tour, which was further than I'd ever got. I even managed to talk him into stubbing out his cigar. "Oh, right," he agreed. "Not good for the baby."

She was hardly a baby but I didn't argue. He called me kid, for crying out loud.

I carried Bridget as Tiger led us to the dressing room. "I can walk," she protested.

"I'd rather carry you." I was worried that she'd fall through a rotten floorboard.

"Are you scared, Ry?" she whispered, pressing her hands to my cheeks.

"No," I whispered back. "Are you?"

"No."

She should've been. We seemed to be walking downhill as we made our way down the poorly lit corridor. The small white door creaked as Tiger pushed it open, adding to the unease. He flicked on the light before venturing inside. "A treasure trove of delights," he announced, stretching his arms wide. "Come and see."

As reluctant as I was to let her go, I lowered Bridget to her feet. She pretended to take her time looking around. She held her hands behind her back, presumably to stop herself from touching anything. I knew Bridget well. The urge to reach out and grab the sparkly wares on offer must have been killing her.

The dressing room was strangely reminiscent of Ivy's living room, just dustier. Coloured feather boas and glittery headpieces hung off a rickety wooden hatstand, and a rail of dresses stood between two dressing tables. It was as if life at the old club has stopped dead one night and everything had been abandoned. There was even a box of old shoes in the corner.

A strange sadness gripped me. Tiger wasn't looking too good either. I doubt he'd been in here for years.

"Good memories, Tiger?" I asked, trying to sound cheery.

"The very best, kid," he replied wistfully. "It was a different world back then."

"Uncle Ryan," interjected Bridget. She'd called me Uncle *and* Ryan. It was a sure-fire sign that there was some serious sweet-talking on the way.

"Yes, niece Bridget?"

She stepped close and whispered. "Can I have one of those?" She pointed to the hatstand. "I really love them."

As expected, Tiger heard every word. He grabbed the hatstand and tilted it so it was at her level. "Take anything you want, baby Bardot."

It was a dangerous offer. She was probably gearing up to stuff the whole lot into her boots.

"One thing, Bridge," I added.

She barely hesitated, picking a gold sequined headband that sprouted a white feather taller than her. I dusted it off as best I could before setting it on her head and pulling the elastic strap under her chin.

"Do I look like an angel?"

"*Oui, ma jolie. Un trés bel ange.*" I reminded her to thank Tiger. "*N'oublie pas le mot magique.*"

Excitement got the better of her and she thanked him in French.

"Well, I'll be damned," he replied, chewing his dead cigar. "She really is a baby Bardot."

***

Keeping an eye on Bridget as she ran around the floor of the main room was easy thanks to the showgirl feather on her head. It acted as a marker beacon.

Tiger used her moment of distraction to pull me aside. The conversation was not one I was expecting. He wanted to talk business. He had completely changed his tune, and the club was back on the market.

"I think you'd be good for the place," he told me. "I don't think you'd demolish it or remodel it into flashy condos."

Altering the building to that extent would be nothing short of criminal. It needed to be brought back to its former glory, not destroyed.

I couldn't deny that I was excited by his change of heart, but my poker face when it came to business was stellar. "I need to talk to my brother. He's my business partner."

"Do what you need to do," Tiger agreed. "Bring your brother over to check it out and then we'll talk." He wanted to meet with Adam and I that night. All I had to do was get Adam to agree. I decided to strike while the iron was hot and call him.

"I'll leave you to it," announced Tiger, already walking away. The double doors to the foyer swung shut and he was gone.

I must've caught Adam at the right moment. He agreed to come to the club on his way home from work. I gave him the address and ended the call before he changed his mind.

Bridget called out to me. I spun around to see her flat on her back in the middle of the floor.

"Bridge, get up," I ordered. "It's filthy."

She didn't move a muscle. "We found it, Ry," she announced.

I walked over to her, hooked my hands under her arms and lifted her to her feet. "Found what?"

"Secret North!"

"How do you know?"

My eyes followed her pointing hand. "Flowers on the roof," she sang.

I hadn't noticed the pressed tin ceiling, which was a shame because it was one of the nicest features of the place. Too many layers of white paint covered the intricate details, but the pattern was unmistakably floral.

"There *are* flowers on the roof," I agreed. "You think this is the place?"

"Yes!" She lurched forward and hugged my legs, making her feather wobble. "Happy, happy day, Ry," she beamed. "You found your place."

I thought back to the other characteristics she'd told me to look for while searching for the elusive Secret North. As well as the flowers on the roof, it was supposed to be special.

It was definitely special. I'd fallen in love with it before I'd even made it through the door. But Bridget had also promised a great view, claiming that I'd be able to see everything from there. That's where her La La theory began to crumble – I couldn't see anything other than a potentially great restaurant location. But I wasn't about to burst her bubble.

Perhaps now that she'd found the secret place we'd been seeking for over a month, we could spend time at the playground instead of wandering around with a compass.

"Well, Bridget," I told her. "If this really is my place, I think we should buy it."

44. PASSIVE AGGRESSIVE

Bente

It was beginning to feel as if I was living two lives. As far as life with Ryan went, I was happier than I'd ever imagined I'd be. On the job front, I was probably at the lowest point in my life.

Spare time after my shifts at Billet-doux were spent scouring the internet for positions better suited to my qualifications. I was getting desperate and trying not to let it show. I didn't want to burden Ryan. I wanted to keep the good in my life good so I called my sister and hit her with it instead.

"Why are you stressing about it, Bente?" asked Ivy. "I'm sure your boyfriend will take care of you."

I matched her caustic tone with one of my own. "I don't want Ryan to take care of me. I want to write for a living."

"Keep looking then," she urged. "Sooner or later something will come up." That was the most encouragement I was going to get from her because her focus was elsewhere. The girls were at war in the living room, using pageant prizes as weapons. "Malibu, put the sceptre down!" she yelled, right in my ear. "If anyone's going to get whacked with it, it'll be you!"

"I'll talk to you later, Ivy," I said dully.

"Wait," she replied. "Are you sure you're okay? I need to know you're okay."

"I'm good, Ivy," I assured. "Thanks for being there for me."

"I'm always here," she said sincerely. "And you're a good writer, Bente. Don't let anyone tell you otherwise."

Despite the mayhem in the background, my sister's words were hugely calming. I couldn't be sure that she heard me thank her. As I spoke, she yelled Malibu's name and the line went dead.

***

I knew I had a few hours before Ryan was due home. I decided to keep my good life good by surprising him with dinner. I stopped at the gourmet deli on the way home and grabbed a few different salads, an antipasto platter and a couple of blueberry bagels for no other reason than they looked delicious. Dinner was prepared, which left me plenty of time to concentrate on the things I planned on surprising him with after dinner.

I took a long bath, blow-dried my hair, painted my nails and still had time to kill. That was the moment I decided I could never be a stay-at-home girlfriend. It would kill me. I was so bored that I was actually hoping one of Ryan's ex-playthings would pick that afternoon to show up. I looked good, which meant I was ready for battle.

When the intercom buzzed half an hour later, I almost squealed in delight as I rushed to answer it. "Yes?"

"Bente, darling." My heart both dropped and began thumping. It was Fiona Décarie. "I can't get in. Who changed the code?"

"I'll buzz you in," I replied, holding my finger on the button. "Come on up."

I spent the five minutes it took her to get upstairs to figure out the reason for her visit. Ryan hadn't mentioned she was coming so I could only assume that she wasn't there to see him.

I opened the door as soon as she knocked. "Hello darling," she crooned, leaning in to kiss my cheeks. She was carrying an armload of dresses so I lightened her load by grabbing a few.

"How are you, Fiona?"

"Wonderful, darling," she replied, making her way to the couch and draping the stack of dresses over it. "I know you're attending that strange girl's wedding soon. I thought you might like something pretty to wear."

I didn't know whether to take offense or not. I had a closet full of pretty dresses thanks to Ivy's brilliant dressmaking skills. Trieste, on the other hand, probably would've been offended by being referred to as strange. "Trieste is a sweet girl." Defending her seemed odd. I'd only met her once but Ryan and Adam were fond of her so it felt like the right thing to do.

"Sweet but whacky," she amended, taking the dresses from my arms. "I'm terribly relieved she's not marrying into my family. One is enough."

"One what?"

It was a redundant question. I knew she was referring to Charli.

"One sweet but whacky girl." Fiona smiled. "I'm thrilled that Ryan has finally settled down with a nice girl."

Hiding the embarrassment that burned my cheeks was impossible. Ryan hadn't settled. Ryan was *trying* to settle, but that was a difficult concept to explain, especially to his mother.

"Are these dresses all yours?" I asked, changing the subject. "They're lovely." I wasn't lying. From what I could tell, they were all couture and stunning.

"No, darling." She sounded amused. "They're all yours."

Charli had warned me that she liked to dress people. It was something that the youngest Mrs Décarie had struggled with for years, and I now understood why. It was an extremely passive aggressive gesture. The struggle came because the clothes were too damned gorgeous to turn down.

"Charli favours vintage dresses," she explained, spreading a black silk dress across the couch. "She's petite and whimsical. I think she looks lovely in pastel chiffon and soft lace."

"She does," I agreed.

"You have a more exotic look," she declared. "Velvet and silk and dark colours."

I was back to toying with the idea of being outraged, but couldn't bring myself to tell her off. Standing my ground became even more difficult when she held up the most beautiful dress I'd ever seen. It was navy blue silk halter dress.

"What do you think?" she asked.

"I love it," I replied honestly.

She thrust it at me. "Try it on."

I changed into the dress as quickly as I could, unwilling to leave her alone in the living room for a second longer than necessary. Despite the rush, I just wasn't quick enough. When I returned she was in the kitchen, snooping around in the fridge.

"Are these leftovers, darling?" she asked, holding up one of the containers of salad I'd just bought.

"No, it's dinner."

Clearly unimpressed, she put the salad back. "Ryan is a wonderful cook," she boasted, closing the fridge. "He gets it from me."

In order to keep the peace, I agreed with her. "Ryan cooks most nights," I explained. "He has a late meeting this afternoon. That's why I picked up a salad."

"Don't you cook?" she quizzed.

"I can, but Ryan prefers to. It makes him happy."

Fiona walked around to my side of the counter and took my face in her hands. I endured it as best I could. "You'll make a wonderful wife," she declared before releasing me.

A few thoughts spun through my mind, and all were troubling. I got the impression that she'd lost all hope of Charli becoming the obedient little wife for Adam, but saw potential in me. I was also bothered that she was already marrying us off. We'd barely been together a month.

I took a step back, out of her space. "He has to ask me first." It was a foolish thing to say. I'd given her hope that it was a possibility.

"It's time he settled down," she told me. "I want that for him."

I nodded, at a total loss for words. I picked up the hem of my dress and fanned it out. "What do you think?" I asked.

"It's lovely," she approved. "Everything about you is lovely."

45. HAPPY HEART

Ryan

I delivered Bridget home and rushed back to the club to meet Adam. She probably could've stayed but I didn't want the distraction of having her running around while we were discussing business. I met Adam outside and gave him the rundown before going in.

"I can already tell it needs a lot of work, Ryan." He ran his hand along the iron balustrade. "Are you sure it's viable?"

I grinned at him. "Wait until you see the inside."

One thing that impresses Adam is good architecture. I knew he was sold before he even made it through the foyer. Once he started tapping walls and stamping on floorboards I knew he was hooked. "It's freaking gorgeous," he admitted.

"Isn't it?" asked Tiger, making his way down the roped-off stairs.

I quickly introduced them. "Baby Bardot's father?" he asked, unhooking the rope barrier.

"Yes," I confirmed, speaking for him. "Bridget's dad."

Adam smiled. "You've met her?"

"Earlier today," confirmed Tiger. "She left her mark." Not even I knew what that meant – until he waved us through to the main room. A million tiny boot prints dotted the dusty floor.

"You should've given her a broom," said Adam.

"I don't have one," replied Tiger making us both laugh.

***

The tables were still set up from the party on Saturday night. We sat down at the poker table and negotiations got underway.

In my head, it was a pretty cut-and-dried deal. I planned to offer Tiger a fair price, take possession of the building, restore it to its former glory and reopen as a classy cocktail lounge. It didn't take me long to work out that the deal was going to be anything but cut-and-dried. If you ask the right questions, you get the right answers, and Adam was good at asking the right questions.

"What's upstairs?" he asked.

"My home. I live up there."

That wasn't good. Not only was the old man losing his club, he was losing his home – and I didn't think I was cutthroat enough to do that to him. The ground the sale stood on suddenly became shaky and the deal began to crumble before my eyes.

Expecting Adam to reel it back in was hopeless. He had even more of a conscience than I did. He stared blindly at the far wall, absently stacking poker chips. "It's not for us, Ryan."

I glanced at Tiger, seeing a mix of relief, worry and sorrow on his face. "What if we just buy a share?" I suggested. "We can restore it and get it up and running. Tiger can continue to live upstairs."

It was a solution to a few problems. The old man got to keep his home and, if the venture was successful, make a few bucks along the way. Meanwhile, we'd be part owners of one of the most glorious old buildings I'd ever seen.

"What do you think, Mr Malone?" asked Adam.

"This building has seen better days," replied Tiger, leaning back and folding his arms. "I have too. If what you're offering me is a chance to see her brought back from the dead, I'd be a happy man."

"That's what we're offering you," I confirmed.

The struggle to hang on to his beloved club had obviously been going on for a long time. Like the hard old coot that he was, he bit down on his cigar and nodded. "We should celebrate," he declared, levering himself to his feet.

As he made the slow walk to the bar I used the time to ponder what we were getting ourselves into. Adam was probably doing the same thing. Realistically, it could be years before we started turning a profit. The renovations would be costly, and we were behind the eight ball before we even started, thanks to years of back taxes that needed cleaning up.

"Do you think we're doing the right thing?" I asked quietly.

Adam's eyes drifted to the stack of chips in his hand. "It's only money," he replied. "And it'll make your heart happy."

I usually kicked up at La La comments, but for once I kept quiet. He was right; and I was beginning to enjoy having a happy heart.

***

I should've known when Tiger returned to the table with whiskey and three dirty glasses that we were in for a long night. He spent the next few hours plying us with booze and regaling us with stories. I wasn't convinced that they were all true, but they were interesting. Tiger Malone had lived a rock star life. He'd dabbled in everything from running the club to owning racehorses.

"Came close to snatching the Kentucky Derby in '63," he claimed. He brought his glass to his lips and threw back the last of his whiskey. "Funny business, horses."

He'd also spent time in prison for racketeering in the sixties. We didn't ask for details but considering the revelation came straight after the horse story, I concluded the two were somehow linked.

"Things worked differently back then," he explained. "We were tougher. Not like you nancy-boys of today."

"We do alright." I cracked the lid on the whiskey and refilled his glass.

"I know *you* do," he agreed. "I've seen the broad you spend your nights with." He turned his attention to Adam. "What about you, kid? What's your story?"

Adam frowned. "I'm not sure I have one," he replied. "I've never spent time in prison, though."

Tiger chuckled blackly. "You're a lawyer. It's only a matter of time."

***

Tiger's stories became more crude and outlandish as the night wore on. I had an aversion to cheap whiskey. Adam had a problem with dirty glasses. As a result, we both sat on one drink all night and left stone cold sober. Tiger Malone was in rougher shape. We offered to help him upstairs before we left but he refused, and wasn't gentle about it.

"I've been climbing those stairs since 1958," he slurred, gripping the balustrade to steady himself. "Sometimes with three women on my arm. I manage just fine by myself."

I imagine it had been a while since he'd had three women on his arm, but we weren't about to challenge him. We waited at the base of the stairs until we heard a door upstairs slam.

"Do you think he's okay?" asked Adam.

I hooked the 'staff only' rope across the stairs. "He's probably feeling better than he has in years. We've just saved him from losing his home."

Adam grinned. "Feels good, doesn't it?"

"Ask me next week when we're forking out to cover his back taxes."

***

It had been a long day. By the time I arrived home, it was after ten. I was tired and craving sleep. Unfortunately for me, Bente was pissed and craving an argument. "You didn't think to call me? I was worried about you."

"No, I didn't," I replied frankly. "Time just got away from me."

Honesty wasn't necessarily the best route to take. It riled her even more. I stayed in the kitchen while she ranted at me from the couch. This was completely new territory. Coming home to an irate woman was another first and it wasn't a milestone that brought me joy.

"I tried calling a hundred times, Ryan. I was worried about you."

"I turned my phone to silent – I always do when I'm in a meeting. You knew where I was."

My blasé attitude didn't go down well. Bente marched across the room until the only thing separating us was the island counter.

"How was I supposed to know you'd be out half the night?" she growled. "All you had to do was call and tell me you were going to be late."

I was exhausted and I was annoyed, which was a dangerous combination. It made me say dumb things. "You sound like my mother," I told her. "Don't be my mother. It's not cute."

Everything quickly went to hell after that. Bente was so angry that her hands were shaking. I decided that the best defence was to ignore it in the hope that she'd get a grip.

"Have you eaten?" I asked casually.

"No."

"Well you should," I told her, staring into the fridge. "It might make you feel better."

I couldn't have anticipated her next move even if I'd been facing her. I didn't have time to react as something bounced off the back of my head. I spun around and looked to the floor to see what it was.

"A bagel?" I asked incredulously. "You hit me in the head with a bagel?"

"You should feel privileged!" she screamed. "I really wanted that bagel."

"Bente, you just hit me."

She grabbed another bagel, drew back her hand and lined up her second shot. "Stand still," she ordered. "I have one more."

I closed the fridge and bravely took a step closer. "If you hit me again, I swear, I'll walk out that door."

She dropped it on the counter, brushed off her hands and burst into tears. "Don't bother." She grabbed her purse off the couch. "I'm out." The front door slammed and she was gone.

Our first argument was short and ugly, and there didn't seem to be a victor. I wasn't interested in chasing after her. I was pissed.

46. FROG TRAINING

Bente

I wish the bagel had been a rock.

Staying out half the night without calling was rude. And once I calmed down a bit, I realised that giving him an attitude adjustment with baked goods was rude too.

My exit from the apartment wasn't very well thought out. Summer was slipping away and the nights were getting cool. I hadn't thought to grab a jacket, and the dress I was wearing provided little protection against the night air. The journey to Ivy's house would be long and painful while underdressed and ugly crying so I sought refuge at the closest place I could think of, Charli's place.

Adam answered the door, which wasn't ideal. "Are you alright?" he asked, ushering me inside.

"No," I muttered. "Your brother is an asshole."

I think he tried not to laugh, but it didn't work. "It took you this long to work it out?"

Charli appeared behind him, looking far more concerned. "What happened?"

There was no way of downplaying it so I made sure my explanation was short. "We just had a fight. I hit him in the head."

Now Adam looked worried. "Is he alright? Do I need to go over there?"

"No," I muttered. "Blueberry bagels don't hurt."

He dropped the concerned expression and laughed again. Charli pulled me further into the room. "Ignore him," she said. "Come and talk to me."

"It's late," I blubbered. "I'm sorry. Maybe I should go."

Charli cleared a group of legless dolls off the couch and ordered me to sit. Adam bowed out of the conversation at that point. I wasn't sure if he was being polite or was just unwilling to deal with the drama. Either way, I was relieved.

"I'll leave you ladies to it," he said, stealing a quick kiss from his wife as he passed. "Tomorrow's a new day, Bente." He smiled at me. "You'll be fine."

***

I'd never known Adam and Charli's place to be so quiet. Without Bridget bouncing around, the apartment took on a whole new feel. We sat side by side on the couch, talking and wailing. To clarify, I was wailing, Charli was ripping tissues from a box and rationing them out to me.

"He can be such a jerk," I sobbed. "He didn't even think to call and tell me he was going to be late." Saying it out loud made me realise how trivial it must've seemed from the outside looking in.

"If you're worried about who he was with, don't be," soothed Charli. "He was with Adam. Their meeting ran late."

My inane rambling had paved the way for her to jump to the completely wrong conclusion. I wasn't worried that he was with someone else. My insecurity stemmed from the fact that he hadn't thought to call me.

"I'm so far into this thing, Charli," I told her. "I love him. I think about him all the time."

She shuffled across the couch and draped her arm around me. "I'm sure it's mutual, Bente."

I tore another tissue from the box on her lap. "If he didn't think to call me, he wasn't thinking about me."

"Well, did you explain that to him?"

"Yeah." I sniffed. "With a bagel to the head."

Once she started giggling, I cracked too. Ryan was an insensitive idiot, but I was the one who'd blown it out of proportion by letting my temper get the better of me.

"Do you want to stay here tonight?" she asked.

I wanted to go home and apologise, but I wasn't that brave. "Yeah, if you don't mind."

"Of course not." Charli stood. "As long as you don't mind crashing on the couch."

"It's fine." I leaned forward and picked a doll up off the coffee table. "The girls will keep me company."

***

I'm a morning person, but Bridget Décarie is a dawn person. It was barely daylight when I opened my eyes and found her wedged at my feet.

"Hi Bente," she said cheerily. "Why are you here?"

Because your favourite uncle is a tool, I didn't reply. "I'm just visiting," I said sleepily.

"Okay. My daddy can make you breakfast."

"Yes I can," agreed Adam, walking into the room. "What would you like? Cereal? A bagel perhaps?"

I lifted my head in time to catch him smiling. "Coffee?" I asked.

"Coffee I can do," he replied, disappearing into the kitchen.

"I don't like bagels," said Bridget.

"Me neither, Bridge," I muttered, pulling the blanket up to my chin. If not for the little person chattering in my ear, I probably could've drifted back to sleep. I was that tired.

"I'm going to a dancing school today," she told me.

"That'll be fun," I replied dully.

"Yes, I know." Bridget peeled back the edge of the blanket so she could see me. "Animal goes there too."

I grimaced. Obviously Ryan's slip of the tongue when referring to Malibu as a Muppet wasn't a one-off.

"Does she?"

"Yeah." Bridget pulled at the blanket again. "She's a bit mean, isn't she?"

Bridget's opinion of Malibu was warranted, but agreeing with her seemed wrong. "I'm sure you'll sort out your differences."

I sat up as Adam walked over and handed me a mug of coffee. "Feeling better?" he asked.

Embarrassment was my prime emotion at that point. The cold light of day made the events of the night before seem ridiculous.

"Yeah." I brought my mug to my lips. "Sorry about last night."

Charli called to Bridget from the bedroom, and she took off down the hall. I was glad. Talking was a lot easier when I didn't have to censor my words.

"You've nothing to be sorry for," replied Adam. "You're welcome here any time."

"It was a one off." I didn't exactly sound believable, and judging by the sympathetic look he gave me, Adam didn't think so either.

"Look," he began, "I know Ryan's not the brightest spark when it comes to considering other people's feelings, but don't give up on him yet." I couldn't give up on him. I was all-in, which was the crux of the problem. Ryan clearly wasn't all-in to anything other than himself. "Do you want me to talk to him?"

The last thing I wanted was to enrol him in frog training. Ryan needed to figure things out for himself, just as Adam had done.

"No, thanks anyway," I replied. "I'll handle it."

Bridget came bounding back, looking sweet in a pink leotard and matching tutu. The little girl was so excited that she was practically ticking. I couldn't face that level of excitement so early. I drank my coffee, pulled myself together as best I could, and went home to face the music.

***

I didn't know what sort of mood Ryan would be in, but I wasn't expecting the mess of a man I found sitting at the kitchen counter. He'd looked tired the night before. With his dishevelled dark hair, creased T-shirt and low-slung pants, he now looked shattered.

"Hey," I said weakly, closing the door behind me.

"If you follow up with a wave, I'm going to be seriously unhappy," he warned.

I clenched my fist to stop myself from accidentally waving, not that he would've noticed if I had. He didn't lift his head to look at me. "Have you been up all night?"

It's the only thing I could think of to explain his disastrous appearance. "Most of it." He picked his phone up off the counter and swiped the screen. "I called you nineteen times. Ironically, your phone is switched off."

"Were you worried about me?"

Say yes, Ryan, I silently willed. It was all I wanted to hear.

"I didn't like the way our conversation ended," he replied. "I didn't like the way it started either, but I would've appreciated a chance to make things right."

I waited by the couch, contemplating leaving again. He'd said nothing so far to make me want to stay. "You don't know how to make it right, Ryan," I muttered. "That's the problem. You just don't have it in you, do you?"

I couldn't even be upset about it. Something in his emotional wiring was misfiring. It wasn't a new problem; he'd always been defective.

Finally he swivelled the stool in my direction and looked at me. The dull expression on his face gave nothing away and as expected, relying on him to enlighten me with words was pointless. "Whatever I say is going to come out wrong so it's best I don't say anything."

Ryan could be very cutting when angry. Perhaps he knew it. It was probably in my best interest to agree, but like a dog with a bone I refused to let it go.

"If you don't speak, nothing gets resolved."

Ryan stood. Sitting at the counter must have been a position he'd been maintaining for a while. He raised his arms above his head, stretching out his tired body.

He was an unfeasibly good-looking man, even after a sleepless night. The gap that appeared between his shirt and his pants when he stretched made me reconsider the tough-love stance I was trying to take – but only until he spoke.

"The only problem we have at this point is your temper," he told me. "It's not okay to hit me, Bente."

That was probably the moment that I was supposed to apologise. I refused. His thoughtlessness hurt far more than my bagel to his head.

"I was worried about you," I yelled. "I thought you were holed up in Grover Irwin's basement or something."

Ryan arrogantly folded his arms, but did crack a small smile. "I couldn't sleep last night," he admitted. "I just kept calling your phone and listening to your voicemail message."

"So you know the level of panic I felt when I didn't know where you were," I suggested.

He shrugged, which infuriated me. It was as if he was determined to hang on to the one part of his personality that made him Ryan Décarie, douche bag.

I planned my next words very carefully. "If you don't care, I can't care," I said quietly. "Do you understand that?"

"What do you need to hear from me right now, Bente?" he asked, sounding at a loss. "Tell me and I'll say it."

I wasn't going to coach him. I was tired of trying to teach him how to be a decent person. I took the steps necessary to reach him and put my palm flat to his chest. His heart was pounding, which was a good sign. It proved he had one.

"Why is your heart racing?" I whispered.

"Because you're touching me." His eyes darted between my eyes and my mouth.

I dropped my hand to my side and he groaned.

"Are you mad?" I murmured.

"No."

"Frustrated?"

He smirked. "A little."

"Doesn't feel good, does it Ryan?" I asked. "That's how I feel. You keep me in a constant state of frustration."

His expression morphed into a wily smile. "I could take care of that for you in about five minutes if you'll let me."

"I'm not talking about sex."

"I know."

"So don't make it about sex. Give me something more meaningful. It'll be another first for you."

Ryan pulled in a long breath through his nose, and seemed to hold it forever. I didn't push. I waited for him to speak.

"It bothers me that I keep screwing us up," he began. "I truly didn't give you a thought last night, but that doesn't mean I don't care. I've never had to think about anyone other than myself, Bente."

"I know."

"It took me an hour after you left to work out why you were so pissed with me. That's how stupid I am. I can't change thirty years of selfish stupidity overnight, but I'm going to keep trying if you'll just stick with me."

He'd given me more of an explanation than I thought he would. I knew I had to give too. I wasn't perfect either. "I'm sorry I hit you. I promise I'll never do it again."

Ryan swept my hair off my shoulder and rested his hand behind my neck. "Thank you," he said softly. "I appreciate that." He stepped forward, closing the gap between us. "Do you want to know why my heart's pounding now?"

"Yeah, tell me."

His soft kiss didn't stop at my lips. It travelled all the way through my body. "The Black Plague," he whispered.

I put my hands on his cheek, holding his face in place. "It's not the plague, Ryan."

"No," he agreed, leaning closer again. "It's something much more serious."

47. GERIATRIC GANGSTERS

Ryan

There's nothing worse than feeling inadequate. I was seriously lacking as a boyfriend; therefore I was inadequate. There were probably a million shortcomings in my repertoire, but the ones I focused on that week were being more attentive and considerate. When I tried, I could be a star pupil. Making the effort wasn't anywhere near as taxing as I expected. I wanted to make Bente happy. I loved her.

The sale of the club was progressing nicely. Adam spent all week arranging paperwork, permit applications and other boring junk. I hadn't been quite so diligent. Most of my week was spent in bed with the most beautiful woman I'd ever known.

Bente had barely shown her face at Billet-doux in days. I'd called in three times asking Noelle to find someone to cover her shift, never giving a reason why. "She's going to make my life hell when I go back to work," said Bente, shifting with me as I dropped my phone on the nightstand.

I smoothed my hand through her hair and kissed the top of her head. "No she won't," I told her. "And if she does, tell Charli. She'll set her straight."

She rested her chin on my chest. "Why would you get Charli to deal with it?"

"Because Noelle already thinks she's a bitch," I explained, grinning. "No harm, no foul."

Her warm laugh melted through my entire chest. It was all the encouragement I needed to put an end to the conversation and remind her why my plan of staying in bed for the entire morning was a good one.

***

For some cruel reason, a ringing phone sounds louder than usual when you don't want to hear it.

"Ry," whispered Bente. "Answer it."

"No." I murmured.

The phone eventually stopped, then started again a minute later.

"Please answer it." She breathed the words into my ear, which was a stupid move on her part. There was no way I was going to answer it now. "Ryan, answer it and tell whoever it is to never call you again," she commanded.

I looked into her lovely brown eyes. "Or what?" I wondered, trailing a line down her body with my fingers.

"Just answer the damn phone."

Groaning in protest, I reached across her and grabbed the phone. "Don't ever call me again," I said curtly.

Bente gasped, making me laugh. I wasn't worried about causing offense. I could tell by the ringtone that it was Adam.

"I don't even want to know what you're doing right now," he replied.

"I'll bet it's a damn sight more fun that what you're doing," I responded.

"You might be right," he agreed. "I'm sorting out building permits."

"Is there a problem?"

"No, but we need to clarify a few things. Can you meet me at the club in an hour?"

I was a little taken aback but didn't question him. It was usually impossible to drag Adam out of his office during the day, and this would be his second play at hooky – the first being when he skipped out to take his kid to the park. I agreed to meet him and ended the call.

"Everything okay?" asked Bente.

I dropped the phone and pulled her close. "Yeah. Adam might finally be growing a spine," I marvelled. "I have to go to the club. Do you want to come?"

She turned her head and kissed me. "No, but thank you for asking."

***

Adam and I arrived at exactly the same time. I'd come empty-handed. He had a stack of paperwork, blueprints and a big tape measure.

"You're on time," he noted. "I'm impressed."

"You escaped your office," I retorted, making my way up the steps. "I'm even more impressed."

Before we opened the door, he gave me a quick explanation for the meeting. "I've been looking over the blueprints Tiger gave us, but they're ancient," he said. "I'm pretty sure some of the measurements are out. We need to make sure they're right before we submit any applications."

I unrolled the prints and pretended to know what I was looking at. "You can tell just by looking?"

"Yeah," he replied. "Can't you?"

"No, Adam." I rolled them back up. "I'm not an engineer."

Adam made a grab for the door handle. "It's simple math, Ryan."

"You are such a freaking dork," I complained, following him inside.

I thought that was going to be the inaugural moment that we finally got to check the club out without Tiger breathing down our necks. I was wrong. We didn't make it a foot inside before seeing him, and he wasn't alone. Tiger stood puffing away on his cigar at the base of the stairs, barking orders to his friend Earl, who was at the top of a rickety ladder battling to keep his balance.

"Move to the left a bit," ordered Tiger.

Moving a single inch to the left would've ended badly. I grabbed the ladder to steady him. "Jesus, Earl! What are you doing up there?"

"Changing a light bulb," he replied.

The top of an eight-foot ladder is no place for an eighty-year-old man. I ordered him down and asked Tiger what the hell he was thinking.

"He likes heights," he explained, shrugging. "His last girlfriend was so tall, he used to have to climb a ladder to kiss her."

Adam and Earl laughed, but I struggled to find the funny side.

"You crazy old bastard," I chided, looking up at Earl. "You're going to kill yourself."

"Lighten up, Ryan," urged my brother.

As soon as Earl was on the ground, Adam took the bulb from him and climbed the ladder.

"Did Earl draw the short straw?" I asked Tiger. "Why didn't you climb the ladder?"

He puffed a choking plume of smoke at me. "No ladder experience. All my broads are short."

Adam changed the bulb and gave Earl the go-ahead to turn the light on. It didn't make much difference: the place was still dingy; but the old men were impressed with their effort.

"Job well done, Earl." Tiger thumped his friend on the back.

"Yes," he agreed, staggering back a step. "Time for a drink, eh?"

Adam stepped back to solid ground. "It's ten in the morning."

"That's right, kid," replied Tiger. He donned a brown trilby and flicked the brim. "We're late."

They shuffled out and the door slammed. We stood in silence until Adam found words. "I swear Ryan, they're geriatric gangsters."

"Yeah," I agreed. "Total badasses."

***

Measuring up the main room would have taken less time if Adam hadn't had to keep stopping to answer his phone. It highlighted just how manic his schedule was. The only calls he didn't take were the ones from Dad, and there were plenty.

"He's hunting me down," he explained. "He has no idea where I am."

I pulled my end of the measuring tape taut. "He keeps a tight leash on you, doesn't he?"

Adam read the tape and wrote the measurement into his notebook. "Nothing I can't handle."

"How does Charli feel about you working for him?" My question was redundant. I knew exactly how Tinker Bell felt. She'd complained to me a hundred times about Adam being under the king's rule.

"She knows he's a hard taskmaster," he replied, still writing. "She understands."

"She knows you're unhappy there, Adam."

He ordered me to drop the tape and began winding it in. "Has she said something?"

"Once or twice." We walked to the middle of the room. "You should look for something else," I suggested.

"It wouldn't matter what firm I worked at, Ryan. I hate the job. I hate everything about it," he admitted. "I might as well stay where I am."

"Better the devil you know, huh?"

He grunted listlessly.

"Well, this place is going to need a lot of work." I looked around, struggling to find a surface that wasn't peeling or decaying. "We need a project manager. You'd be perfect." He was shaking his head before I'd even finished speaking. "You could quit your job, work the hours you want to, see more of Bridget and Charli –"

He cut me off. "Don't bring my girls into this."

I frowned. "Just think about it, okay?"

"I don't want to commit to anything new," he replied. "Charli's contract at the gallery is up soon. She might not want to renew. I'm not even sure if we're staying in New York."

"You think she'll want to go home?"

He nodded, smiling. "I'm hoping so."

"Has she talked about leaving?"

"All the time. She's not sure what she wants to do, but I know she misses Alex," he replied. "And she'd love to spend time with her little brother."

"You want to go back, don't you?"

"I never wanted to leave in the first place, Ryan." He handed me one end of the tape measure and began walking to the far wall. "I want to live on the beach and have a bunch more kids and restore boats."

The reversal of headspace between the two of them was almost dizzying. Life in New York the first time around had worked in the opposite way; Charli had been the one desperate to leave. Now Adam's feet were itching.

The sound of Adam's phone echoed in the empty room. He took it out for the umpteenth time. "Speak of the devil."

Charli's fairy ears must've been burning. Adam hit the speaker button, freeing his hand to write down the measurements he'd just taken.

"Hey," he said gently.

"Adam, I have something amazing to tell you." Her words came out in an excited rush.

I was glad when he took the phone off speaker and put it to his ear. It didn't seem like a conversation I was meant to be privy to.

"What's going on?" The silence at his end lasted a while. "Coccinelle, I can't wait until tonight," he told her, eventually getting a word in. "Tell me now."

Fairy Pants was playing hardball. Whatever she had to tell him wasn't going to happen over the phone. She ended the call, leaving him hanging.

"Well?" I asked, too curious for my own good.

"I don't know. She wouldn't tell me."

His bright smile betrayed him. "Don't be a dick. Tell me."

I dropped the end of the tape measure and he began reeling it in again. It was a pointless exercise, considering we weren't done measuring.

"We've been talking about having another baby," he told me. "I'm hoping it's something to do with that."

Bente's speculation was right. There was baby talk in the air, and Adam didn't look terrified at all. I wondered what sort of consideration went into deciding whether or not to extend your family unit. For some crazy reason, I asked him. "How do you know that the time is right?"

He looked surprised, as if it was a stupid question. "Life just keeps moving on to the next step, Ryan. Bridget's four now."

I shook my head. "I can't imagine making decisions like that."

"You will."

"You think so?"

"You're already doing it," he said. "You never thought you'd live with a woman, until you found one that changed your mind."

"I guess so." I grabbed the end of the tape measure that he'd futilely reeled in for the millionth time.

"Before you know it you'll be married and making babies," he told me.

"That's a scary thought," I replied, walking away with the end of the tape. "Why doesn't it scare you?"

"Why would I be scared? You've seen the babies I make. They're perfect."

"If you say so, Adam," I teased, chuckling. "Your kid has a hole in her cheek like her father and a hole in her logic like her mother. There's definite room for improvement."

48. SILENT WORDS

Bente

Trieste Kincaid's wedding to William Best was to be a small affair held in the gorgeous Conservatory Garden in Central Park. Ryan and I wandered in through the Vanderbilt Gate entrance and took our time walking through the lilac and magnolia trees in the English garden.

"Nice day for a wedding, huh?" he asked, squeezing my hand.

It truly was. The sun was bright and the gardens were gorgeous. Daylilies and Astilbes were enjoying their final run before cooler weather set in.

"It's perfect," I agreed. The idyllic setting wasn't the only pleasant thing to look at. Ryan looked even more handsome than usual in the charcoal suit and crisp white shirt he was wearing. Seeing him suited up wasn't unusual, but something about him seemed extra special that day.

I felt like I belonged right by his side. I'd gone with the navy silk halter dress that Fiona had given me, topped off with a pair of heels I'd swiped from Charli's collection. If I was honest, I'd have to concede that they were a little too small. My feet were killing me, but I worked hard to pretend otherwise.

We caught up with Adam and Charli at the Burnett fountain. They looked like they'd just stepped out of a fashion magazine, and like Ryan they made it seemed effortless. Adam greeted me with a kiss. He smelled so incredibly good that I almost told him so. Charli greeted me with a click of her camera.

Ryan made a half-assed attempt to admonish her. "You're not the freaking paparazzi, Tinker Bell."

"I am today." She aimed it at him.

"Are you photographing the wedding?" I asked.

"Unofficially," she replied, "which is good because I'm more interested in photographing the gardens."

The official photographer looked much more intense. I didn't notice him until Charli pointed him out, then I couldn't take my eyes off him. He kept busy while waiting for the bridal party by snapping pictures of anything that moved. At one point he seemed to be taking photos of thin air.

"He's taking it very seriously, isn't he?"

Charli giggled. "I don't think he's going to miss anything, that's for sure."

Adam and Ryan killed time by discussing the work at the club. To me, the topic was so overdone that it was boring. It made me wonder what they talked about before they bought it. "Where's Bridget?" I asked. "I thought she'd be flower girl or something."

"Trieste did ask her, but it was conditional," Charli explained. "She wanted her to lose the boots for a day. Bridge wasn't interested. She's hanging out with Mamie instead."

I shook my head. "That kid is of another world."

***

I'd never been to a wedding where a flutist played the Wedding March, but it was sweet and romantic. I noticed the groom for the first time when the music started. He stood at the end of the invisible aisle, wringing his hands while he waited for his bride.

Trieste made her appearance looking nothing like the girl who'd shown up at our apartment a few weeks earlier. Her hair was piled high, trailing curls down her back. Her white dress was simple but lovely, and clearly worth the massive price tag. The only fault I could pick was her shoes. I couldn't see them, but the awkward steps she was taking as she clung to her father's arm proved they were too high for her. They were too high for William, too. She would've towered over him in flats.

The way the overenthusiastic wedding photographer kept stepping in front of her to get his shot as she walked amused me, but it annoyed Ryan. "What a fool," he muttered, taking it too personally.

I glanced at him, then at Adam. Both were scowling, looking like the protective older brothers Trieste had never had.

I'd asked Ryan about his friendship with Trieste, trying to understand how she'd inadvertently captured the hearts of both brothers. "She's one of the most honest people I've ever met," he told me. "You can't help but like her."

She could only have been the most decent of people. There's no way she would've gained the affections of Ryan Décarie by being anything but, and I'd seen a hundred try.

***

The small group of guests gathered around and the ceremony got under way. With the exception of the dull noise of background traffic, it was quiet, peaceful and incredibly romantic. Even Ryan thawed a little. He reached for my hand and gave it a few squeezes at certain points in the service, making my heart fly.

I allowed my mind to drift, wondering if we had a chance of ever making it this far. I wanted that kind of euphoria. I believed in it. I just wasn't sure if the man squeezing my hand possessed the same kind of faith.

The two people standing beside him certainly did. It was hard not to be envious of Charli and Adam. I could tell purely by looking that they fitted together. They could speak to each other without a word, and knew each other back to front.

I realised something important when Ryan squeezed my hand for the umpteenth time. He was speaking without words too. We were on our way. All I had to do was figure out what he was saying.

49. CHANGING WAYS

Ryan

Hosting a wedding reception at Nellie's was a first. I'd offered Trieste the use of Billet-doux but she'd turned it down in favour of a more casual option. My first inclination when we walked in was to take charge and manage the reception myself, but Bente held me back.

"You're a guest," she reminded, pulling me away from the podium.

"I just want to make sure it all goes smoothly for them."

"Look at them, Ryan," she urged. "They're ecstatic with the way their day has gone so far."

I looked across at the couple, who were milling around the room chatting with their guests. There was no look of relief that it was over, or nerves because they'd locked themselves into a lifetime together. They simply looked happy.

The wedding ceremony had sent my thoughts in directions they'd never gone before. Listening to Trieste and William declare their love for one another showed that happy-ever-afters are achievable. Some prove it, some die trying – but at least they try. I was in the stupid minority who had never been willing to try, and now something huge was gnawing at me, begging me to change my ways.

The torture of my internal musing became physical over the next hour. My brother was the first to notice. He put his hand on my shoulder and steered me to a quiet spot near the stairs. "What's going on?" he asked. "You don't look so good."

"I'm fine," I assured him. "I just don't like weddings."

"Is that all it is?" He looked amused. "I thought you were going to pass out or something."

In a move that must have seemed nothing short of bizarre, I grabbed him by the upper arms, forcing him to look at me. "Adam, I'm in big trouble," I said desperately. "I really love her."

He frowned, looking slightly alarmed. "We're talking about Bente?"

"Of course."

"Right," he muttered. "Well, that's good news because Trieste is taken now."

I turned my head, searching for Bente while maintaining my unreasonable grip on my brother. She was at a table, chatting with William's parents as if she'd known them for years. I'd told her how beautiful she looked a million times that day, but it wasn't enough. Coming from me, it never sounded credible. I'd spent too many years wasting the compliment on women who didn't deserve to hear it.

"She's so freaking special," I muttered. "She knows me and she puts up with me and she loves me."

Adam hadn't protested at my grip, but he drew the line at being shaken. The sharp shove he delivered to my chest brought me back to my senses.

"I'm sorry." I reached out to straighten him up.

He slapped my hand away. "Get off me," he ordered, punching out a hard laugh. "What are you going to do about it, Ryan?"

"Do about what?"

He motioned to Bente with an upward nod. "The girl who knows you and still doesn't think you're a dick."

I gazed at Bente for a long time before replying. "I think I'm going to marry her."

50. PET PREFERENCES

Bente

Conversing with William's parents was tricky for a few reasons. First, I'd never met them before. Second, I don't speak a single word of Cantonese. If I did, I would've asked how a Chinese family ended up with a last name like Best.

Mrs Best was lovely. I had no idea what she was saying, but she smiled a lot and stole one of the flowers off the table to put in my hair. Mr Best was much quieter, perhaps due to the language barrier. The only time I saw him break a smile was when William came and talked to him.

Ryan and Adam had generously closed Nellie's for the afternoon, which seemed to be overkill considering there were only twenty guests at the reception. Most of the empty tables had been put in the storeroom, which left plenty of room for a dance floor. Trieste was keen to make use of it.

"Dance with me, Bente," she ordered, appearing out of nowhere and pulling me to my feet. Her request was unorthodox, but nothing about Trieste was run of the mill. I'd never danced with a bride before but was prepared to give it a go, right up until she pulled me into a waltzing stance – then I just felt silly. I pulled free, deciding that a solo side to side shuffle was the best I could manage. If the need for distance offended Trieste, she didn't let on. She called out to a passing waiter, "Music please, maestro."

"Don't you think you should save the first dance for William?" I asked.

Her smile was blinding. "We danced in the limo on the way here."

I couldn't begin to imagine the logistics of that manoeuvre so I didn't ask for details.

The song that started playing was slow, which was probably a good thing. Trieste's solo technique was questionable to say the least. I barely moved, but her hips were swinging and her arms were flailing like a hula girl. Perhaps her family and friends were used to her. No one except the wait staff batted an eyelid as I took the occasional slow step to the side to keep up with her. I ignored their looks and focused on the conversation at hand, which progressed much faster than the dance.

"Are you in love with Ryan?" she asked getting straight to the point.

"Yes."

She grinned. "He's hopeless, you know," she warned. "But one of my favourite people in the whole world."

I wanted to snap at her and defend him, but thought better of it. She wasn't being disparaging. She was being honest.

"He likes you too, Trieste."

"I know." Her confidence made me smile. "I think he's serious about you," she mused. "You're smart and brunette and don't take any of his crap. I think he likes that."

"That's good to know."

"I'm glad you gave him a chance." She leaned forward to compensate for her quiet tone. "Most people think he's a mean jerk, but I can tell that you see past that."

"You do too, right?"

"I see through both of them," she replied, as Adam and Charli walked past. "They're not as tough as they pretend to be."

Trieste was an unexpected wealth of information. In a few short minutes she gave up a glut of Décarie secrets. Apparently Adam had mentored her at school. In return, she schooled him on how to be less-frog-more-prince and go after the little family he had waiting for him in Australia. Her friendship with Ryan stemmed from the three years she worked at Billet-doux while attending law school. She told me he nearly cried when she left, and I believed her.

"I have an eidetic memory," she explained. "It's a talent that comes in handy when waitressing. Ryan appreciated my efficiency."

I understood why he liked her so much. In Ryan Décarie's world, everything was black or white. He had no tolerance for indecision, drama or treading gently – unless you were four years old and related. Like him, Trieste was blunt and didn't suffer fools. In many respects, they were similar creatures.

***

Dinner was a quiet affair. Twenty people in a large restaurant don't make much noise. Ryan was particularly quiet. It bothered me so much that I questioned him about it.

"I'm okay," he mumbled from the corner of his mouth. I turned my head to get a better look at him. He didn't look okay; he looked pale.

"Do you need some air?" I asked. "We could go outside for a minute."

He nodded and stood. It was left to me to excuse us. Ryan didn't seem capable of words.

Rather than heading outside, he led me up to the mezzanine. He wasn't looking quite so ashen anymore, but he was still acting strangely.

"What on earth is wrong?" I asked, reaching out to feel his forehead. He grabbed my wrist and took a step back. That wasn't a good sign.

"I have to tell you something," he said gravely.

"Okay, can you do it while standing still?" His pacing was making me dizzy. "What's this all about?"

Ryan stopped walking. He ran both hands through his hair and rested them on the back of his head – but still didn't speak.

"Ry, you're scaring me now."

The look on his face was one I'd never seen before. I couldn't even place the expression. He dropped his hands in a motion that looked like defeat. "I've been putting a lot of thought into this, so I don't want you to think it's a spur of the moment thing," he began.

Oh, God. He's breaking up with me. "Okay," I squeaked, sounding exactly like Noelle.

"And I don't want to do it at an inappropriate time," he added. "Like when we're in bed. But we're always in bed, so my opportunities are limited."

He's definitely breaking up with me.

He waved his arms around. "This probably isn't ideal either but –"

"Just get to the point, Ryan." I folded my arms tightly across my chest to stop myself whacking the side of his head. I'd promised I wouldn't do that any more.

He blew out a long breath I hadn't noticed him take. "We should move to the next level, pecan pie girl."

I consider myself to be pretty quick on the uptake, but I had no idea what he was almost saying. The blank stare I gave him had no effect. He stared back looking just as flummoxed. After a long and excruciating pause, he finally elaborated. "We should get married and make a few babies, and buy a dog. I'm not sure I could handle a big dog, but a little one might be okay. Or a cat. We could get a cat. Do you prefer dogs or cats?"

I couldn't speak. I played the first four words over and over in my mind. Even then, I wasn't entirely sure what he was suggesting.

My lack of reaction seemed to cause him physical pain. A sheen of sweat appeared on his forehead and he grimaced. "Bente?" He managed to squeak out an awesome Noelle impersonation too. "Dog or cat?"

I shook my head, trying to get a grip on the ridiculousness. "Are you really asking me about pet preferences?"

"No." The word got caught in a nervous laugh. "I'm asking you to marry me."

51. A RYAN PERSON

Ryan

It was probably the worst marriage proposal in history, but I'd somehow gotten through it. Bente's reaction wasn't exactly the stuff of fairy-tales either.

"I need to sit down," she whispered. I grabbed the nearest chair and positioned it behind her. For a quick moment, I let myself think it was because she was overcome with emotion. The reality wasn't quite so romantic. "My feet are killing me." She kicked off her shoes and let out a groan of relief.

I dropped to my knees and grabbed her foot. "Well?"

"I'm not really a pet person, Ry."

It was my turn to groan, but not in relief. I dropped my head, mumbling my next question as I massaged her foot. "What about a Ryan person, Bente? Are you a Ryan person?"

She put her hand under my chin and tilted my head, locking my eyes to hers. Her brown eyes were warm and shining. Mine probably just looked terrified. "I am a Ryan person," she confirmed. "And if you promise to keep rubbing my feet like that, I'll gladly marry you."

The first part of her I kissed was her foot, then her knee, her thigh and almost her elbow by accident when she suddenly lurched off the chair and into my arms. That's when I found her gorgeous garnet lips.

We spent the next half hour on the upper floor of my restaurant making out like a couple of teenagers, which was ironic because I'd never felt like more of a grownup in my whole life. I was getting married.

52. QUALITY OVER QUANTITY

Bente

I couldn't wait to leave. As soon as William and Trieste bade farewell to their guests and skipped out the door, we bolted. Ryan called for a car and we stood on the sidewalk waiting for it to arrive. Ryan looked much better. The Black Plague symptoms had given way to a grin that refused to fade.

I felt blissful. I'm not a foolhardy girl. I'm sensible and cautious and careful. Making rash decisions wasn't something I was particularly good at, but nothing about accepting his proposal seemed wrong. I loved him and wasn't afraid to admit that I probably always had.

As sure as I felt, it didn't stop me questioning him. I wanted to know why the career bachelor had suddenly decided to move things up such a big notch.

"Because you're the truest thing that's ever happened to me," he replied.

"The truest?"

"Yes," he replied simply. "And I want to keep you forever."

"Just me, forever?" I wanted to be sure he understood that the commitment he was making extended further than cats and dogs.

His gorgeous smile broadened. "I'm honestly ready for you. That's what makes you true. Are you ready for me?"

I didn't even need to think about it. "Yes."

"Excellent." He let out an exaggerated sigh. "We're going to close this deal quickly. I don't want to waste a minute."

I should've been perturbed that he'd likened getting married closing a business deal, but I wasn't. To him, it probably made perfect sense. I reached out and he took my hand, kissing it before tangling his fingers through mine.

"A short engagement then?" I asked.

"Yes." He barely hesitated. "Two months seems reasonable, don't you think?"

"I'm not sure," I choked. "There's a lot to organise."

"Charli and Adam organised their wedding in less than a week."

"They didn't have a wedding, Ryan," I pointed out. "They got hitched at the marriage bureau. I'm not sure I want to go that route."

He dropped my hand and stepped in front of me. "I'm sorry. I should've asked what you wanted."

"I was hoping for something a little more special," I replied. "Nothing huge."

He leaned down and softly pressed his lips against mine. "You can have whatever you want – as long as you can pull it together in two months."

"What's your rush?" My words hummed against his mouth. "Are you afraid you'll change your mind?"

I felt his smile. "No; are you?"

I'd been worried about him changing his mind since day one, but I didn't admit it out loud. I chose to say nothing and kissed him instead.

***

We didn't go straight home. I didn't recognise the address Ryan instructed the driver to take us to. I couldn't quite decipher the cryptic phone call he made along the way either.

"Who was that?" I asked when he ended the call.

"A man called Mr Shultz," he said vaguely. "Our jeweller."

I almost laughed out loud. "*Your* jeweller?"

He looked sheepish enough to let me know he realised how conceited it sounded.

"My family all use the same jeweller," he replied. "Is that weird?"

"Not at all." I snickered. "It's perfectly normal to have a family jeweller."

"You're making fun of me?" he teased. "That's hardly acceptable behaviour considering we're engaged to be married."

"*Au contraire*, husband-to-be. It's licence to make fun of you for the rest of my life."

***

Mr Shultz, the jeweller, didn't seem put out by Ryan's request that he open his store at ten on a Saturday night. I suspect he knew it would be a worthwhile inconvenience. He greeted Ryan with a hug and asked about his family, specifically his mother. "Such a beautiful woman," he enthused. "Your father is a fortunate man."

"I'll pass on your regards," replied Ryan.

"Yes, please do," he urged, before turning his attention to me. "And who is this lovely lady?"

Ryan introduced me as his fiancée. The only person more surprised by the title than me was Mr Schultz. He threw up his hands. "I never thought I'd see the day. Congratulations to you both." His reaction made me wonder how many times he'd opened his jewellery store to accommodate Ryan's late-night shopping sprees. Playthings probably love jewels. "Perhaps now you will buy something worthwhile," he suggested, and turned to me. "Watches and cufflinks. Always watches and cufflinks!" he exclaimed. "I keep telling him to find a nice girl and buy her some diamonds. Then he will forget about cufflinks."

His words instantly put me at ease. It was a plaything-free zone.

Mr Schultz wasn't anywhere near finished. He had a few other gripes to get off his chest. "Your brother." He pointed at Ryan. "He didn't buy his wife's ring from me. He is a stingy man."

I almost jumped in to defend the frog. Half a diamond mine went into the making of Charli's rings, but Ryan saw no need to enlighten Mr Schultz. Instead he agreed with him, which was all the encouragement he needed to continue. "He came to me with one gold wedding ring." He held his finger in the air. "He made me cut it in half and make two rings out of it. What kind of man does that?"

"A total cheapskate," replied Ryan, grinning wickedly. "He's always been a tightwad."

Mr Shultz nodded so emphatically that his glasses slipped down the bridge of his nose. "I met his wife for the first time a few months ago," he replied, pushing them back into place. "He still hasn't bought her diamonds. The poor woman still wears half a ring."

Ryan could've set him straight, but didn't. "I know," he agreed. "It's pitiful."

"I showed them all of these." Mr Schultz swept his hand the length of the glass cabinet. "You know what they walked out of my store with?" Ryan shook his head. "A silver bracelet for their daughter. Not even gold! The wife gets half a ring and the girl gets silver for her birthday."

Ryan looked at the display in the cabinet. "Well, I'm not after half a ring. It will only be the best for my wife."

Lightning flickered deep in my chest, powered by his lovely words.

Ryan pulled me forward. I stood in front of the display cabinet, blinking at a rate of knots. The store was small but most definitely exclusive. Most of the rings were huge; some were so flashy that they were downright gaudy.

I'd never thought about what sort of engagement ring I wanted, but I got the impression that nothing was off limits. The next words out of Ryan's mouth confirmed it. "Pick one," he urged. "Anything you want."

Mr Schultz got the ball rolling. He set a tray of rings on the counter. I stared down at them before turning to Ryan. "What do you like?" My voice was tiny.

"I'm not good at this junk, Bente," he said sheepishly. "But I prefer quality over quantity. I want you to have something special."

"A solitaire?" suggested Mr Schultz, pointing at the tray.

I nodded.

Choosing a ring was a group exercise. Mr Schultz kept steering us towards massive rocks. Ryan urged me to try them on.

Refusing graciously was difficult, but I tried. "They're a little too big." All I could think of was trying to type while wearing a golf ball on one hand. It was craziness. I finally managed to get them to scale it down, and settled on a pretty, bright solitaire diamond in a platinum setting. It was far more modest than most we'd been shown, but I was still too afraid to listen when the topic of price came up – so afraid that I excused myself and went outside.

It was getting late. The cool night air felt crisp against my cheeks that were hot with excitement, but nothing was going to cure me and calm me down. I was getting married.

53. POMP AND CEREMONY

Ryan

Like our courtship, our engagement would be short – just two months. I wanted to be married to Bente yesterday. I wanted the world to know that I'd somehow got lucky enough to close the deal and make her my wife. If I'd had my way, I would've gone the same route as Adam and Charli and whisked her off to the marriage bureau, but Bente's ideas were different and I respected that. I wanted her to have whatever she wanted, and if a big wedding was it, then I was on board.

Ivy and the squealers were the first to be privy to our plans. There was no pomp and ceremony when it came to telling them. We laid it all out over dinner at their house two days after Trieste's wedding. Ivy and Fabergé took the news well. Malibu, not so much. "I'll be good," she wailed, smashing her plastic mug on the edge of the table. "Don't be my uncle!"

The last thing I wanted to be was her uncle, but for the first time in my life I was prepared to take the good with the bad because the good was so freaking perfect. "I'm a great uncle, Malibu," I told her. "Bridget will vouch for me."

The little girl calmed down in an instant, moving on at the mention of Bridget's name. "Why doesn't she go to dance class any more?"

I had no idea. I didn't even know Bridget took dance lessons.

"She quit?" Bente asked Ivy. "She was so looking forward to it."

Ivy reached for the salad. "She only lasted a few lessons, I'm not sure why."

"Is Bridget going to be in the wedding?" asked Fabergé.

I looked to Bente for answers. If by chance she didn't want her, I was prepared to bump Adam aside in favour of Bridget as my best man.

"You can all be in the wedding," she replied, inciting a round of excited squeals that made me wince.

Ivy loaded up my already full plate with more food. She was a feeder. It was almost a term of endearment. "We'll go over some dress ideas next week," she suggested.

"You're not going to have much time," hinted Bente.

"Why?"

Bente put her hand on my knee. That was the moment I realised I'd been agitatedly bouncing it. "Because we're getting married on October twenty-fifth," she announced.

Ivy quickly totted up how much time she had to work with. "That's barely two months away!" she barked. "What's the hurry? Are you knocked up?" She glared at me. "Did you knock her up?"

"No," I replied calmly. I wanted to add a really crass comment to put her in her place, but held off because the girls were staring me down from across the table.

"We just don't want to wait," explained Bente.

"Where's your ring?" She glanced at her sister's bare left hand before glaring at me again. "What kind of idiot proposes without a ring?"

"You need to buy a ring," Fabergé agreed disapprovingly. "A really nice one."

"Inconsiderate schmuck," mumbled Ivy. "How do you even sleep at night, Ryan?"

"Usually naked, next to your sister." The highly inappropriate comment tumbled out, earning me a stiff elbow to the ribs from Bente. I chose not to remind her of our no violence agreement. I deserved it.

"I have a ring, Ivy," she explained. "It's being resized."

Ivy pulled a sucking-lemon face, but didn't apologise. Perhaps realising we weren't going to get one, Bente moved on. She reached across the table and rested her hand on her sister's forearm. "Everything is wonderful," she assured her. "Be happy for me."

Ivy covered Bente's hand and almost cracked a smile. "I am happy."

"I'm happy for you too," chimed Fabergé. "He'll be a good uncle."

I smiled at the unlikely ally. "Thank you, Fabergé."

"I was happy first!" roared Animal.

Exchanges like this made me wonder what the hell I was getting myself into. Then I had the good sense to look at the beautiful woman next to me. It was the only reminder I needed that I was exactly where I was meant to be.

54. TRAITOR

Bente

Informing Ivy and the girls about the wedding was a cakewalk compared to sharing the news with the Décaries'. Nothing worked simply in that family. I could only surmise that Fiona had caught wind of something because a simple request to meet at their house turned into a full-blown gala dinner.

Attendance was mandatory, which pissed Charli off no end. Her mood was foul from the minute she walked in. Everybody got a curt hello and very little else.

"Why the long face, Charli?" Jean-Luc asked.

"I'm fine," she muttered unconvincingly.

I didn't catch his next remark, but Adam did. "Stop, Dad," he warned. "Leave her alone." Most of the time Charli could hold her own. When she couldn't, Adam stepped in. It was one of the things I liked best about him.

Jean-Luc moved his attention to Bridget, who was her usual bubbly self and oblivious to the tension. He scooped her off her feet and kissed her.

"Where's Mamie?" she asked, putting both hands to his cheeks.

"Upstairs," he replied. "She'll be down shortly."

Bridget wriggled and Jean-Luc lowered her to her feet. "I'm going to get her," she announced, making a beeline for the foyer.

After some stunted conversation, Charli sat beside me on the long couch, looking no happier than when she arrived. Adam opted for the couch opposite. The sweet wink he gave her as he sat was supposed to be discreet, but I saw it. She gave a tiny smile in return, which led me to think her bad mood wasn't frog related.

Even Ryan realised something was going on, and he was usually clueless. Probably looking for a reason to leave the room, he offered to organise drinks. "Yes, champagne would be lovely, darling," interjected Fiona, making her usual grand entrance through the glass doors. Bridget trailed behind her wearing a red Pashmina shawl like a cape. She jumped onto her father's lap forcefully enough to make him groan. "Slow down, baby," he told her.

Bridget pulled her shawl around her body. "This one's a good flier."

Adam kissed her head. "Just fly slowly."

Ryan stood up and offered Bridget his hand. "Let's go, Bridge. I saw cake in the kitchen." She didn't need asking twice scrambled off Adam's lap and grabbed Ryan's hand.

"Bring some champagne back, darling," called Fiona. I was certain her demand wasn't in anticipation of our announcement. Champagne flowed like water in that house.

This dinner shaped up to be nothing like the last one I'd attended. The air was thick. Ryan was smart to get out. I wished he'd taken me with him instead of Bridget. When Charli left the room for the first time, I grabbed the opportunity to talk in private and followed her into the foyer.

"Charli, what's going on?"

She stood stiffly. "Nothing."

She'd left me with nowhere to go but I pressed on. "You don't seem very happy."

Her muted whisper didn't quite match the gesture of throwing out her arms. "Everyone's entitled to a bad day, Bente. Today happens to be mine."

I nodded, unwilling to press her any more. The conversation should've ended there but Ryan appeared.

"How are you, Tink?" he asked. "You're a little out of form this evening."

"I'm not here to entertain you," she replied dully.

"Lucky," he slyly replied. "Because you're not even remotely entertaining tonight."

I grabbed his arm in an attempt to pull him into line. It didn't work. "We have some news to share, so if you could put on a smile and pretend to be happy, I'd appreciate it," he told her.

The sour face she pulled lasted only seconds. "When's the big day?"

I widened my eyes. "You know?"

"Of course I know. Ryan told Adam and Adam told me." She smiled for the first time and I gratefully smiled back. "I'm happy for you," she whispered, hugging me. "Truly."

The conversation was cut short when the glass doors slid open and the queen appeared. "Bente, darling, there you are," she crooned, hooking her arm though mine and wrenching me away. "Come. I have something for you."

Ryan said nothing as she led me in the direction of the stairs. When he dared to wave at me when I looked back at him, I almost reconsidered my decision to marry him.

The second floor of the Décarie home was as opulent and vast as the first. The longest carpet runner I'd ever seen extended all the way to the end of the hall. I counted six doors before we stopped at the last one. Fiona waved me in ahead of her. My eyes involuntarily darted in every direction as I checked out the room. I quickly worked out that I was standing in the king and queen's private domain – the master bedroom.

It was so magnificent I could barely breathe. The room was huge and the ceiling was high. The four-poster bed looked like something out of a fairy-tale, and there wasn't a thing out of place. Everything was expertly coordinated, including the row of silver photo frames lining the dressing table. I desperately wanted to get a closer look but remembered my manners and stayed by the doorway.

Fiona must've noticed the Cinderella moment I was having. "This is my favourite room," she told me, smiling. "It's not masculine, unlike the rest of our home."

It was definitely girly. The lacy canopy over the bed, sheer white drapes and crystal chandelier didn't strike me as being design choices Jean-Luc would've made.

"It's beautiful," I said truthfully.

Fiona smiled again, brighter this time. "Perhaps you and Ryan might settle in a lovely big home once you're married."

My heart began thumping. She was on to us. "You know?"

Her trademark demure giggle answered for her. "I'm far more perceptive than you might think," she replied. "And I know my sons better than they think. I knew Ryan was close to proposing. He clearly adores you."

"I love him too."

"Are you ready for this life, Bente?" she asked curiously.

I wasn't sure how to answer her. I found the Décarie lifestyle fascinating. I'd never seen such grandeur in all my life, but it didn't scare me. The three Décarie men worked extremely hard. They were savvy, brilliant businessmen. As far as I was concerned they deserved to reap the benefits associated with that.

"I'm not sure," I admitted. "But I'm not planning to revolt against it, if that's what you're worried about."

"No plans to live in a shack on the beach?" she hinted.

I smiled down at the plushest beige carpet ever made. "No, I'm a New York girl through and through."

"And what about the wedding?" she asked. "What are your plans?"

"I'd like to share the day with family and friends. It's a celebration, right?"

"Indeed," she beamed, clasping her hands together. "It will be wonderful to see Ryan walk down the aisle. It would mean the world to me. We didn't have that privilege with Adam. "

I suddenly felt like I was betraying Charli in the worst way imaginable. She'd spent the past six years standing her ground and bucking the system, and I was undoing all her good work by agreeing to play by the rules. That made me a traitor.

Fiona seemed to pick up on my angst, and the root of it. "Just to be clear," she stressed. "I sincerely adore my daughter-in-law."

"I do too," I whispered.

She walked to the dresser, picked up a frame and studied it. "I couldn't have wished for a better mother for my granddaughter," she continued. "And I know how much she loves my son."

It wasn't a confession I expected to hear. It made me wonder if she'd ever shared the sentiment with the girl in question. She held out the frame.

The photo of Adam, Charli and a tiny Bridget made me smile. Charli had shorter hair. Adam had messy hair and baby Bridget had no hair.

"I just wish she was more mindful of the fact that her family extends further than the three of them," she continued.

"I'm sure she knows," I said weakly.

"When Charli opted out of this life the first time, she stole my son and granddaughter away too," she said. Dread washed over me as I waited for her to speak again. I should've known she couldn't shower praise on Charli without it being conditional. "I won't tolerate losing Ryan the same way," she warned. "You need to be very sure this is what you want. If you marry him, your life is here."

The queen was laying down the law and I had no skill when it came to handling her.

"I love Ryan," I promised. "I'm not going anywhere."

She smiled at me, brightly enough to make me think she wasn't about to claw me again. "Wonderful. That's all I needed to hear." She walked to a chest of drawers near the window and took out a familiar small orange box. I used the time it took her to walk back to plan my look of surprise.

"I was in Hermès yesterday." She handed me the box. "I saw this and immediately thought of you."

I pulled off the brown ribbon and held the scarf out in front of me. I wondered why it made her think of me. Then I wondered how Ryan would work a seventh scarf into his designer outfit. I killed the thought when I felt my cheeks prick with heat.

"It's lovely," I replied. "Thank you."

She drew me into a hug. "All manner of lovely things await you, Bente," she whispered, sounding far more threatening than she'd probably planned. "Starting with the wedding."

55. MEANINGFUL SMILES

Ryan

I had no idea what was behind Charli's black mood. As soon as Mom and Bente were out of sight, I asked.

"I. Am. Fine."

I pulled a face. "O-kay."

She cracked a tiny smile. "I just have a few things on my plate at the moment," she explained. "Nothing to worry about."

"How's work?"

"Busy. I need more hours in the day."

"For making babies?" I hinted.

She widened her eyes and her mouth fell open. No words followed so I spoke again. "Adam told me."

She shook her head, looking more pissed than before. "You know something, Ryan?"

I grinned slyly. "No; tell me something, Charlotte."

"If I were you, I'd be less concerned about our business and more concerned by the fact that the queen is upstairs interrogating your fiancée."

"She brought her a gift." I shrugged. "That's all."

"That's never all," she taunted. "I'll be surprised if you still have a fiancée when she comes back down."

I looked up the stairs. "Do you think I should go up there?" I asked, sounding more worried than I was comfortable with.

259

Charli didn't answer. She was already walking away, cackling like a demon.

***

Announcing our engagement to my family was unnecessary. It turned out to be the worst kept secret in the room because everyone except Bridget already knew.

Marriage was a concept that my little niece didn't quite grasp. Her questions flew thick and fast across the dining room table. "So we can't go to the park any more?"

Her father answered for me. "Not unless his wife lets him."

Two things stopped me from stabbing Adam with my cutlery. First, the boardroom-sized dining table meant he was too far away. Second, my mother would've throttled me.

"Nothing changes, Bridge," Bente assured her. "You can go to the park whenever you want."

An odd look flashed across Adam's face. It took me a moment to work out that it was probably jealousy. I had the sneaking suspicion that I'd been spending more time with his kid than he had of late.

Charli cottoned on too. She moved quickly to change the subject. "Do you have a ring yet?" she asked, darting her eyes between the two of us.

"It's being resized," replied Bente.

I'd picked the ring up from Mr Shultz earlier that day. News of the engagement might not have been a surprise, but the presence of the ring was. I took the box, flipped the lid and angled it toward Bente.

The list of things I knew about women was growing daily. Bente burst into tears, but because I'm well versed in craziness I knew it was because she was happy. My mother cried too, but her tears quickly turned into unadulterated wailing. "It's lovely," she sobbed, craning her neck to peer into the small box. "I'm so proud of you, Ryan."

I took the ring out and slipped it on Bente's finger. "Perfect," I told her, leaning to kiss her.

Mom grabbed Bente's hand, twisting it in every direction so the diamond twinkled as it caught the light. "Look, Jean-Luc," she ordered. "Isn't it lovely?"

Dad didn't look like he cared either way. He downed a mouthful of wine before replying. "Exquisite."

Charli rolled her eyes at me from across the table, annoyed by his indifference. "Congrats, guys," she said quietly. "I hope you have a wonderful life together."

Adam charged his glass and winked at Bente as he wished her luck. He then held his glass in my direction. "To meaningful smiles."

I'm not a sentimental man, but his words got to me. My reply came out in a croak as I swallowed the lump in my throat. "Thank you."

Bridget held up her tumbler of juice, somehow managing not to spill it as she thrust it forward. "Let Ry come to the park every day, Bente." Clearly, making toasts was another concept Bridget didn't quite grasp.

Bente played along and clinked her glass against hers. "Monday, Thursday, and all days in between."

56. FIFTY-EIGHT FACETS

Bente

Fiona Décarie must've been planning her eldest son's wedding in her head for years. Before we'd even made it through the main course she'd overloaded me with a hundred suggestions for the big day. "We need to book a venue straight away," she demanded. "Good places are booked out many months in advance."

"They're not suitable for us, then," replied Ryan. "We're getting married October twenty-fifth."

He might as well have told her we were eloping. "That's not enough time to plan properly!"

Ryan was unmoved. "It will have to do," he said. "We don't want anything over-the-top anyway."

"You'll need time to get your affairs in order, Ryan." Jean-Luc had barely said a word since we'd sat at the table. The sound of his voice was almost startling and his words were downright terrifying. He made it sound like Ryan was dying.

I wasn't sure what he meant, but Charli and Adam did. The way he slipped his arm behind her and rubbed her back seemed designed to comfort her.

"I'll work it out," replied Ryan.

"I can do it for you," offered Jean-Luc.

"I've got it, Dad," snapped Ryan.

I stared at Charli, silently pleading for the explanation I knew she couldn't give me. Perhaps picking up on my discomfort, she changed the subject. "Why did you choose a solitaire diamond?" she asked.

Ryan glanced at me. "Because it's sleek and simple and gorgeous," he replied.

She nodded. "It denotes unity and decisiveness," she told him. "It's important."

Ryan leaned back. The cocky stance was a tell-tale sign that he was about to take her to task. "So I pledged unity and Adam gave you a finger-load of little diamonds. What does that mean, Charlotte?" He didn't give her a chance to answer. "You got indecision and separation?"

She shook her head, but she smiled, which was a good sign. "Adam didn't give me diamonds."

Ryan laughed derisively. "I knew it," he said looking straight at his brother. "You gave her CZ's."

Adam dropped his head, chuckling down at the table.

"I like BC's," announced Bridget, waving her fork like a wand.

"They're not CZ's," corrected Adam, glaring Ryan. "They're stars."

"Absolute nonsense," barked Jean-Luc.

Everyone ignored him, except Fiona who swatted her napkin at him.

"The number of diamonds isn't the most important detail," continued Charli. "It's the shape. Round diamonds have fifty-eight facets for a reason." I looked at the ring on my hand, trying to figure out where she was headed and how the heck she could be sure it had fifty-eight facets. I was grateful when she elaborated. "Years and years ago there were two young lovers from India called Mahir and Nayana," she began. Jean-Luc groaned but Charli continued without paying him a skerrick of attention. "They shared absolute true love – the kind of love that makes your heart hurt even when things are good."

Ryan reached for my hand under the table. He was silently talking again and I loved it.

"The problem was, Mahir's father was a tyrant." She actually dared to glance at her father-in-law as she said it. He pretended not to notice but it was obvious that he had. Tension was practically steaming off him. "He owned a diamond mine, the biggest in the world. It was deep underground and the conditions were terrible."

"Were there lots of diamonds under there, Mummy?" Bridget asked, leaning across her dad to see her.

Charli leaned too, sandwiching Adam in the middle. "So many, Bridge," she confirmed. "Thousands of them."

Bridget smiled. She was no more awed than I was, but the difference was she was permitted to show it. I got the impression I was supposed to find the tale implausible and crazy.

"Mahir's father decided to separate the young lovers by sending his son underground to mine for him, but it didn't go so well," continued Charli.

"It never does," murmured Ryan, fidgeting with the edge of his napkin.

"Before he left, Mahir gifted Nayana the one thing that was in abundance, a big diamond. It wasn't pretty and sparkly like the diamonds we know. It was rough and uncut. Mahir told her that no matter what happened, the diamond would keep them together."

"Cute story, Charli," mocked Ryan. "Nothing to do with the shape of Bente's ring, but ten points for effort."

"You didn't let her finish," scolded Fiona. She looked at Charli, softening her expression. "Continue your tale, darling."

Charli flashed her mother-in-law a tiny smile. "Mahir told Nayana that nothing could separate them. Not the earth, or his awful father, or even death. They were destined to be together and he was convinced that the diamond would play a part."

"So what happened?" asked Ryan. "Get to the point."

"Hear, hear," grumbled Jean-Luc.

"Mahir got caught in an underground rock fall," she said. "He died, leaving Nayana on the surface mourning him."

"Awesome," said Ryan. "Another heart warming Tinker Bell tale."

Adam swept his hand under the fall of Charli's hair and rested his hand on the back of her neck. "Special, aren't they?" he teased, wiggling his eyebrows.

Ryan laughed. "Your wife is special, and not always in a good way."

"Ryan!" admonished Fiona. "Apologise."

"One day, Ma," he replied, smirking at Charli. "But not today."

Charli didn't seem to be taking offense. She was probably used to it. "I could leave it at that and say no more," she threatened.

"Please do," replied Jean-Luc.

Her shoulders straightened up. "Fine, but when you're awake at four in the morning because you're still wondering about it, don't call me."

Jean-Luc didn't seem bothered, but Ryan seemed to think it through, almost as if he'd been in that predicament before. "Continue," he ordered. "Just get to the point."

Her smile was understandable. She was winning, and she knew it. "Well, the heart-hurting love she'd felt for Mahir turned into the angry kind of love that comes with the frustration of separation. Mahir's father told her she deserved to be alone. He'd never thought she was good enough for his son. Nayana was so angry that she grabbed her diamond and took off to the edge of the river."

"Was she sad?" asked Bridget. "Did she go swimming to get happy?"

"No, she was mad, Bridge." Charli shook her head. "She grabbed the biggest stick she could find and began whacking the big diamond as hard as she could."

The little girl piped up again. "Why was she mad?"

"Because she thought Mahir had lied to her. He'd told her that the diamond would always keep them together, no matter what. But he was gone and she was alone."

"So what happened?" asked Fiona.

"She hit the diamond over and over again, each time chipping away at the stone," Charli explained.

Jean-Luc let out a condescending laugh. "The woman must have possessed superhuman strength to damage a diamond."

Charli continued as if he hadn't spoken. "It wasn't until she hit the stone for the fifty-eighth time that something extraordinary happened. The splinter that chipped off speared straight through her heart, killing her instantly."

"Oh, my God, Charli." Ryan, was appalled. "That's a woeful story."

"No," she insisted, rolling her wineglass between her fingers. "Mahir had been right all along. They found each other again in death. The diamond kept them together, just as he promised."

"You're unbelievable," he told her.

She was unperturbed. "Maybe, but I can guarantee that every time your fiancée looks at her ring, she's going to be thinking about how the fifty-eight facets came to be."

Ryan glanced at me and I flashed him an awkward smile. She was right. And he knew it.

"I think your stories are romantic, Charli," said Fiona wistfully.

"It's a bad story," scolded Bridget. "Whacking is dangerous."

Jean-Luc motioned to his granddaughter but looked only at Charli. "This is what you teach your child?" He sounded truly appalled. "Terribly tragic, violent rot."

Adam answered for her. "Calm down, Dad."

Jean-Luc belted his hand on the edge of the table, making everyone jump. "It's ridiculous and strange."

Adam leaned over and spoke to Bridget. "Go get your boots, baby," he told her. "They're near the front door."

Bridget wasn't too young to know that any reason to escape the table was a good one. She jumped off the chair and took off running.

"Fairy-tales are all as true as you allow them to be, Jean-Luc," said Charli bravely.

He glowered. "This is really what you want Bridget to believe in?"

Charli replied without skipping a beat. "Yes. I want her to find the bone crushing, heart-hurting love too," she insisted. "It's all any of us can hope for."

"Nonsense!"

She frowned back at him, more out of pity than anger. "Maybe you've never felt it," she told him. "I have, and if Bridget —"

"I'm not listening to this any more," he barked.

"Don't cut her off," scolded Adam. "Don't ever do that."

Jean-Luc turned on his youngest son in a flash. "The minute your wife contributes something worth listening to, I will hear her out."

Adam grabbed Charli's hand and pulled her to her feet. "That's it," he declared. "We're done."

Bridget picked that moment to come rushing back, waving a boot in each hand. "Help me please, Daddy." Adam crouched and helped her pull them on.

"Stay," begged Fiona. "This is supposed to be Ryan and Bente's evening."

Adam straightened up. "It still is, Mom."

"Yes," assured Charli, screaming a silent apology at me with her eyes. "Congratulations again. I'm really happy for both of you."

"So am I," agreed Adam. "Just make sure you get that pre-nup wrapped up nice and tight, Ryan." He glanced at his father before continuing. "Bente will have a half a chance of being accepted into the fold if there's no danger of her ripping you off in the divorce." Fiona sucked in a gasp as if he'd just sworn. I was actually pleased he'd said it. It explained his father's comment from earlier. "And if you can make sure she keeps her opinions to herself, that'll score points too," he added.

"Sit down, Adam." Jean-Luc's tone was calm but menacing. "You're being ridiculous."

"No, we're leaving."

"Now?" asked Bridget.

Adam scooped her into his arms. "Yeah, are you ready?"

"Born ready."

"Bye Bridge," said Ryan. No matter how forced it might've been, he sounded cheery.

"Park tomorrow?" she asked.

"Of course."

"Maybe I'll go too," added Adam, already heading for the door. "I may or may not be at work tomorrow, Dad. Sometimes you just need the day."

Adam's attempt at defending Charli backfired a little at the end. After he stormed out with their daughter, she was left standing there.

"Thanks for dinner," she said quietly.

Fiona jumped to her feet and practically ran to her, hugging her tightly. "Of course, darling. Thank you for coming. Say goodnight to Bridget for me."

"I will," she promised.

"Make sure Adam is at work tomorrow, Charli," instructed Jean-Luc brusquely. "And let him know I don't appreciate his attitude."

That would've been the point that I either apologised on his behalf or burst into tears. Charli was much braver. "I'm not telling him anything," she replied. "I encourage bad behaviour from Adam. It doesn't happen very often these days."

57. LOOSE CANNON

Ryan

I had no right to complain about the craziness of Bente's family when mine were just as bad. I would've been content to put the disastrous dinner behind us and never speak of it again, but Bente had other ideas. Thanks to my brother's need to sink the boot into Dad with a heavy parting shot, the topic of a pre-nup was high on the agenda. To her credit, she held off mentioning it until we got home. I was in the bathroom brushing my teeth when she appeared in the doorway.

"Do you want me to sign a pre-nuptial agreement, Ryan?"

I rinsed my mouth, buying time to work out a tactful reply. It was impossible. Nothing kills the promise of enduring love quicker than the mention of a pre-nup.

"If things don't work out, you'll be taken care of," I replied diplomatically. "But things will work out because you're my pecan pie girl."

I switched the light off and kissed her on my way into the bedroom. Bente remained near the bathroom.

"Just so you know," she began, "it doesn't offend me. I'll sign whatever you want me to."

I turned back, trying to hide my relief. "I appreciate that. We'll get it signed and never speak of it again."

"Okay," she replied, ambling toward me. When she put her arms around my neck I was hopeful that the conversation was over. Then she spoke.

"Your brother and Charli don't have one, do they?"

The low groan from the back of my throat was impossible to hold back. "No," I replied. "They don't."

"It makes your dad nervous."

"Charli makes Dad nervous," I corrected. "She's a loose cannon."

"Do you believe her stories?"

"No, and if you tell me you do, I'm going to have to seek treatment for you."

"There might be some basis to them," she replied. "I did a bit of research while you were in the shower." I wasn't surprised in the least. "Diamonds were first recognised and mined in India. Mahir and Nayana were from India."

I rested my hands on her hips. "All that means is that her father paid attention in school."

She frowned, confused. "What do you mean?"

"All her crazy stories come from Alex," I explained. "Most people teach their kids to ride bikes and tie their shoes. He taught Charli how to surf and be crazy."

"I think it's kind of cool."

"So does Adam." I grinned. "He was so enchanted by it that he married her without a pre-nup."

"You know what else I found out?" she asked. "Round cut diamonds actually do have fifty-eight facets."

I shook my head, refusing to buy into the nonsense. "She's a smart girl, Bente. I never said she was silly. Charli is an amazing story-teller, but that's all there is to it."

My grip on her tightened as she pressed herself against me. "So you're not a believer?"

I dropped my head, kissing a long line down her neck. "I believe in many things," I murmured against her skin. "Just not idiocy."

270

58. RICH OR POOR

Bente

Weddings tend to take on a life of their own, especially when you have an overbearing sister and a soon-to-be mother-in-law with a desperate need to show off. Ivy turned up at our apartment with a truckload of supplies including Dora, her favourite dressmaker's dummy. "Help me bring her in," she instructed, battling to keep a grip on it.

I stuck my head out the door. Three bolts of fabric, her sewing machine and a couple of boxes of goodness knows what were stacked on the floor.

"How did you get all this up here by yourself?"

"I made a few trips." Ivy set Dora down in the corner. "Is here okay?"

Ryan entered from the hall, doing up his tie as he went. "Anywhere you like," he told her.

"Ry," I whispered, grabbing him as he passed. "Are you sure?"

His tie tying didn't falter as he leaned and kissed me. "Of course." Clearly he underestimated the work involved in making a wedding dress. Dora and all her accessories weren't going to be taking over the living room for a few hours. Ivy was a perfectionist when it comes to dressmaking. She was also messy. We'd be living with stray pins and material scraps for weeks.

"Are you superstitious?" I asked. "It's supposed to be bad luck to see the dress before the wedding."

Ryan shrugged on his jacket before taking my face in his hands. "I'm not superstitious, but if you are, move it to another room."

"I'm not superstitious either."

"No problem then." He kissed me again. "I'll see you tonight."

Ivy was shrewd. As soon as Ryan was gone, she dropped the diligent seamstress act and slowed her roll to check the place out.

"This is magnificent," she praised, prowling the room.

"See how tidy it is, Ivy?" For some reason, I spoke quietly as if we weren't alone. "You've got to work neatly, okay?"

She glowered at me. "What happens if I don't? What will he do?"

I shook my head, unsure of how to reply. She'd made it sound as if I'd be in for a lashing. "Ryan wouldn't do anything," I replied. "But he likes things neat. Just be respectful of his space."

Since moving in with him, I'd come to realise that I liked order too.

"He's spoiling you," she accused.

"I like being spoiled."

She pointed at my left hand. "I can see that."

The pretty diamond on my finger suddenly seemed massive. Ivy and I hadn't grown up with the privilege and wealth afforded to the Décaries. The life I'd stumbled into was a world away from anything we'd known.

"Be happy for me, Ivy," I begged in a hushed voice.

She took a few steps forward, grabbed my hand and studied my ring. "It's really beautiful," she praised, dropping my hand. "You're a real life princess now. You deserve it."

I lurched forward and hugged her tightly. "I love him, Ivy," I declared. "Rich or poor."

She took a step back, breaking my hold. Her grin was absolutely wicked. "But rich is better, right?"

***

Ivy didn't leave until it was time to collect the girls from school. We'd spent the entire day poring over magazines and drawing bridal stick figures.

No sooner had I gotten rid of her than Fiona showed up. The only good part about her impromptu visit was that she missed Ivy. Allowing those two to meet would require days of planning.

"No, no, no," she scolded, marching over to Dora the dummy. "Why would you have a dress made? We'll buy you one."

"My sister is making my gown for me," I explained. "She's very clever and it's important to her."

Fiona studied the makeshift paper template pinned to the mannequin. "You need it to be perfect, darling." She looked so full of pity that anyone would think I'd just run over her cat. "Are you sure about this?"

I was determined to stand my ground. "She's very talented."

Fiona eventually unlocked my eyes from her forceful stare and invited me to sit down – on my couch – in my home. "Have you thought about the guest list? The invitations have to go out as soon as possible. We need to start on the arrangements for the reception too. "

"Okay."

"You can have whatever you like," she declared, throwing her arms wide.

She didn't mean it. She already had it all worked out. My mind shut down just a few seconds in and her words became nothing more than a posh English drone. My lack of enthusiasm didn't seem to faze her. She didn't seem irate when I walked her to the door a few hours later. Her mind was elsewhere.

"I've much to do, darling." She waved her almost full notebook at me before dropping it into her purse. "It's going to be a wonderful day."

59. COMPLICATED RAMBLINGS

Ryan

I was beginning to have some serious doubts about our sanity by week four of operation wedding. Our apartment had become a working sweatshop. Every spare surface was covered with bits of dresses and sparkly junk. Like me, Bente seemed to have lost interest in the planning weeks ago, mainly thanks to Ivy and the queen's hostile takeover. The unlikely duo met for the first time over lunch and had been firm friends ever since. Ivy had grand ideas and my mother had a grand bank balance to accommodate them. "She's a little rough around the edges," commented my mother, "but her talent is extraordinary."

She'd gone as far as visiting Ivy's home to check out some of her creations. Whether she'd meant to or not, Ivy had garnered my mother's interest in the pageant scene. I was subjected to all the details over coffee at Billet-doux.

"Do you think Charli would allow Bridget to enter a pageant?" she asked hopefully.

I almost choked. "Charli wouldn't be the loudest opponent, Mom," I warned. "Adam would freak out if you gussied up his daughter like a two-dollar whore."

"Ryan!"

"It's true. You can't tell me you approve of that."

Her shoulders slumped as she thought it through. "No, of course not," she admitted. "But those dresses are a work of art."

***

I knew Bente was struggling with the out-of-control wedding plans, but wasn't expecting to be woken by the sound of sobbing coming from the bathroom at one in the morning. I rested my head against the door and called her name.

"I'm okay," she sniffed. "I'm sorry I woke you."

"Can you open the door, please?"

It took a long moment, but the door finally opened. I'd reached another unwelcomed milestone. I'd never had to comfort a woman before, probably because I was usually the one who reduced them to tears in the first place. Seeing Bente standing in front of me with tears streaming down her face made me feel terrible. I had no idea what to say. "We'll call it all off," I offered. "We'll go to Vegas."

Bente almost smiled. "No, it's nothing to do with the wedding."

Now I was stumped. I had no clue what was upsetting her, but was hopeful it had nothing to do with me. "Tell me," I urged.

"I'm hopeless, Ryan," she wailed, pushing past me. "A noose around your neck." She waved a piece of paper at me and I stepped forward to grab it. She explained before giving me a chance to read. "I've had twenty-six rejection letters in less than two months."

I read the letter in my hand, instantly realising the reason for her hysterics. As far as rejections go, it was particularly nasty:

An above average vocabulary does not make for interesting writing. While I appreciate your attempt at gaining employment in this field, I have no desire to read the complicated ramblings of an amateur.

"I'm sorry, sweetheart." I scrunched up the letter and threw it on the bed. "Some people are dicks."

"She could've just said no," she wailed, collapsing against my chest.

I stroked my hand through her hair. "Don't give up," I whispered. "You're an excellent writer."

"Twenty-six people beg to differ," she mumbled.

I knew she was frustrated because she hadn't secured work, but I had no idea she was at the point of midnight meltdowns. "Why didn't you tell me this was upsetting you so much?"

She sniffled. "I didn't want to burden you with drama."

"I want to know if you're unhappy," I told her. "We're a team now."

"Okay, I'm sorry."

I kissed her lips, tasting her tears. "Something will come up," I assured her.

"What if it doesn't?" she asked, sounding worried. "Then what will I do?"

I rested my forehead against hers. "Keep doing the things that make you special. Write and sing and love me."

60. LIGHT BULB MOMENTS

Bente

As usual, I felt better by morning. Late night tantrums were never a good idea, but the drama was definitely dulled by the concern of the cute boy I lived with.

I didn't have much time to dwell. I had a long shift ahead of me at Billet-doux. And thanks to my less than exemplary attendance record of late, Noelle was gunning for me.

"Nice of you to show up, Bente." She barely slowed her walk to squeak out the snarky comment.

"Where do you want me?" I asked, determined to play nicely.

Giving her attitude wouldn't have been fair. I was in the wrong.

Noelle snatched a piece of paper off the bar. "It's a large high tea today," she said, thrusting it at me. "Forty kids."

I nodded, pretending to study the menu. "No problem."

Noelle walked away without another word.

My plan was to lie low and do my job. As far as I was concerned, the longer Noelle went without talking to me, the better. Setting the tables as meticulously as I did was probably pointless. Fairies were messy creatures, and depending on the level of alcohol consumed, their mothers could be worse. The set up was complete an hour before service was due to begin. Trying to keep out of Noelle's way in an empty restaurant wasn't easy but I gave it my best shot, right up until Charli and Bridget walked through the door.

Bridget called out to me, gaining the instant attention of Noelle who stormed over and intercepted them.

"What are you doing here?" She was already ramped up, despite the fact Charli hadn't yet uttered a word to upset her. "We're busy today."

Charli darted her eyes in every direction. "You don't look busy."

"Ugh!" Noelle waved her hands around. "Just go."

"I'm going," growled Charli. She motioned to me with a nod. "But I'm taking Bente with me."

"Charli, I'm working," I protested.

"You can play with me," offered Bridget.

"Not today, Bridge."

Charli grabbed the little girl's hand. "Please Bente," she begged. "I have a meeting with an art dealer in an hour. Mrs Brown bailed, Adam's at work and Ryan's across town. I just need you to watch her for a few hours."

"I would but I can't. I just got here," I told her. "What about Fiona?"

"She has plans with Ivy today."

I bit my lip to stop myself asking what they were. I didn't want to know.

"Please," she begged. "It would really help me out."

It was too much to hope that Noelle hadn't seen the tiny nod I gave her in reply. She was furious. Her head bobbed from side to side as if she wasn't quite sure who to direct her anger at. Mercifully, she went for Charli.

"You can't just come in here and take staff whenever you want."

"I know and I'm sorry, but it's an emergency, Noelle."

My irate manager turned her wrath on me. "If you walk out that door, you're fired."

"Yes, yes," rushed Charli. "She'll be fired. And then Ryan will rehire her tomorrow."

As far as light bulb moments go, that was a big one. Working at Billet-doux wasn't working out for me any better than it was working for Noelle.

I used to be a great server. I also used to like doing it. Those days were long gone.

"Noelle, I'm sorry," I told her. "I think I should just quit."

I winced, bracing myself for a squeaky reprimand, but it didn't come. "Oh, thank God," she groaned, pressing her palms together as if she truly was thanking him. "You're of no use to me."

"No hard feelings?" I asked quietly.

"None if you leave straight away," she replied making Charli laugh. "I'll call someone in to cover your shift."

"Excellent," said Charli, already leading Bridget to the door. "Let's go."

Noelle called out to her. "Now all I need is for you to stay away too."

Charli replied without turning back. "I'll work on it."

***

I'd never spent any time alone with Bridget before, and even though I was happy to help Charli out of her bind, I was nervous.

"I'll only be a couple of hours," she promised. "I don't usually work Fridays but the bloke I'm meeting is from out of town."

"It's fine, Charli," I assured her. "We'll meet you back at your place later."

Charli stooped and kissed Bridget. "I love you so much. Be good please."

That was the only instruction she gave. Two seconds later, she turned on her heels and hailed a cab.

***

Predictably, Bridget wanted to spend the few hours we had together at the park. It was a place she never tired of, and spending time with her helped me understand why.

"You see how it's changing?" she asked, pointing at the yellowing elms lining the path. "Soon the leaves will all be gone."

I looked at our surroundings, studying them as intently as she did. Fall was setting in and the big green canopy that the trees provided in summer was slowly morphing into earthy shades of orange and brown.

"The colours are lovely," I told her.

"You know how they get the colour?" she asked.

I shook my head. I was sure her explanation was going to be far more interesting than anything I could come up with.

"The sprites do it," she said. "They fly around painting yellow and orange and brown."

"Why?"

"To play tricks on squirrels." She screwed up her pretty face. "They don't like squirrels. I don't either. They growl at me."

I looked up at the trees overhead so she wouldn't see my smile. "I've never seen a sprite."

"Me neither," Bridget confessed. "They come at night time."

We took a detour and sat on the next bench we came upon. "What do sprites look like?" I asked.

"I don't know. I can't see any." Her head flicked so wildly from side to side that her blonde hair lashed her face. "They must have wings because they can fly."

"I see," I replied. "What else do you know about them?"

Bridget frowned at me. "You ask me lots of questions, Bente."

Her tone made me giggle. "I do. That's my job, really."

At least, it should've been.

"Oh. Is it a good job?"

"Yeah." I leaned back on the seat and settled my hands in the pockets of my coat. "It's nice work if you can get it."

My answers weren't really cutting it for her. She spent the next few minutes questioning me, trying to grasp the job description of a writer.

She took my explanation a little too literally. By the end of her Q and A session, she was of the opinion that newspaper journalists handwrite the newspapers each day. Her questions were becoming too left of centre to answer honestly. When she asked if my hand ever got tired of writing or if my pen ever stopped working, I told her yes.

"How many papers did you write today?"

I shook my head, feeling entirely too sorry for myself. "None. I'm not working for a newspaper at the moment. I wish I was, though."

Bridget put her tiny hand on my knee. "Keep your wishes and it might happen," she said sagely.

Saving wishes hadn't been part of my childhood, which was a shame. I might have had a few to spend by now if it was.

"How many wishes do you have saved up, Bridge?" I asked curiously.

"A thousand and sixty twelve."

"Awesome." I chuckled. "That's a nice stash."

She grasped the silver locket around her neck. "I keep them in here. My grandpa gave me this," she explained. "Not Papy, the Rex one."

I leaned in, pretending to notice it for the first time. I'd never seen her without it, but until then I'd been unaware that she kept wishes in it. "It's very pretty," I told her.

"Yes, I know."

We were quiet for a minute. I wasn't sure what was holding Bridget's attention but I was content to sit and let life drift by for a while. I knew we weren't going to be able to stay much longer. The dark sky was threatening rain, and the wind had picked up. When a strong gust whipped down The Mall sending dry leaves skittering past, I stood and reached for her hand. She shuffled along the seat out of my reach. "Not yet," she replied simply.

Things were about to get tricky. I had no authority where Bridget was concerned because she didn't allow it. She wasn't the least intimidated by me. I, on the other hand, was marginally scared of her.

"Now, Bridget." I tried to sound firm, but wasn't sure I'd pulled it off. "The weather is coming in. We need to get home before it rains."

Her unusual dark blue eyes shone as she looked up at me. "I can catch a wish for you in a minute, but you have to sit with me."

Common sense told me I should've dragged her out of the park kicking and screaming. Curiosity told me to sit back down.

Catching wishes is far more complex than I imagined. Judging by Bridget's refusal to give me the scoop on how it worked, it's also a highly secretive business.

"Shush Bente," she commanded. I was actually becoming slightly alarmed. She sat completely still, watching dry leaves barrelling past us. If I didn't know better, I'd say she was conjuring up the wind herself. "Just wait." I was relieved to hear her voice. It was the only proof I had that she was still a little girl and not a witch. "We have to wait for a leaf to land on you. If it does, that's a wish."

"That's all there is to it?" My voice was just as tiny as hers.

"Yes, just wait."

I did as I was told and was rewarded early. Just a minute or two later, the wind whipped a bunch of elm leaves into the air and a couple of strays landed on my sleeve.

"You got two!" beamed Bridget. "Good girl!"

I couldn't help laughing. "Now what?"

A big smile lit her face. When she was concentrating or pouty, she was her mother all over. Smiling Bridget was a carbon copy of her dad. "You have to put them in your hair," she told me. "Near your ears."

I was in too deep to back down, even at the risk of looking stupid. "Like this?" I asked, tucking them behind my ears.

"Yeah, just like that," she approved.

"Can I make a wish now?"

"Not yet." Bridget climbed off the bench and scraped up a pinch of dirt off the ground. I might've stopped her if I'd realised what she was doing; it was damp and muddy and I had nothing to clean her with. "You have to paint it on your head, right here." She rubbed her forehead with her clean hand. "Then you make your wish."

I realised I didn't have much to lose. I was already sitting on a park bench wearing leaves behind my ears. "Fine." I edged forward. "Just do it."

She reached out, but stopped. "What's your wish?"

"I haven't made it yet."

"Tell me and I'll make it for you," she offered.

I didn't even need to think about it. A few months earlier I might've considered wishing for true love. I wasn't in the market for love any more. There was only one thing my heart desired.

"I just want a job, Bridge." I sounded pathetic but she took no pity on me. Her little fingers ground the pinch of mud into my forehead while she repeated my wish out loud.

"There," she announced, brushing her hands. "All done."

I went to wipe the muck off my face but a firm little hand grabbed my wrist. "You have to leave it on."

"How long?"

Anything longer than five minutes, I'm out.

"You can wash it off when we get home. The wish will be done then."

I'd come this far so I might as well see it through. If I was stopped by the relevant authorities and committed on the way home, I was sure they'd call her parents.

***

Charli was home when we arrived at the apartment. Bridget leapt into her arms at the door and was showered with a ton of kisses. "I missed you today," crooned Charli. "What have you been up to?"

"We found Bente some wishes," she replied.

Charli looked at me for the first time. Her confused expression troubled me. If anyone should be accepting of a woman with leaves in her hair and mud on her face in the name of wishes, it was her.

"What happened to you?" she demanded.

I looked at my little charge as if that explained everything. Charli looked confused but cottoned on that it was to do with her daughter. "Bridge, go and hang your coat in your room, please," she instructed.

The little girl took off down the hall, dragging her coat behind her. As soon as she was gone, I demanded to know the process of wishing on autumn leaves.

"You can wish on fallen leaves," she confirmed, still staring wide-eyed.

"Okay," I replied. "Job well done then, right?"

She nodded and shrugged, which was a gesture as clear as the mud on my face. "If a leaf lands on you, you're entitled to a wish," she explained.

I waved my hand, prompting her to elaborate. "And?"

She shrugged again. "And nothing, Bente. That's it."

"No, no, no," I whispered forcefully. "What about the wearing it behind your ear and rubbing mud on your head to make the wish come true part?"

"I have no idea what you're talking about."

I'd been duped. I swept my hand through my hair, flicking the leaves to the floor. "Your kid belongs on the stage, Charlotte," I informed her.

She didn't dare laugh until I did, and then there was no stopping her. "I'm so sorry." She didn't sound sorry. She barely got the words out because she was laughing so hard.

"Don't worry about it."

I wasn't mad. I was kind of impressed, but it didn't seem appropriate to admit it. Bridget Décarie was a perfect mix of brilliance, wickedness and charm. It was a combination that made me want to kiss her and whack her in equal measure.

61. OLD TIMES

Ryan

Finalising our partnership with Tiger Malone was a welcome distraction from the wedding planning from hell. Adam and I weren't keen on taking Tiger up on his offer of celebrating. He had money in his pocket now, which meant his whiskey would be cleaner and his stories would be dirtier.

We kept it professional and arranged to meet at the club to discuss the upcoming renovations with him. Adam bounded up the steps. "I can't stay long," he said, handing me the latest round of blueprints he'd had drawn up.

"It's after five." I double-checked the time. "You're not seriously going back to the office?"

"No," he replied. "Bridget starts a new dance class tonight. I promised I'd be there."

The mention of dance classes reminded me of an earlier conversation with the squealers. "Ivy said she'd quit."

"Yeah, that class didn't work out." Adam grimaced. "Charlotte enrolled her in a different one."

I didn't ask why because I didn't care. Bridget had Animal issues. Attending the same dance class as Malibu was begging for trouble.

"We'll give Tiger ten more minutes," I said, checking my watch again. "He was supposed to be here."

The club took on a new feel when the crusty old owner was absent. I'd never admit it, but it was almost as if something was missing. Adam took an opposite view. It was hard to get anything done while Tiger was around. He appreciated being able to walk around and explore without the distraction of cigar smoke and dirty stories.

Exploring didn't last long. Tiger shuffled through the front doors a few minutes later with Earl in tow. "Am I late?" he asked, looking surprised.

"No, you're fine, Tiger." Adam made his way to the door. "But I've got to go. Ryan can bring you up to speed. The builders start next week."

"Stay a while." The old man held up a bottle of whiskey in a bid to tempt him. "We'll celebrate."

Adam shook his head. "I can't, Tiger. I've got a date with my little girl."

"I respect that," he replied, throwing a wily grin my way. "I'd leave too if I had somewhere better to be."

***

It didn't take long to work out that Tiger Malone wasn't the least bit interested in hearing details of the renovations. Earl was even less interested. He sat on the dusty old chair near the stairs and promptly fell asleep. The lack of enthusiasm annoyed me but I forged ahead, explaining how the tin ceiling in the main room needed to be sandblasted. "It'll be messy, so you'll have to stay out of there until it's done," I instructed.

I wasn't sure that he heard me. He was too busy prodding Earl with his walking stick. "Wake up," he ordered. "We've got whiskey to drink."

Staying here when I could've been at home with Bente was nonsensical. I was done. "Well, gentlemen," I announced, "I'm out of here." I gathered the plans and headed for the door. Tiger called out to me, just as I knew he would.

"See that hole in the wall?" He pointed to the left of the door. "Do you think that'll get fixed?"

"Of course," I replied. "Everything will be fixed."

"It was a poker game gone bad." He pointed at the wall again. "Harry Taylor was a dirty cheat." I looked at the damaged wall, now realising it was a head-sized hole. "He was caught marking the cards," explained Tiger. "We asked him to leave."

"Head first," added Earl, suddenly wide awake.

Both men dissolved into rumbly chuckles. "What year was that, Earl?" Tiger asked, barely composing himself enough to speak.

Earl didn't even need to think. "'73."

Tiger turned to me. "We haven't seen him since."

I refused to put too much thought into it. If I allowed my mind to wander too far, I would start wondering if *anyone* had seen Harry Taylor since 1973.

"We'll fix it up," I muttered.

"All the stories will disappear, kid," called Tiger.

I dropped my grip on the door handle and turned back. "Are you worried about that?"

The old man's posture crumpled. "My mind isn't so good any more," he replied. "If I didn't have the hole in the wall to remind me, I might forget the story."

It wasn't just Harry Taylor's head hole that reminded Tiger of old times. Every dirty glass, poker chip and feather boa was a visual reminder for him. Perhaps that's why he'd fought for so long to hang on to them.

"Leave it with me, okay?" I asked.

He nodded stiffly. "You got it, kid."

62. BUCKET FULL OF HOPE

Bente

It had been a good few weeks since Ryan had been an inconsiderate jerk, but I was still shocked when he called to tell me he'd be late home after his meeting at the club. "Something's come up," he said vaguely. "I shouldn't be late." He could've arrived at dawn and I wouldn't have minded. For the first time ever, he'd thought to call me. I didn't have to wait until dawn. Ryan arrived home just before eight.

Walking into the apartment after a long day didn't bring either of us much joy these days. The place looked like a bomb had hit. Ivy's dressmaking clutter had multiplied over the past week. She'd temporarily abandoned my dress and moved onto creating the bridesmaid's dresses. There were now three little dummies keeping Dora company in the living room.

Ryan had been a trooper, never once complaining, but it wasn't hard to tell it grated on him. He never usually paid the dummies any attention, but tonight they caught his eye. He walked over to get a better look.

My only input had been choosing the colour. The idea in my head was much simpler than the actual works in progress. Pretty, simple, age-appropriate burgundy dresses were what I wanted. Ivy stuck to my vision for as long as it took her to sew them. Then the glue gun came out.

"Do you like them?" asked Ryan. I chewed my lip while I deliberated. "You don't," he concluded. "I can tell."

"I'm trying to pick my battles, Ry." I tweaked one of the dresses. "They're just dresses."

It wasn't just Ivy I had to contend with. After seeing Ivy's pageant room, Fiona had developed a penchant for glitter. She thought the creations were beautiful, and they were. They just weren't what I wanted for my wedding.

Ryan picked up the hem of Fabergé's dress, feeling the weight of it. "The dresses are heavier than the girls."

I pulled him away. "Forget the dresses," I ordered. "Tell me where you've been."

I forced him onto the couch and flopped down beside him. He looked worried. "I called you, Bente. Are you still mad at me?"

"No," I assured, amused by the terror I'd incited. "I'm just trying to shift the topic away from the wedding."

Ryan relaxed and loosened his tie. I went a step further and dragged it off his neck. "I caught up with an old friend of mine," he explained. "I wanted to run an idea past him."

"Anything you'd like to share?" I twisted the top button of his shirt undone.

"I saw Tiger today," he began. "The man has fifty years of memories invested in a place that we're preparing to tear up."

His tone led me to think he was having second thoughts. I tried to reassure him that the renovations would only improve the place. "He'll love seeing it look so amazing again."

"He's worried that he'll forget how it used to be," he said pensively. "But I might have solved that problem. I thought maybe you could spend a bit of time with him. Just listen to him and write his story. One of these days, Tiger will be gone and the history of the place will go with him."

I felt the sudden urge to kiss him to within an inch of his life, but I needed him alive so I kept it short and sweet with a quick peck on the lips. Ryan had other ideas. He pushed me back into the cushion, covering my body with his. "Don't start what you're not prepared to finish, Miss Denison," he murmured.

It was a blissful position I could've held all night, with a few minor adjustments, but I wasn't quite done with the conversation. I held his face in my hands, keeping him at bay while I questioned him. "Do you want me to write a book for him?"

"Not exactly." The corner of his mouth lifted forming a handsome crooked smile. "I contacted a guy I know. He's an editor at The Manhattan Tribune."

I wasn't feeling amorous any more. He'd just doused me with a bucket full of hope. I was back to being ambitious and desperate for employment. I wriggled beneath him, trying to force him to sitting position. Thankfully, he helped me out and moved. "You know someone at The Tribune?"

"Yeah," he confirmed.

"How?"

"We went to school together," he replied casually. "We were ballroom dancing partners." He winked at me, making me smile. "I asked him if he'd consider pulling a few strings and running a story on the club as the renovations progress – sort of a riches-to-rags-to-riches story. Tiger would get a kick out of it, and the publicity would be good for us."

"It would be huge," I agreed.

"I also asked him if he'd be interested in letting a gorgeous up-and-coming young journalist write the article."

"Me?" I asked with wide eyes and a tiny voice.

"No sweetheart, some other gorgeous journalist I know."

"And he said yes?"

Ryan nodded. "If it's good, he'll run it. That's the best he could promise."

Unable to contain my excitement, I threw my arms around him and forced him back into the cushions "All I want is a chance," I choked. "I won't let you down."

"You've never let me down."

"I wished for this, Ry."

"No, you worked for this," he corrected. "Don't downplay it."

"No, you don't understand. I actually did wish for it. I spent the afternoon with Bridget."

Ryan wasn't interested in hearing how his niece had caught an autumn wish for me until I got to the part about wearing a mud mask and leafy ears. He laughed so hard his body trembled. I had to grip a handful of shirt to steady myself. "She's so crooked," he told me. "She got you good."

"I don't even care," I replied. "It worked. My wish came true."

He put his hand behind my head, pulling my face to his. "A good day all round then."

"Exceptional," I agreed, kissing him. "Oh – and I quit Billet-doux."

If Ryan was curious as to why, it didn't show. He'd lost interest in chatting. We hardly said another word for the rest of the night.

63. HARSH REALITY

Ryan

The next few days were extremely busy, which suited me fine. Anything that kept me out of the wedding loop was welcome. It wasn't as if I was being excluded – my mother tried hard to keep me up to date on the decisions via daily phone calls. The subject today was wedding cakes.

"You must have an opinion, Ryan," she complained, annoyed by my indifference. "Traditional fruit cake or a more modern sponge?"

I chose fruitcake, possibly because I knew a few.

"Wonderful, darling! That was Bente's choice too."

I doubt she got there on her own, but questioning Mom would've taken time, and I was done discussing cake. I had a mountain of work and an antsy four-year-old to occupy.

I knew we weren't going to make it to the park before I'd even picked Bridget up, but held off telling her until we got to my apartment.

"Why do we have to stay in today?" she asked, trudging through the front door. "It's not too cold."

"I'm busy, Bridge. I've got heaps of work to do." I pointed to the mass of club-related documents on the kitchen counter.

"What am I going to do?"

"Well," I picked up the remote and pointed it at the TV, "you can watch your movie, or play with your girls."

"I don't want to, Ry."

I didn't often take a hard line where Bridget was concerned, but it probably wasn't going to kill her if I did.

"I don't really care, Bridget," I replied indifferently. "I'm busy today so you're just going to have to make do."

"But I don't want to." Her sad little voice was one of her most dangerous weapons. I instantly felt like a jerk.

Bridget didn't look at me when I scooped her up. Her focus was on twisting the top button of my shirt. "Please can we go to the park?"

I lowered her onto the couch. "Watch a movie or play quietly for a while," I instructed. "When I'm done, we'll go to the park."

Bridget wasn't pleased, but agreed. I switched on the redheaded mermaid and left her to it.

My niece's idea of playing quietly differed from mine. For once the movie wasn't holding her interest. I sat at the counter trying to ignore the squeals that accompanied her bouncing until I could take it no more. I looked up, preparing to growl. The instant I saw her, I realised she didn't need reprimanding. She needed an intervention. The four-year-old daredevil was standing on the back of the couch, gearing up to launch herself onto a pile of cushions she'd set up on the floor.

"Stop!" I yelled, leaping off the stool to grab her.

I caught her mid-flight. I couldn't be sure if I'd spoken too late or if she'd defied me. Either way I was livid.

Bridget Décarie was fearless, and it was dangerous. And on days like today, I couldn't handle it. I lowered her to the floor. "You're going to really hurt yourself. Stop this stupid jumping."

Her bottom lip quivered. I was so angry that I managed to ignore it.

"I was just flying," she whimpered.

I cleared a space and sat her on the kitchen counter. "Listen to me, Bridget," I began. "Birds fly. Aeroplanes fly. You don't fly."

"Butterflies fly."

"They do, but you're not a butterfly."

"Some fairy girls fly, Ry."

I couldn't stop the low groan that escaped me, nor did I try. "You need to stop this nonsense," I ordered. "Your mama is filling your head with silly stories that endanger your well-being."

She shook her head. She had no clue what I'd said. In a moment of pure frustration, I brutally broke it down for her. "None of it is real, Bridget. You're a flesh and blood girl – totally breakable."

"I might do it right one day."

"No little girl on earth can fly, no matter how many times she practises. If your mother was more honest with you, she'd tell you the same thing. Flying girls don't exist. Fairies are not real and magic doesn't happen."

I watched as my words speared through her. It started with a confused look and ended in a flood of tears.

I couldn't apologise for anything I'd said. The way I saw it, telling her the truth was the only hope I had of keeping her safe.

"No magic?" she whimpered.

"None." I imagine my expression of pity still had a tinge of anger to it. "There's no such thing."

Bridget threw out her little hands. "What do we have then, Ryan?"

She'd stumped me. I had no idea how to answer, and judging by the way she'd used my full name her question was deadly serious. "We have reality, Bridget." It was a miserable explanation to give a four-year-old, but it was truly the best I could come up with. "Try living in the real world."

***

I had a guilty heart, and the only way I could think to ease the wretchedness was to give in and take the kid to the park. Thankfully Bridget was a forgiving soul. She headed to the playground, squealing just as gleefully as she usually did at the sight of swings and slides. I hung back on the edge of the play area, keeping half an eye on her while I caught up on the emails that I should've been dealing with from home. "Watch me, Ry!" Bridget ordered.

I alternated glances between her and the screen on my phone. "I'm watching, sweetheart," I assured. "Don't climb any higher."

She was hanging off a climbing frame, upside down because that was Bridget's thing. Assuming she'd do as she was told was a mistake. The next time I looked across she'd climbed higher.

I trudged through the sand to rescue the kid who didn't need rescuing.

"How about you climb something a little less impressive," I suggested, peeling her off the frame. Bridget didn't argue. I lowered her to her feet and she took off to find her next conquest. I walked back to the edge of the sand and went back to checking my emails.

"Watch me, Ry!" ordered the very familiar little voice.

"I'm watching," I told her, barely casting a glance her way. The same conversation happened a few more times. I was too engrossed to notice that she'd hightailed it back to the climbing frame.

It wasn't her demanding little voice that alerted me. It was the horrible thud of something hitting the sand. My head whipped up, quickly realising the thud was Bridget.

Everything moved in slow motion after that. I barely touched the ground as I ran, but it seemed to take forever to reach her. I wasn't even first on the scene. By the time I came to a halt and dropped to my knees, a woman was already tending to her.

My tiny niece was out cold. I'd never seen anything more horrifying in all my life. "Oh Jesus!" I dug my hand between her and the sand, trying to lift her.

"You mustn't move her," ordered the woman, holding me back with a hand to my chest. "What's her name?"

"Bridget," I choked. "Please, please, please…"

The woman stroked her hair, calling her name as if she was trying to coax her out of an afternoon nap. It wasn't working. Nothing was happening and I was close to losing my mind.

Someone behind me announced that they'd called 911. The only other thing I could hear was the pounding of my heart as terror took over.

"*Allez, réveille-toi mon poussin,*" I whispered, holding her little hand. Willing her to wake up was a useless contribution, but I had no idea what else to do.

Seconds passed like minutes then Bridget let out a strained little cough and opened her eyes.

The woman tending to her smiled down. "Hello, little one. Welcome back."

I studied her face. "She's not back," I insisted, terrified all over again.

I'd been looking into those blue eyes long before Bridget was born. They were exactly the same shade of blue as her father's and grandmother's. They were dark, deep and clear. Bridget's were blank. She was also deathly quiet, and Bridget was never quiet.

"She might be having a seizure," suggested the woman, sounding worried.

I put my hand on Bridget's chest, but wasn't sure why. She let out a little cry and asked for her dad.

I breathed out, utterly relieved. "She's back."

Bridget's crying got louder as the minutes passed. I took it as a good sign, but I wanted her to stay put until the EMTs arrived so I gently held her in place on the sand.

By the time they finally got there, she was inconsolable. We both were, which is why I let the lady who hadn't left her side since the fall do all the talking.

"She was out for less than a minute," she reported.

Allowing her to be the spokesperson was a good move. In my mind, I'd been begging her to wake up for at least an hour, and probably would've told them so. "It took her a long while to come round once she opened her eyes," she added.

The two EMTs began talking between themselves as they checked Bridget over. The decision to take Bridget to hospital was made quickly. I wouldn't have settled for anything less, but it did nothing to dull my terror.

"Are you her father?" asked one of the men.

"Her uncle." *Her inattentive, incompetent uncle.*

"You're going to ride with her?" he asked.

There was no way they could've stopped me if they'd wanted to.

***

Bridget was whisked out of my sight as soon as we arrived at the hospital, but I could still hear her. She sounded as scared as I was, crying out for Charli and Adam. If she'd had a preference, it would've made my next move much easier. I had no idea which of her parents to call first. I stood in the corridor, trying to stay out of everyone's way while I decided.

Adam was less likely to freak out and kill me, so I called him. The conversation was quick. He didn't want details. All he wanted to know was which hospital his little girl was in.

"Will you call Charli or do you want me to?" I asked.

"I'll call her."

I'd transferred all my panic to her father. My panic had given way to guilt. I trudged back to the waiting area and slumped in the first empty chair I came across, burying my face in my hands. After a long moment, I glanced up at my surroundings, quickly deciding that Emergency Room waiting areas are close to hell on earth.

A miserable looking woman sat across from me. I dropped my head again purely to avoid her unnerving stare. A small child sat behind me, coughing right in my ear. That wasn't unnerving. It was just plain gross.

I don't know how much time passed before a nurse got my attention by putting her hand on my shoulder. "Mr Décarie?"

I straightened up. "Yes?"

She smiled kindly. Obviously she had no idea that I was the baby-sitter from hell. "Bridget is asking for you."

I shook my head. "No," I corrected, clearing my throat, "she's asking for her dad."

"You're Ryan?"

"Yes."

She nodded. "Then she's asking for you."

I followed her without question. Despite the fact that the only thing separating us from the rest of the busy emergency room was a curtain, things seemed a little calmer. One nurse remained with us, writing on a chart at the foot of the bed. Even Bridget had settled. Her wailing had dulled to a sad little whimper.

She reached out as soon as she saw me. She looked so little and so scared that I was afraid to touch her, but I took her hand.

"Have her parents been notified?" asked the nurse, glancing up.

"They're on their way."

Considering Adam was at his office when I called, I was amazed to see him arrive as quickly as he did. He threw back the curtain and half scooped Bridget into his arms, almost roughly.

I backed up to give him space. Adam didn't acknowledge me. I doubt he even saw me. As soon as he'd checked Bridget over, he set his sights on the clipboard-wielding nurse, firing off a quick round of questions without giving her time to answer.

"A doctor will be in shortly," she said perfectly calmly. "He'll explain everything."

Ambiguity and Adam are not friends. If I'd known that was her MO, I would've warned her against it.

"Get someone in here now," he demanded. "If you can't tell me what I need to know then get someone who can."

"Let her do her job, Adam," I muttered.

He twisted in the chair to face me, still holding his daughter. The nurse took the opportunity to slip out. "What the hell happened?"

Whatever I told him was only going to be summation. I was about to confess that I hadn't actually witnessed her fall when Bridget threw up – straight down the front of his shirt. She followed up with hysterical crying. Adam did his best to calm her, pretending that being covered in vomit didn't bother him. I ripped a handful of paper towel from the dispenser on the wall and handed it to him. Pathetically, it was the best I had to offer. I had no idea what to say or do.

"Thank you," he muttered, futilely dabbing the front of his shirt.

"I'm going to wait outside," I said weakly. "Is Charli on her way?"

Mentioning her name wasn't smart. Bridget's wailing now included calling for her mother.

"She's on her way, baby," Adam promised, before turning back to murmur a more truthful answer to me. "Her phone went to voicemail. I left her a message."

I nodded. "I'll keep trying her." I slipped back out to the waiting room and sat on the same chair I'd vacated earlier.

I had every intention of trying to call Charli but an incoming call sidetracked me. I stared at the phone before answering, watching Bente's name flash across the screen.

"Hey," I answered quietly.

"Hey. Where are you? I thought you'd be home by now."

"Are you at home?"

"Yeah, have been for a while," she replied. "I've just come from the club. I spent all afternoon with Tiger. We –"

"I'm at the hospital," I interrupted. "Bridget fell off the climbing thing at the park."

"Oh my God," she gasped. "Is she okay? Do you want me to come down there?"

I could think of nothing I wanted more, but it wouldn't have done any good. I had no place there. She'd just be another person in the way.

"No," I said quietly. "But I'd be really happy if you were there when I got home."

"Of course I'll be here, Ryan," Bente replied. "Always."

***

I never got as far as calling Charli. Just as I ended the call with Bente, she came rushing in, looking more damaged than Bridget. She was carrying her shoes in her hands, and limping thanks to a nasty scrape on her knee. She didn't see me but I caught her arm as she passed.

"Where is she?" she demanded.

"Adam's with her," I replied. "She's okay."

She stared blankly at me, seemingly processing the information, which was very odd because I really hadn't given her any. Her eyes welled with tears. "I fell off my shoes," she whimpered.

Charli was strange, but not usually this strange. "Do you want me to get someone to have a look at your knee?"

Charli looked down at her bloody knee. "No. Where's Bridget?"

"I'll take you to her," I replied.

The nurse at the triage desk buzzed us in and Charli's urgent pace kicked in again. I almost had to run to keep up with her. "Slow down, Charli," I pleaded. "You don't know where you're going."

She came to a grinding halt and spun back to face me. "Where were you, Ryan?" she hissed. "You were supposed to be watching her."

"I know. I'm so sorry."

She said a million words with just the expression on her distraught face. I said nothing. I pointed to the door that her child was behind. I didn't follow her. I stayed in the corridor, continuing the excruciating wait for news.

Eventually two orderlies wheeled a gurney into Bridget's ward. When they reappeared a minute later, my little niece was on it, still sobbing her heart out. They stopped midway down the hall while they studied the chart at the foot of the bed, ignoring the little girl's distress.

Bridget was a happy kid. I'd never heard her cry for longer than a few minutes, even when she was a baby. She'd been crying solidly for well over an hour now, and it was entirely my fault.

Adam and Charli walked out a few seconds later. He was talking softly, trying to reassure her. Charli nodded incessantly but I knew she wasn't hearing a word he was saying. Adam knew it too. He turned her to face him. "Do you want me to go with her?" he asked. "You can stay here and get someone to patch up your knee."

"No," she whimpered. "I want to go with her."

Adam kissed her, resting his forehead on hers. "I'll wait here for you. She's going to be fine, Charli. I promise you."

Charli didn't reply. She broke free and limped after the gurney.

Adam watched until they pushed through the double doors and disappeared. He might've stood there indefinitely if I hadn't spoken and snapped him back to the moment. "Where are they going?"

He turned to face me, looking weary and worried. "They're doing a CT scan, just as a precaution."

I slowly nodded. "I'm so freaking sorry." I punched out the words. "I only turned my back for a minute and – "

"Do you think we can get coffee here?" he asked, cutting me off. "I could really do with one right now."

***

I couldn't remember the last time I'd bought coffee from a vending machine. After one sip, I remembered why.

We ended up in the vile waiting room, side by side on a row of joined plastic chairs. I chose the far side of the room where we had some little privacy, but the miserable woman with the scary stare was still eying me from a distance – and the closest child to us was coughing.

Neither of us spoke. I spent minutes trying to come up with something reassuring to say, but failed. Adam spoke first. "I can't wait to get this shirt off," he muttered. "It's foul."

He was right. It was nasty. But it wasn't what I was worried about right now. "I should've been watching her. I didn't even see her fall."

"She didn't fall," he replied.

"Huh?"

"She didn't fall. She jumped. Bridget told me she jumped."

I shook my head. "One minute she –"

"She jumped, Ryan," he insisted. "She's been taking flying leaps off things for a long time. You've seen her do it." Adam glanced at me. "It just so happened that this one ended badly on your watch."

I stared straight ahead. "I'm sorry. It shouldn't have happened."

Adam huffed out a noise that almost sounded like a laugh. "Yeah, I'd be in a much happier place if she'd made the landing."

After my harsh lecture earlier that afternoon, her flying ambitions were supposed to have been permanently shelved. I knew Bridget well. I should've known that I hadn't curbed anything. I'd only made her determined to prove me wrong.

"She'll be okay," I told us. *Please let her be okay.*

"I know she will." He sounded absolutely truthful. "She has to be."

I had no idea why he was being so reasonable, but I was grateful. "I'm still sorry."

Adam dropped his coffee into the trashcan. "Me too," he replied. "I'm sorry I wasn't the one at the park with her and I'm sorry I didn't get here sooner."

"You were at work," I reasoned.

"I'm always at work," he said sourly. "I don't even know why anymore."

The conversation had shifted, and I had no idea where he was going with it. "I'm going to quit," he quietly announced. "Dad can find a new whipping boy and I can spend more time with my daughter. That's how it's supposed to be."

I glanced at him. "Because of today?"

"Partly. It was a wake-up call."

"Just take a bit of time off," I suggested. "You might want to go back to it later."

"No, I won't."

"How do you know?"

"Because I'm not a lawyer, Ryan." He stared at the floor. "I just pretend to be. I freaking hate the job. I hate everything about it."

"So you'll take on the work at the club?"

"Maybe. I'm looking forward to smashing stuff up. I don't want to oversee it. I want a more hands-on role. That's what I do best. I smash stuff up and then I make it new again. That's my bliss."

Fairy-speak was creeping in. It wasn't his fault. It was a side effect of being married to Tinker Bell – the same Tinker Bell who stupidly encouraged their daughter to practise flying.

"I used to spend every day hanging out with Bridget." It was a dizzying exchange. Adam's mind was so shot that he was drifting between two conversations. All I could do was try to keep up. "Now I'm gone all day and she's in bed when I get home at night. Who in their right mind would choose to do that? What's the point?"

I had no answer.

"Charlotte and Bridget are everything to me, Ryan." His voice cracked. "I don't know what I'd do if anything happened to them." He hung his head, resting his elbows on his knees.

I put my hand on the back of his neck. "She's going to be okay," I replied unconvincingly.

He said nothing.

64. SUPPORT

Bente

The afternoon dragged on. When Ryan finally walked through the door, I was beside myself with worry. He stood with his back against the door, staring at me but not speaking.

I kept my position on the couch, studying his dire expression. Unable to draw any positivity from it, asking after Bridget took effort.

"She's okay," he said quietly. "Concussed, but she's going to be alright. If she gets some rest tonight, they'll let her go home tomorrow."

I jumped up, rushed over and pulled him in as close as I could. His whole body was rigid and tense, so I held him tighter. He finally reciprocated by wrapping his arms around me and burying his head in my shoulder. "Are you okay?" He answered with a warm kiss to my neck.

"Please talk to me," I begged. He didn't talk. The strong, aloof Ryan Décarie just needed to be held.

He finally broke the embrace. "Today has been awful," he said, swiping both hands down his face.

"I know," I replied. "But everything's okay."

"She could've died, Bente." His jaw tensed as he swallowed hard. "I was supposed to be watching her."

My heart broke for him. I knew there was nothing I could say to make him feel better, but I could at least get him cleaned up. "Ry, you stink."

He choked out something between a sob and a laugh. "I know. Bridget puked on Adam." I frowned at his stained shirt. "We swapped shirts."

"You gave your brother the shirt off your back?" I joked.

Finally he smiled. "It was the least I could do considering I nearly killed his kid."

***

A long shower almost revived him. I'd showered earlier, but joined him anyway in a ruse to keep him talking.

Ryan was worried about more than Bridget's well being. He was anxious that he'd somehow damaged her by smashing Charli's fairy theories to pieces.

"You should've seen her little face, Bente," he muttered. "I broke her heart."

I rubbed his shoulders with soapy hands, trying to work the knots out of his stressed body. "You said she jumped," I reminded.

"So her dad says."

"Well, if that's true she's still a believer," I reasoned. "She obviously thought she was going to nail it."

"It wasn't my place to set her straight."

I stayed silent because I agreed, and he didn't need to hear it. I was fascinated by Bridget's take on the world. Unlike Ryan, I didn't find it odd. I thought of it as endearing and innocent – and a perfect mindset for a little girl.

"You should've seen the look on Charli's face," he continued. "I've never seen her so upset."

"Her baby is in the hospital, Ryan. Of course she's upset."

"I think she blames me," he mumbled. "I don't know how to cope with that."

***

Bridget was released from hospital the next morning. I declined Ryan's offer to visit her at home. He didn't question it, which led me to think I'd made the right decision.

"What am I going to say to her?" The desperate tone of voice was very unlike him. "I'm not sure what I should say."

Guilt is a terrible burden, especially when it's undeserved. "No one is going to blame you," I promised. "Tell her you hope she's feeling better and give her a big hug."

He nodded. "It's a start, right?"

65. CONFESSIONS

Ryan

Turning up empty-handed seemed awfully cheap. Under normal circumstances I would've taken flowers, but my sister-in-law had a problem with cut flowers and I wasn't prepared to rock the boat that day.

Adam met me at the door, looking worse than he had the day before. I soon realised why. Mom was busy in the poky little kitchen, and I could smell something bitter and burnt.

"Hey Ma."

She rushed over, shushing me. "The girls are asleep." She pointed at the couch. Bridget and Charli were tangled up together looking remarkably peaceful.

"Sorry," I whispered, looking back at Adam. "I just came to see how Bridge is."

Mom brought me up to speed. "She had a nasty fright but she's going to be fine. She just needs rest."

"Charli didn't sleep last night," added Adam. "They both just need sleep."

"And how are you?" I asked.

He ruffled his hand through his messy hair. "I didn't sleep much either."

"Would coffee help?"

Adam almost smiled. "Yeah, coffee sounds good."

Mom had no problem with holding the fort for a while. It gave her purpose in an otherwise hopeless situation. "Of course, darlings," she said softly. "I'll keep an eye on the girls. If they wake, I have cookies for them."

I hoped for their sakes they slept the rest of the day.

Adam kissed her cheek. "*Je suis bien content que tu sois ici, Maman,*" he murmured.

"Where else would I be?" she asked, straightening his collar.

***

Gabrielle's apartment was cramped at the best of times, but when there were more than two people in it, it felt like an overcrowded bus shelter on a rainy day. Getting out of there brought instant relief. We didn't walk far, opting to stop at the first café we came across. Clearly it was one of Adam's local haunts. The barista greeted him by name.

We sat at a small table near the window, mostly in silence. Adam was probably enjoying the quiet, but I found it awkward.

"Have you put any more thought into your job situation?" I asked, grasping for conversation.

"There is no situation," he replied. "I quit, effective immediately."

"You told him already?"

Adam grinned wryly. "Yeah, and you're back to being favourite son."

I shifted uncomfortably, unhappy that I'd regained pole position that way. "Was he mad?"

"You might say that," he replied indifferently. "I got the same lecture I always get. My wife is my downfall, I'm setting a terrible example for my child and I'll never amount to anything." He picked up a spoon and scraped the foam off his coffee.

"You know that's not true."

"I don't care. None of it matters. As long as Bridget is okay, everything is fine."

"I'm so sorry for what happened," I said for the millionth time.

Adam grimaced. "Ryan, unless you tell me you pushed her, I don't want to hear sorry from you again. It was an accident. Accidents happen."

I might as well have pushed her. I'd metaphorically given her a shove. It seemed like a good a time as any to confess. "She was jumping off the furniture at my place yesterday. We had words."

Adam obviously knew there was more to it. He stared me down from across the table, waiting for an explanation.

"I was angry and my mouth got the better of me."

"What did you say?"

I rehashed the whole sorry tale, ending with the most damaging part. "I told her there was no such thing as magic and that her mother's stories are a crock."

His cool expression morphed into a pissed-off frown. I wasn't surprised by the turn. "Why would you do that?" He sounded calm, but wasn't. "She's four years old, Ryan."

"And I want her to live to see five," I defended. "You can't have her jumping –"

"It's not even about the jumping," he interrupted. "Why didn't you go the whole hog and enlighten her about Santa and the Easter Bunny while you were at it?"

I shook my head. "I know I shouldn't have said anything. It was a mistake."

"It's not me you're going to have to convince. Charlotte is going to kill you," he warned. "And I'm not sure that I'll stop her."

I should've been eating my dose of humble pie and accepting that I'd done wrong but my mouth kicked in again. "Charli needs a reality check too. If she keeps filling Bridget's head with nonsense, she's going to make her crazy."

"That's not your call to make," he angrily replied, drumming his forefinger on the table. "Charli's not stupid, Ryan."

"I said crazy, not stupid," I clarified. "There's a difference."

Adam pushed his cup away. If I'd put him off coffee, things were really dire. "Look, Bridget has a lifetime of harsh reality ahead of her," he began. "I'm her dad. I want her to stay little forever, but eventually she's going to grow up and meet a jerk just like me." He grimaced at the sight of me. "Or worse, someone like you." I reined in my smile, acutely aware that it was an inappropriate reaction. "He's going to promise her everything and deliver nothing," he added. "He's going to break her heart over and over, and there will be nothing I can do about it. I want her to have a happy heart, Ryan. La La Land is where it's at for now."

Not any more. Even if Bridget did manage to hang on to her faith, I knew she had to at least be questioning it. "Do you think I should mention it to Charli?" I asked. "I will if you want me to."

Adam pulled his coffee back. "No. She has enough to deal with at the moment. Just wait and see what happens."

It wasn't the first time someone had alluded to Charli having a full plate. I wasn't in a position to demand an explanation, but I tried anyway. "Is there something going on that I should know about?"

His blank stare lasted for an uncomfortably long time. "No," he said eventually. "Everything is fine."

66. ONE DAY

Bente

When drama hits the Décarie family, it does so with the force of a freight train. Adam had quit his job, earning the wrath of his father. Escape was impossible, but lying low was Adam and Charli's plan. We hadn't seen them or Bridget in over a week.

Ryan didn't seem concerned by the fact that they'd fallen off the radar, but that was because he had avoidance issues. He knew Charli would be furious over his little misplaced heart-to-heart with Bridget, but in typical Ryan style he played it down.

"Adam wanted more time with Bridget and Charli," he explained. "He's unemployed and making the most of it, that's all."

I didn't press the issue. Fiona was doing enough of that for all of us. Jean-Luc was on the warpath and the queen was trying hard to keep her family together. "He won't take his father's calls," she confided. "It breaks my heart." I couldn't blame Adam and Charli for wanting to step off for a while. I'd been feeling like doing the same thing for weeks. I wished I were as brave as them.

"Just give them some time, Mom," urged Ryan. "They just want some time together. If one gets hurt, they all get hurt. They're a tight little family."

The queen was unimpressed. "We're all family," she said angrily. "Adam would do well to remember that. I miss Bridget terribly."

"So do I," admitted Ryan.

Hanging out with Bridget was good for Ryan. She slowed him down to a pace that I could keep up with. Without her, he slipped back into a manic schedule that he couldn't possibly enjoy. Long, lazy mornings in bed were now a distant memory. Lazy everythings were a distant memory. Work at the club was in full force, and he made a point of showing up every single day. I took heart in the fact that it would be temporary. When Adam was back on board, Ryan could take a step back.

I visited the club most days, but not to check out the renovations. Tiger Malone was proving to be a perfect distraction from the drama overtaking our lives. I'd spent many hours over the past week, scribbling until my hand ached, trying desperately to capture the wild and sometimes implausible stories he told me. Any nervousness I had about my ability to construct a print worthy article for the Tribune was long gone. Tiger Malone was a writer's dream.

***

Now that she was temporarily one son down and her granddaughter was off limits, Fiona threw herself into the wedding. The plans for our big day were spiralling further out of control with every passing day.

"It's not that bad, surely," reasoned Ryan.

"Ry, we're having a champagne fountain at the reception," I retorted. "It's madness."

"Wow." He screwed up his handsome face. "Tacky."

I agreed a hundred percent. Fiona had impeccable style, which led me to think the fountain was my sister's doing. But it wasn't worth questioning. If I kicked up about the fountain, there would be no stopping me.

I had a million wedding-related gripes, and I had no one to blame but myself. I'd given Ivy and Fiona free run weeks ago. My punishment for lack of enthusiasm was being forced to star in an over-the-top gala event that I had no interest in attending.

"It's only ten days away," I said, thinking out loud.

Ryan wrapped his arms around me and whispered in my ear. "And then we get our lives back."

I twisted to get a better look at the sewing area in the corner of the living room. The three small red bridesmaid dresses were all glitzed up and good to go. My dress was hidden under a sheet. It wasn't a tactic to hide it from Ryan – I was hiding it from myself.

Ivy had worked incredibly hard. Hundreds of hours had gone into hand sewing each bead and button. I didn't have the heart to tell her that it now looked nothing like my vision. I dreaded the thought of wearing it, and it took huge effort not to let my disappointment show every time she made me try it on. "I'm going to look like one of Tiger's cocktail waitresses, Ryan," I bleakly warned.

He kissed my neck. "You'll be beautiful," he mumbled. "Sparkly and beautiful."

Every time the subject of the wedding was raised, I wished Ryan would reconsider my suggestion to call it off, but he never did. "It's one day," he kept repeating. "It'll make our mothers happy and we'll be married."

I didn't even know what my mother's take on it would be. We hadn't spoken since I told her I was engaged. All I knew was that they were due to arrive in New York the day before the wedding, and were leaving the day after. I wondered why they were bothering at all, but like everything else, I didn't question it.

67. THIEF

Ryan

I missed Bridget more than I let on, and tortured myself by wondering if she missed me too. Adam had completely wiped Dad off, and rightly so. The king was hurt and disappointed, which seemed to be the only time he was capable of putting his feelings into words. Charli bore the brunt of it, and if there was one thing Adam wouldn't tolerate it was Tinker Bell bashing.

I wasn't part of the communication ban, but phone calls were so awkward that I gave up. I still didn't have a clear take on how Charli had taken the news that I'd burst Bridget's fae bubble, and was too cowardly to ask. Waiting for them to come to us was my plan, and it happened ten days after Bridget's fall.

Bridget was coming over for her final dress fitting. Ivy arrived early to add the finishing touches, but had the good sense to leave the squealers at home, acutely aware of my niece's dislike for Malibu. "Unless she's had a growth spurt it should be okay," said Ivy, brushing her hand down the dress.

"I wouldn't know," I mumbled. "I haven't seen her in a while."

Bente sidled up beside me. "She's probably going to be bouncing off the walls when she sees you," she said encouragingly. "I'm sure she's missed you."

It was a sweet notion, but not true. The little girl who turned up at my door wasn't bouncing at all. Thanks to me, her bounce was gone. I didn't even get one of her famous leg hugs. I got nothing but a tiny little hello.

And it killed me.

I got even less from her mother. Charli made a beeline for Ivy and Bente, completely ignoring me. Bente gave me a tiny smile that was probably designed to be supportive. I tried to smile back.

In just a few minutes, the dress was on and Bridget was glammed up like a little doll.

"Do you like it?" Ivy asked the little girl.

"A little bit," she replied, looking down. "I like diamonds."

"You've done a great job, Ivy," praised Charli, almost sounding believable.

Bridget turned to me. "Do you like it, Ry?" Her tiny voice had never sounded sweeter.

"I do," I replied smiling. "I think it's lovely."

"Can I take it off now?"

Charli helped her out of her dress and hung it back on the mannequin. The tension in the room was crippling. Even Ivy picked up on it. She made a few excuses to leave and practically bolted out the door. I'd never known her to move so quickly.

As soon as Bridget had her own clothes on, she wandered over to her toybox, presumably to check on her girls. "I haven't been playing with them," promised Bente, holding her hand to her heart. "I'm sure they missed you."

Bridget shrugged. "You can play with them if you want to, Bente."

"How about you stay and play with them for a while?" I suggested. I switched on the coffee machine. "I'll make your mama coffee and you can play."

The whole conversation was painful. It felt contrived and unnatural and pointless. Bente must've picked up on my hopelessness. She walked over, took Bridget by the hand and suggested they go for a walk. She looked at Charli. "We'll be back soon, okay?"

Charli replied with a stiff nod.

They took none of the tension with them when they slipped out the door. I was glad I was on the opposite side of the counter. It offered me the protection I was sure I was about to need. Charli looked as angry as I'd ever seen her.

"Are you mad at me?" I foolishly asked.

"You know I am," she replied, pulling out a stool.

"I wasn't trying to cause trouble, Charli," I muttered. "Honestly."

She didn't take her eyes off me as she sat down. "She's not yours, Ryan," she said simply.

"Pardon?"

"Bridget isn't yours."

I almost smiled. "Well that's good to know. You had me questioning the laws of nature for a second."

"I feel the need to remind you of that," she said seriously. "Maybe it will stop you trying to parent her."

Maintaining eye contact with her suddenly became impossible. I dropped my head and allowed her to continue verbally thrashing me. It was the least I could do.

"You stole something from me," she accused. "And for the life of me, I don't know how to get it back."

The only thing worse than dealing with Charli while she was angry was dealing with her when she was crazy. "Help me out, Charli," I said. "I don't know what you mean."

She pulled in a long breath, steadying herself before she explained. "Adam connected with Bridget straight away. As soon as she was born, he just knew what he was doing." She clicked her fingers. "It was as if he'd been waiting for her all along. It took me a lot longer to find my feet."

I couldn't link what she was telling me to the conversation at hand, but played along anyway. "You're a good mom, Charli."

"Some days I am," she retorted. "And some days I have no clue what I'm doing. You want to know why I think that is?"

I looked at her, which was all the encouragement she needed to continue.

"I had no mother, Ryan. How am I supposed to know what the hell I'm doing?"

"I don't know."

"My connection to Bridget isn't going to the park or speaking French or reading books," she added. "It's the stories that my dad gave me. That's how I connect with her, and that's how he connected with me."

I struggled to come up with a defence that wasn't going to get me killed. For some reason I still felt the need to get my point across. "She knocked herself out trying to fly, Charli," I reminded her. "You can't possibly think that's okay."

She put both hands flat on the counter, probably to stop herself lurching forward and ripping my throat out. "Perhaps if you hadn't stolen her wings she might've done it."

"Wings?" I asked incredulously. "You think I stole her wings?"

She could not possibly be serious. Now that she was spouting foolishness, I could feel my contrition slipping.

"We all lose them eventually, Ryan," she said quietly. "The moment you doubt whether you can fly, you cease forever to be able to do it."

I was in no position to be getting angry with her, but it was impossible not to. "Don't preach fairy nonsense to me," I demanded.

"It's from *Peter Pan*, idiot."

"That doesn't make it any more credible."

She shook her head and groaned. "You just don't get it. I'm not crazy. I know the difference between a fairy-tale and real life, but what if there's the tiniest ring of truth to it?"

I put serious thought into her question. I owed her that much. "Impossible," I finally concluded.

"Deny it all you want to, Ryan, but one day something extraordinary is going to happen and you're not going to be able to explain it away," she told me. "You won't think it's impossible then. You're going to think it's magic. I just hope I'm around to see it."

"If you're not, I'll be sure to call you."

In a move that looked like defeat, her posture crumpled. "Whatever, Ryan."

"Look, I'm sorry for what I told Bridget," I said sincerely. "I overstepped the mark and I shouldn't have. If you want me to talk to her about it, I'll do it. I'll do whatever you want me to to make things right."

Charli sadly shook her head. "Short of giving her her wings back, I don't know how you can."

"I'm not going to encourage the kid to fly," I shot back. "She's going to really hurt herself."

"Wings aren't literal, Ryan!" she shouted. "Of course she can't fly, but it hurts me to think she knows it so soon."

The position I'd put myself in was a bleak one. There was no way I could make it up to Bridget, or to Charli for that matter. "Is she mad at me?"

"No," she replied calmly.

"So why hasn't she been hanging out with me lately?"

"It's not personal," she muttered. "Adam's been home. Daddies trump uncles."

It was a perfectly sound reason and I accepted it immediately – but still felt a hole in my heart. "I'll make it up to her, Charli," I pledged. "I don't know how but I will."

She stared straight at me. "I believe you."

68. LOIS

Bente

Tiger Malone ran hot and cold, and when he was running cold, he was freezing. Some days he didn't cope well with the intrusion of workmen tearing up his beloved club. It made him petulant and grouchy.

"The damn noise is irritating," he complained, meeting me at the base of the stairs.

I waved my notebook at him. "Do you feel up to talking today, Mr Malone?"

"Upstairs," he said gruffly. "It's quiet up there."

It took forever to follow him up the stairs. If I'd given him a ten minute head start I still could've beaten him. I'd never been to the top floor before, and I knew Ryan and Adam hadn't either. It was a privilege to be invited.

I was expecting it to be as dusty and unkempt as the rest of the building and I wasn't far wrong. The cluttered apartment was more like a cheap bedsit. The room was dark, with maroon walls and sheets of newspaper over the windows. The newspaper drapes were dated March 1991. Clearly he hadn't decorated in a while.

"Sit," he ordered, pointing to a small wooden chair in the corner.

I did as I was told and Tiger took up position in a huge recliner. I usually started by asking him about a particular decade in the club's history. After a slow start, something would jog his memory and then there would be no shutting him up. Today was a little different. Tiger had a few questions for me.

"When are you getting married?"

"Saturday," I replied, smiling.

"Do you love the kid?"

I lowered my notebook. "With all my heart, Mr Malone."

He pointed a shaky finger at me. "Watch him," he warned. "Ryan's a lady's man, you know." He spoke as if he was letting me in on a big secret.

"He used to be," I corrected.

Tiger pulled the lever on the side of his chair making the recliner tip backward. "I nearly got married once," he revealed.

My pen started twitching. "Will you tell me about her?"

"Her name was Lois." He smiled fondly. "She was a nice broad. Good legs."

He might have been talking about a piece of furniture, but I let him go on. The description of Lois didn't get any more flattering, but I could tell that at one time she'd meant the world to him.

"I waited a long time to find the right woman," he told me. "I tried a lot out." He winked and took a break to light up a cigar. "I met her at Solito café." He blew out a quick puff of smoke. "Down on 48th. Do you know it?"

I shook my head.

"She thought I was a fool at first, but I talked her round," he continued. "The minute I saw her I knew she was the one I'd been waiting for."

"How did you know?"

"Because she had fire in her eyes. I like that," he replied. "And good shoes. You can tell a lot about a woman by her shoes."

I looked down, paying more attention to my black heels than I ever had. "What do my shoes say about me?"

He grinned and I warned him to keep it clean. "You're a tall girl who's not afraid to add more height. Confidence is an attractive quality."

"Thanks, I think." I tapped my pen on my notebook. "Let's get back to Lois."

"What do you want to know?"

I wanted to know what had gone wrong. I guessed that the lovely Lois had probably put up with all manner of grief from Tiger. He was brusque and reckless with people's feelings. He'd also admitted to being a huge womaniser back in the day. She'd probably taken as much as she could stand and then called it off.

"I saw her every single day for two years." He announced it proudly, as if he should've been rewarded for such dedication. "We talked and we danced – she could really dance, Ginger. Just like you."

"Where did you dance?"

"Here, of course."

Of course.

"I made her a promise that I'd dance with her every day, and for two years, I did." A look of misery overtook him then and I knew the tale was on the downward slide. "We talked and talked, and you know something, Ginger? I listened. She was the first woman that I actually listened to."

"There were a lot before her?" There had probably been just as many after her too. I doubt a broken engagement would've slowed him down for long.

Tiger gave a rumbly laugh. "Too many, some might say. I've never liked whiny women," he explained. "Sure, they usually look good but there's no substance. I waited until I found the whole package."

"And Lois was it?"

"Yes she was," he said with reverence. "She could dance, she could cook and she looked good. She sounds perfect, right?"

I couldn't help laughing as I agreed. He'd just described Ryan to a T. "Definitely a keeper, Tiger."

"That's what I figured, so I asked her to marry me." He stubbed his cigar out in a filthy ashtray. "Lois was prepared to take the chance. She thought I was dashing and looked like Montgomery Clift. I liked that she was a betting woman – and that her eyesight was poor."

I shifted on the tiny chair. It was as hard as a rock and my butt was going to sleep. "But you didn't make it to the altar?"

Tiger's eyes glazed. It took me a few seconds to realise that he was tearing up. I prayed he wasn't about to cry. I had no idea how I'd handle him if he did. "I lost her." Even his whisper sounded gravelly. "She passed away."

My heart hit the floor at the news. I'd imagined Lois jilting him at the altar in favour of the best man, or running off to Vegas to be a showgirl. Those scenarios were perfectly fitting for the feisty young woman I imagined in my head.

"I'm sorry to hear that, Mr Malone."

"I waited a long time for her, Ginger." He cleared his throat. "She was the one I'd been looking for. Life has a way of kicking you in the guts."

It was absolutely none of my business, but I wanted to know more. Tiger never held back when seeking information, so I decided to try the same approach, hoping he wouldn't be offended. "What happened?"

Tiger leaned back, tilting his recliner even further. He smiled, but it was awkward. "She was eighty-one," he replied. "I lost her last February."

I stared at him. I hadn't been doing my job properly that day. I'd assumed too much, conjuring a tale in my head to fit the party-hard, womanising old man I'd come to know. And I'd got it completely wrong – so wrong that I almost apologised. "You did wait a long time for her," I mumbled.

"Sixty years," he agreed. "After sixty long years of whiny broads, I finally found the one I wanted to dance with every day."

I didn't know I'd begun to cry until a tear hit the notebook. I swiped my eyes with the back of my hand. The last thing I wanted to do was cry in front of him. Tiger was having a hard enough time holding himself together.

"I'm sure you'll remember her forever," I said quietly.

"Of course I will." His gruff reply implied that it was a stupid thing to say. Perhaps it was. "I have her heart. I might've lost the girl, but I'll always have her heart. That's all that matters."

I was done. The emotional roller coaster I'd been riding for weeks had just taken another huge dip. Between the drama of the wedding, Bridget's escapades and Tiger's tragic tale of lost love, I was in danger of having a breakdown. "I think we should call it a day, Mr Malone," I suggested, packing up. "I've plenty to go on with for now."

I was almost out the door when something caught my eye and stopped me dead in my tracks. Fifty-something years of memories spanned the wall in the form of framed pictures, but only one called to me. I glanced back at Tiger. "Ryan hasn't been up here, has he?"

"No."

"Can I bring him back to see this?" I pointed at the picture.

The old man shrugged. "If you think he'd be interested."

I smiled brightly. "I think he's going to be very interested, Mr Malone."

69. CRYSTAL CLEAR

Ryan

Since Bridget had dropped me like a hot potato in favour of her dad, I had no excuse for not spending time at the office. That day was particularly busy, but it didn't stop Noelle bugging the hell out of me with inane interruptions.

"Nine bottles of Azure Champagne have been ordered in the last three hours," she said poking her head around the doorway.

"Okay," I said dully. "Good to know."

Unhappy with my reaction or lack thereof, Noelle carried on. "They're two hundred and sixty dollars a pop, Ryan. That's a super result."

I stared blankly. What was I supposed to say? "Okay." It was the best I could come up with.

She smiled, and for the first time ever, I realised she looked remarkably like one of Bridget's dolls with the big heads and the little bodies.

"You don't look very happy these days, Ryan," she told me, abandoning the grin. "Is everything okay?"

Like a lot of things Noelle said, I found her comment to be right out of left field. Apart from a few minor dramas I was happier than I'd ever been. I would've told her so but I was trying hard not to engage her in conversation.

"I'm fine."

"No nerves about the wedding?" she asked, taking a seat.

I leaned back, trying to figure out the angle she was working. "I'm excited to be getting married." My voice rose at the end, making it sound like a question.

"Of course."

I was done playing so I cut to the chase. "Do you have something to say, Noelle?"

She shrugged, running both hands up and down the arms of the chair. "No, if you're happy, that's all that matters."

"Why would you think I'm anything but?"

"You've just never struck me as the marrying kind, that's all," she replied. "I like that about you."

I frowned. I didn't want Noelle to like anything about me – I'd done nothing to encourage her and wasn't about to start. "I appreciate your concern, but I'm more than content with where I'm headed."

"Soon it'll be children and mundane day to day life…"

"What's the alternative, Noelle?"

"I'm not sure, but it doesn't have to be mundane," she declared.

I was appalled. Noelle had been trying to catch my attention for a long time. Perhaps realising that time was running out, she was making a last ditch attempt to win me over.

"Please don't go there," I warned. "It's going to make working here really awkward if I'm scared of you. I'll probably have to sell."

Her huge eyes widened. "I'm scaring you?"

"Totally freaking me out," I confirmed with a rigid nod.

Noelle headed for the door. "You've changed, Ryan." She sounded saddened by it. "I didn't believe it at first, but I'm pretty sure you do actually belong to her. Good luck with everything."

"Wait." I couldn't believe I'd called her back. "What were you hoping for?"

She shrugged. "Nothing serious."

I almost smiled but feared she'd misinterpret it. There was a time when Noelle would've been exactly my type. She was pretty, blonde and, most importantly, willing. But I'd never even been tempted by her and the thought of being propositioned was downright terrifying. "How long have you worked here?"

"Nearly a year."

It proved to me that the search for pecan pie girl had begun a long time before Bente got thrown out of a cab at my door. It brought me hope. It meant I'd been working at being a more decent man for a long time, which was epic because my fiancée deserved nothing less.

"You've just made my day, Noelle," I told her.

"Why? Because I hit on you?"

I shook my head. "No, because I'm scared of you."

***

Bente and I had both spent a lot of time at the club lately, just not usually at the same time. When she called and asked me to meet her there later that afternoon, I was a little surprised.

"I have something to show you," she said excitedly.

I checked my watch. "I can meet you there in an hour."

"Okay, but you need to hurry, Ryan. It's important."

"Why sweetheart?" Her urgency made me smile. "Does Grover Irwin have you holed up in the basement?"

"No." She giggled. "Just get here as quick as you can."

I was intrigued enough to escape the lunch time rush at Billet-doux and head down there, managing to arrive much earlier than promised. Bente met me at the door, pulling me inside by the lapels on my coat. I didn't get a chance to speak. Before I knew what was happening, her mouth was on mine and I was fighting the urge to take things further.

"Hi," she eventually murmured, barely breaking free to get the word out.

"Hello," I breathed.

Her hands moved to my face as she inched my head back. "You're not going to believe what I found today."

I lurched forward, chasing her ruby lips. "Maybe not, but I like it so far."

"I love you, Ryan," she said solemnly. "We can dance every day if you want."

Despite the randomness, it was probably the most endearing thing she'd ever said to me. "Are you alright?"

"Perfectly fine." She sounded calm, but she'd tightened her hold on my face. In fear of being crushed to death, I shifted her hands, holding them at her sides while I waited for her to speak again. "I spent the morning with Tiger."

"I spent the morning at Billet-doux," I retorted. "Noelle hit on me."

"She did?" she asked, interested. "How did that go?"

I smiled apathetically. "I appreciated the effort."

Bente nodded. "She does try hard."

I laughed at the absurdity of the conversation. "Can you please show me whatever it is you found so we can get out of here?" I asked.

"It's upstairs." She gestured with her head.

I couldn't believe the audacity of the old man. I owned one third of the building and had never been invited up. If not for Bridget, I wouldn't have been permitted to see the backstage area either.

"What's up there?"

Bente pulled me to the stairs. "Come and see for yourself."

***

I left it to Bente to knock on the door.

"Do I look like a doorman?" came a crotchety voice from the other side. "It's open."

I tentatively turned the handle and ushered Bente in ahead of me. I wasn't being polite. It was her idea to go up there so it only seemed fair that she'd be first in the line of fire if things turned bad. Tiger was lying back in an old recliner. "Hello again, Mr Malone," she said cheerily.

"We meet again, Ginger." His voice was rumblier than usual, which led me to think we'd woken him up.

"I brought my handsome man with me this time." She waved her hand as if showing me off.

"Beauty is in the eye of the beholder," he growled, looking at me. "How's life treating you, kid?"

I stepped forward and shook his hand. "Fine, sir."

Tiger reached into his pocket and pulled out a cigar. I used the time it took him to light it to survey the room. As expected, it was a dive. Even the cobwebs on the light fitting were dusty.

"So what do you think of the place?" asked Tiger, pausing midway through his question to cough.

"Nice digs, Tiger."

"You're a rotten liar, kid." He looked at Bente. "Don't ever let him near a poker table. He'll send you to the poor house."

Bente giggled. "I won't."

I reached for her hand. "So what did you want to show me?" The putrid cigar smoke was making me feel sick. I wanted to hurry things along and get out of there.

She pointed to a row of pictures near the door. "Magic," she whispered.

I took a step closer. It took me all of three seconds to work out what she was talking about.

"You like horses?" asked Tiger.

I stared at the picture, unable to find the breath I needed to answer him. The old black and white photo of the racehorse didn't interest me. The name on the silk sash around the horse's belly is what stole the air from my lungs.

"Secret North," I whispered.

Bente hooked her arm around mine. Perhaps I looked in danger of dropping to the floor.

"The finest horse I ever saw," Tiger announced proudly. "He had a muscly back end and a good broad chest. Better than that, he could run like hell. We almost snatched the Kentucky Derby with him back in '63."

Tiger had regaled Adam and I with his Kentucky Derby tale weeks ago, but not once had he mentioned the name of the horse. I wondered if things might've been different if he had.

"Bridget called it," I whispered to Bente. "How did she know?"

Her shoulders lifted. "I don't know, Ryan."

I stood for a long time, trying to come up with a logical reason for what I was seeing. Coming up blank, my mind drifted to the conversation I'd had with Charli. "Deny it all you want to, but one day something extraordinary is going to happen and you're not going to be able to explain it away," she'd told me. "You won't think it's weird then. You're going to think it's magic."

I took a step back, convinced I was going a little mad. I'd somehow wandered into La La Land.

Bridget's description of Secret North had been dead-on. There were flowers on the roof, it was very special, and today the view was crystal clear.

For the first time in my life, I could see magic.

I couldn't focus enough to string a sentence together. Luckily, I didn't have to deal with Tiger any more. He was fast asleep in his chair. Bente gallantly took the cigar from his fingers and stubbed it out.

We didn't say anything until we were at the bottom of the stairs. "What happens now?" she asked.

I shook my head, frowning. "I'm not entirely sure, but I know one thing: I've got to find a way of giving baby Bardot her wings back."

70. GOOD ENOUGH

Bente

I'd known Ryan for a long time, but there were certain quirks that I'd only recently begun to notice. I was sure they weren't new – I was just seeing him through different eyes these days. One habit was the way he shut down when he had a lot on his mind. He could go a full hour without speaking when his brain was busy. His brain was definitely busy that night, and I got the impression it was all magic related.

The silence didn't bother me. Conversation wasn't high on my agenda. Distracted or not, he was mine for the rest of the night.

***

Weird sleeping patterns were one of my quirks. Wide awake, I untangled myself from Ryan's arms a little after two in the morning and crept to the living room. I had a mountain of notes from my sessions with Tiger that I could've worked on but I wasn't up to writing. I checked my emails instead, and immediately wished I'd stayed in bed.

There was one from my mother. Before I opened it I knew it was bad news, and reading it just confirmed it. My parents had decided to give my wedding a miss in favour of an extended Caribbean cruise.

We got a great deal. I know you understand, Benny. Good luck with the wedding.

My mom's nickname for me had always vexed me. Not only did she curse me with a stupid name that no one could pronounce, she went on to shorten it to the ridiculous moniker of Benny.

I could count on one hand the number of days I'd spent with my parents in the last five years. Ivy and I were pretty good at pretending not to take it personally. The truth was a little sadder. They were selfish and always had been. Their decision to blow off my wedding confirmed it.

I hated that it upset me so much. I hated it even more when Ryan stumbled into the room just as angry tears took over.

It wasn't the first time he'd woken and found me sobbing. If he'd made a bolt for the door to escape the craziness I wouldn't have blamed him.

"I'm not upset," I sniffled, dropping my head in a stupid attempt to hide. "And I'm definitely not crying."

Probably at a complete loss, he grabbed a bottle of water from the fridge and took a long sip before even acknowledging me. "Are you sure you're not crying?" he finally enquired. "Because if you are, I can handle it. I've got this moral support thing in the bag now."

I lifted my head to look at him. Ryan stood half naked, leaning against the kitchen counter. Obviously he had being insanely handsome in the bag too.

I dried my eyes with the cuff of my sleeves and focused on breathing. "Definitely not crying," I assured him.

Ryan leaned forward. I stretched to meet him half way and was rewarded with the most perfect of kisses. "Why are you *not* crying?" he murmured, resting his forehead against mine.

I explained the email from my parents with the lack of detail it deserved.

"They're really not coming?"

I straightened up and shook my head. "Do you think Adam will give me away? I don't want to walk that huge aisle by myself." Fiona's choice of marriage venue was every bit as grand as the rest of her plans, and it wasn't the intimate setting I was hoping for. A jumbo jet could safely land on the mile long carpeted aisle.

Ryan moved to my side of the counter and pulled me to my feet. "He's best man," he reminded me.

I melted against him, resting my cheek on his warm chest. "This wedding is shaping up to be a nightmare."

"Don't say that," he soothed, stroking my hair. "What about Dad? Would you be okay with him walking you down the aisle?"

"Yeah," I muttered. "Good enough."

Those two words summed it up perfectly. Everything to do with the wedding was just good enough. We were merely performers in a huge production orchestrated by Ivy and Fiona. And I sucked at acting.

71. NAKED AND SINGING

Ryan

Stealing her mother's number from Bente's phone didn't seem like such a major crime considering my intentions were good. I planned to call her on the sly while Bente was in the shower, but hesitated because my little songbird picked that morning of all mornings to break into song.

Naked and singing was a stellar combination, but I knew I'd only get to enjoy one or the other: if I walked in on her she'd stop singing. I sat on the edge of the bed and listened instead. I got Bente naked all the time. The sultry, mind-scrambling singing was a rare treat. I wasn't sure that I had the right to feel as proud of her as I did. I contributed nothing to her brilliance. But I could feel proud that she was mine, and I was still pinching myself that I was lucky enough to be able to keep her forever.

After a few minutes of eavesdropping, I tore myself away and dialled her mother's number.

Evie Denison sounded a lot like Ivy, and instantly grated on me because of it. In fairness, she'd got my back up before uttering a single word. Anyone who was prepared to bail on their daughter's wedding wasn't worthy of polite chitchat, but I remembered my manners and introduced myself.

Evie seemed happy to hear from me until I asked her to reconsider their decision to stay abroad.

Negotiations went nowhere fast. Nothing I tried tempted her – not even the offer of first class plane travel. "Just come for the weekend," I urged. "You can be back on board the ship by Monday morning."

"No, I don't think so." She didn't even sound regretful. "It's sweet of you to offer though, Ryan."

As hard as it was to hold my tongue, I pressed on, using everything I could think of to talk her round. When I resorted to offering to pay for their next cruise, I realised that the woman just wasn't worth the effort. If she'd taken me up on it, I probably would've reneged.

I admitted defeat and called it quits. "Your daughter is the most amazing woman I have ever known, Mrs Denison," I declared. "And I want to thank you for that."

"My pleasure, young man." She replied as if she'd done me some great service. "I'm glad she's met a nice boy."

What did she know? I could've been an axe murderer or a bank robber. In-laws were supposed to be hard to win over. My brother was nearly drowned by his father-in-law, and I know for a fact he was threatened with bodily harm more than once. I almost felt ripped off. I wasn't getting even a hint of intimidation or threats. The woman was practically palming her daughter off to me like an unwanted gift. As angry as I felt, I didn't let it show. I wished her well and ended the call while I still had my manners in check.

I set my phone down, staring at the black screen while I plotted my next move. There wasn't one. I'd given Evie Denison ten minutes of my time, which was ten too many. I wasn't interested in ever doing it again.

∗∗∗

I had never voluntarily visited Ivy's house before, and the second she came to the door I remembered why. "What do you want, Ryan?" she barked through the screen. "I'm busy."

"It's not a social visit," I shot back. "I'm busy too."

She pushed the screen door open and stepped aside to let me in. I was immediately struck by how quiet it was when the girls weren't home. The hours that they spent at school must've been a godsend to her, although the peace hadn't lifted Ivy's mood much. She looked downright miserable.

"I'm making coffee," she told me. "You want one?"

"Yeah." I spoke as glumly as she looked. "That'd be great." I followed her through the glitzy little front room into the kitchen.

It was impossible not to notice the stack of papers spread out across the dining table when I walked in, and clearly I wasn't supposed to. Ivy scooped them up, shoved them in a drawer and ordered me to sit. Nothing was said in the time it took her to brew coffee, and it seemed to take forever. I swear I heard every single drip filter through to the jug. But the result was worth it: Ivy's coffee was as good as I'd ever had.

"Why are you here?" she asked finally, setting a mug in front of me.

She wasn't one for small talk so I didn't try. "I need your help with something."

"Something for Bente?"

I shook my head. "No, for Bridget."

"I'm listening."

It took longer to explain than I expected, which led me to think my plan for redeeming myself with my niece was half-baked at best. Ivy didn't look impressed, but at least she had the good manners to hear me out. "I've got it all worked out," I explained almost truthfully. "I just need you to make me some wings."

"How big and what colour?"

How did I know? "You're the designer. You decide. Just make them pretty and girly and junk."

"They'll need to be lightweight," she mused.

"Whatever you think is right."

Ivy looked at me through narrowed eyes. "You're a decent guy, Ryan." I nearly keeled over in shock at the rare compliment. "Bente deserves someone decent."

"I love her, Ivy. Make no mistake about it."

"I know you do."

"I'm glad."

"I don't like you," she added making me laugh. "But I respect you."

I had to concede that I felt a certain level of respect for her too. She'd done her best to hold my feet to the fire. Ivy was the in-law I'd had to work hard to win over.

It seemed like an appropriate time to let her know that her parents had bailed on the wedding. I was fairly sure that Bente wouldn't have rushed to tell her the news. Ivy sat motionless as I told her. She didn't seem surprised at all. "I knew it," she stated calmly. "They're hopeless."

It occurred to me that I really didn't know much about the dynamics of the Denison family. It was a now or never moment. I used it well, got brave and asked.

"They've never been around," Ivy revealed. She told me that her parents had received a windfall by way of an inheritance from a distant aunt. "Bente was only sixteen. They signed the house over to us and took off travelling. We see them once a year if we're lucky."

Ivy was six years older than Bente. It had been left to her to look after her while their parents gallivanted around the world on their endless cruises. It was no wonder Ivy mothered her sister so much – she'd been picking up Evie's slack for years.

"We weren't exactly kids, but Bente was nowhere near cooked." The image made me smile. "I did the best I could. She turned out alright."

"Better than alright," I corrected. "She's perfect. I told your mom that too. I wouldn't have bothered if I'd known the truth."

Ivy stared at her mug of coffee. "They're not bad people, Ryan," she said slowly. "They're just not cut out to be parents. They honestly don't see that they did anything wrong."

I suspected Ivy took a lot on board by herself, and probably always had done. Raising two squealers, running a household and trying to keep her sister on track was bound to get on top of her at times. I probably should've been more forgiving of her pissy moods. It was a state of mind that she was entitled to. I also should've been making more of an effort to get to know her. As frightening as it was, we'd soon be family. I didn't even know what Ivy did for a living.

"I make pageant dresses, Ryan," she replied. "Some sell for a lot of money."

There was no denying that the woman was talented. It seemed only fair to tell her so.

"Thanks," she muttered, bringing her coffee to her lips. "Unfortunately it's not steady work. Sometimes it's hard to make bills on time."

I pointed to the drawer that she'd stuffed full of papers. "How much do you owe?"

"None of your business."

"I could help you out, Ivy,"

She slammed her mug down, making the table wobble. "I'm not a charity case."

I leaned forward, speaking slowly and strongly. "I'm not offering you charity. I'm offering to pay you for the wings you're going to make for my niece."

After deliberating for a long moment, Ivy grabbed the papers out of the drawer. While she looked them over, I used the time to check my emails on my phone. I'd deleted all the wedding-related emails from my mother by the time she'd tidied them into a neat stack.

I retired my phone to my pocket. "Just give me a number."

"Eighteen hundred," she replied weakly.

I extended my hand across the table. "Deal. Eighteen hundred for spectacular fairy wings sounds more than fair."

Ivy reluctantly shook my hand. "Thank you, Ryan." Her voice was barely louder than a whisper. I didn't know she was capable of such a soft tone.

I walked my mug to the sink and told her I needed to get back to the office. "Just give me a call as soon as the wings are ready."

Ivy called me back as I got to the doorway. "Please don't tell Bente about the money situation," she pleaded. "I don't want her to worry."

"What money situation, Ivy?" I winked at her – another first. "I don't know what you're talking about."

72. BABY BARDOT

Bente

Two days before the wedding, Ryan dragged me down to the club to show me what he'd set up in a bid to woo Bridget back to the land of La La. I complained the whole way, but was secretly thrilled to escape the wedding talk going on in our apartment.

"We don't have time for this, Ryan."

"Yes, we do," he insisted. "Besides, would you rather be out with me, or at home with Mom and Ivy drinking tea and discussing last-minute changes to the seating plan?"

"I'd rather be anywhere than there."

"Stop whining then," he suggested, "or I'll take you back and tell them what you really think of their champagne fountain."

"You wouldn't!"

His laugh was positively sinister. "No," he agreed. "I'm not that heartless."

"You're not heartless at all, Ryan."

His brown eyes locked on mine and he smiled coyly. "You don't think so?"

I closed the gap between us. "Your heart has always been there," I whispered, laying my palm on his chest. "You just weren't sure how to use it."

"I've had an excellent teacher," he murmured.

I wasn't going to take any credit. Ryan's journey from douche bag to husband material started long before I arrived. The little girl with the missing wings had been the first to show him the error of his ways. I just got to reap the benefits.

***

Like his mother, Ryan Décarie does not do things by half measures. I had no idea what he was planning, but if he needed to carry it out at the club it was going to be a big deal. His mood led me to think it probably involved circus performers or fireworks or both.

The place was eerily quiet when we got there. I was used to the noise of power tools and hammering, but today there were no workmen on site.

There weren't any circus performers either. In fact, there was nothing out of the ordinary. The only change I picked up on was that the ceiling in the main room now looked pristine. I craned my neck to look. It was now bright white, and the intricate pattern of the flowers stood out brilliantly.

"Bridget's going to flip when she sees this," I told him.

"Yeah, maybe," he replied, uninterested. "That's not what I want to show her, though." He pulled me toward the stage area. "Look up there." He pointed at the overhead lights and stage rigging. "I've had a guy working on it all morning."

Working on what? All I could see was framework and cabling.

He didn't get a chance to explain. Adam, Charli and Bridget came through the big doors.

"Wow, this is gorgeous," commented Charli, taking everything in as she crossed the room. They hadn't been given details of his grand plan either, and probably assumed they were there to check out the progress of the renovations.

"It will be," replied Adam. He looked up. "Ceiling looks good."

"Yeah," agreed Ryan, still uninterested.

Bridget ran the last few feet as she approached Ryan, launching herself at him at the last second. It was a good sign that she was on the way to being her usual bubbly self.

"I have something to show you," he said, deftly catching her.

"Really?" She pressed her hands to his cheeks, making sure his focus remained on her. "A surprise?"

Ryan twisted to see Charli. "You were right," he quietly told her.

She frowned at him. "I'm always right."

"I'm sorry I stole from you," he said vaguely. "I'm going to give everything back to you today."

Charli nodded and I could tell by the look on her face that she knew exactly what he was referring to. Clearly I wasn't the only one out of the loop. Adam looked as confused as I was.

Ryan set Bridget down on the stage. Like a little wind-up toy itching to get going, she set off running in circles the second her boots hit the floor.

"I love it up here," she told him. "Really love it."

I moved to stand beside Charli, who was hanging on Adam's arm as if she was expecting something terrible to happen. I had no clue what to expect, but prayed for Ryan's sake that everything went according to plan.

Ryan disappeared behind the curtain at the back of the stage, reappearing a few seconds later with a pair of the prettiest fairy wings I'd ever seen. They had to be Ivy's handiwork. They were sparkly, detailed and perfect. Bridget squealed at the sight of them, so shrilly that we all winced. "I just love them, Ry!"

His wonderful deep laugh echoed in the vast space. "*Tu aimes tout.*"

"Yes I just do!" she shouted, making Adam and Charli laugh.

Putting her wings on wasn't simple. Ryan spun her around so she was facing her audience. It was the perfect distraction. She couldn't see that he was trussing her up with more than wings.

"Are you sure about this, Ryan?" asked Adam cautiously.

I could understand his nervousness. From what I could make out, his daughter was being connected to a pulley system.

"I didn't rig it," he replied. "It was done professionally."

"She'll be fine," whispered Charli, leaning in to him. "There are no rules in magic."

"There are rules in safety, Charlotte," Adam muttered back.

"Are you ready, Bridge?" asked Ryan.

She stumbled back as he tugged the cable. "What for?"

Ryan crouched in front of her. "I want to tell you something," he began. "These wings are magic."

"I know. I love them."

"They're going to make you fly."

Bridget's big blue eyes grew enormous. "Really?"

"Yes," he confirmed. "They're super special. The only time you can fly is if you're wearing these wings. Do you understand?"

She nodded at a rate of knots. "Okay."

"I mean it, Bridget," he warned sternly. "You mustn't ever try flying without these wings."

"I won't," she promised, getting impatient. "Make me fly now, please."

He took a step back and held both hands up. "I can't make you fly," he told her. You have to wish for it."

The curtain at the back fluttered and a man appeared from behind the stage as if cued. He walked to Bridget and began fussing with her back. The little girl was so keyed up she didn't even notice. I could feel the relief wafting off Adam. If there was a chance that Ryan hadn't hooked her up safely, she was definitely good to go now.

The man gave someone out of view a thumbs up.

The uncle-of-the-millennium stepped aside. "Ready?" he asked.

"Born ready!"

"Wish hard, Bridge," called Charli, between fits of giggles.

The little girl squeezed her eyes shut as if wishing took a mammoth effort. Perhaps it did. Wishes certainly couldn't be seen. Maybe they could be felt.

The pulley above Bridget started turning and the girl with the ambition to fly lifted off. If that didn't make a believer out of her, nothing would. By the time she opened her eyes, she was already a couple of feet off the floor.

"Get me higher to the sky, please." She asked politely but it was definitely a demand.

"Wish harder then," Ryan urged.

The more height Bridget gained, the more she moved. Her body swayed from side to side, ten feet off the ground. Her legs flailed and her arms waved as if she was treading water. It was impossible not to laugh – at least, that's what Adam and I were doing. Charli was clinging to Adam, racked by silent sobs. I expected no less from her. For her, the moment would've been huge.

It was a big moment for Ryan too. I studied him as he stood looking up at the girl butterfly. He looked completely victorious, and rightly so. He'd just pulled off the impossible and given Bridget her wings back.

73. SWEET NOTHINGS

Ryan

If beauty sleep was an integral part of a bride's preparations on the night before her wedding, Bente was screwed. I woke just after five to find her trashing the bedroom.

"What are you doing?" I mumbled.

Clothes were flying thick and fast as she pulled them out of the pink drawers and tossed them over her shoulder. "I can't find your tie. I need to find it."

"It's hanging up with my suit." I closed my eyes and pointed blindly at the closet. "Right where we left it."

"Are you sure?"

The absolute panic in her voice woke me properly.

"Positive." I propped myself on my elbow. "Come back to bed," I suggested with a jerk of my head.

"I can't," she replied. "I have stuff to do."

I looked at the clock and quickly did some mental math. "We're getting married in ten hours. You can spare a minute."

After a bit more coaxing, Bente reluctantly crawled into my arms. She was so stiff that trying to mould her into a decent cuddling position was akin to bending wire.

"Do you think we're ready for this, Ryan?" she asked. I slid my hands down her legs. "What are you doing?"

"Checking the temperature of your feet," I teased, grabbing them.

Finally she laughed and the effect was immediate. Tension slipped away and her body melted against mine.

"No cold feet," she assured me, curling against my side. "I just don't know if I'm ready for today. This wedding is going to be a big deal."

"It's one day, sweetheart." I'd used that line a million times lately. Even to my ears it was wearing thin.

"I get stage fright," she admitted. "It's horrible. I can't even breathe it's so bad."

I pulled her in closer, tucking her head under my chin. "You'll be fine."

"I hope so," she uttered. "That's why I don't sing in front of people. Big crowds freak me out. It never used to bother me as a kid."

"That's because you had wings back then." I grimaced, unable to believe that I'd actually said that out loud.

"I wish I still had them," she whispered.

"You sang at the club," I reminded, drawing a lazy pattern down her spine with my fingertips. "You had an audience then."

"I kept my eyes shut," she confessed. "I didn't see any of them."

I thought back to the night in question, picturing my little red firecracker up on the dusty stage. Her body was moving, her hands were drifting – and her eyes were welded shut. "I thought you were just in the zone."

"I was in the zone, Ry," she agreed. "The zone between peeing my pants and collapsing. I got through it by closing my eyes."

I tried not to laugh, but failed. "Do the same thing at the church then," I suggested.

"You want me to walk down the aisle with my eyes closed?"

"Yeah. We'll attach a lead to Malibu and she can guide you, like one of those Labradors that assist the blind."

Tightening my hold on her as she tried wriggling free was only effective for a few seconds. The sharp elbow she delivered to my ribs ended the battle quickly. Bente leapt off the bed and stood too far out of my reach for me to make another grab for her. "You are not funny, Ryan Décarie!"

"Look," I contritely began, "all you have to do is make it to the end of the runway without peeing your pants – and if by chance you do pee your pants, I'll still marry you."

"Wonderful." She slapped her hands down on her sides. "You're all heart."

"I'm only half hearted these days, Miss Denison," I corrected. "You have the other half."

Her scowl slipped in an instant. Even I was impressed by the impromptu sentiment. Until then I hadn't realised I was capable of sweet nothings.

"I got your heart?" she asked in the tiniest of voices.

"Yeah," I confirmed. "Just like you promised you would."

The second she threw herself across the bed and back into my arms where she belonged, I knew that for now the crisis had been averted. All we had to do was make it through the next ten hours. If we could pull that off, the rest of our lives would be a cinch.

74. BAD OMENS

Bente

The instructional phone calls from the queen began just after eight. I was sitting at the counter trying to eat the breakfast Ryan had insisted on cooking when she rang for the third time.

"One more thing, darling. You need to be at Charli's no later than ten," she told me. "The hair and makeup team will be there at quarter past."

"There's a team?" I asked, horrified. "We need a team?"

"It's a figure of speech, darling," she soothed. "As far as I know there are only three."

I only had one head. How I was supposed to cope with three people pawing at me at once was beyond me, but like the good bride I was trying to be, I promised to be there on time. As a reward, Fiona ended the call. "I have to go, darling," she crooned. "Much to do."

I went back to pushing eggs around my plate "You've got to eat something," Ryan told me. "You might not get chance again for a while." He made it sound as if I was gearing up for battle, which did nothing for my appetite.

I slid the plate away. "What are your plans for the day?"

He glanced at his watch. "Well, I'm getting married at three."

"What about before three?"

He smiled at me, and it was perfect. "I'll probably get dressed, watch *The Little Mermaid* for the last time as a single man and then wait for Adam to get here."

"Sounds like an easy day." I felt jealous.

"I need to take it easy," he said, wiggling his eyebrows. "I have a long night ahead of me."

I hung my head to hide my smile. He needed no encouragement. I could never have predicted three months ago that the arrogant man with the smart mouth and painful sting would turn out to be the best thing that had ever happened to me. I was just about to tell him so when my phone rang again.

"I'll get it," offered Ryan.

I pushed his hand away. "It's okay. It's Ivy."

He swiped it off the counter anyway. "Ivy."

As hard as I tried, I couldn't make head or tail of the conversation. Ivy was doing most of the talking. Ryan's responses were grunts, but his eyes never left mine, which was my biggest hint that the conversation wasn't pleasant.

As soon as he ended the short call, I demanded an explanation.

He walked around the counter. I knew it was terrible news. All I could do was brace myself.

"There's been a slight change of plans," he said, easing into it.

Working quickly to offload the drama, he explained in a jumbled rush.

Ivy, Fabergé and Malibu were sick.

"She thinks it's food poisoning," he told me. "It's pretty bad. They're not going to be able to make it to the wedding."

"But I need them, Ry," I replied.

Ryan didn't speak. He just stood there, giving me time to let the news sink in.

"They have to be there," I whispered desperately. "Do something."

I don't know what I was expecting him to do. He might've been a recent convert to magic, but we needed a miracle to sort this mess out.

"You know Ivy would give anything to be able to make it," he said quietly. "They're really ill."

I couldn't believe it was happening. Apart from a few distant relatives, none of my family were going to be at my wedding.

"It's a bad omen," I warned, wringing my hands. "We broke too many rules."

"What rules?"

"You saw my dress." My tone made it sound like a wicked deed. "That's bad luck. We spent the night before the wedding together too. More bad luck."

"We're not superstitious," he pointed out; "therefore the rules don't apply."

I nodded a hundred times, willing myself to accept his words as true. "We can do this," I gritted, trying to psyche myself up.

His hands moved to my face, holding my head still as he spoke. "Promise me you'll be there," Ryan demanded. "I'll look like a total dick if you leave me standing at the altar."

I tried to laugh. "I'll be there."

"Awesome." He kissed me hard. It wasn't sweet and romantic. It was more like a moral building exercise. "I'll be there too."

75. STUPID MEN

Ryan

It wasn't our regular driver who picked Bente up and delivered her to Charli's apartment that morning. I knew that because I watched her leave from the front window, making sure that she got in the car instead of making a run for it. I hadn't let on, but her nervousness had rubbed off on me. When my brother arrived a few hours later I was a wreck, and his cheery demeanour did nothing to settle me.

"Ready?" he asked, strolling through the front door in a suit identical to mine.

I made no attempt to get off the couch. "I'm having trouble with this," I confessed, waving my black tie at him in surrender.

Adam ordered me to get up. "How many times have you tied a tie in your life?" he asked, taking it from me.

"More times than I've been married."

Adam threw the tie around my neck. "Nervous?"

"Only because I'm not convinced that she's going to show up."

"I wouldn't blame her if she didn't," he teased. "You'd be a lot to take on permanently."

"Not helping, Adam," I told him. "Seriously."

He slapped my shoulders, shaking me. "She'll be there," he assured me. "She was getting dressed when I left."

That was a good sign. Other than church, I could think of no other place she could go wearing a big white dress and a veil.

"Would it be bad manners if we got drunk now?"

"Yeah," he replied, finishing off the knot at my throat. "But one drink won't hurt."

***

On a day of many firsts, drinking a glass of scotch at one in the afternoon was added to the list. I felt better for it. Without the distraction of shaking hands, explaining the drama of the morning was much easier.

"So the whole family bailed?" Adam asked incredulously.

In fairness, Ivy hadn't bailed. I knew her well enough to know she would've moved heaven and earth to see her sister, the squealers and her sparkly dresses walk down the aisle.

"All three of them are in a bad way. I heard puking in the background." I shuddered at the memory. "Food poisoning."

"Ugh." Adam, pulled a face. "Tough break."

"Bridget's good to go, though. Right?" Bente needed the support of at least one little girl in a red dress, even if it was Bridget.

He grinned at me, doing his best proud papa impersonation. "She looks so freaking cute, Ryan," he boasted. "She wouldn't lose the boots though."

I laughed. "Mom is going to kill someone if Bridget turns up in galoshes. It's bad enough that she's two bridesmaids down already."

Adam was shaking his head before I'd got the words out. "Mom bought the boots. She found red ones to match her dress."

"Huh." I set my glass down. "She must be mellowing."

"Maybe," he replied. "I wish Dad would."

It was probably going to be a tense day for Adam and Charli. They hadn't seen or spoken to the king in the three weeks since Adam pulled the pin on his job. I made a mental note to be as far away as possible when they crossed paths. Even being in a church wasn't likely to save them from his wrath. I tried to play it down. "What's the worst he can do?"

"Nothing," he replied confidently. "There's nothing he can do, which is the main reason he's so mad."

I shook my head, trying to shake free of the ugly family related tension. "He's giving Bente away."

"That's nice of him."

"Yeah."

"He likes Bente, Ryan."

"He likes Charli too…. way down deep in his soul."

Adam grinned wryly. "I know he does."

"If she wasn't such a fruitcake, he'd go easier on her," I added.

"I like that she's a fruitcake. She's my fruitcake," he said proudly.

I couldn't help smiling. As deluded as I thought he was at times, it was really impressive that six years down the road, he still considered Charlotte his biggest coup.

"Do you think we'll be as happy?" I asked.

Adam leaned back in the cushion, picking invisible lint off his trousers. "It's not difficult, Ryan," he replied. "Accept that you're an idiot and let Bente take care of the rest."

I didn't understand. He explained carefully.

"Décarie men are stupid," he began. "It started with Dad."

"What did?"

"The stubborn, selfish thoughtlessness that makes us deficient."

I felt my shoulders sag. It was impossible not to feel disheartened. I was all these things, despite the huge effort I'd made to change my ways.

My brother reached across and slapped me on the back. "Don't stress about it," he urged. "The universe came up with a solution." Despite the fairy-speak, I let him continue. "We're sent beautiful, forgiving wives who are ten times smarter than we can ever hope to be. It evens the score and balances things out."

I glanced across at him, immediately noticing his stupid grin. "Bente is much smarter than me," I agreed.

"She needs to be," he told me. "You need all the help you can get. You're even dumber than I am."

76. FOLLOWING RULES

Bente

I freaking hated my dress. It was so weighted down with beads and diamantes that walking was difficult. I'd given up trying, and spent the last hour parked on a chair in the middle of the living room – not that I had much choice.

The stylists Fiona had commissioned to transform me into a bride befitting her son had been primping and tugging and pulling at me since they walked in the door. Finally deciding that enough was enough, Charli all but kicked them out. "She's done," she said firmly, handing the women their supplies. "She's gorgeous. Thank you. Good job."

"What about the little one?" asked one of the women.

"She's four," replied Charli. "She's not being made up."

"But what about her hair?" asked another, waving a brush at her.

Charli opened the door and herded them out like wayward sheep. "I'll take care of it," she assured. "Thanks for everything."

She closed the door and I took my first breath of the hour.

"Better?"

"Thank you."

"Are you okay, Bente?"

Her question opened a floodgate of emotions I'd been holding back since dawn. I inexplicably burst into tears, ruining my inch-thick makeup in an instant.

Bridget got to me before Charli did. "Don't cry, Bente," she soothed. "It's a happy, happy day today." She patted my knee.

A painful sob caught in my throat. "I know, baby. I am happy."

Charli thrust a handful of tissues at me. "It's okay to be nervous."

Dabbing my eyes was futile. I could practically feel the mascara running down my cheeks. "Were you nervous before your wedding?" I asked.

"I can't actually remember." She half smiled. "I can remember being really excited, though. It was like setting off on a huge big adventure without having a clue where we were headed."

There was still excitement in her voice. It made me wonder what the hell was wrong with me. I desperately wanted to marry Ryan. I'd spent weeks promising myself that I could get through this day to make that happen. I was beginning to realise I'd been lying to myself the entire time. How I handled that would probably determine my whole future.

From the minute I broke into the Décarie circle, my game plan was to lie low and gain acceptance by toeing the line. I wasn't like Charli. I didn't resent the trappings of wealth and I found no joy in rebelling against the lifestyle. But there were consequences for being easygoing and agreeable. The consequences that day were champagne fountains, beaded dresses and a hopeless feeling of dread.

I looked at my dress. "Look at me, Charli." I thumped my hands on my lap. "This is just the beginning of a day of madness."

"Oh, Bente," she said pityingly. "How did you wind up in this mess?"

Admitting to treason was harder than I thought it would be. The words came out in a pathetic mumble. "I just went with the flow and followed the rules." And now I was drowning. "I knew this wasn't what I wanted. I should've been braver and spoken up weeks ago."

I waited for her to say something encouraging enough to pull me out of my funk. It took a while, but she finally came through. "Following the rules only takes you so far," she said gently. "Sooner or later you have to forget them and play by your heart."

I nodded in complete agreement.

"What are you going to do?" she asked.

I bunched up my skirt as if I was screwing up paper. "Not this," I whispered hoarsely. "I can't go through with it."

77. MITIGATING DAMAGES

Ryan

Not a single phone call that day had brought good news, so when Adam's phone rang I was preparing for the worst. When he turned his back on me and began speaking in a muted whisper, I knew I was right to be worried. An excruciating length of time passed before he turned to me.

"Now don't panic," he warned, "but there's been a slight hitch."

"What hitch?"

Even with extra thinking time he wasn't able to word it gently. "That was Charli," he began. "Bente just called off the wedding."

That wasn't a slight hitch. It was a catastrophic disaster.

I fell back onto the couch and buried my face in my hands. "Just freaking perfect."

I wasn't even shocked. I knew it was on the cards from the minute I woke that morning, which meant I should've been better prepared for it. Instead, I could feel my hands beginning to shake as despair set in.

"I said don't panic," Adam repeated. "Charli wants us to go over there."

I shook my head. "I can't deal with this, Adam."

Adam grabbed my arm and forced me to my feet. "You have to," he demanded. "Some things don't go according to plan, Ryan. Just change course and get back on track."

"How?" I demanded.

"I'm not sure," he admitted. "Let's just get over there and figure something out."

***

Along with the rest of the day, the weather had taken a nasty turn. If I was superstitious, I'd probably consider it to be another bad omen to add to the list. But I couldn't allow craziness to take hold, so I put it down to it being stock standard October weather. I leaned my head against the window of the cab, enjoying the coolness of the glass while rain beaded on the outside.

The usually short journey seemed to take forever, made even longer by the fact that neither of us said a word. I don't know what was occupying Adam's thoughts, but I was busy trying to work out how I'd cope if Bente had called us off as well as the wedding.

I knew I didn't deserve her, but no matter how deficient I was in some areas I'd given her my all. That had to count for something, and I planned to remind her of that while I was begging her to change her mind.

Avoiding the rain gave me a good excuse to run from the cab to the door without seeming desperate. I bolted through the foyer, quickly thanking the doorman on the way past. But by the time we got to the eighth floor I'd well and truly slowed my roll. I had no idea what to expect when I walked in, and no clue what to say.

Bente was on a chair in the centre of the room, looking miserable and swamped by an excess of white fabric that she'd bunched up on her lap. Charli was nowhere to be seen. At least Bridget was happy to see us. She scooted across the room to her dad, pausing briefly to gift me a quick leg hug on the way.

"Look at my dress, Daddy," she demanded. "I'm still very clean."

"Nice work, baby." He scooped her up and turned to me. "We'll leave you two to talk," he offered before carrying Bridget down the hall.

I appreciated the gesture, but a private moment was all but impossible in that apartment. Ignoring the fact that my brother and his family were holed up in the bedroom, I set about trying to reclaim my happy-ever-after.

I crouched in front of Bente. "Hi," I said weakly.

356

"Hello," she whispered.

I put my hand under her chin and tilted her head so she'd look at me. "What's going on?" I asked gently.

"I can't go through with it, Ryan," she replied. "I'm so sorry. I thought I could but I can't."

Her demeanour was perfectly calm, zombie like. She looked a bit like a zombie too. Long streaks of black marked the tracks of tears. I shouldn't have been surprised that she'd finally had enough and called it off. I was the worst offender when it came to pressuring her. I'd pushed for an early wedding date and then had the nerve to take a step back when the drama of planning it took hold. She'd tried to tell me a hundred times that it was becoming too much to bear. I was under the assumption that we'd both be able to suck it up and handle it. Clearly I was wrong. Pecan pie girl folded at the finish line.

Begging her to change her mind seemed pointless, but I was desperate enough to try. I plotted a very good argument in my head. It was long and detailed and perfectly summed up my feelings. What came out of my mouth was somewhat lacking. "I love you. I wonder if you know that?" I couldn't be sure. At that point, I wasn't sure about anything.

Hope flooded my body as she answered. "I know how you feel about me, Ry."

"It's not about what I feel for you, Bente," I clarified. "It's about what I've never felt for anyone *but* you. Please don't take that away from me."

She let go of her bunched up dress and fell forward, throwing her arms around my neck. "I'm not taking anything away," she whispered in my ear. "I just don't want to do it this way."

I felt a moment of relief until thoughts of the bigger picture kicked in. Calling off the wedding was going to be a logistical nightmare. In just over an hour, three hundred guests were due to front up at church expecting to see us get married.

I released my hold on Bente and stood. The zombie bride remained glued to the chair.

"Right," I muttered, trying to figure out some semblance of a plan. "We can still make it work. A quickie wedding at the marriage bureau. What do you think?"

Bente nodded weakly. "Sounds good."

It wasn't ideal. She'd vetoed that idea when I first mentioned it, hoping for something slightly grander. But the alternative now terrified her so much that a quick civil ceremony had become her dream wedding by default.

"I'm going to have to call my parents," I said bleakly. "It's the least I can do."

"I'm sorry, Ryan," she whimpered, getting upset again. "I've put you in a horrible position."

I reached for her hands and pulled her to her feet. "No you haven't. As long as we're together, my position is good."

That wasn't entirely true. Mom was going to be devastated, embarrassed and probably hysterical. And when she recovered she'd surely kill me, which meant my position wasn't good at all. But Bente didn't need to hear this, so I didn't share the thought. I turned around at the sound of little feet stampeding down the hall.

"Can I come out now?" asked Bridget, rounding the doorway.

"Of course." I forced a smile. "Where's your mama?"

"Getting changed," replied Adam, appearing behind her.

"I'm keeping my dress on," announced Bridget, grabbing the hem of her skirt and flipping it over her shoulders. "It's like big wings, but I won't fly with them, Ry," she promised.

"I'm pleased to hear it," I replied.

Adam picked Bridget up. "So, what's the plan from here?"

"We're going to head down to the marriage bureau," I explained, looking at Bente. "I have to marry this girl before she changes her mind again."

"I won't," she said quietly. "As long as I don't have to do it in a church or in this dress."

I stared at Adam feeling a woeful expression creep across my face. "I have to call Mom."

"No, you don't."

"Of course I do," I insisted. "She'll be beside herself. You smashed her wedding dream to bits years ago. I'm about to do the same thing."

Adam shrugged as if it was no big deal. I wanted to smack him, or at least shake sense into him. I only held off because he had my niece in his arms. "It's the right thing to do, Adam."

"Maybe," he agreed. "Or maybe you could just come up with a way of keeping her happy."

Impossible, I thought. There was no way around it, and for a man who claimed to be smarter than me, he should've realised it too. "I hope you've got a plan, genius, because I haven't," I snapped.

"I have, as it happens." He was way too smug to be bluffing. "Three words for you. Mitigate. Your. Damages."

Lawyer-speak. I understood it better than the fairy nonsense he usually came out with.

"How?"

"What does Mom want most out of this day?" he asked.

"Power and glory," I muttered.

"No she doesn't," Bente corrected. "She wants to see her son get married. She's been telling me that from the beginning. She has photos of the family on her dresser. It kills her that she doesn't have wedding pictures." She turned to Adam. "Charli is a photographer and you didn't get a single picture of your wedding day."

"I know." He grinned. "We forgot."

"That's all she wants, Ryan," Bente told me.

I threw my hands up in exasperation. "So how do we fix that?"

No one needed to say a word. Charli appeared, solving every single problem we had without speaking.

The long ivory gown she was wearing looked vaguely familiar. When she slowly twirled to show it off, the bow on the back jogged my memory. It was her wedding dress.

"What do you reckon?" she asked, smoothing her hands down the front. "Still fits, right?"

Adam answered by hauling her in close and crushing her with a kiss.

"You're a bride girl, Mum," chimed Bridget, trying to wriggle out from between her parents.

"I am," she confirmed, making space for her.

"Get married to my daddy, okay?" came the demand.

"Yeah," she agreed, smiling at her daughter. "I haven't had a better offer."

"What are you doing, Charlotte?" Overwhelmed, I choked out the question. Bente wasn't faring much better. She'd started sniffling again.

"We'll be your ring-ins," Charli offered. "That way, the queen will still get to see one of her precious princes get hitched. Hopefully she won't mind the unscheduled change to the programme."

"You're okay with this?" I asked Adam.

"Of course." He laughed blackly and gestured at his wife. "Look at her, Ryan. Tell me I'm wrong."

I shook my head. "Not today."

Not any day. I wasn't too much of a jerk to admit that my younger, smarter brother had had it right from the beginning. Tinker Bell and her crazy ways were perfect for him. I just wasn't going to admit it out loud.

I lurched forward, catching all three of them in a hug. "Thank you," I mumbled inadequately.

"Thank us later," replied Charli, shrugging free. "You're going to make us late for our wedding."

"Can I come?" asked Bridget, grabbing Adam's attention by taking his face in her hands.

"You have to come." He turned his head and kissed her palm. "You're my best girl."

78. LOW KEY

Bente

I'd selfishly pushed us dangerously close to the edge of disaster that day. I wasn't sure that I deserved a second chance, but was eternally grateful for the one offered to me by the people who'd soon become my family. I had no hope of properly expressing it at that moment so chose to stay quiet and concentrate on pulling myself together instead.

Ryan seemed a little shell shocked too, and it lasted a long time. He hardly said a word to me on the cab ride back to our apartment, which could only mean he had a lot on his mind.

I reached for his hand. He squeezed my fingers in reply, silently assuring me that we were okay. The tiny gesture brought me hope. My inability to follow through might've smashed the day to pieces, but I hadn't damaged us.

***

Getting undressed brought instant relief. I demanded that Ryan stay in the living room while I changed. "We have a chance at a do-over," I reasoned, bundling up my sparkly dress and throwing it in the corner. "We're going to do it right. No seeing the bride before the wedding."

"That might be difficult," he called through the closed door. "I only called for one car."

"No seeing the bride before she's ready then," I amended. He followed up with a wonderful low laugh that I'd given up hope of hearing again that day.

"I love you, Ryan," I declared for no particular reason.

"Can you love me from this side of the door, please?" he asked. "It's lonely out here." His pitiful tone made me giggle. He sounded as if I'd locked him in a cupboard.

"Two minutes," I promised.

I pored through the rack of clothes in the closet, trying to find something to wear. Only one outfit stood out. I slipped into Ryan's favourite red dress and moved onto phase two of operation low-key bride.

Washing my face worked wonders, although I would've spent more time redoing my makeup if not for the impatient demands coming from the other side of the door. It wasn't perfect by any means, but looking at my reflection made me realise I'd achieved something far more important than flawless makeup. I looked happy. And for the first time in weeks, I looked relaxed.

I unpinned my hair and brushed it out. "What do you think?" I asked, swinging the door open.

A slow smile crept across his perfect face. "I think I'm the luckiest guy in the world right now."

Once in a while, right in the middle of mayhem, life throws us a moment of clarity. I'd completely screwed up our wedding day, burdening him with unimaginable drama in the process and he still felt lucky. "You must really love me," I concluded, thinking out loud.

"At Black Plague level, sweetheart."

I refused to give into the urge to get him naked. We had a wedding to go to. "Do you have everything?"

Ryan patted his pocket. "I've got the rings and I've got the licence."

"We need ID," I added.

"I think we need a couple of witnesses too," he said.

"Who?" Every person we knew was sitting in church waiting for us to arrive.

"What about Tiger and Earl?" Ryan suggested. "We could swing by the club and pick them up."

I couldn't help smiling. "You want a couple of grizzly old gangsters to bear witness for us?"

"Yeah. Do you have any objections?"

I shook my head. I'd objected enough for one day. As far as I was concerned, it was a perfect idea.

79. DEAD ENDS

Ryan

It took longer to round up Tiger and Earl than Bente. Fifteen minutes after being told to wait, I stood at the base of the stairs and called up to them. "Nearly ready, Earl?"

No reply.

"Now what?" Bente asked.

I shrugged. "Just give them another minute."

I'd expected to have to talk the old men round when it came to bearing witness. I'd done a lot of pleading that day and was becoming embarrassingly good at it. But they hadn't needed convincing. They just needed time to get spruced up.

Earl and Tiger finally made their way down, both clinging to the balustrade to steady themselves.

It wasn't hard to see why it had taken them so long. They were dressed to the nines, making me wonder where they thought they were going.

"Vintage threads, Tiger?" I had to ask. No reputable tailor in the last forty years would've been caught dead working with olive plaid tweed.

"I've had it a while," he confirmed, brushing his knuckles across his chest.

Earl went for the vintage look too, opting for a brown pinstriped blazer. It would've been a great cut on someone a foot taller, like his friend Tiger who'd lent it to him.

Tiger donned a black trilby, Earl grabbed his cane, and we were good to go. "You ready?" grumbled Tiger. "I'm tired of waiting."

I frowned at his audacity. "Yeah, of course."

"So why do you look like a long tailed dog in a room full of rocking chairs?" He thumped me on the back. "It's your wedding day. You might as well be happy. I've heard it's all downhill from here."

"Tiger Malone, you take that back," demanded Bente. My blushing bride stood with her hands on her hips and a scowl on her face. "You believe in this just as much as we do," she told him. "I know you do."

Tiger tipped his hat, silently apologising for being his usual bolshie self. "He'll do alright, Ginger," he told her. "You just keep him in line."

I didn't need to be kept in line – I just needed to get married, and at that point it was proving difficult. I bundled the motley wedding party out the front door and steered them in the direction of our waiting car.

"Holy smokes!" Earl whistled in approval at the long black car parked on the street. The driver held the door open, impressing the old men no end.

Tiger nudged his friend. "It's going to be a good afternoon, Earl. I can feel it in my bones."

***

Tiger's bones were wrong. As it turned out, the marriage bureau isn't open for business on the weekends.

Bente and I were at the top of the steps to trying to come to grips with the latest dead end before the old men were even out of the car.

"We just can't catch a break," I growled.

"What now?" Bente asked.

The irony was laughable. I'd spent my whole adult life running from commitment. Today I was desperately trying to do the opposite and being shut down at every turn.

Bente didn't look too distraught. She just looked freezing. Her thin red dress was no match for the October air. I shrugged off my jacket and draped it around her shoulders.

"I'm out of ideas, sweetheart," I said, defeated.

She smiled brighter than she had all day. "We'll come back on Monday," she said. "No big deal."

She was right. There was no urgency. If we waited until Monday, Ivy and the squealers might be better, and Adam, Charli and Bridget could be there – Mom and Dad too, if they were still talking to us.

She hugged me, probably seeking warmth more than comfort. I held her closely, rubbing her back to warm her.

Tiger appeared at the base of the steps. "There's a big poker game in Queens tonight, kid."

I turned to face him. "So?"

"So we need transportation." He motioned to the car behind him with an upward nod. "One good turn deserves another."

Tiger's reasoning was shady at the best of times. I didn't bother pointing out that he hadn't actually got as far as doing us a good turn.

"Unbelievable," I muttered. Bente buried her face in my chest, laughing between shivers. I held her tighter. "Take the car, Tiger," I called. "We'll make our own way home."

He grabbed a cigar from his top pocket, gritted it between his teeth and grinned at me. "You're alright, kid."

80. DÉJÀ VU

Bente

Mercifully we managed to pick up a cab before hypothermia set in. I interrupted as Ryan gave the driver directions to our apartment and asked him to take us to Nellie's instead.

"You're sure?" asked Ryan.

I didn't feel like going home, and hanging out at Nellie's for the evening would be perfect. "Yeah. It's closed. All your staff are at the wedding."

He frowned, looking like he was hearing about it for the first time. "She really did invite everyone, didn't she?"

"They'll all be having a blast," I reasoned. "Half of them don't even know us so they won't even notice the imposter bride and groom."

Ryan chuckled darkly as his thoughts turned to Charli and Adam. "I'm going to owe those two hugely for this. They took a bullet for us."

I had to agree. I grabbed his wrist and checked his watch. It was just after five. The ceremony would be over and done with and the happy couple would be gearing up for phase two, the five-course reception dinner. I didn't regret bailing, and sincerely hoped they didn't regret their decision to stand in for us either.

I blew out a long breath and fell back limply into Ryan's arms. "No more wedding talk," I mumbled. "We're done."

***

Creeping into an empty Nellie's wearing my red dress and clinging to Ryan's arm gave me a massive sense of *déjà vu* – especially once he started moving tables around.

"Dance with me?" he asked, holding out his hand as he crossed the space he'd cleared.

I took his hand and he twirled me into position. "Music?"

"We don't need music." He smiled. "Everything we need is right here, but feel free to sing if you'd like."

"I'll sing for you," I bravely offered.

"You will?"

"Sure." I nodded, just once. "You don't freak me out."

He dipped his head, murmuring against the curve of my shoulder. "You freak me out every day."

I took half a step back, forcing him to straighten up and look at me. "How?"

"Because you know me, and you still love me," he replied. "That's freaky."

Something deep in my chest shifted, and I realised it was probably the last piece of doubt that I'd been holding on to for the past three months. The conceited, egotistical man who'd made an art form out of breaking my heart was gone. In his place stood a much improved version who wasn't afraid to be loving and vulnerable. And after my antics of the day, he'd also proven that he was protective and willing to step up when I couldn't.

"I think I should keep you forever."

The corner of his mouth lifted. "You should," he agreed. "I'm pretty close to being the complete package."

Clearly, the war against his massive ego was one he'd never completely win.

My head fell back as I laughed and Ryan moved in, wrapping his arms around me and pressing his lips against my throat. I seemed to be the only one who heard his phone ringing.

"Ryan, answer your phone," I muttered.

"No."

"It might be important."

Depending on who the caller was, there was a fair chance it might be also be painful and horrific. Ryan knew it too, which explained why he ignored me. I slipped my hand into his pocket and grabbed his phone, reading the screen. "It's Trieste."

Ryan's expression changed in an instant. He put the phone to his ear. "Hey."

If it was supposed to be a private conversation, he had no chance. Thanks to the deathly quiet surroundings of the restaurant, I heard every word.

"I just wanted to let you know something," she began. "Apart from mine, your wedding is the best I've ever been to. I wish you were here to see it."

"It's going well then?" he asked, winking at me.

"It's spectacular, Ryan."

"Can you see my mom anywhere?" he asked curiously.

After a long silence Trieste answered. I was relieved; Ryan seemed to be turning green while he waited.

"Oh, I see her," she told him. "She's dancing with Adam."

"Does she look okay?" he asked. "Happy?"

Trieste's guffaw was so loud that he held the phone away from his ear. "She looks ecstatic. I can't say the same for Adam, though. That man can't dance."

I could see relief wash through Ryan at the news that his mom wasn't an hysterical wreck. He smiled. "That's good news, Trieste. Thank you."

"Don't thank me," she shot back. "I should be thanking you. William and I are spending your wedding night at the Four Seasons."

We were so far out of the loop that neither of us even knew we'd been booked into the Four Seasons. Standing in for us didn't extend as far as a night in a hotel for Adam and Charli. With Bridget in tow, romance was out of the question. Generous to a fault, Adam had offered Trieste the room instead.

"Enjoy," urged Ryan.

"Oh, we will." Her suggestive tone made me giggle. "Can we order room service?"

Ryan huffed out a quick laugh. "Sure."

"And the movie channels?"

He pulled a face. At least I wasn't the only one disturbed by the prospect. "Whatever you want, Trieste." He worked quickly to end the call, perhaps fearful of what she might come out with next. "I'll talk to you soon," he promised.

If she spoke again, we didn't hear. Ryan put his phone away.

"Let's never speak of that conversation again," he suggested with a shudder.

81. SECRET INGREDIENTS

Ryan

After an emotionally trying day, my body and mind felt depleted. Desperate for an energy kick, I thought food might help. I took Bente by the hand, spouting a round of menu suggestions as I led her through to the kitchen.

"You know what I'd really like?" she asked, tugging my hand to slow me down.

"Room service and the movie channels?"

"No." Her raspy laugh made me wish she'd answered differently. "Pecan pie. I've had lots of pecan pie in my time but none compare to Nellie's."

"Do you mean that?"

She nodded. "Heaven on earth. You should try it."

I didn't need to try it. I knew it was spectacular. The recipe was mine and I proudly told her so. "I tried a hundred different variations until it was perfect." I tapped the side of my nose. "It has a secret ingredient."

"Your parents got it so wrong," she said, sadly. "They didn't raise lawyers. They raised a carpenter and a chef."

There were no words to explain the emotions I was feeling at that point so talking was senseless. There were other ways to tell her how I felt, and I quickly got lost in the moment. Bente did not. Her mind was fixed on pie.

"What's the secret ingredient?" she murmured against my mouth.

"I can't tell you," I murmured back.

"You have to tell me," she insisted. "We're as good as married. We're supposed to share everything."

"Not secret pie business."

Working her into a frustrated frenzy was easy. All I had to do was keep quiet. Withholding information drove her inquisitive mind insane – and I loved that about her. There wasn't a single thing I didn't love about Bente, including her great pitching arm and sharp elbow. I wasn't sure which she was about to unleash on me so I stepped out of range and put her out of her misery. "Apple cider vinegar," I said.

"That's it?"

Her disappointed tone made me laugh. "What were you expecting? Truffles infused with the laughter of a thousand babies?"

A smile crept across her face as she stepped toward me, stretched up and linked her arms around my neck.

"Just get me pie, Ryan," she whispered.

***

Sharing a life with someone was far more complicated than taking on pink furniture and sharing closet space. It was about sharing myself and taking more on board than I ever thought I could. It was also about being adaptable when plans changed, which seemed to be happening to us a lot that day.

We were sitting in the deserted restaurant eating the world's best pecan pie when our Monday wedding plans were shot to pieces.

Bente didn't know the man who called her. I knew him well – at least, I used to. I'd gone to school with Reid Bachman. We lost touch after graduation. I went on to law school and he pursued a journalism degree. Law hadn't worked out for me, but he ended up landing a gig as an editor at The Manhattan Tribune. If we'd stayed in touch he probably would've been at the wedding watching my brother remarry his Tinker Bell. But we hadn't, so he was clueless that he'd picked an odd day to call.

It wasn't hard to work out why he'd called Bente, but I listened to her excited explanation as if I had no clue.

"He loves my work, Ryan!" She waved her phone at me. "I sent him some of the stuff I'd been working on with Tiger. He wants to meet me on Monday."

I pushed my pie plate to the centre of the table. "I told you things would work out."

Bente mistook my pride for smugness, narrowing her eyes as she jumped to a conclusion. "Did you have something to do with this?"

"Like?"

"Like, pulling strings and calling in a favour."

"Trust me sweetheart, there were no strings to be pulled and Reid owes me no favours. If anything, it's the opposite."

"I thought you were friends," she reminded me.

"I might've embellished that part," I admitted. "He doesn't like me much."

Bente dropped her napkin on the table. "Girlfriend or sister?" she asked casually.

"Excuse me?"

A wry smile swept her gorgeous face. "You heard. Did you sleep with his girlfriend or his sister?"

"Sister." I grinned. "Prom night. Nothing else to report."

Bente shook her fork at me. "You're impossible."

I reached for her hand. "I'm not, you know. I've been told I have huge potential."

"Perhaps I should marry you, then."

I feigned disinterest with a heavy sigh. "Well, Monday's out."

"Does Tuesday work for you?" she asked, smiling.

"No, actually. I'm meeting with contractors most of the day."

I would've cancelled if she'd asked me to, but she didn't. She continued to play along. "Hmm, I see," she mused. "Do you think we should just play it by ear and see what happens? Wait for a free day?"

The urgency I'd been feeling to get her to the altar had slipped in the last few hours. It dawned on me that winning didn't necessarily mean closing the deal. Winning just meant being together, hanging out in an empty restaurant and sharing pecan pie.

"What if we just get married in La La Land?" I suggested. "That would count, right?"

"Count as what?" Bente looked nervous, which was perfectly understandable. I took out the ring box that had been burning a hole in my chest all afternoon, flipped it open and took out the smaller of the two rings.

"What are you doing, Ry?" Her voice was barely louder than a whisper.

I motioned for her hand. As soon as she was in reach, I slipped the ring onto her finger. "I love you. You're mine. I'm yours. Happy ending. We're married."

Bente let out a sharp laugh. "In whose eyes?"

"I'm sure God's watching." I grinned. "And if you believe Charli and Bridget, there's probably half a dozen fairies and an elf looking on too."

She reached for the box and took out the other ring. When I offered my hand, she slipped it on my finger. "Happy, happy day, Ryan Jean Décarie," she murmured. "I love you. You're mine. I'm yours. Happy ending. We're married."

I leaned across the table and kissed her, ignoring the glass I'd knocked over in the process. "All that drama for nothing. See how easy it was?"

"I'm not sure that was a lawful ceremony," she replied, righting the fallen glass.

"No, probably not," I agreed. "But it's enough for now, right?"

She held up her left hand, studying the newest ring on her finger. "It's perfect for now."

"We'll have to make it legitimate sooner or later," I told her. "The four Ryans might not appreciate being born out of wedlock."

Bente stood and walked around the table. As soon as she was in reach, I pulled her onto my lap. "It turned out to be a good story of the day, Ryan," she said quietly. "We're going to have an amazing life together."

I held her tighter, prepared to hang on forever. "Bring it on, sweetheart," I replied. "I'm ready for you."

THE END

www.ingramcontent.com/pod-product-compliance
Lightning Source LLC
Chambersburg PA
CBHW071202250626
47159CB00001B/175